VERTICAL COFFIN

STEPHEN J. CANNELL

D0009610

St. Martin's Paperbacks

VERTICAL COFFIN

Copyright © 2004 by Stephen J. Cannell.

Cover photo © Bill Ross / Corbis.

Library of Congress Catalog Card Number: 2003058567

ISBN: 0-312-93479-3
EAN: 80312-93479-8

Printed in the United States of America

St. Martin's Press hardcover edition / January 2004
St. Martin's Paperbacks edition / March 2005

St. Martin's Paperbacks are published by St. Martin's Press, 175 Fifth Avenue, New York, NY 10010.

10 9 8 7 6 5 4 3 2 1

MORE . . .

HOLLYWOOD TOUGH

"Cannell, creator of such TV shows as *The A-Team*, clearly knows the ins and outs of the entertainment industry, and the detective story, with its wry, subtle humor, doubles as Hollywood satire . . . the cops-and-robbers sequences hit the mark as well. Well-drawn characters and keen observations on the similarities between Hollywood and the mafia make this a winner."

—*Publishers Weekly*

"Scully has ample opportunity to prove how 'Hollywood tough' he is . . . veteran writer/TV producer Cannell has concocted his special brand of reader candy."

—*Kirkus Reviews*

RUNAWAY HEART

"A cop thriller with a futuristic, sci-fi twist . . . Cannell has a genius for creating memorable characters and quirky, gripping plots . . . this is a fun read."

—*Publishers Weekly*

THE VIKING FUNERAL

"Stephen J. Cannell is an accomplished novelist."

—*New York Daily News*

"Stephen J. Cannell's *The Viking Funeral* is the sort of fast and furious read you might expect from one of television's most successful and inventive writer-producers."

—*Los Angeles Times*

"Solid plotting with nail-biting suspense and multiple surprises keep the reader guessing and sweating right up to the cinematic ending . . . Cannell has a knack for characterization and a bent for drama that will satisfy even the most jaded thrill lover."

—*Publishers Weekly*

THE TIN COLLECTORS

"I've been a Stephen Cannell fan since his remarkable *King Con*, and he keeps getting better. *The Tin Collectors* is an LAPD story that possesses both heart and soul; a fresh and different look at the men and women who, even more than the NYPD, are the most media-covered police force in the world. Stephen Cannell has the screenwriter's fine ear for dialogue and great sense of timing and pacing as well as the novelist's gift of substance and subtlcty. Cannell likes to write, and it shows."

—Nelson DeMille

"Cannell turns out another winding, suspenseful thriller."

—*New York Daily News*

Also by Stephen J. Cannell

Runaway Heart

Hollywood Tough

The Viking Funeral

The Tin Collectors

King Con

Riding the Snake

The Devil's Workshop

Final Victim

The Plan

This one's for my old friend, Chuck Bowman.
As young men we shared far-fetched dreams and now
we're actually living them.

ACKNOWLEDGMENTS

As always, there are many people to thank. Without the help I get from my friends in law enforcement, both city and federal, I would be lost. Bill Gately, U.S. Customs (Ret.), has been a great friend and a constant source of information and realistic detail. I dedicated *The Viking Funeral* to him because that novel was based on one of his cases. This time around, as always, he supplied valuable insight and advice. Dick Weart, ATF (Ret.), an old friend, hooked me up with several people at Alcohol, Tobacco, Firearms, and Explosives—most notably, Joe Dougherty, ATF Baltimore. Lieutenant Eric Parra of the L.A. County Sheriff's Special Enforcement Bureau welcomed me and gave me a tour of the facilities. He introduced me to a heroic bunch of guys who spent hours talking to me with the tape running. Thanks to Sergeant Phil Barth and Deputies Jeff Riggin, Mark Schlegel, Carlos Parga, William Robert, George Cramer, and Willie Robinson. I would also like to thank Stan White, LASD (Ret.).

Any mistakes I made in portraying either the operations or the tactics of ATF Special Response Team or the Sheriff's SEB are mine alone.

As always, I have great help in the office. My mop-and-pail crew of crack assistants unscramble my dyslexic spelling and work tirelessly, running down info, checking facts, and doing endless manuscript cleanups. I owe them a huge thanks. Grace Curcio, my friend and assistant for twenty-five-plus years, has retired, but she still types my weekend pages. Kathy Ezso is now on point and makes this work go smoothly, juggling more details than would seem possible. Jane Endorf is tireless and without peer. Thanks, guys. Jo Swerling is the first one to see the manuscript after it's ready. I hand it to him with shaking hands and he does the first cold read with an expert but gentle eye.

Thanks to my new agent, Robert Gottlieb at Trident Media. He has helped me redesign my thinking and career. Robert, we're on a roll.

I would like to thank all my friends at St. Martin's, especially my editor, Charles Spicer, who has been a constant source of strength, and my publisher, Sally Richardson, who has not hesitated to step up for me. Also a big thanks to Matt Baldacci, Joe Cleemann, and Mathew Shear.

At home is where my real strength lies. My children are a constant source of joy and wonder. Tawnia, you have made your dad a happy man. You are a magnificent mother and it has been a joy for me to watch you work your way up from gofer to sought-after television director (without my help). Your gifts are personal and professional. Chelsea, you continue to grow and become more awesome. Your life choices and sense of fairness signal a wonderful spirit and true heart. You are all a father could hope for. Cody, you have proven what can happen when you work for a goal and don't give up on your dreams. I have watched you mature and see that success in life comes from the inside out. You have made me proud. My wife, Marcia, holds my circus together, keeps the family on course, and changes the air in my head when it gets too full of helium. You have made all our dreams come true, babe.

VERTICAL COFFIN: A term used by SWAT teams to describe any threshold. When clearing a house, police are most vulnerable to gunfire while passing through doorways.

PROLOGUE

July 14
These Colors Don't Run

They swung wide off Trancas Canyon, thirteen bikes clutching down to make the turn; high-octane Harley engines growling loudly, tearing an ugly hole in the still afternoon. Right ear down, one by one they all finished the turn and straightened up on the Pacific Coast Highway, the old Camino Real. They were ten miles northwest of Malibu, hurtling along the four-lane, timing their moves to roar around slower-moving traffic. Thirteen Harley V-twins in formation. Metal locusts growing larger and more dangerous as they swarmed, the two-second rule be damned.

They called Emo Rojas "Maniac." He was prez, so he was out front, riding point. Emo's giant shoulders reaching high to grab polished ape hangers that stretched like chrome wings over his black Harley Softail. His four-stroke roared angrily: intake, compression, combustion, exhaust. A growling black-and-silver she-devil.

Next was the ride captain Darren Zook, called "Goat." Big, with sleeveless black leathers and arms from Gold's Gym. Hard to tell where his arms stopped and the vest began—he was that black. Outrageous wraparound, chrome-rimmed darks hugged his square face like clip-on bug filters.

Behind Goat was Jabba the Slut. She'd arrived just minutes before the ride, patched in club colors. An American flag do-rag wrapped her head while ink-black shades the size of welders' goggles hid her porcelain-white face. She was club treasurer and had the ride money, so she rode third. Bulging biceps and man-sized thighs straddled the 95 V-twin of her yellow-and-black Screamin' Eagle Deuce; scuffed boots thrust forward on highway pegs.

After Jabba the Slut came the two-by-twos. Blam-Blam, on a chrome-and-black Harley Super Glide. A tub of guts in too-tight leathers with vibrating love handles. Next to him was Drill-Bit, then Johnny Bravo and Pebbles, Wart and Shooter, Mean Mike and The Rooster.

Then came Chooch and Shane Scully. Since they were not patched members of the club, only guests, they rode last: tail-gun charlies. Chooch on Emo's backup bike, a red Harley Fat Boy with a dry clutch. Shane rode Swede Petersen's modified Road King. They came out of Trancas Canyon at the end of the line, completed the turn and accelerated, hurrying to close ranks, bunching tight again, until they blocked both southbound lanes like scurrilous outlaws—riding four across, lane splitting, the throaty animal rumble of all that horsepower redefining them, the exhaust; a self-induced steroid.

You could see awe and revulsion in the eyes of the Sunday drivers they passed. The beach crowd in their SUVs looked over and saw thirteen thugs on custom choppers with mean-looking, radical fork rakes. They saw the head wraps and greasy leathers and quickly looked away. The club patch—the colors—rode their leathers defiantly. Across the shoulder blades in a death font was their name: IRON PIGS. Under that the logo: a fierce warthog with curling tusks and fire blowing out of its nostrils. The bottom rocker said "California."

Only the baddest club in the state was allowed to wear

a bottom rocker. In the eighties that was the Hell's Angels. Then the Mongols blew in and changed all that. They shot a few Angels, ripped the bottom rockers off the dead bikers. The Mongols said you wore the California patch at your own risk. It had been the rule ever since. All bikers knew that if you were caught by a Mongol with a bottom rocker under your colors, you were dead. Mongols alone wore the patch.

Mongols, and of course, Iron Pigs.

The thirteen riders snaked down PCH. The Pacific Ocean glittered on the right, the Malibu Mountains dressed in dry, beige summer colors framed the left. Finally they turned on Mulholland Highway, climbing into the hills. Now the roar of bored pistons and straight pipes bounced off mountains, pinging loudly in the granite canyons. Another left turn off Mulholland took them to Las Flores Road, the hawgs slowing as the road wound dangerously. The late afternoon sun glinted off polished chrome and lacquered paint. A few people heard the deafening rumble and came out of their houses to watch them pass. Then up onto Puma Road, two-by-two, a growling metal centipede making its way slowly along the narrow highway.

Shane looked over at Chooch and saw him grinning. Hard not to feel the rush of all that energy and power. They were nearing the end, rolling in, loud and dangerous. Around the corner, up ahead, was a biker hangout high in the Malibu Mountains.

They rounded the last curve and saw The Rock Store. The parking lot was full. Almost a hundred bikes lined up like soldiers at parade rest, all dressed right, leaning on metal kickstands. Mostly, it was American iron, Harleys and Indians, with a few Japanese rice-burners. The Rock Store was Mecca for Southern California bikers. It was the high church—hawg heaven.

Maniac pulled in and, one by one, the Iron Pigs backed

their bikes into a line, then shut them down. Silence filled their ears, laid tight against their skulls. Goat dismounted and turned to face the Pigs.

"Ride captain buys the beers," he said. A cheer was followed by a round of vicious insults.

"I got your ride money, Goat. Right now, you couldn't buy a Hoover Street hooker," Jabba the Slut scoffed. Then she threw a canvas bag full of cash at him. The Iron Pigs whistled and hooted.

Chooch and Shane climbed off their borrowed bikes. "I'll buy you a beer if you don't tell your mother," Shane whispered, instantly realizing he sounded like a Boy Scout at a truck stop.

"I own you now, Dad," Chooch teased. "If I tell Mom about this, you'll be in honey-do jail until Christmas."

"You gotta take a few chances in life," Shane grinned, and threw an arm around his son's shoulder as they all walked toward The Rock Store.

Shane heard a bike start up and looked around just in time to see Jabba the Slut pulling out on her custom Softail. Then he remembered she said she was on the midwatch and had to get to work. She deep-throated the yellow-and-black Harley, roaring down the road, laying rubber, kicking ass on her way back to L.A.

"I wonder what she looks like under those goggles and do-rag?" Shane pondered.

The Rock Store had been a stagecoach stop in the early 1900s. Ed and Veronica Sazko owned it since the sixties. They made it into a convenience store. The rock foundation was responsible for its name. Two old red-and-white gas pumps sat out front dinging off the gallons like antique slots. In the seventies, the Sazkos had added a dining room and bar. They'd sold one hell of a lot of beer since then. Most L.A. bikers eventually hit the Rock Store. Everybody from Jay Leno to old-time, bee-in-the-teeth

Harley roughnecks hung there. Shane, Chooch, and the remaining Iron Pigs found three open booths, crowded in, and drank beer as the roof shadows grew long, stretching across the porch into the dirt yard. The place started to clear out by seven. By seven thirty most of the Iron Pigs had left. Maniac, Goat, Chooch, and Shane hung on stubbornly, not wanting the ride to end. Alexa was in Chicago at a police convention so Shane and Chooch were spending some guy time together. Maniac and Goat took off their head wraps and the cool biker handles disappeared with them. They were back to being Emo and Darren.

Chooch was explaining the Wing-T offense he quarterbacked at Harvard-Westlake High School, finger painting plays on the table using the moist condensation from their beer cans. Emo watched closely as the play was diagrammed on the sawed wood.

"Don't you run any options off that formation?" Emo asked. His overdeveloped shoulders and muscular build made him look like a linebacker, but Shane knew he'd once played quarterback at Cerritos Junior College.

"Yeah." Chooch drew another play as he talked. "You can fake to the halfback, coming across like this; or do a naked rollout pass run option. We also have a pitch to the trailing back."

Emo leaned over and looked down at the diagram painted in water on the chipped cedar table. Then he added a play of his own.

"You should tell your coach to put in a Z-Option off the rollout. You throw back to the wingback on the far side." He drew the pass pattern and Chooch looked carefully at the play.

"Countermotion," he said, and Emo Rojas nodded.

Shane thought this was just about perfect. He and his son were making the important, but difficult, transition from parent and child to buddies.

They heard the four Harleys pull in, but nobody paid too much attention. Darren Zook went to the restroom to tap a kidney. Shane went to get another beer from the bar. He had just paid when he heard angry voices coming from the other room.

"Do I look like I give a fuck?" he heard somebody shout.

Shane moved out of the bar and stood in the threshold of the dining room. He saw four scruffy looking bikers leaning over the booth where Emo and Chooch sat. Shane knew at a glance these were outlaws. One-percenters. Chooch was trying to get to his feet, but one of the large thugs had his hand on the boy's shoulder holding him in place. Hard to do because Chooch, at eighteen, had grown into a six-foot-three, 225-pound college football prospect. These four outlaws were patched. When one of them moved, Shane saw the Mongols' colors riding his back like a dangerous insult.

"This ain't gonna work, dickhead," one of the Mongols said to Emo. He was big. At least two hundred and fifty pounds, with a red beard and deep-set eyes. He looked mean, but slow.

"Hey Rainman," one of the other Mongols said to red beard, "this kid ain't patched. Maybe he's a prospect."

Rainman leaned in and glared at Chooch. "Then you're prospecting for dead people." He turned and growled at Emo. "You wear the bottom rocker in our state, you eat shit and die."

Chooch was still being held in place. But then without warning, he bolted up, spun, and shoved the Mongol behind him hard, using a forearm shiver. Suddenly everyone was moving at once. Emo Rojas ducked under Rainman's wild right and bolted out of the booth. Chooch scrambled out beside him.

A hard-eyed Mongol with GEEZER stitched on his

pocket was holding the door. He pulled a cut-down out from under his three-quarter-length coat—a shotgun with a four-inch barrel. Cut-downs were illegal in California, but these guys made their own laws. Geezer chambered the piece and everybody froze.

"You got one way outta this place," Rainman said to Emo. He was smiling through his red beard, but his slit eyes offered little humor and no hope. "You get down on your belly and ya crawl out the door. I'm gonna break you up, rip that bottom rocker off, and stuff it up your ass. Then if you suck this prospect's dick, I might let you run."

Now a slight smile appeared on Emo's face. Adrenaline, or some form of street insanity. Chooch was on the balls of his feet and ready.

Shane left the bar threshold and moved quietly along an adjoining wall, then looped right and ran through the service door. Geezer didn't see it coming until it was too late. Shane dove over a table and hit the gunman between the shoulder blades, right in the middle of the ugly, snarling Mongol logo, taking the man to the ground. The shotgun flew from his hands, discharging into the air. It landed, then bucked out the door into the dirt.

How long the fight lasted was a topic of dispute for months. Darren Zook, who heard the shotgun blast and ran out of the can, said he thought he was only in the brawl for about thirty seconds. Shane and Emo felt it had lasted over three minutes—but to be honest, fish and fight stories always get bigger with each telling.

Most dustups end up on the ground, so the LAPD and the L.A. Sheriff's Department teach a version of Brazilian jujitsu, which is a ground-fighting technique. Tough guys and heroes like to stand toe-to-toe and trade punches, but Emo, Shane, and Darren all took their guys down fast, wrapping them up in arm locks and leg holds. Geezer screamed as Shane applied too much leverage and broke his right wrist. Rainman hit Chooch, who shook it off and countered with two sharp left hooks that dumped him.

Whether it took a minute or an hour, the end result was the same. Shane, Darren, Emo, and Chooch were standing over the four dazed Mongols. It was a moment that would bond them forever.

"Los Angeles Sheriff's Department. You're under arrest," Emo said, as he flashed his deputy's star and cuffed Rainman.

Shane flashed his LAPD badge, then grabbed his cuffs and hooked Geezer up. Darren and Emo cuffed the other two, who called themselves Crash and Nasty, then went through the bikers' pockets and finally found enough meth in their saddlebags to add Possession with Intent to Distribute to the charge sheet. Afterwards, they escorted their captives outside and waited for the LASD transport van.

The Mongols shook their heads in dismay. "You guys are cops?" Rainman asked. "I thought you were outlaws."

Darren said, "Iron Pigs don't ask if they can wear the bottom rocker, because you gotta be a cop to join." Then Emo reached out and tore Rainman's California rocker off his leathers and stuffed it in the trash can out front. He tapped his own club logo. "These colors don't run."

When the sheriff's van pulled away with the four Mongols, it was almost dark. Shane and Chooch said goodbye to Emo and Darren, then walked back to their borrowed bikes. As Chooch turned to get on his Fat Boy, Shane saw that he had a cut on his eyebrow trickling blood. His lip was also beginning to swell.

"Your mom's gonna kill us," he said.

"We didn't run, Dad," Chooch said proudly.

"Yep. We hung solid," Shane agreed. As he started his Harley he thought this boy had surely been sent to him by God.

ONE

Vertical Coffin

It was mid-September, hot and dry, the kind of hot that makes you think of frosty cans of Coors and long swims in the ocean. I was standing in a small, burned-out shack ten miles east of Palmdale in the high desert. There wasn't much left—a rock chimney and some blackened footings. My shoes were already covered with soot from kicking at scorched rocks and the remnants of charred furniture. It was ten on a Tuesday morning and the lizards had already abandoned their flat rocks to slither into the shady crevices between granite outcroppings.

This had been a Palmdale P.D. crime scene a month ago. Now it was mine. I'd driven out here in a primered Ford Bronco along with Sonny Lopez. The truck was his privately owned vehicle, known in police circles as a POV. Sonny was a sheriff's deputy working L.A. Impact, a multijurisdictional law-enforcement task force located in Los Angeles County, in Lancaster. The TF was a bad pork stew made up of LAPD and state cops, LASD, and a smattering of feds from the FBI, Customs, and ATF. All of them pretending to be a kick-ass unit, while at the same time trying to get past their deep jurisdictional prejudices.

Sonny Lopez was in his mid-thirties, tall, and movie-star handsome. He was working meth labs for L.A. Impact. This one had exploded and burned to the ground. At first it was thought to be a gas leak, but the county fire teams had learned to call the cops if they saw chemistry glassware in the ashes. When they were raking the debris cold, too many test tubes came up in the furrows. Since crystal kitchens tended to explode more frequently than Palestinian suicide bombers, the Palmdale P.D. did tests on the soil and found high quantities of methamphetamine. In fact, the dirt was so laced with amp, the site started to get nightly visits from local crankheads. They hauled away the soil, taking it home to mine it for meth. A dirt lab is what we called it. L.A. Impact did a lot of meth investigations, so they were called in.

I came from a far more depressing direction.

Two kids had starved to death in a house in Fullerton; fourteen-month-old Cindy and her four-month-old brother, Ben. Their mother, Paula Beck, was a crystal addict with half a dozen meth-cooking busts in her package. Paula was currently in the Sybil Brand Institute facing two involuntary manslaughter charges. The D.A. wanted to boot it up to murder two and had asked Special Crimes at LAPD to look for extenuating circumstances. Since my partner, Zack Farrell, was on a temporary leave of absence to be with his ill mother in Florida, and since it was mostly a background check, which required no partner, I got to work on that grisly little double homicide. The D.A. thought if he could file the bigger charge against Paula he could get her to roll on her ex-boyfriend, Paco Martinez, a high-profile drug dealer. Paula had been banging him until a month ago, when she'd finally gotten so tweaked and crankster-thin he kicked her out.

Once Deputy Lopez determined that this burned out hacienda had been Paula Beck's pad, the sheriff's and LAPD crime computers played "Let's Make a Deal" and that's how we ended up in Palmdale together. Because

Paco Martinez was such a major player, I'd been expecting to find a big crystal plant. But now that I was here, I knew I'd wasted the trip. This was just a user lab, a Beavis and Butt-head kitchen where poor, strung-out Paula Beck cooked her own personal bag of crystal, then fried her brains. I wondered if little Cindy had crawled in the dirt out front while Ben lay screaming in soaking diapers watching his mommy shoot the moon. I wondered if she'd gotten so tweaked in Fullerton that she just forgot she had left her two babies locked in their room till they starved to death.

So now Sonny and I were standing in Paula's kitchen, both silently wondering, if somebody had taken notice sooner could this whole terrible tragedy have been avoided?

But crystal is the oxymoron of narcotics. Technically, methamphetamine is the artificially synthesized version of the body's natural adrenal hormone. Cook up a good batch and it makes you feel beautiful, sexy, attractive, and alert. The problem is that it also takes away whatever it was that you wanted from it. If you use it for sex, you can't have an orgasm. Take it for work, you become totally inefficient. And very quickly it goes negative. You start to get so drowsy you need to load up just to keep your eyes open. It's a nightmare drug. I've seen recovered heroin users, but not one recovered meth addict. They all check off the ride at the first possible stop.

Cindy and Ben had paid Paula's trip ticket and now I was out here trying to cash her in for a D.A. who really only wanted her boyfriend. It was part of an endless cycle of death and destruction.

More and more I was finding it difficult to do this job. All I saw was human wreckage. Even when I succeeded in doing something that felt right, more often than not, I'd been cursed for it. People didn't want cops around. Even my victories produced confusion. I had been fighting these feelings by not thinking about them, pushing them aside like bad food, knowing that if I ate much more it would soon make me sick. But you can't run from moral dilemmas, and I knew my days in law enforcement were numbered unless I found an answer.

"This lab burned a month ago?" I asked, jerking my ruminations out of this deep rut and back onto Paula's cratered family.

"Yep." Sonny looked around the flat, dry desert, his dark good looks clouded by his own elusive thoughts.

A hawk wheeled high overhead, a black shadow against the cobalt sky. The bird called softly to me. A mournful sound: too late . . . too late . . . too late.

"You gonna write any of this up?" Sonny asked. "I got the PFD reports. I can burn you a copy if that'd help, but there's nothing much here. It's been baked and raked. Whatta ya say we head back?"

"She's out here cooking up a batch, gets so amped out, she burns her own place. It's a wonder those kids lasted as long as they did."

Sonny nodded and looked up at the sun. "Man, it's hot. How did my ancestors put up with this heat?" He wiped his face with a handkerchief, anxious to get moving.

"Let's roll," I said.

We trudged back to the Bronco. Sonny cranked the air up, but it blew hot for almost three minutes before things got better. We took the Grapevine over the hill and in less than an hour dropped back into the Valley. My car was at the Agoura sheriff's substation where we'd met. We rode in silence most of the way.

Finally, somewhere near Sunland, Sonny looked over and shook his head angrily. "How do you get so wired you forget your own kids?" he grumbled. "It's bummin' me out."

"We both shoulda gone into retail," I replied.

When we arrived at the substation all hell was breaking loose. Sonny almost hit a black-and-white Suburban that was careening out of the parking garage. I could see the wide-eyed, adrenaline-charged face of the uniformed driver as he bounced the vehicle out of the lot and squealed away up the street.

"That's our technical command vehicle," Sonny said. "The area commander uses it to roll on hot calls." Seconds later, ten sheriff's deputies ran out of the station carrying shotguns and Kevlar, trying to buckle into their Tac vests as they ran.

"This don't look good," Sonny said. He squealed into a parking spot, jumped out, and ran toward the substation.

I was LAPD and this was an L.A. Sheriff's Department rollout. As I picked up my briefcase and headed toward my black Acura, I told myself, leave it be, I've got enough action on my own beat.

The joke in LAPD is that the sheriffs are just rent-a-cops on steroids. The reason is that LASD sells their services to any unincorporated city in L.A. County that needs them. They contract out, just like the square badges who work the malls. The rip is they wear stars not badges, and that *star* is just *rats* spelled backwards. Of course, that's just a sleazy, jurisdictional cheap shot. The LAPD, gods that we are, are paid by the almighty taxpayers, giving us superior placement in the jurisdictional universe. All of which is worth about what you paid for it. Nothing.

I was unlocking the Acura when Sonny Lopez ran back into the lot with four deputies and a lieutenant. The "LT" was cradling a Tactical Operation Tango 51, which I'd read was their new Remington 700 Action sniper rifle. It was an extremely accurate long gun that fired a 168-grain Boattail .308 hollow point. Huge stopping power. Something big was definitely going down. The deputies and their watch commander piled into a new sheriff's Suburban with a Mars Bar, hit the cherries, and squealed out fast. Sonny never even glanced back at me. He was that pumped.

I reached into my car and switched to the Impact channel on my police radio. The LAPD and LASD work on completely different radio frequencies, but since I had worked with L.A. Impact twice before on overlapping cases, I had put their TAC frequency on my scanner. This was a major scramble and I figured some of the Impact crew was undoubtedly rolling on it. If so, I'd be able to crib their transmissions. They used Tactical Frequency 4. I switched it on and immediately heard somebody screaming:

". . . Deputy down! Thirty-Mary-Four is down! He's layin' up on the porch right in the door. Every time we try and get to him, the sonofabitch inside starts pourin' lead out at us." You could hear the adrenaline in his voice.

Somebody else came back yelling an order. "Forget Emo! We can't get him out of there—not yet. Set up your fire lines. Cover the back. Get a secure perimeter and somebody run over and tell those fucking SRT SWAT guys not to canister the place with hot gas. I don't have their frequency. Tell 'em we can't take a fire. This neighborhood is too dense and the brush is too dry."

Emo? I thought. *Emo Rojas?*

I pulled out of the substation parking lot as I triggered my mike. "This is LAPD Sergeant Scully. What's your location?"

"Get the fuck off this channel," somebody barked.

"Where is this?" I yelled. "What's the Twenty?"

"Hidden Ranch Road," someone else answered.

I don't ride that much in the county and had no idea where that was, so I pulled over and programmed the street and city into my Acura's GPS. A map appeared on the LCD screen. It was the main road in a housing development called Hidden Ranch. The street dead-ended at a cul-de-sac in the foothills of Agoura two miles behind me. I swung a U, put the hammer down, and made it there in two minutes, with my on-line bitch goddess screaming directions. *In two hundred feet turn right,* she ordered.

You could hear the gunfire from almost half a mile away. Not the flat popping sound of 9 mm handguns, or the hard crack of an Ithaca pump, but the BLAPBLAP-BLAPBLAP of an AK-47, or some heavy-ordnance machine rifle on full auto.

When I reached Hidden Ranch Road I saw a residential area full of two-story builder houses in the mid-to-expensive range tucked up against the dry San Gabriel foothills. Fifteen LASD's cars were already on the scene. At least twenty-five deputies were fanned out hiding behind garden walls and parked squad cars. Some were pouring 9 mm rounds into a house at the end of the cul-de-sac.

Just then a shooter appeared in one of the downstairs windows and let loose with an AK-47. The weapon tore holes right through the sheriff's van parked in the center of the street. Then the gunman ducked back out of sight. Two sheriff's air units and a TV news chopper added to the wall of noise as they circled relentlessly overhead. I rolled out low from the Acura, hung my badge case open on my jacket pocket, grabbed my Beretta and ran toward the sheriff's vans and the Suburban TCV parked in a semicircle in the middle of the cul-de-sac.

The shooter's house was a phony Georgian with fake trim and Doric columns. Sprawled across the threshold of the front door was a uniformed deputy. He wasn't moving. But I recognized those shoulders, that short black hair. It was Emo Rojas. Flat on his face, lying in the vertical coffin.

TWO

Barricaded Suspect

As I approached I heard a uniformed sheriff's captain screaming into his cell phone.

"The shit just jumped off! We got an active shooter and a deputy down. I need an incident commander and a Special Enforcement Bureau team on site now! There's an SRT unit here, but they're pinned down across the street. They're not on our frequency, so I can't communicate with them."

Just then, a four-vehicle sheriff's SEB convoy rolled in, sirens wailing, flashers on. The SWAT van squealed to a stop near the three sheriff's vehicles already parked in the center of the cul-de-sac. Two deputy cars and an armored rescue vehicle, an ARV, followed. I had done some cross-training with the LASD at their facility in Spring Ranch, so I knew how they were set up. Special Weapons Teams were comprised of a team leader, usually a sergeant, the second in command was a scout, who did the onsite tactical operation plan. A back-up scout assisted him. The fourth man stayed at the truck to gather intelligence. The fifth and sixth men were responsible for equipment. There were two snipers, called long guns. The weapon of choice for the long guns was a Tango 51 or its predecessor, the 40-X. Both rifles fired armor-piercing .308s. Each long gun had a spotter with him to help isolate targets and to give him tactical support and cover.

The team leader unlocked the SWAT van and the long guns swarmed inside to grab their weapons while the backup scout started passing out flash-bang grenades.

The fourth man opened the office on the side of the truck where the incident board and the weapons team roster hung. He pulled out a graphed Lucite desktop, grabbed a piece of paper, and started to diagram the house and the cul-de-sac, eyeballing it from where he stood, doing a rough but reasonably accurate layout, including all the vehicles parked on the street.

"Get in touch with the city planning office and see if you can get somebody to fax us the plans of this house," the fourth man said to the fifth.

Just then the barricaded suspect popped up again in an upstairs window, firing his AK-47. From where I was hiding, it looked like the weapon held a hundred-round drum mag. The slugs started tearing up the police cars out front and blowing holes in the brick walls where deputies were proned out trying to take cover.

The team leader grabbed his shoulder mike. "All deputies on this channel, get back! You aren't safe. This guy's using lead core rounds. You can't hide behind walls or car doors. Get behind a house, or at least find an engine block."

He opened an ammo box and started handing out .308 mags. His two long rifles and spotters jammed the clips home, then deployed quickly, running low, looking for a good place to set up shop. I ran up to the SWAT van, took cover, then glanced at the team roster clipped to the door. This was the Gray team. The team leader, Sergeant Scott

Cook; scout, Rick Manos; first long gun, Gary Nightingale; and spotter, Michael Nightingale. *Brothers?* As I was reading the board the fourth man spun me roughly around.

"Who the fuck are you, Chester?"

"Scully. LAPD."

"Get lost. This ain't your rodeo."

I held up my Beretta. "This guy's in Kevlar. My nines are useless. Can I borrow some Teflon rounds?"

"Shit," he said, but turned, grabbed a box, and tossed it to me. "Stay behind something dense. Those lead cores he's using are brutal."

"Right."

I moved away and ducked down behind the engine compartment of a sheriff's car. The deputies pinned behind the brick wall were trying to retreat, but every thirty seconds or so the shooter would appear in another window of his house and start firing. His twenty-round bursts tore up everything they hit. I knelt and thumbed the useless, standard 9 mm Winchesters out of my clip, then started feeding in the Teflon mag rounds. Once I had all thirteen loaded, I slammed the clip home, chambered the gun, then peeked up over the hood of the car. Emo was still up on the porch. It didn't look like he'd moved at all. Nobody had the stones to try and go up there. If you made a run and timed it wrong, it was pretty much suicide. You were gonna get chopped in half by that AK.

I told myself that even though Emo wasn't moving, it didn't mean he was dead.

Ten yards away I spotted Sonny Lopez crouched down behind a squad car with another deputy. Both held shotguns at port arms. Their Ithacas were useless in this situation, and you could tell from their strained expressions that they knew it. I moved up from behind and tapped Sonny on the shoulder.

He jerked around to look at me. His face was pulled tight. "Scully, whatta you doin' here?"

"Not to be a critic, but shouldn't we go get our guy off the porch?"

"Can't. The perp's got armor-piercing shit. He's blowing holes right through car doors. We're calling for more backup."

"Why doesn't somebody get him on a cell phone, try and cool this down?"

"The lieutenant tried talking to him. Guy won't come out. An incident commander's on his way. Captain Matthews wants to sit tight and wait for him."

Then, in an attempt to explain why all these cops were on their faces eating dirt, Sonny added, "This asshole's nuts," which was more or less obvious.

"Look, that's Emo Rojas up there, right?" I said.

"You know him?"

"Yeah. If we could get one of those two SWAT teams to work the right side of the house, maybe they could draw the guy over there and you and I could make a run and pull Emo off the porch."

"You outta your mind?" Lopez said.

"Probably," I answered. "Wanta try it?"

He thought about it for a moment, looked skeptically toward the house.

Just then the shooter popped up again. He was upstairs this time, and let go with a five-second burst, aiming at the squad car we were hiding behind. The black and white rocked hard with the impact from a stream of lead that sliced through the door panels like they were plywood. Windshield glass and side mirrors shattered and flew. Then the man ducked back down. It seemed to help Sonny make up his mind.

"Let's go," he said hotly. "Lemme get my Loo to sign off on it." He moved off to find his lieutenant.

There was walkie-talkie madness all around me. People screaming, shouting counter-instructions, stepping on each others' transmissions. While all this was happening, I decided if I was going to try to get Emo off that porch, I was going to need some better intel. I looked up and saw that there were now three news helicopters swirling overhead. Pinned down, I couldn't really risk rising up to case the situation. I looked behind me. The neighbors' houses across the street had all been evacuated. I waited until the shooter popped up and greased off another burst. After he finished I sprinted across the street to the nearest house. Luckily, the front door had been left ajar. I hit the front porch, crossed it in two steps, and kicked the door wide, entering the house.

I ran through the downstairs and collected two small portable TVs, one in the kitchen and one in the office. Then, carrying one in each arm, I ran through an Early American–style living room into the den, where I found a big-screen TV. I turned it on and plugged in the two portables. Every thirty seconds or so, the AK cut loose out front. Bullets whined and ricocheted in a deadly concert of tortured metal. I couldn't hook up all three sets to cable, but I was able to pick up the local news stations with the rabbit ears on the portables. I flipped around the channels, stopping at three different stations that were carrying the shootout. KTLA had a bird up. So did KTTV and KNBC. For the first time, I could see the entire scene.

The sheriffs had the house completely surrounded, front and back. The long lenses from the news cameras kept zooming in tight, and now, when the shooter appeared and fired, I got a pretty good look at him. This asshole was dressed head-to-toe in black body armor and was wearing a gas mask. He would pop up, looking like an extra in a Steven Seagal movie, and squeeze off a five-second burst, then disappear. His window choices seemed random.

I took off my watch, set it on the table in front of me, and started to time him. First he worked the downstairs. He'd shoot through three or four different windows at random, then move upstairs. After watching for about three minutes I could see the pattern.

Downstairs, he was all over the place shooting short, twenty-round bursts. But he always ended at the window on the far left side of the house. He'd fire a long stream of lead from that position, and then be gone for thirty to forty seconds before reappearing upstairs. He'd shoot randomly out of the upstairs windows, then be downstairs again. But his last firing position on the ground floor was always that same window on the far left of the house. My guess was that the staircase was over there.

It took him thirty seconds to get upstairs and start shooting again. He was triggering off five-second bursts, which I estimated at about fifteen or twenty rounds. He probably needed another ten seconds to change C-clips at the top of the stairs before again going to work in the upstairs windows. The time for me to make my move up to the porch was after he shot the long burst through the far left downstairs window.

I turned off the TVs and decided to test my theory. Moving to the front door, I waited for him to shoot out of the last window downstairs, then ran out of the house and across the street. I settled down behind the same squad car where I had been earlier, easily beating the next burst of gunfire from the upstairs window.

Sonny was already there and turned when I arrived. "Where were you?" he asked.

"Watching TV."

Sonny gave me a strange look, so I said, "Are we good to go?"

"Loo says no. The captain wants to wait for the incident commander from the downtown bureau."

"What is he, some kinda desk commander?" I said.

"More or less," Sonny agreed.

"Then I say screw him. Emo could be pumping dry. He could be dying. We can't just leave him up there."

Sonny didn't speak, but after a second he nodded.

I told Sonny my plan. We both tried to watch the shooter take one more lap around the house so Sonny could see for himself. But in truth, it was damn hard to keep your head up while he was pouring those lead cores down on us.

"Next time, after he does the last downstairs window on the left, we go," I said. "Okay?"

Sonny licked his lips and nodded grimly.

We waited until the shooter finished his last downstairs pop-up, then both of us exploded out from behind the car and ran low, heads down, across the lawn and dove under the porch. I don't think the shooter saw us, but then, I wasn't looking either. The minute we started our run there was a lot of yelling from the sheriff's troops behind us. Somebody started screaming and calling us assholes.

Once we were under the porch, Sonny pulled his transmitter off his Tac vest and spoke clearly into it. "We're gonna pull Emo off there," he said. "Lay down some cover fire, but aim high. Don't hit us! Get our SWAT van up here on the lawn. Give us a place to take him. This is going down after the next time he shoots."

A few seconds later another lead burp ripped the air: BLAPBLAPBLAPBLAP! Fifty sheriffs and two SWAT teams responded, pouring lead into the house as Sonny and I rolled up simultaneously and grabbed Emo by the

ankles. Bullets thunked and glass shattered from the sheriffs' volley as we started pulling Emo off the deck. He
streaked a wide stripe of bright red blood and brown
stomach matter on the porch behind him before flopping
down onto the lawn with us. As soon as he hit I knew he
was dead. There was a huge hole in his gut, another in the
center of his chest, his pants were messed. His bowels had
let go; urine soaked his leg.

I held his head anyway.

Just then six SWAT guys who were all tricked out in
black jumpsuits opened up with grenade launchers, mor-
taring hot gas canisters through half a dozen windows in
the house: THUNK-THUNK-THUNK. A few remaining
windows shattered. Smoke billowed.

"Who the hell are those guys?" I asked Sonny. "That's
hot gas. They should use the cold canisters. They're
gonna set the house on fire. The whole hillside could go."

Sonny shook his head. "Don't know," he said.

They looked like SRT to me.

Two minutes later the house flamed. Black smoke billowed out of the upstairs windows. But the barricaded
suspect had a gas mask, and kept shooting, popping up,
firing short bursts. Sonny and I were trapped under the
porch.

After about ten minutes we heard on the radio that the
man had stopped shooting out of the upstairs window and
was now running back and forth downstairs. The roaring
fire covered the sound of everything but the occasional
high, shrill wail of a late-arriving fire unit and the short,
choppy bursts from the AK-47. Eventually, as the fire
raged, his gun went silent.

It was getting so hot where Sonny and I were that we
had to pull back or be incinerated. The shooter hadn't
fired for more than two minutes, so we grabbed Emo's

body and dragged him across the lawn to the SWAT van. The sheriff's department SEB long rifles covered us, firing a deadly volley into the raging fire and billowing smoke. The heat from the blaze seared my back as we dragged Emo's body behind the van and laid him down.

When I turned I wasn't at all prepared for what I saw. Every room in the house had flames and black smoke pouring out of the windows. The roof was on fire. Ten minutes later the entire second floor collapsed. Then, one by one, boxes of ammo started going off in the garage. Armor-piercing .308s and .223s whizzed through the neighborhood like deadly hornets. Without warning, huge explosions rocked the cars we hid behind. Whatever just went up, it wasn't conventional ordnance. It was some kind of high-grade explosive. Everybody out front hit the deck and stayed down until it was over.

Finally, when they were sure that whatever caused the explosions had detonated, the fire units moved in, concentrating on keeping the dry brush in the foothills from going up, and working to keep the sparks from igniting the houses next door.

I found out from one of the deputies that Emo Rojas, who was a sheriff's motorcycle officer, had volunteered at roll call that morning to serve the warrant at end of watch.

Apparently, one of the home owners, a guy named Vincent Smiley, had been walking around the Hidden Ranch neighborhood flashing a badge and impersonating a sheriff's deputy. The neighbors called the department and found out that Smiley wasn't a sheriff. A warrant to pick him up was issued. Emo borrowed a D-car at the substation and came out here with his partner, Dave Brill. It was a nothing bust. A class-B felony. So Emo just walked up and rang the front doorbell with the arrest warrant in his hand while Brill stayed in the car filling out the incident report. Nobody was expecting trouble.

Then Smiley opened the front door and shot twice.

Emo was probably dead before he hit the ground.

THREE

Crime Scene

After Emo's corpse left in the ambulance I tried to disappear. I wanted to hide in some dark place and check my psyche for damage, to see how I really felt about this, before something I couldn't fix broke inside me. The Agoura substation's area commander, Captain Matthews, was still in charge because the incident commander from LASD headquarters didn't make it to the site until Vincent Smiley had changed categories, going from an active shooter to a crispy critter. When the IC finally showed up the site was already Code 4. He didn't want any part of it and gave this disaster a kiss and a wave, leaving a dead deputy, a smoldering house, and angry neighbors for Captain Matthews to deal with. Naturally, Matthews was pissed. He recognized career leprosy when he saw it.

He grabbed my arm and stopped me from leaving. "Gonna need your statement," he growled.

"Right, Skipper. Solid," I said, trying to sound hard-boiled and competent.

"Wait in that patrol car by yourself," he instructed. "I don't want you talking to anybody, changing your story around to fit somebody else's account."

So I sat in a sheriff's car alone, and watched the rest of the place burn to the ground, fueled by the hot gas grenades and Smiley's illegal explosives. It didn't take long either. The place burned down faster than a Skid Row hotel. The fire crews kept the hill from going up and managed to keep the structures next door wet. Even though those houses didn't catch fire, the adjoining walls were scorched from the intense heat.

I tried to think about the brand of insanity that had made Vincent Smiley, whoever he was, strap on all that body armor and trade rounds with half the uniforms in the Valley. He'd stayed inside his burning prefab Georgian, raining death indiscriminately out the windows, endangering his entire neighborhood until he was buried in a collapsing inferno. Was he trying to get the sheriffs to kill him?

Suicide by Cop was the new hot category in law enforcement. It covered situations like this, where the perp's actions defied conventional rules of behavior. I thought hard about it, because I was trying to keep my mind from sinking into a painful memory of Emo Rojas. I wasn't sure I could face where that would take me yet.

I had really liked Emo. He was one of those cops who could wear a badge without letting it change what he weighed.

The fire crews hosed down the smoldering remains of the house, then raked the embers cool. When it was over there wasn't much more left than at Paula Beck's shack out in Palmdale. Just a chimney and a mound of steaming ashes.

I watched the neighbors gather in little knots, looking on with wide, blank expressions—staring at the charred ground that hours ago was a fancy, two-story Georgian.

The M.E. and SID arrived shortly after the smoke monkeys knocked down the flames, then stood around and waited. Once it was cool enough, a team of CSI techs started sifting through the ash and bagging brass, while the coroner's people began searching for Mr. Smiley's remains. They found him in a bathtub. He'd been parboiled, then charbroiled. When they tried to get him out of the tub, he was so cooked he broke into pieces. God knows how hot the fire had been downstairs, but it sure didn't leave much for the coroner to identify. They loaded him into three rubber body bags and rolled him out on a gurney. The neighbors watched him leave with tight expressions of fear and relief. Teenage girls clustered together chewing the sides of their thumbs, muttering platitudes.

"How does this happen?" whispered a young mother who was standing near the car I was in.

It was my question, too.

"You Scully?" a voice asked, interrupting these thoughts. I looked through the side window and saw a tall angular man in a tan suit. Old-style Ray-Ban Aviators were perched on his face with fifty-mission swagger. The plastic nosepiece had yellowed years ago. He was chewing a toothpick, his hair was one week past a buzz cut, and his face had the weathered, no-nonsense look of somebody who'd spent a lot of time squinting down a barrel at big game.

"Yeah," I said. "Shane Scully, LAPD."

"Right." He looked me up and down—a quick, professional appraisal. "Sergeant Bob Dodds. I'm running point on the shooting review for SEB. We got a division commander and somebody from the D.A. headed out here. Gonna do the OIS review at the Agoura substation." OIS stood for Officer Involved Shooting. "I'm gonna need your preliminary statement now."

He climbed in the back seat with me, turned on a tape recorder and held it between us. "This is Sergeant Robert Dodds and I'm conducting a post-incident statement given by Sergeant Shane Scully, LAPD. It's one forty P.M. September fourteenth." Then he turned to me.

"So what's the story here, Scully? Can't get enough action in town, you gotta jump out on county calls?" It was an old interrogation technique. Start with an insult, see what happens.

I smiled back at him. "Are you planning to ask me what I saw, Sergeant Dodds, or would you rather just chew on that toothpick and act like an asshole?"

We sat looking at each other, breathing in that funky squad car smell. They all smell pretty much the same: Lysol, vomit, warm plastic. The M.E.'s Black Mariah rolled past, taking Vincent Smiley to the morgue for his last earthly checkup. Dodds and I both watched him leave, then he looked back at me.

"This is a mess," I said. I pointed out the window. "That SWAT team over there, the men in black, hit this hood like Rommel's Africa Corps. Nobody stopped to call for a qualified negotiator. Half your Valley day watch and an SEB team also rolled, everybody's cranking off rounds. . . ." I motioned again toward the black-suited SWAT team that had fired the gas grenades. "That bunch starts lobbing hot gas canisters while we're still up under the porch. Almost turned this neighborhood into a mini-Waco." He said nothing. I could see my warped reflection in his Ray-Bans. "This isn't my jurisdiction," I continued. "I'm a non-sheriff and a potentially friendly witness, so what I say will carry a lot of weight. I can tell this two or three different ways." I smiled thinly. "Now, how we gonna play it?"

Bob Dodds took off his shades. "Why don't we start over?" he said, then put out his hand and we shook. "Emilio Rojas was a friend of mine," he added.

"Me too. It's why I came up."

Dodds picked up the tape recorder, rewound it and hit record, reslated it, then began recording over our false start.

"Begin with why you came up here," he said in a much friendlier voice.

"I heard it on TAC-four. Heard somebody say Emo was down, lying up on the porch. Since I knew Emo, I came. Got here and basically hid behind a car."

"The lieutenant says you and Sergeant Lopez disobeyed his direct order not to attempt to pull Rojas off that porch. He's a little torqued about it. 'A foolish stunt,' is what he called it. You could have been killed rescuing Rojas, who was already dead."

"Here's how that story tells," I said. "I don't work for the lieutenant, don't even know his name, so, in a strict command sense, he can't order me to do anything. On the other hand, if I'd heard his order, I certainly would have obeyed it in the spirit of interdepartmental cooperation."

"You would, huh?" Dodds frowned. "Am I gonna need to roll up my pant cuffs here?"

"I'm a book guy," I said. "But here's what happened. Nobody knew then if Emo was alive or dead. I saw him lying up there, and since he was a friend, I kinda freaked. I took off without asking anybody . . . I can see now it was a big mistake. Sergeant Lopez was just trying to stop me. Chased me right up the lawn. Next thing you know, we were both under the porch. Once we were there, seemed like there was no reason not to pull Emo down."

Dodds shut off the tape again.

"Is that the way Lopez's gonna tell it?"

"It is, if you give me a minute to explain it to him first."

Sergeant Dodds smiled. "So it's like that, is it?" he said.

"Yep. How 'bout we cut this brave deputy a little slack?"

Dodds smiled, and after a moment he nodded. "Okay," he said. "If you get to him before I do, I guess there's not much I can do." He turned the tape back on.

"So who's in charge of those trigger-happy kazoonies in the cool black jumpsuits?" I asked.

"They're feds," Dodds answered, confirming my guess. "An SRT unit from Alcohol, Tobacco, Firearms, and Explosives."

SRT stood for Situation Response Team—federal SWAT. The media-conscious feds had stopped using ballsy acronyms for their urban assault team, preferring nonviolent handles like SRT or SWT. Even after all the flack that the LAPD had taken of late, we still cling stubbornly to kick-ass unit designations, preferring names like CRASH or SWAT. It seems some lessons are impossible for us to learn.

Dodds handed me his card. "You better call your watch commander and tell him you'll be here most of the afternoon. Drive down to the substation and check in with Jan Micklyn. She's with our Internal Affairs Shooting Review Board. She'll find a place for you to hang out. We'll get your complete statement, wrap you out fast as we can." He snapped off the tape.

I started to get out of the car, then turned back. "A Situation Response Team from ATF? They're located downtown. What were they doing way the hell out here?"

"It's a good question. Their team leader says they were doing range work, practicing clearing houses at their training facility in the foothills. They were driving back and heard it on the L.A. Impact frequency."

"Sounds good." I shot him a little smile. Even though we were buddies now, my smile didn't seem to warm him much. He squinted at me with that weathered shooter's expression, making me feel like game in a laser sight. Then, without saying anything else, he got out of the car and walked away.

I found Sonny over by the van, sitting on a curb look-ing at the burned-down house. He had soot and Emo's blood on his shirt, a frown on his face. I filled him in on my statement to Dodds and he looked up at me and nod-ded. "Thanks, Shane. I owe you for that."

"No you don't. We did the right thing. Why let a bad order and a dumb section in the rule book change it?"

On the drive back to the substation I called and checked in with Lieutenant Jeb Calloway, who was a twenty-year LAPD vet and my new boss at Special Crimes. Cal, as everybody called him, was a big African-American with a shaved head who looked like he should be working event security at a rap concert.

"That shoot-out is all over the news," Cal said after I explained where I was. "Sounds like the IC up there got froggy and pulled the string early."

I told him the incident commander didn't make it and that Captain Matthews, the area commander, got caught wearing the hat. After I explained the rest of what hap-pened he just grunted. He'd seen enough CYA in his ca-reer to know everybody was probably ducking.

When I arrived at the substation the ATF SRT truck was parked in the secure lot in a visitor parking stall. As I walked past it I banged on the side to see if anybody was home. Nobody answered. The back was a locked box that contained all their high-tech toys and deadly ordnance. But I didn't want what was in the back. I walked around to the driver's side and checked to see if the alarm was set. All SWAT vehicles have very sophisticated alarms, and the trucks were never supposed to be left unattended without that alarm set. However, this one was open, the alarm light off. Probably, with all the adrenaline over-load, the cherry in charge of team security just forgot. He was going to catch a ration of shit later, but I didn't care. I stepped up on the running board, opened the door, and jumped in. Then I turned on the police scanner and started flipping through channels.

The unit didn't have TAC-4. I knew that channel had to be specially programmed by a communications tech, because I'd had to have it done on my scanner.

So who was kidding who here? If these guys didn't hear the call on TAC-4, how the hell did they know a shooting was in progress?

FOUR

OIS

I found Sergeant Micklyn setting up shop in the substation. She was a dark-haired, no-nonsense member of OIS and had taken over two I rooms for interviews. She said she wasn't ready for me yet, but settled me in an empty office in the back where I put in a call to DSG at Parker Center.

"My God, Shane," Alexa said after I told her what happened, sounding for a minute more like my worried wife instead of the acting head of the LAPD Detective Services Group.

Alexa and I had an easy, professional relationship on the job. That was because I always did what she said. She wasn't my direct supervisor; she was five layers above me on the command structure. But she was my division commander. If one wants a career in police science, one does not give one's division commander any substantial grief.

At home it was different. We had a completely open and balanced relationship, although I had always suspected that in most complicated, emotional, or political situations Alexa could outperform me. Of course, I could beat her at arm wrestling. She is also the most beautiful woman I have ever known. Tall, with an athlete's body and a face that belongs on the cover of a glamour magazine: black hair, Irish eyes, and strong cheekbones that ride high above the flat plains of her face and frame a strong but sensuous mouth.

I, on the other hand, look like something you'd find in the center ring at the Main Street Boxing Gym. My hair is always ruffled and unkempt, no matter what I do, so I keep it short. My body language is the trademark shuffle of a street brawler, which for a while in my teens I'd been. It always surprised me when women found all this nonsense intriguing. But the only thing that mattered was that Alexa had bought the package.

After I told her about Emo and the shoot-out, she remained quiet for a minute. "But you're okay," she said again.

"Yeah, physically I'm fine. Not a scratch. But emotionally I'm having trouble with it. Emo's dead. He was serving a warrant on some guy for impersonating an officer. Got hit standing in the perp's doorway."

I didn't tell her I'd exposed my scabrous hide to gunfire in an attempt to pull him out and had only managed to rescue a corpse. Hopefully, that detail would be confined to sheriff's department internal documents, and she wouldn't be copied.

"I'll be back as soon as I can, but they're cooking a three-layer cake out here. Active shooter, lotta deputies at the incident, all of 'em cheesing off rounds. Sheriff's SEB had a SWAT team on the scene, ATF rolled a truck. It's gonna take some time for OIS to get all the stories coordinated so it plays okay for the six o'clock news."

"Don't be such a cynic," she said. "I love you. Call if you get outta there in time to meet someplace for dinner."

"Right." I hung up and stood out in the waiting room where I practiced trying to be invisible, which is hard to do when you're in a sheriff's substation wearing a sports jacket with a dead deputy's blood and stomach contents spattered all over it.

I finally got a chance to make my statement at four o'clock. I was led into one of Sergeant Micklyn's I rooms and seated at a wood table in front of a tape machine. Captain Matthews sat in a chair across the room and kept quiet. He glowered as a young lawyer from the D.A.'s office took notes. Sergeant Micklyn ran the interview, Sergeant Dodds stood against a white concrete wall and listened. I started telling my story, adding my one embellishment to keep Sonny Lopez straight with his lieutenant. After I finished I looked at Dodds, who still had on his Ray-Bans, even though we were inside. He had been leaning his thin frame against the wall, chewing his toothpick, looking like a cowboy in a Bull Durham commercial. He finally pushed away and straddled a straight-back chair facing me.

"You sure you didn't fire your weapon at the scene?" he asked. "Even though you got them rounds from SEB?"

"I didn't fire," I answered.

"You have any psychological misgivings here? You and Emo were friends. You got the heebie-jeebies? You want me to call your supervisor, get you some time off . . . arrange for a visit to a psych?" It was a standard post-interview question, asked after all shootings to protect the department from a cop's lawsuit, in case he cracked up later.

"No, I'm fine," I said.

Captain Matthews, who had said nothing, got up and walked toward the door. Then, without warning, he swung back.

"Tell me something, Sergeant. Did you see that fed SRT truck parked at the scene when you were coming up Hidden Ranch Road?" he asked.

"I think they got there ahead of me, Captain," I said.

"That's not what I asked you."

"I didn't see them until after I was there. Then later they started lobbing hot gas, like I already said."

"So you didn't see them arrive?" he said.

"Excuse me, Captain, but why don't you just go ask them when they got there? They're still in the station."

"Because they won't agree to be interviewed," he said, repressed anger bubbling to the surface like toxic waste.

"They were on the scene at your shooting," I said. "They fired shots. They gotta sit for your internal review."

"Tell *them* that," he said. "They're saying they'll only talk to their own Internal Affairs."

I thought that might be the new low in interagency cooperation, but I didn't say anything.

Then Sergeant Micklyn, whose first name was Jan, officially closed the interview, picked up her tape recorder, snapped it off, and popped out my cassette. She labeled it, then set it in a stack with some others.

"Since that tape is off, maybe I can help you with one thing," I said.

"What's that?" Dobbs said.

"You told me that ATF arrived quickly because they were coming from a training day and heard the cross talk on the L.A. Impact channel."

"That's their story," Dobbs agreed.

"Kinda hard to do when you don't have TAC-four on your scanner." Dodds let one eyebrow climb his forehead. "On the way in here I looked in their truck. Not on there," I said.

Dodds glanced at Captain Matthews. Neither said anything or changed expressions, but a lot was going on between them. Then someone knocked on the I room door. Dodds opened it. A uniformed deputy was outside.

"Captain, I've got the ASAC from ATF outside. Name's Brady Cagel. He wants to talk to the incident commander. Guess that's still you," the deputy said.

Matthews groaned. Dodds took off his sunglasses and carefully wiped them with a handkerchief, not looking at Matthews, who moved to the door and said, "Where's SRT? They still in my office?"

"Still there," the deputy said, and both of them left.

Dodds turned to me.

"I'm done with you for now, Scully. We'll get this typed up and you can sign it in a day or so."

"Okay." I got to my feet and walked back into the substation. You could feel the tension. Everybody's nerves were frayed and sparking. Dangerous energy was arcing around like loose bolts of electricity.

Brady Cagel was your standard-issue fed in a suit. He was in the waiting area alone. Medium height, with a tight build. His regular features, short hair, and square jaw made him look rugged, not handsome. But he was angry. His eyes, like lasers, were zapping around, peeling the paint off walls in the underfurnished lobby.

I wasn't about to miss this, so I ducked into the coffee room and started searching my pocket for quarters to feed into the vending machines. After a moment a lock buzzed and I heard Captain Matthews come through the electric door into the waiting room.

"Agent Cagel?" I heard him say. "I'm Matthews, the CO." There was a pause while I guess they shook hands.

Then Cagel said, "I'm the ASAC for SRT. I understand you're keeping my people here."

"I need your unit to all make statements. I can't close our shooting review without it. We need an account from everyone who discharged a weapon on the scene."

"You'll get statements. We'll just do it over at our shop, is all. We're gonna use our review apparatus. I'll shoot everything over to you after it's done."

"They'll have to make the statements in my presence," Matthews said, his voice getting hard.

Then I heard feet shuffling and it got quiet out there, so I went to the coffee room door and took a peek. They had gone to the leather club chairs in the waiting area and were now seated, leaning toward each other. I couldn't quite hear what they were saying, so I crossed to the vending machines, bought some candy, then moved back to the door and looked out again. I could now hear them again, because their voices were raised in anger.

"We're not going to sit for your shooting panel, get used to it," Cagel was saying.

"Your guys were firing Parabellums and hot gas without coordinating with me. It was my incident. You were operating out there without even being on the same radio frequency," Matthews said. "Your guys set the house on fire. I have a lot of questions. I wanta know how they got to our crime scene less than three minutes after the shooting started."

"I talked to my team leader. He says they were coming back from a training exercise, heard it going down on the IMPACT channel."

"Only their truck doesn't have the Impact frequency on its scanner," Matthews said.

"You're mistaken," Cagel replied. "Now, where are my people? I have an IAD inquiry convening downtown. We're already keeping a lot of people waiting."

Matthews was losing this one. He had no way to force SRT into his review if they didn't want to do it. They worked for a separate agency.

"There was a lot of armor-piercing ordnance stored in that house," Matthews finally said. "Grenades, at least fifty thousand rounds of three-oh-eights or two-twenty-threes. We had some big explosions, which could have been dynamite, or even C-four. You sure ATF wasn't already teed up on that guy for some illegal firearms complaint, and that's how you got there so fast?"

Brady Cagel stood. "Look, Captain, we're going to do a thorough investigation. I haven't interviewed my team leader yet, but we will pursue everything by the book. Once our IAD says the investigation is completed, we'll make sure you get a copy. Then you can add it to your review. Now where is my team? I'm not going to ask you again."

"They're in my office," Matthews said tightly.

I didn't need to see him to know he was seething. I heard the ASAC move past the coffee room and ask the desk sergeant to let him into the rear area.

I waited until I heard the electric lock buzz, then went into the bathroom and tried to get Emo's blood and guts off my jacket. I scrubbed with wet paper towels but wasn't having much luck. The sports coat looked like a complete loss, but I stripped it off, folded it over my arm, and carried it out with me anyway.

In the parking lot I found Sonny Lopez waiting by my car. He still had Emo's DNA on his uniform. We stood looking at each other for a long moment, not sure how to wrap this up.

"Thanks for helping me get him down off the porch," I said. "If he'd stayed up there, we woulda lost the body."

"I was waiting out here to tell you I shoulda suggested it first. He was my *carnal*, my station mate. I kinda froze."

"Not when it counted," I said, and put a hand on his shoulder. I could feel his nerves and muscles twitch under my hand.

"This is really fucked, huh?" he finally said.

"Yep."

"SRT just rolled out of here in their new LAV." The feds called their SWAT van a light armored vehicle. "I've never seen Captain Matthews so jacked up. He's usually pretty mellow."

"That's 'cause SRT won't sit for your shooting review. They're doing a parallel investigation. His ass is on the line. He lost a deputy, the perp is barbeque, the house in ashes. There's gonna be beaucoup legal trouble over this," I said.

"It's even worse than that, Shane. I just found out from the desk sergeant that ATF called us. They got the initial complaint, but since Smiley was impersonating a sheriff's deputy and lived in the county, ATF handed us the collar. The neighbors up there told me an hour ago that Smiley had been wandering around, showing his neighbors a sheriff's badge for months. He'd been telling 'em he works for our antiterrorist division. They said last week Smiley took some of the guys who live up there into his garage and showed them his armory. Boxes of ammo, grenade launchers. They said he even had plastic explosives up there, some C-four."

"That's what blew the roof off the garage," I said.

Sonny nodded. "The neighbors called ATF and reported it because they didn't want some spook in their neighborhood with a garage full of explosives. Matthews thinks after they gave us the impersonating charge they were parked nearby, waiting to see what would happen about the guns. That's how they got there so fast."

It didn't sound right to me, then Sonny's handsome face contorted.

"The feds didn't want to serve a warrant on a guy with an AK-forty-seven and a garage full of C-four so they sent Emo up there thinkin' he was arresting some ding on a class-B nothing, and he walks into a bullet. All the while ATF was waiting down the road to see whether he got the cuffs on or not." Lopez was shaking with anger.

I knew part of it was just a post-shoot-out adrenaline burn, but I didn't like the dangerous look in Sonny's black eyes. His chest was rising and falling as he took deep breaths to calm himself down. His heartbeat pulsed a vein on his forehead.

"Listen Sonny, I think you need to go end-of-watch, hit a heavy bag or something, then get a beer and chill out."

"I'm gonna go get a fucking riot gun and chill out the ATF building downtown . . ."

"Good idea. Real smart," I said softly.

"Damn it, Shane, they might as well have just killed him themselves."

"Sonny, let their shooting review panel deal with this. If there's a problem, their Internal Affairs guys will flag it."

He dropped his head and looked at his shoes. When he glanced up again he was crying.

"I know his wife and kids," Sonny said. "I help him coach Pop Warner football. He was my *carnal*. My amigo . . . Those fucking guys . . ." He couldn't finish, overwhelmed with emotion.

"Get outta here, man. You need to get your feet under you."

"I loved him, Shane."

"Me too," I said softly.

FIVE

Getting Ready

It was ten o'clock on Saturday morning six days later, and Emo's funeral was scheduled for two that afternoon. I was sitting in the backyard of my little house in Venice, California. Our adopted marmalade cat, Franco, lounged at my feet, taking in the view of plastic reproduction gondolas floating in two feet of brackish seawater and narrow, arched, one-lane bridges spanning shallow saltwater canals. Venice, California, had been built in the twenties by Abbott Kinney, who had designed it to resemble a scaled-down version of Venice, Italy. It was an architecturally challenged throwback to the fifteen hundreds. Run down now, and a little sad, the neighborhood still clung proudly to its tacky, old-world heritage like a stubborn drunk refusing to get off a barstool. I don't know how Franco felt about it, but I loved it for its corny pride.

Chooch was inside doing his homework. Delfina, his girlfriend, whom we had taken in after her cousin, American Macado, died last year, was now living in Chooch's old room. He had willingly moved into makeshift quarters we'd set up in the garage. Delfina was proving to be a great addition to the family. She was a beautiful, black-eyed Hispanic girl who usually brought a soft, relaxed point of view to our mix. This morning she was off at a rehearsal at Venice High School where she was now enrolled. They were putting on a production of *West Side Story,* and Delfina was playing Maria. All week she had been rehearsing songs, her slightly thin, true voice floating through the house. She had left an hour ago, visibly nervous because they were doing the first run-through with music.

I was stretched out on my patio furniture reading a disturbing follow-up article on the Hidden Ranch shoot-out in the morning edition of the *L.A. Times.* It was under the same grainy photo of Vincent Smiley the newspaper had been running all week. In the shot the dead killer appeared young and expressionless. A vacant smile split his lips like a poorly drawn line that didn't foreshadow his violent end.

He looked small. Small eyes, small neck, small life. It was hard to think somebody like Vincent Smiley could have killed a man like Emo Rojas. But all of society has come to understand that guns in the hands of idiots are mindless equalizers. I was trying to get a handle on my emotions and prepare myself for the funeral ahead.

I hate cop funerals. After the Vikings case, and Tremaine Lane's over-the-top grave site production, I had promised myself that I would never attend another brother officer's burial; that I would try and find a quiet place to say my good-bye alone. But there wasn't much I could do about ducking this one. In fact, to be blunt, it was my second cop funeral since making that hollow promise. So it seemed I was just blowing off steam and lacked the courage of my own convictions.

I steeled myself to get through it. It had been six days since the shooting on Hidden Ranch Road. The incident was still a front-page, above-the-fold feature in the *L.A. Times.* The fickle electronic media had played it big for

three news cycles, then returned to their endless fascina-
tion with celebrity mischief. But new facts kept rolling
out on the pages of the *Times*. Since I wasn't part of the
active sheriff's investigation, I was getting most of my information from the unreliable rumor mill downtown, and
from the morning paper.

In a profile of Smiley earlier in the week, the paper revealed that he had once been a member of the Arcadia
Police Department. He'd been on the job for about ten
months in 2002, made it through their academy training,
but had been rolled out as a probationer shortly after he
hit the street. Apparently his training officer observed
some critical flaws in his psyche and submarined him.
The Arcadia police had not shared the reason for his dismissal with the press, saying, since Vincent Smiley was
dead and not being tried, his psychiatric records would
remain locked up in his 10-01 file.

The county coroner couldn't do a standard print or
dental match on Smiley's corpse because the body was
too badly burned. His teeth had turned to dust from the intense heat, but the M.E. had positively identified the body,
using DNA. Apparently Smiley had given a sample to the
Arcadia P.D. when he was still on the force—something
I found very unusual, if not downright strange. Police
unions were adamant against letting their officers give
DNA, citing a list of probable cause and Fourth Amend-
ment statutes. But for some reason Smiley had voluntarily
given up a sample. It made me wonder if his dismissal
might have stemmed from charges of sexual misconduct,
and he had given the sample voluntarily in an attempt to
beat the rap.

As far as anybody knew, Smiley didn't have any family that was still alive, so he was to be held in the morgue
for the required two weeks. In another eight days, if his

body wasn't claimed, he would be dumped in a pauper's grave, courtesy of the county, destined to spend eternity in a ten-foot hole full of the very homeless miscreants he had once hoped to police.

The crisis had lurched along for almost a week, like a cartoon cowboy with a slew of arrows in his back. On Friday, the L.A. County Board of Supervisors, headed by a broken steam valve named Enrique Salazar, got into the act. Salazar had picked up the sheriff's fallen shield and was charging the hill at Justice. He repeated the charge that ATF had not shared all the pertinent details of the arrest before sending Emo out to serve the warrant, speculating that this probably happened because Emo was a Mexican. Of course, nobody at ATF could have possibly known that a Mexican-American sheriff would serve the warrant, so that was just Enrique playing to his Hispanic base. But he also reasoned that ATF had not told the sheriffs about the illegal weapons cache, because, had the sheriffs known, they would have said, "Serve your own damn warrant." The Salazar piece was this morning's front-page ticking bomb.

Far more troubling than that was the fact that the temperature between these two law enforcement groups was at slow boil. Only the LAPD had managed to stay neutral.

Alexa came out, sat on the metal chair beside me, and took my hand. I showed her the front-page article in the *Times*.

"Saw it," she said. "Two thousand of Emo's friends and co-workers gathering this afternoon to cry over his body, and Salazar picks today to say ATF thought he was just another dumb Mexican. Guy needs a new public affairs consultant."

"This isn't going to go away," I said. "Salazar is going to make it an election issue. He'll go to the governor."

"In that case, he won't have to go far. The governor is going to be at the funeral. My office was notified that his security detail was going to need special parking at Forest Lawn."

"Great," I said.

She turned and looked at me carefully. "Shane, we need to talk about this."

I thought we had been talking about it, but apparently Alexa had something else on her mind.

"This whole thing with Emo—it's been eating at you. Even Chooch asked if you were okay."

"Yeah, I'm okay, it's just . . ." I stopped and let it hang there, not sure how to phrase what I was feeling.

"Just what?"

"I just wish I hadn't been up there. I wish I hadn't seen it. I can't get the memory of his blood off my skin."

"And?"

"And I hate cop funerals. I'm dreading this thing this afternoon. Bring in a TV camera and every publicity-seeking asshole in the state shows up. The governor comes, the city council, all the chiefs, sheriffs, and under-sheriffs—even you and Tony. No offense intended."

"None taken." She cocked her head, thinking for a moment, then smiled. "I think."

"You saw what happened when we buried Tremaine. It'll be just like that. All the department ass-kissers who didn't even know Emo swarming like flies on garbage. All telling the brass what a great guy Emo was, how they were in the same foxholes with him, all spinning their dumb war stories. Most of the people making speeches this afternoon will be strangers. The ones who really loved him will get pushed to the back. We'll all be listening to guys like Salazar turn Emo's funeral into a campaign issue. Once they're done, down Emo goes into the hole, awash in crocodile tears and bullshit. Then everybody leaves, hoping the governor will remember they were there."

"Then why are you going?"

"I don't want to go, but I have to. How do you not go to a good friend's funeral?"

"Why is Chooch going?" she said, hitting me with a blind shot that I hadn't seen coming. I looked away to buy time, gather my defenses.

"Huh?" Not much of a response, I admit, but I'm not too good at dodging her.

"He's in there finishing his homework so he'll be able to go."

"Oh. I guess that could maybe be because I sorta told him he could go."

"He didn't even know Emo."

"Yes he did." I heaved a sigh. Once again I was going to have to bust myself. I took a deep breath. "He knew him because he went on an Iron Pigs ride with us two months ago."

"Right. Sure he did. He doesn't even know how to ride a Harley."

"Last July—the week you were in Chicago, I borrowed two bikes. We practiced every night for five days. Got him licensed Friday afternoon. I swore him to secrecy because I knew you wouldn't want him riding a hawg."

"You're damn right I wouldn't." She fell silent and let go of my hand. "And he sure doesn't need to go to this funeral."

"Let him go. He wants to. It's part of growing up. People you know and care about die. It's a bitch, but it happens. He liked Emo. They're both quarterbacks."

"When cops die, you know he puts you in the coffin, Shane. Emotionally, he sees you in the box."

"I suppose."

"No suppose about it. It's true." She was mad about the Harley ride but had the good sense not to bang me around about it now. Instead, her anger was coming out over Chooch and the funeral.

"Look, I'll talk to him, okay? I'll make him understand," I said.

"Make me understand," she challenged.

"You already do, sweetheart. It's why I love you." I gave her a hopeful smile.

She looked at me and her eyes softened. "Damn you, Shane. I'm really pissed off here. Acting goofy and sweet is no fair." Then she got up and went in to get Chooch.

SIX

Godspeed, Thirty-Mary-Four

Delfina would be at rehearsal until six. Chooch went to the funeral on crutches, because he had a broken foot.

Here's how that happened. About a week after the Iron Pigs ride in mid-July, during the first week of two-a-day football drills, he tried to escape a blitz, spun right, and rolled over on his right foot, cracking one of the small bones on the outside. Chooch was being recruited heavily by half a dozen big Division 1 universities and was afraid that the tiny bone break in his foot was going to cost him his entire multimillion-dollar pro-football career.

I gave him my "Life Is a Journey" speech. Net effect, zero. I gave him my "You Only Grow from Adversity" speech. Nothing. Finally, Alexa convinced him that his football career wasn't as important right now as his academic career, and he'd better make sure he kept his grades up; because, if he didn't get the athletic scholarship, he'd need to get into college on pure academics. She reminded him he could always walk on if he didn't get the ride. This made sense to Chooch, and he had a 3.8 going into midterms. All of this is noteworthy only when you realize that, as usual, Alexa's pragmatic approach had carried the day.

It was a bright, cloudless Saturday afternoon as we drove to Forest Lawn. The San Gabriel Mountains were almost purple against the cobalt sky. A light Santa Ana wind had cleared the basin of smog for Emo's funeral. As we neared the off-ramp to Forest Lawn Drive, I could see this was going to be a mob scene. Traffic was already piling up on the 210 Freeway before we reached the L.A. River. You could tell it was for Emo, because even the people who weren't in squad cars were wearing uniforms with black ribbons pinned diagonally across their badges.

I wanted to drop Chooch off as close as possible. I've spent my share of time walking with birch under my arms, and I know that handling crutches on grass is a bitch. I managed to sneak up next to the chapel where the hearse and limos were parked. When I dropped Chooch and Alexa off there were already more than a thousand people milling in front of the church, most in tan deputies' uniforms. A smattering of LAPD blue punctuated the crowd. A sound system and some video screens had been set up for the overflow crowd that couldn't squeeze inside the church.

The LAPD white hat working traffic at this event turned me around and sent me back down toward the mortuary office. Forest Lawn was inside the city limits of Los Angeles, so, even though 80 percent of the attendees were county deputies, we were working the event. I found a parking place down by the office and wedged the Acura into a no-parking zone, putting two wheels up on the grass. I didn't think our traffic control officers would be handing out too many greenies at a cop's funeral.

As I was locking up I heard the loud, familiar rumble of straight pipes. I turned and saw almost a hundred Iron Pigs from different chapters all over the state making their way solemnly up Forest Lawn Drive, riding two-by-two. They had their uniforms on. Green from the Highway Patrol, tan and brown from the Sacramento P.D., tan and blue from the L.A. sheriff's and Orange County, blue and white from Los Angeles, Pacoima, Newhall, and San Diego.

The bikes were all custom Harleys, and both men and women alike wore their lightweight summer colors, most stitched on sleeveless jean or leather vests, worn over police uniforms. The club motto stitched on some of the jackets now seemed a dangerous threat: "Cut One and We All Bleed." They snaked up the drive as everyone stopped talking and turned to watch.

Darren Zook, the local chapter's ride captain, was out front leading them. He slowed to a stop in front of the church, then turned and backed his bike against a sixty-foot stretch of curb that had been coned off in preparation for their arrival. One by one the officers dismounted, kicked their stands down, leaned their bikes, and stepped away. The lacquered yellow, orange, and candy-apple red paint jobs dappled colored sunshine against polished chrome manifolds. Then the Iron Pigs moved silently toward the church.

I finished locking the Acura and followed. I was almost up to where Alexa and Chooch were standing when I heard a voice raised in anger. The tone made my adrenaline kick. An angry curse uttered with deadly sincerity. I moved closer.

"You fucking people don't belong here!" I heard Darren Zook say. He was near the concrete steps of the old church glaring at six guys in dark suits. At first I didn't recognize them, but as I approached I knew who they were. Men in Black—the ATF Situation Response Team from the Hidden Ranch shootout. They were standing in a group on the church steps, unsure how to handle this.

"We came to pay our respects," one of them said. I'd seen most of their pictures in the newspaper for a week, and I think he was the one named Billy Greenridge.

"You paid your respects on Hidden Ranch Road. Now get the fuck out of here," Zook said.

The feds started to look around for backup or support, or maybe just for a friendly face, but the Iron Pigs quickly closed ranks around them.

"Get out or get thrown out," Darren Zook growled dangerously.

"Look, we feel—" Greenridge began.

But Darren cut him off. He and three other Iron Pigs grabbed Greenridge roughly by his arm, spun him around, and started to march him down the walk to the cars. Then a dozen more of the police bikers grabbed the remaining ATF agents and quickly hustled them out behind him.

Before they reached the parking lot, the ATF ASAC, Brady Cagel, pushed through the crowd and blocked the path. "You people are way out of order," he said.

"Get these assholes out of here," Darren said. "And you go with 'em. I won't have you guys at Emo's funeral."

Two more sheriffs grabbed Brady Cagel. Then they half-pushed, half-dragged the entire SRT unit, plus their ASAC, down the steps and pinned them against some parked cars across from the church.

"Get out," Darren Zook repeated, his voice thick with rage.

"I'm going to write this up," Cagel said.

"Get out or get thrown out!"

"Let's go." Cagel motioned his team to follow. Then he and his brother agents walked down the road to their cars, while almost two thousand pairs of eyes glared holes in their backs.

Emilio Rojas Jr.'s funeral started late. It was two thirty before the organ in the big church began to play. There were more than a thousand people who couldn't squeeze inside and were watching the service on two big-screen TVs. Alexa and Chooch had managed to get in and save me a seat near the back.

The LASD Chorus sang "Ave Maria." Emo's brother Miguel spoke about his brother as a boy, mentioned his sense of humor and how he always had a smile for everybody. His widow, Elana, sat quietly and listened, dabbing her eyes with a handkerchief. Emo's six-year-old son, Alfredo, was beside her, ramrod straight, eyes brimming with tears, but somehow he kept them from running.

The service was a Catholic mass that seemed endless to me. After the coffin was blessed and sprinkled with holy water, ten Iron Pigs from the local chapter carried the box out of the church and slid it into the hearse for the short trip up the hill.

We followed the winding road to the grave site. Then the crowd gathered on the hillside while the family sat under sun tents for the political speeches. The governor, who hadn't known Emo, told us what an exceptional officer he had been, how bright and friendly. He said Emo was the gold standard by which all others would be judged.

Supervisor Salazar, who never knew Emo, talked about his courage on the job and how he represented the Mexican-American dream, how he had made a difference to his family and to his people, and how he would always be remembered.

Next came the command structure. Sheriff Bill Messenger, the diminutive head of LASD, spoke of valor under fire. Next to him stood Tony Filosiani. He was wearing his dress-blue LAPD chief's uniform. Four command stars gleamed on each of his wide shoulders. At five foot seven, two-hundred plus pounds, the chief of the LAPD was shaped like a blue lunchbox with medals. Because this was a sheriff's deputy's funeral, Tony had elected not to speak. The undersheriff spoke next. Then Captain Matthews offered a personal apology, because he had been in charge the day Emo died. His voice was choked with emotion. One by one they all came to the mike, standing erect in starched uniforms, their rank emblems glittering. They said Emo represented the brightest and best. Some of them searched for poetic metaphors. One commander from Ad Vice actually said that Emo reminded her of a California cactus: tough and dangerous on the surface, but sweet inside.

It was hot, and sweat started running down the back of my shirt. I couldn't help but think that Emo was up there shitting bricks over some of this. The cactus simile was priceless. Most of these testimonials were from people who wouldn't have taken the time to have coffee with him when he was alive.

Six officers on black-and-white police Electra Glides came over the hill in the Missing Man motorcycle formation, a V with an empty space in the corner. They rode across the grass slowly. Somebody released six white doves. A man I didn't know walked over to Elana and handed her the seventh. She kissed the dove on its back, then released it into the sky. We all watched as it flew away.

Next, the LASD Helicopter Air Unit did a flyby. Four Bell Jet Rangers passed low over the grave, then peeled off and climbed away in separate directions.

After Elana was handed the folded American flag, it was supposed to be over. People were starting to leave when Emo's last backup, Dave Brill, decided he had something to say. He had not been asked to speak, but stepped up and took the mike anyway. He looked frayed and empty, like a man whose soul had been leaking slowly out of him. He cleared his throat and the sound system barked loudly.

"I just wanted to say . . ."

He stopped and looked around at the politicians, who had turned back to face him but were stealing impatient looks at their watches—meetings to take, flights to make.

"Emo . . . Emo was . . ." Then Brill broke down and started crying. He sucked it up and tried again. "Emo . . . I . . . I'm sorry. I . . . Y'see, we . . . At the academy, we . . ."

He couldn't continue. He faced the grave, his face contorted in pain. As he turned toward the speakers, the microphone squealed feedback. Dave Brill looked at the coffin, unsure now of how to get off or how to say what he felt. What he really wanted to tell Emo was how sorry he was that he hadn't been able to protect him. That he'd been sitting in the D-car doing paperwork, with his gun in his holster, when his friend died.

Overcome with grief and emotion, and using Emo's police call sign, he finally said the only thing he could think of: "Godspeed, Thirty-Mary-Four."

Then Brill laid the microphone on the coffin and walked away from the grave. The governor and most of the brass were already ten steps ahead of him.

God, I hate cop funerals.

SEVEN

Wake

There were seven of us wedged in a back booth at the Pew and Cue on Barham Boulevard, four blocks north of Forest Lawn Drive. It was an hour after the service. We were supposed to be Emo's "tights"—the guys who loved him most. Two were fellow motorcycle officers, Darren Zook and Dave Brill. Next to them, were Gary and Mike Nightingale from SEB. The Nightingale brothers were on the sheriff's Special Weapons Team that had been at Hidden Ranch Road. Their expressions were grave, carved from granite. I remembered the mission board I'd seen on the side of the truck. Gary was a long gun, Mike his spotter. In the corner was a deputy named Christine Bell and, across from her, Sonny Lopez. I sat at the end.

The Pew and Cue was small, dark, and crowded. Wooden tables and straight-backed wood pews lined the room. The barroom adjoined a pool hall, but none of our little group of mourners was shooting eight ball. We were there to drink and brood. Alexa had driven Chooch home. I was going to catch a ride back to Venice with Gary Nightingale who, it turned out, lived less than a mile from me.

Emo's last backup, Dave Brill, was pounding down scotch shooters, leading choir practice, telling an Emo war story. "There was this time in the hills," he was saying, "him and me, up there cruising the twisties on Angeles Crest. We'd been riding for hours and were both getting sorta iron-assed, so we decide to go ten-ninety and crib for a while. So Emo turns and rides down this dirt road. We round a corner and, lo and behold, here's this fucking meth lab and fifteen armed shitheads with Harleys doing a drug deal outside a beat-up motor home. And I think, 'That's it, we're dust.' Y'know? But Emo just looks at these stringy-haired SOBs, gets off his bike, walks up, smiles, and starts pitching them tickets to the Sheriff's Inner City Fundraiser, the kid's concert thing. Acting like that's the only reason we rode down there in the first place. These guys don't know if they're busted or not. But it's only ten bucks a ticket, so they figure it's cheaper than the grief they're gonna get shooting two deputies. Sold 'em two hundred dollars' worth. Then Emo, he turns to this one ink-strewn asshole with an eye patch and he says, 'Hey, partner, this concert is gonna be Barry Manilow and elevator music. You guys are probably into bands like Tool or Rage Against the Machine, and won't go. But ya want, you can donate your ticket back. That way, we can send extra kids to the concert.' Then one by one, all of these guys are giving their tickets back. We ride out of there with two hundred dollars cash and we still got all the fucking concert tickets. Come back with twenty cops an hour later, hook 'em all up. The guy was amazing."

The stories went on like that. Little by little, they were working the ache of Emo's passing out of their souls.

Gary and Mike Nightingale started talking about the shoot-out. "That guy, Vincent Smiley," Gary said, "it really sucks when these suicides ain't got the balls to just do it. Gotta get us to fire the bullet for 'em. He can't do the Dutch, so he dumps Emo to get a shoot-out going. What bullshit."

Darren Zook got up to go to the bathroom. He wandered into the pool room, which is where the restroom arrow said the men's can was. I was drinking beers, trying to be part of this, but not finding much solace either. War stories about dead cop buddies never made me feel better. I was thinking instead of Emo at the Rock Store, leaning over the table with Chooch, both of them drawing football plays in water with their fingers.

Then I remembered Sonny had told me that Emo coached a Pop Warner team. Pop Warner was tackle football for kids in the nine- to fifteen-year-old age brackets.

"Who's gonna take over and coach his football team?" I asked, as a thought tickled the back of my brain.

"My kid plays on that team," Christine Bell said. "Sonny, you helped him coach, you should do it."

"Not me." Sonny Lopez slowly brought his head up. He'd been looking down into his beer, as if the answer to life was floating in there. "I coach blocking and tackling, that's my thing. Emo was running some kind of Veer offense. I wouldn't know a tight-end from a chorus boy. You need somebody who understands that offense."

"Somebody'll step up," Brill said, emotion bending his voice. "Emo had friends, man. People were always standin' in line t'carry that man's flag."

Darren Zook came back to the table. His face was tight, his black skin stretched white around his jaw. "Those fucking guys are in there," he whispered, pointing to the pool hall.

"What guys?" Christine asked, but everybody else at the table knew. SRT had come here, just like us, because it was the closest bar to Forest Lawn.

Darren turned and started towards the poolroom. I scrambled out of the booth, grabbed his arm, and spun him around.

"Whatta you doing?" I said.

"I got some things to say to those assholes," he snarled.

"No you don't. Sit down."

"Hey, fuck you. Who are you anyway? You came on one ride with us. You're blue, we're tan. You're not even in our tribe."

He yanked his arm away from me and started into the pool hall. I looked over at the booth. Four sheriff's deputies all sitting there trying to decide if they wanted to stop it or join it.

"This is no good," I said softly. Then I turned and followed Darren into the poolroom.

There were two SRT commandos shooting a rack on the far side of the room. The other four members were in a booth drinking. Brady Cagel must not like hanging with his troops, because he wasn't around. I looked over and saw Darren Zook by the cue rack, carefully selecting a weapon. He was making a big deal out of running his hand over the stick, checking it for cracks. Then he pulled it down and headed toward the six SRT agents. I cut between pool tables and intercepted him.

"Darren, you're drunk. This ain't it," I said, holding one hand against his chest. Now the SRT agents looked up and saw us for the first time.

"Hey Billy," Gordon Grundy, a big, square-headed federal SWAT commando said, "yer fucking moolie's back." All the feds looked up at us. The vibe was so nasty that the four civilians playing pool at the next table laid their cues down on the green felt and just walked out of the bar. On the way they passed the four sheriffs from our table, who now stood in the threshold: Brill, the Nightingale brothers, even Christine Bell.

"Here come the rent-a-cops," a stocky, Hispanic fireplug fed in a black suit said. I thought his name was Ignacio Rosano. He stood, and as he did, three other feds rose with him. Now everybody was on their feet.

"Let's cool down," I said. "We don't need this, guys."

"Get the fuck outta here, Scully," Zook said. Then, without warning, he pushed me hard to the right and swung the pool cue. It hit Rosano on the shoulder and bounced up hard, into his throat, landing with a loud *THWACK*.

The dance was on.

Bar fights, like bad parties, are no fun and hard to remember afterwards.

I paired up with Billy Greenridge. He was a SWAT-trained commando about my same height, and had good moves. I tried my Brazilian jujitsu, but he was fast and I couldn't take him to the ground. We traded right hands. I caught the first few body shots on my elbows, then one slipped through and cracked a rib. *This is not the way police officers are trained to behave,* I whined to myself as I covered up. Then I saw his square jaw loom into view—a clean shot. I swung hard, but he spun and I missed, catching his shoulder and throwing myself badly off balance in the process. Out of the corner of my eye I saw people wheeling and trading punches. Darren and one of the SRT guys were doing some kind of *Quo Vadis* thing with pool cues. Christine Bell seemed hard pressed to find an opponent. The feds kept ignoring her, turning away and going for one of the guys, until she stepped up and kicked Grundy between the legs and brought him down like a bag of sand.

The worst part of this fight was that it was so stupid. Our side was also going to be shamefully easy to identify afterwards, all in our nice police dress uniforms, complete with name plates.

Two of the feds were now lying on the floor. As I turned to find a new opponent, I caught it from behind with a pool cue. The next thing I knew, I was on my hands and knees under the table trying to remember what continent I was on. That's when one of the feds put me out of my misery. I caught a shiny, black brogan with the right side of my head.

I was done. Down for the count. Gone.

Oh well.

EIGHT

Busted Again

"What the hell happened to you?" Alexa asked. It was eight fifteen the next morning. As soon as I stepped out of the shower I put on a baseball cap to cover the six emergency-room stitches in the back of my head. But I guess the shower had opened the edge of the cut, and blood was running down the back of my neck.

"Take off that silly hat," she ordered.

"Oh, I don't think . . ."

She reached out and snatched the hat off. Then we did a little circle dance where she kept trying to get around behind me. "Shane, have you been fighting?" Sounding now like the horse-faced nun in those old Mickey Rooney movies.

Busted again.

Chooch had just hobbled out the door with Delfina, both of them on the way to school. He dropped her at Venice High each morning, then drove out to Harvard-Westlake in the Valley. We were alone, so I couldn't even use the kids for cover. I brought us both mugs of coffee and handed one to Alexa. She sat at the kitchen table and looked unhappy. I knew she couldn't stick around long, because she had a nine o'clock meeting with Tony Filosiani. They were reviewing some detective crime scene tactics in Vernon, where the department had a big public relations problem pending on a bad arrest.

"Who hit you?" she demanded again.

"What makes you think I got hit? This was a . . . I fell off a whatever—a thing." *Great, Shane.* "I was leaning back and tipped over in a chair, hit my head." *Better.*

"I can spot blunt force trauma. Don't forget who you're dealing with," she said.

She was right. It's pretty hard to BS a trained street detective. When it came to skirting the edges of the truth, this was not your normal marriage.

So I told her about the fight that took place the night before at the Pew and Cue. When I finished she was very quiet.

"Well, say something," I said. I hated it when she went quiet. That was always the worst.

"What do you want me to say, Shane? We've got major problems going down between sheriffs and SRT. Lawsuits are bound to get filed, so how do you help? You and a bunch of sheriffs go out after Emo's funeral, get plastered, then get into a fight with SRT. Let's see . . . What should I say? How about this: Was it fun?"

"Would it help if I told you I tried hard to break it up before it got started?"

"That might help."

"I tried really, really, really hard to break it up before it got started."

"Y'know, Shane, I love you, but you still have a lotta spots left that need smoothing off."

"And you're slowly sanding them. I want you to know I'm extremely grateful."

"Did the LAPD roll on it? Is this disaster gonna show up on a department green sheet downtown?"

"One of our black-and-whites was called, but Darren talked 'em out of doing anything."

"Darren. Not you."

"I was . . . in the toilet throwing up."

"Shit." Now she looked worried. "You got knocked out?"

"I don't think I was puking because of a concussion. I think it was bad chicken wings. I feel really good this morning. Tip-top. The E.R. docs didn't even want to hold me."

"Because you didn't tell them you were throwing up."

"A lot of it is kinda vague. I've got blank spots."

"Really." She leaned back, tipping in her chair, still watching me.

"Be careful," I said. "I wouldn't want you to go over and hit your head, like I did."

"Shut up, Shane."

But I'd turned the corner, I could already hear a smile in her voice.

"It was just bad luck. We didn't know they'd be in there."

She heaved a sigh. "Look at me. Right in the eye." She leaned forward and started checking my pupils. "You're okay, I guess."

She got up. I stood with her, but got a little dizzy when I did. To be honest, I might have picked up a mild concussion, but the less said here, the better.

She kissed me without passion; still angry, but she was late. "Be home for dinner?" she asked.

"I think so. I'm trying to wrap up the Paula Beck thing today. Once the D.A. files and Zack comes back from Miami, we can move on to something else. I'll be on the fourth floor. Lunch?"

"I don't break bread with lawless brawlers," she said.

"I was not brawling. I barely hit anybody."

"Noon at the Peking Duck," she snapped.

We left in separate cars. I drove my Acura, following her new blue Lexus until she sped up around the 10 Freeway and lost me in the heavy traffic.

I spent most of the morning on the fourth floor at Parker Center wrapping up the Beck investigation. I didn't think I had come up with enough on Paula for the D.A. to file the double-H. Even though the case was tragic, it really was just involuntary manslaughter. The D.A. could try and run his bluff, but if her public defender wasn't a complete moron he'd know it was a stretch. I finished the investigation report and handed it in to Cal, who glanced it over, then smiled at me.

"What happened at the Pew and Cue?" he said, his black, shiny, chrome-dome glinting purple in the overhead fluorescents.

"I wasn't there," I said.

"It's all over the department. Somebody said you got knocked cold." I kept my six-stitch lace-up turned from his view.

"Me?" I said. "Wasn't there. Bum rumor."

I had lunch with Alexa and we didn't say much. She picked at an avocado plate, which I could have told her was a bad menu choice at the Peking Duck. Stick to the Oriental dishes in that joint, the egg rolls and dim sum.

The rest of the day went slowly. I searched through our files on predicate felons, looking for a new target Zack and I could work when he got back. By six I was getting ready to pack it in, when my phone rang. It was Sergeant Ellen Campbell, who works as Alexa's administrative assistant.

"The skipper wants to see you," she said brightly. The skipper was Alexa.

"On my way."

I closed up my desk, logged off my computer, and rode the elevator up two flights to the sixth floor. I figured Alexa was going to suggest we make up over dinner. There was a Greek restaurant called Acropolis, in the Valley, she'd been wanting to try.

I walked down the thick, sea-foam green carpet that covered the corridors of the command floor, entered Alexa's outer office, and found Ellen, a perennially happy, freckled blonde sitting behind her desk. Most lieutenants aren't staff rank officers and don't have private secretaries, but Alexa was an acting division commander, and head of Detective Services Group. She reported directly to the Office of Operations, which was right below the Chief, so she was way up on the department flowchart.

DSG supervised all the detective bureaus, from Forgery and Missing Persons, to Special Crimes and Robbery-Homicide. Normally the head of DSG would be a captain or a commander, but Alexa had taken over the XO position a year ago as a lieutenant. She was made acting head by Chief Tony Filosiani after her boss, Captain Mark Shephard, had been shot and killed. Chief Filosiani liked her and was willing to leave her as acting head until she made captain, which, the way she was going, would probably be in another year.

Ellen was facing her computer as I crossed the office. "Storms blowing. Wear your raincoat," she said without looking up.

Alexa's digs were small. One window, no view. She had portable bookshelves on every wall. Tony Filosiani was a law enforcement junkie and read everything from student doctoral theses on criminology to medical volumes on forensic science. Alexa had picked up the trait. She had books and manuals piled everywhere. It was the new department. The rubber hose was in the Hall of Fame. Now we forced confessions with drops of DNA, luminous light, and blood-spatter evidence.

"Shane, sit down," my wife said, looking harried. She glanced at her watch and I instantly knew we weren't going to dinner.

"What's up?" I asked.

"Big problems. ATF Internal Affairs just sent us over a copy of their findings on the Hidden Ranch shoot-out. They found SRT innocent of any wrongdoing."

"What'd you expect?"

"Sheriff Messenger's in with Tony right now. He's pissed. The mayor is coming over with Enrique Salazar from the Board of Supervisors. The area SAC from ATF is on his way, too."

"Look, Alexa, it's . . ."

"No. Stop talking for a minute and listen. We're going into a meeting on this in seconds. The ATF finding claims that they told the sheriff's warrant control office about the automatic weapons in Smiley's garage. Of course, the WCO denies it, and of course, there's no paperwork substantiating what ATF says."

"Of course."

"But Brady Cagel says they never write any paper on stuff like that when they give over a bust to another agency, and the fact is, he's right."

"But what does this have to do with us? It's a sheriff's department–ATF spat."

Her intercom buzzed. She picked up the phone, listened, then said, "Right. Thanks, Ellen." She hung up and said, "Come on. Mayor MacKenzie's here. We're on."

"Alexa, whatta ya mean *we're* on?"

"We've been ordered by the mayor to reinvestigate it." And she was out of the office and down the hall.

I hurried to catch up, finally grabbing her arm before she got to Chief Filosiani's huge double doors. "You're giving this to me?" Duh . . . Finally getting it.

"Look, Shane, I need you. This is the ultimate red-ball. Either way this goes, nobody is going to come out a winner. The best we can hope for is some kind of mitigating circumstance. But we probably won't get that lucky. The

mayor doesn't want ATF to reinvestigate. He's not happy
with their current finding and doesn't trust their objectivity. He also can't trust the sheriff to be unbiased. He
knows there's going to be multiple lawsuits on the shoot-
out from the neighbors and from Emo's family, so he
came to us. We're your classic uninvolved third party."

"Why me?"

"Three reasons. One: you're a great cop and you're
fair . . ."

"Stop it. You'll make me vomit."

"Two: you're the only L.A. cop that Sheriff Messenger
will accept. He liked the way you handled the Viking case."

"What's the third?"

"You're the only person in this building *I* can trust not
to leak. We're gonna do this together."

The door to the chief's office opened and Tony was
standing there. His round Santa Claus face was red, but
his cheeks were not ho-ho merry. He motioned us into the
outer office.

The chief's waiting room was fronted by a secretarial
area. Bea, his battle-ax with a heart of gold, was sitting
behind a large desk, a murder-one scowl already on her
hawkish face. She nodded at Alexa and me as the chief
led us into his office. You had to be very observant to spot
the twinkle in her eye.

Mayor Richard MacKenzie, known around town as
Mayor Mac, was standing by the window. He was a tall,
skinny, hollow-chested man with riveting blue eyes and a
ridiculous blond comb-over. His double-breasted suits all
fit like hand-me-downs. Also in the office, looking like he
wanted to throw an ashtray, was Bill Messenger. Half Ar-
menian, half Egyptian, he was a second-generation deputy
who had been elected county sheriff two years ago.

Across the room, wearing charcoal stripes and a purple
tie, looking exactly like what he was, a slightly over-

weight politician working on a sound bite, stood Enrique Salazar.

Tony closed the door behind us. "Shane, you know Mayor MacKenzie and Sheriff Messenger," he said.

"Yes," I said, shaking hands.

"And Supervisor Salazar."

Enrique didn't cross the room. He waved a ring-laden hand at me instead.

The office was strangely underfurnished. Chief Filosiani was a no-nonsense commander, known by his troops as the Day-Glo Dago because of his New York Italian demeanor and his penchant for flashy pinky rings. He had stripped out the expensive antiques and artwork that was the legacy of his predecessor, Burl Brewer, then sold them at auction and used the money to buy new Ultima Tac vests for his SWAT teams. He had installed utilitarian metal office furniture in the room, but there was damn little of it.

"Have you filled Shane in?" Tony was saying.

"A little," Alexa said. "I've explained the—" She stopped when Bea opened the door and admitted a sandy-haired, brown-eyed, compact man in a tan suit who looked like a carefully tailored gymnast. Behind him was the ATF ASAC, Brady Cagel.

Tony shook hands with the first man, then introduced him to the room. "Garrett Metcalf is the new SAC area commander. He and Mr. Cagel are here to make sure we don't blackjack ATF. Supervisor Salazar is looking after the county's interests."

"We're already late for a briefing at Justice," Metcalf said. "We can't stay but a minute. What's so important here, you had to demand an emergency meeting?"

Mayor Mac turned away from the window. "We have the IAD shooting review you faxed over," he said. "You guys should scare up a literary agent and start publishing fiction."

"Whatta you want, Mr. Mayor? You want me to lie?" Cagel snapped back. "Want me to fire shots at my own people when they didn't do anything?"

"They sent one of my deputies up to Hidden Ranch without all the pertinent details," Messenger said.

"I'm not going to argue this with you, Bill," Metcalf responded. "Our ASAC told your warrant control office there was a possibility of automatic weapons up there. Your guys didn't act on it or include it in the warrant. What am I supposed to do?"

"You're just whitewashing," Messenger said. He looked like he was on the verge of throwing one of his well-known Egyptian conniptions.

Garrett Metcalf said, "Your warrant guys dropped the ball. We're not gonna pay the freight."

"I'm asking LAPD to reinvestigate," the mayor said. "Detective Scully is a neutral party. I've asked him to re-hang the investigation."

"He can investigate all he wants," Metcalf said. "It won't matter. It's closed. This is it as far as ATF and Justice are concerned. Not to get pissy, but a municipal investigation just isn't gonna cut it. This is a federal finding from Justice. It's over."

"Municipal crimes are tried in municipal courts," Salazar said, speaking for the first time. "The federal government can't change that." His words flew across the room like chips of ice.

Metcalf walked to the door and turned: "You people are looking at lawsuits on your dead deputy. Some of those neighbors are probably also gonna file. You turned that block into a fire zone. I sympathize, but it's not our problem."

"*You* turned it into the fire zone," Salazar said. "Your guys fired the hot gas. The L.A. County Supervisors are holding hearings, not only into the death of a Mexican-American sheriff, who looks like he was just sent in there and wasted, but into the entire behavior of the Justice Department on cross-jurisdictional matters."

"We're not gonna be scapegoats," Cagel said. "In case you haven't read your own county codes, an incident commander is responsible for everything that flows down from his scene. Your guy Matthews was in charge, so he's wearing the hat." He threw the LASD Manual onto Tony's desk. "Section thirty-one, paragraph eighteen. Great reading." He turned, and both feds walked out of the office.

"You've got to get this investigation done and a report written in less than two days," Tony said to me.

"I want a deputy on it with you," Messenger said.

"I agree," Salazar added.

"Nothing doin'," Mayor Mac replied. "I want only LAPD. They've got no stake in it. No axe to grind. Enrique, you know better than anybody what the press will do if this looks like a cover-up. We need an independent finding."

"We'll get right on it, sir," Alexa said, and led me out of the office.

Moments later we were standing in the hall.

"Alexa, I'm hardly uninvolved," I said. "I got into a fistfight with that SRT weapons team. There're already rumors about it circulating in the department."

"Shane, I know it's not perfect, but I need you, okay? Something tells me this isn't over yet. Not by a long shot."

Boy, was she ever right about that.

NINE

Football

It was 10 P.M., and I had been reading crime scene reports for three hours. Alexa was inside going over the ATF shooting review. I needed to get my mind off the Hidden Ranch mess for a while, so I took a break and got together with Chooch. We sat in the backyard talking football.

"I'm not hearing from as many coaches as I thought I would. We're already in our second game, and I'm just standing on the sidelines with a clipboard. I'm gonna lose the chance for a scholarship," Chooch complained. He was sitting next to me on the patio under a quarter moon.

The narrow Venice canals were picturesque, the arched bridges and shimmering water tinged silver in the pale moonlight. Venice was a haven for nonconformists and throwback hippies, and I could hear Led Zeppelin leaking from one of the houses on Grand Canal.

Chooch started banging on his cast with the rubber tip of his right crutch, the injured foot his new mortal enemy.

"C'mon. You go back to the doc in a week. Maybe he'll take the cast off. You've still got a chance to get into the last few games, as well as the CIF playoffs."

"College recruiting trips are in December. I'm screwed, Dad."

"You just got another call from Coach Paterno."

"Yeah, I know."

"He saw your video from last year's games. He still seems interested."

"Penn State wants to move me to defensive-back," he said sadly. "I wanta be a quarterback. I know the position."

"You got four recruiting letters. You're gonna have coaches' visits from Arizona, Oregon, Tulane, and Miami of Ohio. The SMU scout wants to talk to you when he comes through next month."

"Dad, I'm not playing. They're not gonna give a full ride to some guy holding a clipboard."

"They understand injuries, son."

"No they don't. I'm missing almost a full year of experience. They're gonna think I'm just some green, two-year high school player. I'll probably do better going to a junior college, where I could at least start as a freshman, then transfer to a D-one school my junior year."

"Chooch—life isn't just about football. What's important is your education."

He sat quietly, looking at his offending foot. He was really in the dumps.

"I had an idea the other day. You know Emo coached a Pop Warner team? The Rams, I think."

"Yeah, you told me."

"With him gone, they're probably looking for a new head coach."

He didn't say anything.

"Sonny Lopez is coaching defensive linemen and line-backers. They need someone who knows how to run a Veer Offense."

"I don't know anything about a Veer. We run a Wing-T."

"Not much difference. They're both option offenses."

"There's a lot of difference, Dad."

"Okay, but you know fundamentals. You could teach the quarterbacks the reason for a three-step drop as opposed to five—how to do defensive reads, or look off a defender, stuff like that."

"I can't coach a buncha twelve-year-old kids. What good is that gonna do me?"

"This was Emo's team. You were his friend. He cared about these boys. Sometimes you gotta do things for other reasons than just, 'What's in it for me?' "

Chooch sat quietly for a long minute.

"Hey, I don't even know if I can get you the gig. I didn't want to ask Sonny to float the idea past the league if you were gonna say no. But it might get your spirits up, give you something else to focus on."

He was still glowering at his foot.

"Son, most of the mistakes I've made in my life, I made because I've been a loner. I started out an orphan, and it's been hard for me to let my guard down, invest in other people."

He still wasn't looking at me.

"You and Alexa have helped me understand that life is about more than just survival, but I don't always share my feelings, and there are times when I feel so desperate and alone I don't think I can stand it. Sometimes I'm not always the best partner, husband, or dad, because some part of me is always holding back. I don't want you to be like that. It's important that you learn how to give parts of yourself to others without wanting something in return."

He didn't speak, but he had a puzzled look on his face.

"Give it some time. Talk it over with your mom and Delfina. Think about it for a day. Will you at least do that?"

"Yeah, sure," he said. Then he got up, grabbed his other crutch, and lumbered back into the house.

I rubbed my eyes. I felt I hadn't said it right. Then I went back to the shooting reviews. But it took me a while to get into it.

I had Vincent Smiley's Arcadia P.D. application, which was dated June 15, 2000. I'd already read it twice, now I looked again at the same vacant picture the *Times* had used. It was clipped to the top of the form. There wasn't much in his police application that helped. He went to middle school in Glendale. There was nothing listed for high school, except a note that said he had done home schooling from grades ten to twelve. He got his GED in '95, then two years of junior college at Glendale Community. His mother and father died in a car wreck in '95. I read a short essay that was attached, where he detailed his reasons for wanting to be a police officer. It was filled with the kind of vacuous nonsense that beauty contestants utter. *I want to be a policeman to help people and foster peace among diverse segments of society.* ZZZZZ.

An hour later, Alexa came out and handed me a cold beer. She plopped down in the chair Chooch had vacated, and we clinked bottles.

"Where you gonna start?" she asked.

"Out at the crime scene. Hidden Ranch Road, first thing in the morning."

"Shane, far be it from me to tell you how to do your job . . ."

"But?"

"But the guy is dead. Smiley is gone. His DNA is patched and matched. What's the point of starting out there? The neighbors have been interviewed. There's nothing much in their statements, except he acted like his elevator got stuck between floors and he was storing illegal weapons in his garage. We already know all that."

"I always start with the inciting incident, then work out from there. That's the way I was trained to do it."

"Except, we only have two days. Maybe you should take a shortcut."

"No shortcuts in a thorough investigation, babe. You know that."

"But . . ."

"You can always get another detective," I said, and sipped my beer, looking out at the water. "Okay with me, if that's what you decide."

"Nope. Can't get out of it that easy. You're my guy. Do it your way. Now take me to bed and give me a party."

"Thought you'd never ask."

TEN

Rottweiler

The next morning I drove out to Hidden Ranch. On the way I kept thinking about the incident reports I'd read the previous night.

At the beginning of every investigation I start by looking for coincidences and inconsistencies. In police work, you quickly learn it's never wise to trust a coincidence, because coincidences are often caused by criminal lies or mistakes. Inconsistencies occur when two people have conflicting opinions about a shared event, and there is often a lie or a misunderstanding at its core. In both of these circumstances it is generally profitable for an investigator to take a closer look.

After reading the deputies' statements, it seemed that almost all the sheriffs at the scene agreed that Vincent Smiley was a suicide, that he had staged it so the police would be forced to kill him. Death by cop. Even after shooting Emo, Smiley had plenty of chances to surrender. He could have thrown down his weapon, come out and saved his life, but instead he chose to barricade himself inside the house and shoot it out with the police until there was no possible solution but his own extinction.

I had to agree that on the surface it looked like a manufactured suicide. Except for two things. First, the guy had been wearing Kevlar. From my perspective, you don't wear Kevlar when you're trying to get the cops to kill you. It was inconsistent, but not unheard of.

The second inconsistency occurred in two of the neighbors' post-event statements. According to a neighbor named William Palmer, who lived four houses away on Hidden Ranch Road, Smiley had spent most of the previous summer building a bomb shelter in his basement. A woman down the street named Katie Clark had also mentioned the same thing. So the question is, why does someone who is so afraid he might die in a nuclear blast that he builds a bomb shelter in his basement commit suicide, and why was he wearing Kevlar? Those two facts didn't seem to fit in the same emotional quadrant with the death-by-cop theory.

I called Katie Clark, and her baby-sitter told me she was out of town on business until next Friday. That left William Palmer. He agreed to stay home and wait for me until 9 A.M.

As I turned back onto Hidden Ranch Road I remembered the bizarre insanity of my last visit here. I was still shaken by that bloodstained memory. I pulled up and parked in front of William Palmer's two-story colonial. White with dark green trim. Bright purple bougainvillea trellised off the front porch. Birds sang in the sycamore trees. A welcome contrast to the memory of that chattering AK-47.

I trudged up the walkway and rang the bell. After a moment Palmer opened the door. He was a tall, thirty-plus man with short hair and laugh lines framing a friendly smile. I liked him on sight. After I showed my creds, he shook my hand and led me into a large, well-appointed living room.

As we sat down he asked me to call him Tad. "Everybody does," he said, adding that he sold insurance for

Aetna and had a meeting with his district manager in an hour, a not-too-subtle hint letting me know he didn't have much time. So we got right into a discussion of Vincent Smiley.

"The guy was always kinda nuts," Tad said, shaking his head at the memory. "Like, he'd walk his dog early every morning. If you went out to pick up your paper or were even backing out of your driveway late to work, he'd always want to stop and talk. And it was always about nonsense. Like, why didn't you plant out your hedge line? Or, your pool house would look better painted pale yellow. . . . I don't know how he afforded that house of his. Somebody said it was from the life insurance after his parents died. He just hung out, giving dumb advice and getting on everybody's nerves. Since he didn't work, he had no sense of anybody else being on a schedule."

"Nobody said anything about a dog," I said. "That wasn't in any of the statements I read."

"Yeah, a big, slobbering, black Rottweiler. Mean son-of-a-bitch. I was always worried he'd get loose and maul somebody's kid. I know it's not right to be glad he's dead, but it was no fun having Smiley in the neighborhood."

"And he told you about the weapons in his garage?"

"Showed 'em to me. He was all, 'Don't you love this?' Then he'd pull out a grenade launcher or something, and break it open, show you the breech, show you a box of ammo for his AK-forty-seven. Then he shows us boxes of plastic gunk and tells us it's C-four."

"How would a guy like Smiley acquire C-four? That stuff is impossible to get. The government restricts its distribution so terrorists can't get it."

"I don't have a clue," Palmer said. "But I've got kids and a wife. I don't need that shit four doors away. Claire is taking the kids to school right now, but you can ask her when she gets back. She thinks he was one of those antigovernment survivalist nuts. He had this computer in his garage. He bragged about hacking into some military training site called Cactus West. It had all kinds of acronyms like MCAS, YUMA, or TACTS. He showed it to me."

"You have any idea what that stands for?" I asked, writing this down.

"None at all. I tried to find it on my computer, but I couldn't. Like I said, it was a secure military Web site. Add that to the automatic rifles, C-four, and a phony sheriff's badge, and we all knew we had a huge problem."

"Tad, you said in your statement he was building a bomb shelter?"

"Yeah. June, July, all last summer, basically. Said it was in his basement. He was hauling dirt outta that house right through the back door. Had it piled up in the backyard. Took truckloads away at the end of each month."

"And you're sure it was a bomb shelter?"

"That's what he said." Tad was beginning to sneak looks at his watch.

"I'll be just a minute more," I said. "So, if he was building a bomb shelter, what's your take on the idea that he shot that deputy so the cops would come up here and kill him?"

"I agree with my wife. The guy was a survivalist. I don't think he had a death wish. He told me once he went to a camp for training on how to survive in the wild. He was always flashing that badge, but he was also terrified of authority. He said he hated cops."

"He hates the cops, and at the same time he's telling everybody he is one."

"That's why me and Claire, and the Bellinghams, got together and decided to call the sheriff's department and check him out. He didn't seem like a cop to any of us. The sheriff's office said he wasn't on their roster, so we knew the badge was a phony."

"If you had to characterize him for me, how would you describe him? Just a general impression."

"The thing about Vince was he was kinda—y'know, outta sync. He didn't act right. He laughed at stuff that wasn't funny. His vibe was wrong. When he showed us all the stuff in his garage he'd kinda caress it. It was more than just ammo, it was like—manhood."

"And you called ATF, not the sheriff, right?"

"That was because a lot of that stuff in there was illegal. The automatic weapons and the grenade launcher. Chuck Bellingham said we should call Alcohol, Tobacco, Firearms, and Explosives because illegal weapons are their beat."

He looked at his watch again and I stood up to go. "Thanks," I said. "Do you have a card, in case I have any more questions?"

He pulled one out of his wallet and handed it to me as we walked to the front door. After he showed me out I got back in my car, picked up my cell phone, and dialed the LASD bureau downtown and asked for the forensics lab. A criminalist named Robyn DeYoung was in charge of the Hidden Ranch shoot-out. Once I had her on the phone, I identified myself, and asked, "Did you guys find a dog's remains out there?"

She sounded guarded. "No, but you're LAPD. What's your interest? This is a sheriff's investigation."

"You can check with Sheriff Messenger's office. He'll verify my involvement."

There was a long pause.

"I'd like to have somebody go out and rake through the ashes and look for that dog's remains," I continued.

"Why?" she asked.

"Because it's a loose end. There's supposed to be a dog. If you didn't find a dog, then where is it? It's a Rottweiler. They aren't all that cuddly. If he's out and running around loose up in the foothills, we should probably know that, don't you think?"

She didn't respond.

"Also, there's supposed to be a bomb shelter in the basement. We need to dig down and try and find it." She got very silent. I could tell I wasn't scoring many points with Ms. DeYoung.

"I'll check with Sheriff Messenger," she said after another long pause, not happy about having to go back out and sift through all those ashes again, or dig out a ton of soggy rubble looking for a bomb shelter. I had the feeling my request was going to get assigned a very low priority. I took down her direct-dial number and rang off.

My next stop was Smiley's burned-down house. I wanted one last look. I drove up the street and pulled to the curb on the east side of the cul-de-sac. There was already a green Suburban parked there. A blond woman was wandering in the ashes where the house had once stood. She was muscular, with short, spiky, white-blonde hair. As I walked closer I could see the powerful slope of a weightlifter's shoulders. Almost five-ten in low heels, she was wearing a tan miniskirt and a sleeveless cotton blouse. Her arms were cut, her legs were sinewy and tanned. I wouldn't call her exactly beautiful, but she fit into that unique category of strong-faced women who can accurately be called handsome. When she turned and focussed a level stare at me, another unique feature became apparent. Her right eye was blue, her left one green.

I stepped into the still damp ashes, crossed the distance between us, pulled out my badge and showed it to her. She studied it carefully. "LAPD?" she said. "I thought this was a sheriff's investigation."

"Let's start with who you are." I was trying not to sound badge-heavy and territorial, but I hated having civilians wandering around up here, even though the sheriff's yellow crime scene tape was down.

"I'm Kimmy Fox." She smiled at me. Her smile was dazzling, her square teeth bright and even as a row of porcelain tile. "I live right down the road. The two-story Regency on the right." She pointed at a house with a manicured yard.

I looked down and saw that she was holding two ash-dusted brass cartridges. Evidence that sheriff's CSI had missed. "Looking for souvenirs?" I said as I reached for the shell casings. She handed them to me reluctantly.

"I still can't believe all this happened," she said.

"Did you know Mr. Smiley well?"

"As well as you can know somebody like that. He was kinda strange. He had this way of looking at you. Like you were a thing . . . or just property. It was very off-putting."

"You see him with his dog? I understand he walked a dog every morning."

"I'm sorry?"

"A black Rottweiler."

"Oh, yeah. Everybody knew that dog. Vicious. I'm a mom, and I was always worried he'd get loose. I have morning carpool this year, so I saw him out walking that beast a lot when I was heading out." She smiled again. "My kids are on midsemester break. Little rascals conned me into two days at Disneyland this morning." She looked at her watch. "Guess I should get going."

"You ever see mounds of dirt piled in the backyard in June or July? I understand he was building a bomb shelter last summer."

"How could you miss it? Who builds a bomb shelter anymore? That was a sixties thing." Then she smiled at me. "Could I have those back?" she said, looking at the cartridges in my hand.

"Sorry. It's evidence."

"Oh . . . okay. I was just going to show them to my husband. He was curious about all that stuff in Vincent's garage—the guns and boxes of ammo." She started to fidget. "I'm sorry if I did anything wrong coming up here. They took down the crime tape, so I figured it was okay. The guy lived just down the street from us. Then last week, he goes completely nuts, starts shooting up the neighborhood. It's just—I needed a way to close the door on it, is all."

"I understand."

She nodded. "Well, better get going, I have teacups to ride."

"Ride carefully," I smiled.

She walked away from me, picking her way out of the ashes, then down the walk on strong, muscular legs.

There was something about her that seemed familiar, but I couldn't pin it down. I watched as she drove her Suburban up the street and parked in her driveway half a block away. I turned back and surveyed the burned-out house, wondering how the mindless insanity that had caused all this could live in such a peaceful neighborhood.

ELEVEN

The Argument

"You're coming at it from the wrong direction," Alexa said. "You're wasting precious time investigating Vincent Smiley's death. He's not the problem anymore."

We were finally at the Acropolis restaurant in the Valley, sitting at a patio table, but our plates of moussaka were untouched and cooling as we argued.

"Honey, if I don't start there I won't even know what questions to ask."

"You've only got two, or possibly three outcomes. Either ATF knew about the automatic weapons and C-four in that house, withheld information critical to the safety of the deputy serving the warrant, and they're lying, or they shared the information with the sheriff's warrant control office like they said, and the sheriffs are lying."

"What's the third?" I asked, because I sure couldn't see it.

"ATF was just on their way back from a training day like they claimed, and heard the shoot-out on the radio and nobody's lying."

"They couldn't hear it without that TAC frequency in their truck."

"Right. And you can't prove it's not there, because you can bet by now that truck has the frequency installed. Besides, you didn't have a warrant to search the damn thing."

"Picky, picky, picky."

"Hey, Shane, no kidding. You're on the wrong path here. Vincent Smiley isn't the problem."

"He had a dog—a Rottweiler, and the sheriffs didn't find the remains."

"So what?"

"It's a loose end. I don't like loose ends."

"It's nothing."

"If he had boxes of C-four, where did he get them? It's so regulated by the government there's not even a black market for that stuff."

"I don't know, Shane, but it's not what you're supposed to be investigating."

"He wore Kevlar and built a bomb shelter. He was hacked into a secure military computer called Cactus West. People who wear Kevlar and build bomb shelters do it because they want to stay alive. I don't think Smiley was trying to get the cops to kill him."

"We have death-by-cop suicides wearing body armor all the time. Look at the North Hollywood bank shootout. Those guys knew they were gonna die. Smiley built his bomb shelter almost ten months ago. Things change. Maybe he took a bad hit of acid. Maybe he was dusted on PCP and went off the rails. Look, the only reason LAPD is on this thing in the first place is because the ATF shooting review cleared their SRT, and the mayor thinks it's a bad finding. Stick to that."

"If it's a bad finding, then give it to our Professional Standards Bureau." Our new, media-friendly name for Internal Affairs. "They're good at scoping out OIS mistakes." I continued. "What the hell am I doing with it anyway?" I was raising my voice a little, and the people at the adjoining tables were beginning to look over at us with annoyed expressions.

"I can't give it to Professional Standards. It's not an LAPD shooting. And you're the only one Bill Messenger will accept. Don't make it more than it is. Just do the job."

"Is the moussaka not to your liking?" the maitre d' asked. He had drifted over to our table, displaying an elegant presence. His manner and tone made it clear that he thought we were destroying the restaurant's classic ambience.

"It's fine," I snapped.

"Bag it," Alexa barked.

The maitre d' waved a waiter over. He cleared the plates while both of us tried to calm down. After he left I leaned toward her and lowered my voice. "Alexa, you've been a cop for almost as long as I have."

"Are we gonna start comparing pedigrees now?" she hissed.

"In all those years, how many times have you seen somebody who wants to be a cop start by filing applications with the Arcadia P.D.?"

She was silent for a long time. "So?" she finally said.

"So, my guess is that Smiley started out by applying to the LAPD or the sheriff's department, then, once he failed those entrance requirements, he worked his way down the list to the smaller departments. Santa Monica, Pasadena, Glendale, Arcadia."

"Again, so what?"

"Since Arcadia wouldn't give us their psych package on him, how about we look in our own academy apps? We do preliminary psychological tests. Maybe he's in there."

"Why do you keep coming back to him? For God's sake, Shane, do you think he's still alive or something?"

"No. I trust the DNA match. What I think is, maybe a sheriff or ATF agent knew something about Smiley, or maybe Smiley had something on one of them. He gave the Arcadia P.D. a DNA sample, maybe he raped some cop's sister and this was disguised payback. Maybe he had knowledge about some cop's misdeeds and needed to be silenced. Somebody is lying about that warrant, and I'm looking for the motive. I just want to keep my options open."

"Maybe ATF just screwed up and that's why they're lying," she said, voicing the solution both the LASD and LAPD were rooting for.

"I still want to see if he ever applied to our academy."

"Shane, don't make me order you to do this my way."

"And don't force me to disobey my division commander's direct order. At the center of this, something's very wrong. Smiley hates cops, but he's walking around pretending to be one? He has boxes of C-four, nobody knows where it came from. The vest, the bomb shelter, it's all inconsistent. It needs to be looked at."

She studied me for a long moment. "I'm standing on top of a land mine here. I don't need you to tell me how much powder is in the mine. I need you to disarm the damn thing."

"Honey, you're coming at this from a totally parochial position. You already have a theory and you want my investigation to confirm it. That's not the way to go about it."

She sighed and her expression softened.

"I'm through investigating Hidden Ranch anyway," I said to mollify her. "I'm now working my way from the center out. Sheriffs are still in control of all the lab and CSI evidence. I talked to a labbie in their forensics division named Robyn DeYoung. She's the evidence tech for Hidden Ranch and she isn't too eager to follow through on any of my requests. That has to change. I want them to look for the dog and the bomb shelter."

"Okay. I'll make you a deal. I'll unstick that, and I'll see if Smiley's in our academy apps, but you have to start concentrating on whether ATF or the sheriffs are lying."

We both sat back in our chairs and stared across the linen tablecloth like fighters who had gone into neutral corners.

"I can't promise you anything," I said. "I gotta take this where it leads." Then I smiled and said, "Still love me?"

"Jesus!" she snarled.

"An easy mistake. But no, I'm Shane," I teased.

We got home at ten and found Chooch studying in his makeshift room out in the garage. "Have fun?" he asked.

Neither of us answered.

I got a beer while Alexa went to work in her office, answering e-mails. I was sitting in the living room, trying to focus on the eleven o'clock news, when Delfina came in and stood in the doorway.

"Shane?" she said, and I glanced over at her. She had her hair pulled back in a barrette and was holding our adopted cat, Franco, stroking his orange and white fur softly.

"How you doing, Del?" I said. "Thought you had a big chemistry test tomorrow." She was a junior, and chemistry was definitely not her best subject.

"I do," she smiled, "but I need to talk to you about Chooch."

I grabbed the remote and turned the volume down.

"Come on."

I led her out onto the patio. She followed silently behind. We settled into two chairs in my favorite spot overlooking the narrow canals with their Disneyesque bridges. She put Franco down and immediately the marmalade cat began to wind around my ankles.

"I've been talking to Chooch about that job coaching kids," she said.

"What's he think?"

"A lot of things are bothering him right now. He's afraid if he doesn't stay with his own football practices at Harvard-Westlake his coach will get angry and not play him, even when his foot heals. I told him that is not so. He is much better than his replacement. But he is unsure. He's also afraid if he takes over Mr. Rojas's team and doesn't do a good job you'll be disappointed. He wants you to respect what he does, but he is torn. He's afraid to make a decision. I'm telling him no decision is the same as a decision, because they'll get somebody else to be the coach. He needs to make up his mind."

"What do you think?"

"I'm worried about him, Shane. He's not like before. He's not the happy person now. I think it's very important that he does something to take his mind off his troubles."

"It's why I suggested this in the first place."

"I think I can get him to say yes," Delfina said softly.

"How?"

"I'm his *chavala*." She gave me a knowing, worldly smile. "I think, if you tell them now that Chooch will coach the team, I can get him to say yes in a day or two. Then we will have done a good thing."

"But we will have done it behind his back."

"He is *un marvillo,* you know that. But he is also sometimes acting the spoiled little boy. This will be good for him and for others. Sometimes with boys you must give them just a little push to help them decide. You get the job, and I will get the coach."

I smiled at her. Franco looked up and meowed loudly. So, of course, with both of them so vocally on the record, there was nothing much I could do but agree. *"Yo te acuerdo,"* I said.

It was late, but I took a chance and called Sonny Lopez. He was still up. When I threw Chooch's name at him he thought it was a great idea, and said he'd check with the league office and get back to me.

An hour later Alexa and I were slamming around in our bedroom, getting ready for bed. Finally she got in on her side and I got in on mine. We pulled the covers up and I snapped off the lights.

"Yes," she said.

"Yes, what?"

"Yes, I still love you." Then she rolled over and looked at me, propped up on one elbow. I could just barely see her in the ambient light coming through the window. A beautiful, dark-haired vision. "It isn't about you and me, it's about tactics," she said.

"Honey, I know you're getting pressure from Mayor Mac and Salazar, as well as Tony and Bill. I know you think I just wasted one whole day reinvestigating things that didn't need to be investigated. But this is how I do it. If I don't put all the jigsaw pieces on the table, I'll never solve the puzzle."

She scooted over, put her arms around me and held me tight. "I just hate arguing with you," she said softly, "even when you're wrong."

I held her, smelled her hair, and felt the soft textures of her body. I decided I'd rather make love than war.

So that was what we did.

TWELVE

Police Madness

When we got there Billy Greenridge from SRT was dead in a vertical coffin. His feet were still inside the living room, his large body spilled headfirst across the threshold, half in and half out of the front door of his house. The back of his head was a pulpy mess, dripping blood and brain matter onto the oleander bushes that grew just under the railing.

It was nine-fifteen the following morning.

The house was a small, wood-shingled, California Craftsman in the Rampart Division. Rampart is inside LAPD jurisdiction, so, although Greenridge was a fed, for now it was an LAPD crime scene. However, if they pressed, I knew ATF could take it away. He was their murdered agent.

Alexa and I arrived in separate cars from Parker Center. We parked and found three LAPD tech vans already on the scene, along with four LAPD black-and-whites. There were two unmarked cars with federal license plates. I recognized the ATF ASAC, Brady Cagel, already up on the porch looking down at his dead agent. Eight LAPD blues and two other men not in uniform formed a choir around the body. As I approached, I realized that the two non-uniforms were also members of SRT. Gordon

Grundy was on Cagel's right, tall, square-headed, and rawboned. His stoic face looked like someone had painted a straight-line mouth and gunmetal eyes on a block of granite. Next to Grundy was stocky Ignacio Rosano, whom I remembered from the bar fight. I'd learned he was called Nacho. The LAPD uniforms were trying to get the three feds off the porch, but the Justice Department agents didn't seem inclined to cooperate.

"Here's our division commander," one of the LAPD blues said, pointing at Alexa as we walked up.

Brady Cagel pulled out his shield and badged us. "You guys don't belong here," he said. "I'm claiming the crime scene."

"All my uniformed people who don't have a reason to be up here right now, get off this porch and secure the street out front. One of you stay here and start an incident log. The rest of you tape off a staging area, then wait by your cars." Alexa issued instructions and seven uniformed officers turned and left the porch. One of the cops remained behind, opened a notebook and started the crime scene attendance sheet. The CSI techs faded back into the house.

Brady Cagel and his two feds held their ground. "This is a dead federal agent," he said. "That makes it our investigation, according to Title Eighteen of the U.S. Code of Crimes and Criminal Procedures. I have somebody from our homicide division on his way."

"It's in our jurisdiction," Alexa said. "There's also a strong possibility that this is connected to the death of Deputy Sheriff Emo Rojas, which we've been ordered to investigate by Mayor MacKenzie. Until you file a jurisdictional claim and get a favorable ruling, it's gonna stay our case." Alexa looked right at Cagel. "So, for now, you three guys get off this porch, or I'm instructing my officers to come back up here and arrest you for interfering in an active homicide investigation and obstructing justice."

"What horseshit," he growled.

"Get moving or face the consequences," she warned.

Cagel gave it a moment's thought, looked at the eight LAPD officers twenty feet away, realized he was badly outnumbered, then motioned to his two teammates and they stepped back and headed to their cars.

Alexa watched as they walked across the street. But they didn't leave. Cagel was already on his cell phone, probably calling the U.S. Attorney for a legal opinion. Just then, another unmarked vehicle with government plates pulled in. I recognized two more members of SRT: Bill Wagner, who was nicknamed "Ringo," and Bob Zant, called "Happy." This collection of catchy nicknames stood across the street in a tight huddle, looking like a terrorist cell getting set to run a play.

"The case will end up getting transferred, unless I can get the U.S. Attorney to block the Title Eighteen," Alexa said softly.

"How's he gonna come down on our side?" I asked. "We're municipal. He's federal."

"Mayor Mac has to convince him we have a potential SWAT war going on here." Alexa for the first time put into words what everyone feared. "We need a neutral homicide team working this, and right now we're it. So let's do it right. If we do end up transferring the case, I don't want a lot of complaints about the way we handled the preliminary investigation." Then she looked around the crime scene. "Where the hell *is* my homicide team?"

"Rampart homicide dicks and the M.E. are en route," one of the crime techs said.

An LAPD crime photographer was already inside taking pictures. I could hear his motorized camera firing off frames. I took a quick tour of the two-bedroom house. It was furnished with bad art and vinyl furniture. It looked as if Greenridge lived alone. No female accessories in the bedroom, bath, or shower.

Finally, a Rampart Division homicide car slid to the curb and the last cop I wanted to see working this murder hauled his obese, 280-pound ass out of the D-car and started to waddle up the walk. Lou Ruta was fat, red-faced, and out of shape. He'd gained at least twenty pounds since we'd tangled at Carol White's murder scene last year. He struggled up the front steps gasping like a torn windbag, until he finally caught sight of me.

"What's going on here, a Boy Scout meeting?"

"That'll be enough of that, Sergeant," Alexa said, stepping out from behind the front door into his view. Ruta's face whitened, then darkened. Last came a ghastly expression where fleshy jowls pulled away from tobacco-stained ivory in a gargoyle's smile.

"Sorry, Lieutenant, didn't see ya back there," he muttered, then kneeled and studied the corpse.

The bullet had hit Greenridge in the forehead, leaving a delicate, dime-sized hole positioned like an Indian caste mark right between his eyes. Then it blew the back of his head off, leaving bone chips and gore all over the porch.

"Somebody look for the bullet," Ruta told the CSI techs, who were now standing nearby waiting for instructions. "Looks like a drive-by. Guy was comin' out his door. If the shot came from the passenger seat of a car parked down on the street, we got an upward trajectory, so start looking high in the walls across from the front door and in the living room ceiling."

The techs jumped into action.

I pulled Alexa aside, leading her down off the porch. "This guy's a joke, Alexa. The vic fell forward. How's that an upshot? Ruta's gonna screw this up."

She looked troubled. Her problem was that, as head of DSG, she couldn't favor one detective over another. Since Ruta had been next up on the homicide rotation at Rampart, she couldn't just pull him off without cause. He'd go to the union, file a complaint, and he'd win. She also couldn't admit she had a bad detective out here working active shootings. But the truth was, Ruta had lost interest years ago, and everybody was holding their breath until he got his twenty in and pulled the pin in March.

Just then, two sheriff's units roared past the LAPD squad cars blocking the end of the street and chirped to a stop. Four deputies got out and started toward the house, but the LAPD officers stationed there stopped them. The deputies gathered back by their cars. It didn't take long for ATF and sheriffs to start giving stink-eye to each other.

"This is going to the dogs," Alexa said, observing the cliques of angry agents and deputies gathering out on the street.

Happy Zant had picked up the microphone in his federal car and started talking to someone, probably calling in reinforcements.

"You gotta move some of this meat outta here before we have another fistfight," I told Alexa.

She nodded, looked at the street, then turned back to me. "Okay, here's how this is gonna work. As of now, I'm reassigning you to Rampart homicide. You're gonna be the primary on this shooting. Work it with Ruta and his partner, but you're on point."

"What about the Hidden Ranch investigation?"

"This *is* the Hidden Ranch investigation. That's your case, so as far as I'm concerned, all crimes that flow from it are yours. You work this hit, while I try and keep us from getting shot down by Title Eighteen."

Then she turned and addressed the blues who had wandered back up toward the porch. "Get enough police presence out here to move the sheriffs and ATF guys out of our staging area and down the street." One of the uniforms hustled to his car to make a call.

I crossed to where Lou Ruta was standing over the body, peeling a cigar. He let the wrapper fall and it blew away in the morning breeze, landing in the bushes by the far end of the porch. I walked down the steps and picked the cellophane off the oleander. I took it back up onto the porch and handed it to him.

"Got your fingerprints, Sarge. CSI finds it, you could get busted for this murder."

He glowered, but stuffed the wrapper in his pocket, then jammed the cigar into his mouth and started searching for a match.

"And if you light that stogie and spew ash on this site, you're gonna be smokin' it out of your ass."

"Big tough guy," he said. But he pocketed the unlit cigar as well, then started looking out at the street. "Where the fuck's my split-tail partner?"

A few minutes later Alexa took Ruta aside and gave him the news that from now on he was reporting to me on this homicide. His face contorted when she told him, but he said nothing. Then Alexa left to try and cut a deal with the U.S. Attorney.

Five minutes later Ruta's partner arrived. She was a nervous-looking honey-blonde with too-big hair. Her name was Beverly King, and from the way she looked at him, I could instantly tell she hated his guts.

THIRTEEN

Crime Scene

ATF didn't work many homicides. Their beat was illegal party favors—guns, booze, and stogies. Because we worked hundreds of murders a year, normally on homicides that fell in their jurisdiction, they'd send us an agent to help out, but would leave us on point. After the Hidden Ranch shoot-out, that obviously wasn't going to happen.

Ruta was pacing in the living room shooting off orders at everybody. "Get me a phone dump on this hard line and don't forget his cell calls," he barked at Beverly King.

She nodded, her face pinched tight with stress, her body language a concert of uncertainty. She took off through the living room toward the phone.

"Not through the crime scene, you idiot!" Ruta yelled. "Go out the front door, around to the back porch. After it's dusted, use the phone in the kitchen. Who the fuck taught you crime scene tactics, Katie Couric?"

Beverly King muttered an apology and scooted out the front door on her errand.

I walked over to Ruta. "Why don't you cut her some slack?"

"Why don't you suck my dick? Or can I say that to the husband of our division commander?"

"Hey, Lou, you can say anything you want, just don't piss me off, or I'll drag your sorry ass outside and disconnect your dome light." I smiled benignly. "Besides, how would I ever find your dick in all that blubber?" He reddened but didn't respond.

All around us, CSIs were doing their thing. They were getting ready to flip Billy Greenridge, after bagging his hands. In my opinion, there wasn't going to be any DNA under his nails. This didn't look like it was done from up close. He looked like he was shot from a distance with a high-powered round, probably from a sniper's rifle.

Everybody was more or less thinking that someone from the sheriff's enforcement bureau had done this, but nobody wanted to say it because of where that would take us.

Beverly King found the bullet hole in the living room wall. It had punched through a copy of that corny painting of dogs playing poker. The picture hung opposite the front door, the bullet passing right through the head of a fox terrier holding five spades in his paw. Apparently not a winning hand. Then the slug went through the laundry room and back porch, blasting out into the backyard, where it was lost somewhere in the open field beyond. It had to have been a big round, like a .308, to go through Billy's head, three walls, and keep going. Hunting for it in the field behind the house was going to be an iffy project. The bullet would probably never be found.

When the M.E.s were finally ready to transport the body I went over and watched them load Billy onto the gurney, his bloody remains now all zipped up neatly in a rubber coroner's bag. I walked out with the M.E.'s assistant, an Asian man named Ray Tsu, helping him push the gurney. Tsu had a pipe-cleaner build and long hair parted in the middle and pushed behind his ears like black tieback curtains.

We struggled, pushing the load up to the coroner's van. The front wheels of the gurney folded under and we slid the body into the back. Before he shut the van doors, I stopped him.

"Can I take one last look, Ray?"

"Sure." He unzipped the bag and Billy's pasty white face came into view. I examined the bullet hole in the center of his forehead. An ugly red cyclops.

"Up or down?" I asked, referring to the trajectory.

"Ruta says up," Tsu dodged.

"Yeah, but whatta you say?"

"Depends on the attitude of his head when he got hit," he hedged again. "I'm just a tech. You should get all that from the M.E."

Just to keep the conversation rolling, I said, "Bullet fired from some shooter sitting in a car parked out front would be slightly up, right? An upshot would knock his head back. The head's responsible for what? A little over a tenth of a person's gross weight?"

"Eighteen percent."

"Right, eighteen. So it's like a fulcrum, whichever way the head goes, so goes the body. An upshot should blow him back, but he fell forward, head toward the street. How come?"

"There's no rules on this stuff, Shane," Ray said, smiling now, despite our ghoulish subject matter.

"Take a guess," I said. "You see a lot of this. I won't hold you to it."

"Well, two ways it happens, maybe. One, if he was shot up close, like from a few feet away with a big round. The muzzle velocity on a three-oh-eight or a two-twenty-three is so great coming out of the barrel, it maybe blows out the back of his skull without much recoil. So he doesn't fall back, but his head rebounds slightly from the exit kick and that throws him forward. Or it was a down-shot from a ways away, and the shot takes him to his knees. From there, depending how he hit, he could fall anywhere."

"Any other way it happens?"

"I've seen hundreds of drive-bys the last few years. Sometimes there's no reason why a body lands the way it does. Bullets ricochet off bones, change directions. The rules of physics on this can get skewed. He could have even bounced off the door frame and got knocked forward."

Ray Tsu rezipped the bag and closed the van door, then paused before leaving. "Ruta's got his full, fair share of mean, don't he?"

"In our business, it's real easy to go sour. It's something to watch out for."

Tsu nodded, then got into the van and pulled out. The rest of the preliminary crime scene investigation went right down departmental guidelines. We drew a grid of the place, graphed everything, vacuumed for trace evidence, hair, and fiber, in case the shooter had been in the house before he pulled the trigger. A long shot, but you never know. We looked for brass out front. Didn't find any. Photographed and dusted, taped up and backed out. Textbook.

Out on the street Ruta was hovering. I wanted some time alone to run my theories and thoughts, so I told him I was done. He grunted, walked to his car, and pulled away. I saw Beverly King sitting on the curb having a cigarette, trying to get rid of some anger. I walked up to her. Her hands were shaking as she took a drag.

"Good going in there," I said, referring to the fact that she had found the bullet hole in the painting. It wasn't a huge victory, but she needed something.

"Right. Mrs. Columbo saves the case." Her tone was bitter. Angry.

"Detective King, some things we can change, some things we can't. The secret is knowing the difference."

"I guess," she said, looking up and snapping the butt away. It scattered sparks in the street where it landed. "The guy just gets me froggy. Once he starts selling his wolf tickets, I end up getting tentative and start making mistakes."

"Ruta can't define you. Only you can do that. You let him get into your head, you're finished. The trick is to ignore his flack and stay focused. You're in charge of your game; he's in charge of his. Don't get the two mixed up, just because he's got two extra stripes and some attitude."

"Easy to say."

"Think of it this way. You're a homicide dick. A specialist. A lot's at stake when you get a call. You're the last hope the vic has for justice. Billy Greenridge is your client now. Don't let exposure to negativity cheat your client out of the best you have."

She frowned. "Who are you supposed to be, Deepak Chopra?"

"I'm just a guy who's done it wrong too many times and had to pay for it."

Finally her look softened and she smiled. "Thanks, Shane," she said softly.

FOURTEEN

Sighting

I drove across town to the new County Medical Examiner's office located on the southeast corner of the L.A State College campus. They had recently broken ground on a high-tech, state-of-the-art crime lab facility next door and as I pulled in I could see the growling bulldozers working in the adjoining field preparing the site. The coroner's unit was already up and had been in business for about a month. It was a modern three-story building with mirrored glass. I pulled into a slot in student parking, put my handcuffs over the steering wheel—the universal signal to all cruising traffic control officers and parking police that this was a cop car—then I entered the air-conditioned, sterile confines of the new facility.

I was there because I needed some time to pass. I wanted to let things settle down before going back to Billy Greenridge's little house on Mission Street. There was a good chance that the sheriff's black-and-whites and ATF cars would cruise that neighborhood for hours. It was going to be the latest "Whatta-buncha-bullshit" gripe for both agencies.

I didn't want to get caught standing on the front porch chewing my nails with a dumb look on my face, so I came here to satisfy one little detail that I probably already had the answer to.

I badged my way down to the second subbasement floor and found a county M.E. named Lisa Williams, who had done the DNA match on Smiley. She was a thirty-year-old African-American wearing a blue medical smock, slippers, and hair net. A surgical mask was hanging around her neck.

"Sure," she said after I told her what I wanted. She led me down a hallway into a quarter-acre-sized, windowless room full of fluorescent-lit workstations and cubicles. We arrived at her desk and she turned on her computer and waited for it to boot up. "The DNA sample we got from the Arcadia P.D. was taken by their medical officer in 'oh-two. It's a legally obtained sample, witnessed with double signatures. We matched it to the DNA we got off the corpse at Hidden Ranch."

Her computer had loaded, and now the two DNA strands were side by side in the center of her monitor. She started scrolling.

"On the right is the 'oh-two Arcadia sample. The left is the one we took from the charred body last week. It's a perfect match. No variables, intangibles, or dropouts. These strings of base pairs line up perfectly. That corpse in the morgue is definitely Vincent Smiley."

"Thanks."

I left with nothing new learned. Okay, maybe it was a waste of time, but I'm a stickler about this stuff. I looked at my watch. I'd been gone an hour. Time to head back to the house on Mission.

I parked up the street, then walked back to the wooden Craftsman. Ruta was sure that the shooter had been in a car, but according to the location of the bullet hole in the living room, my trajectory estimate put a shot from a car on the street too low. Of course, the doer could have opened the car door, stepped out, fired from a standing position, then picked up his brass and left. That would have more or less lined him up with the bullet hole. But if he did it that way he was risking exposure and identification by a neighbor.

Ray Tsu had said a down-shot might have knocked Greenridge to his knees and pitched him forward with his head toward the street.

I remembered Billy from the bar fight. He and I had stood toe-to-toe trading body shots. We were about the same height. I had measured the height of the bullet hole in the living room two hours earlier, using my arm. When I pointed at the hole, it was about three inches below my shoulder. So now, facing the opposite direction, centered in the doorway where I thought he had been, I extended my arm to about head high, pointed it straight out and raised it three inches. It was now, more or less, pointed up at an apartment building across the street. If the shot hadn't come from a parked car, then maybe the bullet had come from that building.

I knew it was an outside chance, because most street assassins like to have a set of wheels under them when doing a drive-by. Disregarding that logic, I sighted along my arm at the four-story apartment complex. It was an old, sixties-style building. Concrete boxes. Ugly. In my opinion, the sixties had been a decade of architectural blight. I counted windows and realized that, if the shot came from over there, it would have to be from the third or fourth window at the end of the building, second floor.

I walked up the street so I wouldn't be seen by any of the people living in the apartments, then doubled back and came down the sidewalk, hugging the buildings on the other side. I entered the apartment complex and took the elevator to the second floor. It was a groaning, creaking ride. The door finally wheezed open and I exited into a dark hallway. I knew approximately how far down the hall the window I had sighted would be. When I reached the spot, I looked at the closest door. It was ajar. I pulled out my Beretta, and with my toe, pushed it open a crack and looked in.

The apartment was carpeted but had no furniture or drapes. Standing on the east side of the room, looking inside an empty bookshelf, was a woman. I knew those muscular legs, cut arms, that spiky white hair. I stepped inside. She heard me behind her and turned.

"Aren't you supposed to be riding teacups at Disneyland?" I asked.

"Hi," she smiled at me. The smile really was a dazzler. I'm sure it had gotten her out of a lot of tight spots, but not this one.

"Listen, I can explain," she said.

"How?" I replied. Then I moved forward and snatched her purse off her shoulder and went through it. I found her wallet, opened it.

"Look—okay, I'm not Kimmy Whatever. I'm . . ."

"Nancy Chambers?" I said, reading her California driver's license. The picture was definitely her: weight lifter's neck, mismatched eyes, white-blonde hair.

"First you're at Hidden Ranch digging through that crime scene, trying to remove evidence, now you're poking around up here. This needs to be an excellent explanation, Nancy."

"I'm a newspaper reporter. My press card is in there. I work for the *Valley Times*, the crime desk. I'm doing a series of articles on urban violence. The Hidden Ranch thing is this Sunday's Op-Ed piece."

"How's that get you over here?"

"I have a police scanner in my car. I was monitoring federal frequencies. I heard them talking about this. I knew Billy Greenridge was on the ATF SWAT team that was up at Hidden Ranch, so I came over."

By then I had found her press card for the *Valley Times*. Under her picture it read "Nancy Chambers, Reporter."

"People call me Nan." She smiled, again giving me the Pepsodent Challenge.

"Whatta you think you're doing here?"

"Investigating my story. Greenridge was hit by a sniper. I think this might be the firing position. Look at this."

She stepped aside and pointed down at something under the window. I looked down and saw a tripod mark, three little indentations in the carpet next to the window.

"He sets up a shooting stand right here," Nan said, really into it now, "and when Greenridge comes out of his house, ka-pow!" She turned to face me. "This could be where the killer shot the rifle," she announced triumphantly. "I was just looking around for his brass."

"I hope you didn't already steal the cartridge casing, like you tried to yesterday."

"I'm a reporter, not a criminal," she said, "but I don't think it's here. I already looked."

I glanced around the room, then turned and faced the window. "Unless they're specifically made for lefties, most rifles port to the right, so when the brass ejects, it should be over here on the right side of the room."

We both started searching, looking up on the empty shelves, in the moldings around the carpet edge. Then I glanced down and saw a floor heating grate. It was a large, old-fashioned, cast-iron number fastened down with brass screws. The opening was big enough for a cartridge case to drop through, and if it had, my hope was that in his haste, the sniper would have left it there. I took out a pen knife and, while she watched, loosened the screws and lifted the heavy metal. I saw it before the grate came off—a spent casing from a .308. I took out a pen, reached down, and sticking the point in the open end of the case, lifted it out. Sometimes my detective skills astound even me.

"We found it!" she said, beaming.

I was frowning. I knew that now our tool marks section in the ballistics lab would have to go out and test fire all of the long rifles at sheriff's SWAT. Under the circumstances, not an easy request. But if this cartridge casing matched one of their Tango 51s or 40-Xs, we were off on a horrible misadventure.

"I think this could be terrific," she grinned.

"I think it could be terrible," I replied.

FIFTEEN

Fuming

I closed up the apartment using the button lock, wondering how many prints Nan smudged on the way in. I had been careful not to touch anything, but I was pretty sure she had left prints everywhere.

"Whatta you doing?" she asked, as we walked across the street. I still had the cartridge casing upside down on my pen tip. I fished out the key to my Acura and opened the trunk, withdrew a small crime scene evidence kit, then headed toward the back door of Billy Greenridge's house where I knew Beverly King had found the hide-a-key under a pot.

"Aren't you supposed to put that in a bag or something?" she said, dogging my footsteps.

"Latent prints typically fall into two categories," I told her, showing off a little, "porous and nonporous."

"You mind if I get this down?" She fished a notebook and pen out of her purse, flipped to a clean page, and started writing. "I might be able to use some of it." She was scribbling: "Nonporous—okay, go on."

"Porous prints appear on soft surfaces like paper or cardboard, unfinished wood. You can bag a porous print because the finger oil has sunk into the material, basically setting it. If this shooter wasn't wearing gloves when he loaded this cartridge, then any prints he left on here will be nonporous. Nonporous is any hard surface. Nonporous prints are fragile. Anything can wipe them off, even the evidence bag, so I have to fume it first, to set the print before I transport it."

"This is fascinating. Fume it. Okay . . ." She was scribbling in her notebook. "So our bullet is nonporous."

Suddenly it was *our* bullet—of course it wasn't a bullet, it was a cartridge case.

I unlocked the back door of Billy Greenridge's house and walked into his kitchen. She was hot on my heels, writing as she went. I handed her "our bullet."

"Hold the pen like that, don't touch the brass," I instructed.

I removed a pair of latex gloves from the kit and snapped them on, then moved around the kitchen, taking what I needed. I took a coffee cup out of a cupboard, filled it, and put it in the microwave, setting it to boil. Next, I found some aluminum foil in a drawer.

I reached into my evidence kit, removed a tube of superglue, and dabbed about a nickel-sized glob on a square of foil. Then, I shut off the microwave and put the foil inside, next to the steaming cup of water, took the pen with the bullet casing out of Nan's hand, and carefully placed it tail down in the microwave. The microwave was acting only as an enclosed space to hold the superglue fumes and the steam from the cup of boiling water. I closed the door and looked at my watch.

"This is amazing," Nan gushed. "But what on earth are you trying to do?"

"Harden the print. Superglue is basically a chemical called cyanoacrylate. The fumes get heated slightly by the cup of boiling-hot water. They float around in there—attach themselves to the amino and lactic acids, the glucose, sweat, and peptides that are the print residue. You can see the white ridges from the fumes starting to form on the cartridge already. Looks like maybe we got something."

She leaned down and looked through the glass of the microwave door, smiling. "This is so cool," she said. "You're like Bill Nye the Science Guy with a badge."

I groaned at that, then looked at my watch. Long enough. I opened the door, and with my gloved hand removed the cartridge case and held it up to the light. We had a slightly smudged partial print. It looked like an index or middle finger. Besides the print were some striated action marks, which had been left when the casing ported. They could also prove helpful.

"Not a clean print," I said, "but maybe the lab can raise it some more. At least now it's hardened." I took out an evidence baggie and dropped the casing with its preserved print inside.

"I never knew you could do that."

"Easier than getting a crime tech out here, waiting for an hour, and getting the same result. Let's go."

I cleaned up the mess in the microwave, placed the coffee cup back in the cupboard, then took everything else with me as I exited the house and locked the door. I walked Nan Chambers over to her green Suburban parked on a side street and watched while she unlocked the car and opened the door.

"What was your name, again?" she asked, turning back and smiling. "Scully or something?"

She started to write it down, but I took the notebook out of her hands. "Don't bother. It won't be good if we see each other again, or if my name shows up in your paper."

I started thumbing through her notes. Aside from my lecture on latent prints, she had a page on each of the ATF SWAT members. Date of birth, education, time in service—with background information: married, how many kids, etc. She also had a few other statements from the neighbors at Hidden Ranch—and notes from an interview with William Palmer. We had covered a lot of the same terrain. I finished flipping through the book. It looked legit.

"Isn't this illegal search and seizure?" she said, interrupting my thoughts.

"Probably, but it doesn't matter unless I arrest you for this crime and try to get your book submitted as evidence in court. But since I'm in a charitable mood, I'm gonna let you take a pass. Unless you ignore my warning, we should have no problem."

She was pinning me with those strange mismatched eyes. Her expression had hardened. "I haven't committed any crime."

"The crime is interfering with a police investigation, breaking into that apartment without permission, and the possible destruction of evidence."

"What crime scene?"

"That apartment. If it's the shooting position, it's a secondary crime scene."

She didn't look handsome now. She looked pissed and a little frightening. "I went to the manager, got his permission to look inside," she said. "He opened up for me. I didn't see any crime scene tape and I don't need your permission to go inside a place I'm thinking about renting when I have the manager's permission."

"Ms. Chambers—"

"It's Miss. I'm not much on feminism. I do okay without it."

"You are not an uninformed bystander who is interested in renting an apartment, you're a newspaper reporter. You pushed into a room that you knew might be connected to a homicide, possibly disturbing fingerprints or trace evidence. Now I'm going to have CSI contact you and get a set of elimination prints. I'm not going to put up with any more of this from you. If I ever see you again, I'm filing those charges." I handed her notebook back. "Good-bye."

She got into her Suburban and drove out of my life—I hoped.

On my way back to the Glass House, I got a radio call instructing me to switch to TAC-2 for a message from my C.O. Cal came on and told me that I had a "forthwith" from the chief to meet him and Alexa at the U.S. Attorney's office.

"What's cookin'?"

"Your ass. Twelfth floor, Office twelve eighty-nine."

SIXTEEN

Forthwith

It took a full forty minutes to get there. Two of L.A.'s enduring myths are that it's a tropical paradise and that you can get anywhere in the Basin in twenty minutes.

The U.S. Federal Annex is on Spring Street. It's a large, turn-of-the-century Greek monstrosity with a roof fresco decorated with frolicking satyrs. The winds had died down and the flags out front hung like dead pelts. I parked in the underground garage, stowed my gun in the trunk, and cleared security in the basement. Then I rode the elevator to the twelfth floor.

Federal buildings always feel musty to me. Maybe it's all that in-line thinking. The tile halls were polished, the doors dark mahogany or oiled maple, I'm not sure which. The only woods I'm good at identifying are peckerwoods.

I found Suite 1289. When I entered the reception area I heard arguing coming from the inner office. A vanilla-flavored male secretary looked at my credentials and pointed at the door. He didn't speak. Why waste your breath on lower lifeforms like city cops?

Inside the high-ceilinged room was a crowd of angry, misguided people. It was Cole Hatton's office, the U.S. Attorney for the Central District of California. He was a good-looking, dark-haired fifty-year-old with a country club tan who wore his clothes so well that I instantly distrusted him.

Bill Messenger and his area commander Paul Matthews stood on one side of the room. Garrett Metcalf and Brady Cagel were next to the windows in nicely fitted, gabardine suits, easily winning the fashion competition. Tony Filosiani and Mayor MacKenzie looked uncomfortable in the center of the room, while Alexa hovered nearby.

"This is Sergeant Scully," Tony said. I shook hands with Cole Hatton, who barely looked at me before he turned back to the mayor.

"I don't see any rationale for overturning a federal statute," he said. "The Bureau of Alcohol, Tobacco, Firearms, and Explosives should be allowed to investigate the death of one of their own. According to your own criminalists, there was C-four residue on the ashes. Illegal C-four is a mandated statute of ATF. That's basically it, unless the FBI deems that its own absence from the case would materially affect the interest of justice. That's the way the statute reads." His voice was booming in the high-ceilinged room. Everybody winced at the mention of the FBI.

"We've got a dead sheriff's deputy and some very strange circumstances surrounding the service of a warrant given to us by ATF," Messenger said. "Their Internal Affairs investigated and found no wrongdoing, but our IAD sees it differently. The county will undoubtedly face lawsuits. Since the mayor ordered the LAPD to reinvestigate, our opinion is that these cases are related, and that gives Sergeant Scully standing to investigate the Greenridge murder."

"How is the murder of William Greenridge related to Emo Rojas? That's nuts," Garrett Metcalf said hotly. "Unless you're suggesting something pretty damn unfriendly."

"Can we all calm down?" Hatton said, then crossed to his desk. "I'm going to bifurcate the investigations. LAPD can go ahead and reinvestigate the Hidden Ranch warrant problem, but ATF is going to handle their own agent homicide and the investigation into how the hell this nut got his hands on so much C-four."

"And if the two investigations overlap?" Alexa asked.

"Try and keep that from happening. Build a Chinese wall," Hatton instructed.

"Hey, if they overlap, Cole, they overlap." Now Tony was getting mad. "How'm I gonna build a Chinese wall? That's total bullshit."

"Hand over all of your tapes, photographs, forensics, ballistics, and trace evidence from the Mission Street crime scene to the ATF homicide investigators," Hatton said to Tony. "Do it before close of business today. That's it."

We all filed out of his office. The feds looked smug, the cops looked pissed, Mayor Mac, Tony, and Alexa looked dazed.

Technically speaking, the crime scene we had been ordered out of was Greenridge's house on Mission. Nobody had said anything about the apartment across the street. Of course, to be fair, they didn't even know about that yet. But if I played it carefully, and if Nan Chambers didn't blow me in on the pages of the *Valley Times* tomorrow morning, maybe I could keep us in the game. I had to call her and set up a meeting to make sure she'd play along.

The brass casing from the .308 was burning a hole in my pocket as we walked into the underground garage.

SEVENTEEN

Drinks

"We need to talk," I said, stopping the two top cops before they got into their cars. Alexa had stayed upstairs with the feds to work out the details of handing over the evidence from Mission Street. I pulled out the .308 casing and showed it to Tony. He studied the brass in the cellophane evidence bag. "Looks like it's been fumed."

"It has."

I told them about finding the secondary crime scene and how I discovered the cartridge casing with Nan Chambers, then hardened the print in Billy's microwave. I finished by saying, "I locked up the apartment, but I didn't call it in or bring our crime techs out there yet. I was just about to when I got the forthwith."

Messenger was now holding the cellophane baggie with his thumb and index finger, glaring at the casing like it was a dead cockroach he'd found in his salad. It wasn't hard to figure out what was going through the sheriff's mind. If that partial print on the shell casing matched one of his SEB SWAT members, then his department was hip high in trouble.

"We got a big problem," Tony said, his Brooklynese bubbling up. "You turn this over to ATF, first they're gonna demand you print-check all your guys, then they're gonna wanta test-fire them Tango Fifty-ones and Forty-Xes you got at SEB to see if one matches the breach and ejection striations on this brass. The sheriff's police union is gonna start throwing bricks. They'll say you got no probable cause to test those weapons, and this turns from a petty jurisdictional squabble into a shit sandwich."

Bill Messenger was still holding my cellophane evidence bag. "Okay, Tony, how do you wanta do it then?"

"It's your department, Bill. We're only investigating the warrant problem at Hidden Ranch. You wanta take on a U.S. Attorney, have at it."

"I got a compromise," Bill said. Tony listened, rocking back slightly on his heels.

"You let me put an investigator next to Shane and I'll get all my SEB long rifles tested. There won't be any union trouble. I'll do it under the radar, have the range officer take them all out for sight adjustments or something, then we'll collect the brass and look for a match. If this casing fits one of those rifles, or this print is from one of my guys, then I'll find a way to get past the union. I got no room in my outfit for killers. I'll bust 'em myself and hand the whole thing over to ATF."

"I don't want some deputy looking over my shoulder," I said, seizing only on the first thing he said and ignoring the rest.

"Shut up, Shane," Tony commanded. Then he looked at Messenger. "Okay. You get a print run started and have your SEB long guns tested and checked against this brass, and in return, Shane works with one deputy of your choosing."

"Deal," Messenger said. "And as long as all the Hidden Ranch forensic stuff is already at our crime lab, I'd like to suggest we leave it there. My criminalists are as good as yours. It'll save time."

Tony nodded his agreement. Then Bill Messenger turned to me. "Your partner is going to be Sergeant Brickhouse, one of my crack IAD investigators. You two can meet over at the sheriff's main building this afternoon at four."

"No. Your office is too far away, and I have a bunch of stuff to do on this side of the hill. Let's meet at Denny's restaurant at five. The one on Lankershim in the Valley."

"Done." Then Messenger turned, and carrying the brass casing, walked to his car.

After he drove out, I looked at Tony. "How the hell's this gonna work? I'm really supposed to investigate the Rojas shooting with some biased hump from the sheriff's rat squad?"

Tony unlocked his car, took off his coat, and threw it over the seat. "Yeah, because if I was in Messenger's position I'd feel just like him. I'd want my own investigator looking out for my interests, too. He's in a deep crack." Tony settled into his Crown Vic and turned to look at me. "We've gotta turn that secondary crime scene over to ATF," he said. "Why don't you get somebody to rediscover it? Then call the feds and give it to them."

"But we don't give 'em the shell casing I found in there? How's that work?"

"I don't know. I'll think about it and we'll reevaluate all our options as things progress. In the meantime, put this thing down fast, Shane. I don't like where it's going. If SEB and SRT are gunning for each other after work, we're all gonna end up in the bag." He put his car in gear and drove out.

I still had two hours before my meeting with Sergeant Brickhouse. As soon as I was on street level where my cell would work, I needed to make two calls: Lou Ruta and Nan Chambers. The first was going to be Ruta. I finally had a use for that angry asshole. I pulled up the ramp into a smoggy L.A. afternoon and reached for my phone. It rang before I could open it.

"Hello?" I held the unit to my ear as I drove.

"Shane? Sonny Lopez." He sounded a long way away, or we had a bad connection.

"What's up?"

"I got Chooch the coaching job. But there's a league guy you have to talk to. He's got some questions. Like, is Chooch eighteen?"

"Not quite."

"A Pop Warner head coach has to be eighteen, but I can sign up for that job and he can be what they call a demonstrator. Demonstrators in Pop Warner aren't coaches, they're guys who demonstrate to the kids how to do stuff. Technically I'll be in charge, but he'll do the head coaching job. We just don't tell anyone. There's other stuff you need to sign off on. We're meeting with this guy at six tonight."

"I can't. Got an appointment. How 'bout in the next hour or so, for drinks?"

"I'll have to call you back," Sonny said.

We hung up and I dialed Ruta. "Yeah?" he growled.

After I told him we were off the case, I told him about the windows across the street from the murder scene, and that somebody should tell the feds to check the apartments over there in case it was the shooting position.

"Whatta buncha shit," he said and hung up. I wasn't sure if he was talking about my theory or us getting bounced. Then I called the *Valley Times*. Nan Chambers was out, but I left my name and number and the message that I wanted to see her immediately.

Sonny Lopez called back fifteen minutes later. "Okay, the guy will meet you at the Boar and Bull on Ventura for drinks. Be there in twenty."

"Deal," I said.

The place was almost empty when I arrived. I moved through the darkly colorful restaurant. Stuffed boar and bull heads with glassy eyes were mounted over the bar, gazing down like hairy drunks hung on the wall to dry out.

I found my way into the back room where four members of the sheriff's department were sitting in one of the red leather booths under a big-screen TV that was playing a tape of last Sunday's Chargers game, with the sound off.

"Hey, Shane," Darren Zook called out.

I walked over. I knew them all. Darren was at one end of the booth. Next to him was Sonny Lopez, then Gary Nightingale. Rick Manos, who I remembered from their mission board was an SEB scout, sat on the far end. This was obviously not going to be about football.

Sonny said, "Want a beer?"

"Not till I know what's going on." I pulled up a free chair and straddled it, sitting at the end of the horseshoe booth so I was facing them. "So let's just get to it."

"Okay. You were Emo's friend. Word is you're the one looking into all this, so I guess we're looking to you for some cover," Sonny said.

"Cover, or cover-up?" I asked.

Rick Manos leaned forward. I'd heard about him before. Big street rep. His silent jacket said he was not a guy to mess with.

"We know you got the Greenridge homicide," Manos said. "We also know ATF is gonna try and force you to put it on my people. SEB didn't kill that guy, piece of shit that he was."

"Okay, here's my take on that," I said. "I don't know whether SEB popped Billy Greenridge, or if he was shot by some old peckerwood bust of his who crawled out of the woodpile at Vacaville, looking for payback. But it doesn't matter what I think anymore, 'cause ATF Title-Eighteened us. They've got it now, so if you got a problem, talk to the nutsacks over at Justice. But I'll tell you this much, if I was still involved I'd put your request on the record and you'd all lose pay and grade."

"You're taking this the wrong way," Lopez said.

"How is that, Sonny? You guys just asked me to throw an investigation."

"We didn't kill Billy Greenridge," Manos said. His voice was soft, but I could hear the anger. "We just look good for it and everybody wants this thing put down fast."

"I'm sure if you lay back everything will turn out fine." I started to get up and Rick Manos and Gary Nightingale stood with me. Each took one of my arms to keep me from leaving. "You sure this is the way you want to play it?" I said softly.

They hesitated, then let go.

"Shane, they killed Emo," Sonny said. "They sent him up there without knowing what he was walking into. Why isn't anybody investigating that?"

"They are," I said.

"Yeah? And just who's doing that?" Manos said.

"Me. I'm looking into it for Sheriff Messenger and Mayor Mac."

"LAPD?" Nightingale said, but his face clouded with disbelief, as if I'd just said the Girl Scouts of America were working the case.

"I'm not gonna bend the warrant investigation either," I went on. "I'm gonna do it straight up, and my advice to you guys is to back up and hit neutral. Proactive behavior is just gonna make things worse."

"What if their SRT team decides to even the score?" Gary Nightingale said. "We didn't pop Greenridge, but they think we did. What if they snipe at one of us next?"

"That's why you guys get the extra-thick Kevlar," I said, and stepped back from the table.

"You were supposed to be Emo's friend," Lopez said.

"I was his friend, and I know if it had been one of us up there on the porch instead of him, Emo would never be asking for stuff like this." Then I looked directly at Sonny. "And thanks for using my son to lure me out with all that bullshit about Pop Warner. Next time you want to have a police meeting, call my office and make a regular appointment."

"Here." Sonny reached down on the seat beside him, picked up a thick blue binder, and slid it across the table toward me. "That's the play book for the Rams and the rule book for the league. The guy you've gotta call's number is in there."

As I reached for it Rick Manos grabbed my arm and held it. When he looked up at me, his eyes were as dark and empty as two gun barrels.

"If the shit jumps off, be sure you've got a side to be on," he warned.

EIGHTEEN

Rats

At five o'clock I was waiting for Sergeant Brickhouse in a back booth at Denny's, the Pop Warner binder sat unopened on the seat beside me. I was still angry about the meeting at the Boar and Bull. I'd expected much more from those guys. I sat with a cup of coffee, trying to calm down while a growing dissatisfaction with my role in police work festered.

I guess what pissed me off most was how over the years situations like this had forced my expectations down and made me question everything I had once believed in. When I joined the force we were Blue Knights, protectors of the innocent. Centurions. I had worn my uniform with pride, but without realizing why, things had started to change, and I had slowly lost my point of view.

I remember the first time somebody spit on my black-and-white. I was only about three years on the job, still in a uniform, working a neighborhood car in Van Nuys. It was a heavily Hispanic area and a ten-year-old *vatito* ran up while we were at a stop sign and hocked a lugie. It hit and ran down the squad car's windshield. The boy flipped us off, then took off running. My partner said the next time he saw that *flaquito,* he'd slap him silly. I had another reaction. I was angry, sure, but also I wanted that boy to know I was out there in the streets for him. If he needed me I was his backup. Instead, he only saw somebody to despise.

The same thing happened again six months later, when I was working an L-car in Carson. I had parked the unit, and this old African-American woman with her arms full of groceries spit on the windshield of my empty Plain-Jane. I came out of a coffee shop just as she did it and caught her. She started yelling curses at me. If somebody had tried to mug her, I was prepared to risk my life to stop it. She didn't understand that my job was to protect and serve *her.*

Of course, I also knew that in her eyes I didn't exist. As a man, I was invisible. All she saw was the uniform, and it was a symbol of something she hated. What distressed me was that this virulent hatred spanned fifty years and two ethnic boundaries, from that ten-year-old Hispanic boy in Van Nuys, to the black grandmother in Carson.

Rodney King and the O.J. case were part of it. The Rampart scandal put it in overdrive. We were not Blue Knights to some of these citizens, but a gang in blue— thugs with life-and-death power, who kicked ass, took names, and didn't care if we got it right, as long as we got it down. Hook'm, book'm, and cook'm. A bad bust probably just takes another guilty asshole off the street, so don't sweat it. It was the total collapse of an idea I once treasured.

Years ago I thought I should make a difference. Be a one-man cleanup crew. One afternoon I spotted the same old woman carrying groceries in Carson and I followed her home. I guessed her age was about sixty, but she looked almost a hundred. When I knocked on her door she opened it to the length of the chain lock. Our emotional and intellectual view of each other was as narrow as that inch-wide slit.

"Go away," she said, seeing my uniform. "They all dead." Then she slammed the door.

Two days later, while I was patrolling the same area, I saw her again. She was struggling with an especially large armload of packages. Her ankles were swollen, her face shiny with sweat as she toiled along. I rolled up beside her, got out, and opened my squad car door. "Can I give you a ride home, ma'am?" I asked.

She stood at the side of the curb and looked at me with contempt. "I told you, they all dead," she said, exasperated. "You killed ever' one. Now you think I be gettin' in dat damn *po*-lice car?"

"But I didn't kill them," I said. "I never met them."

"You *po*-lice, ain't ya? Two boys and one baby girl— my grandchildren, all dead, shot by *po*-lice." And then she spat again, this time on me. I felt it spray across my face and run down into my collar.

I got back into my car, drove half a block away and parked. I was shaken by the incident. I didn't know why the police had shot her grandchildren or even if they had a valid reason. But I knew it didn't matter. A valid reason or a legal justification wouldn't change the hatred in that woman's ancient, yellow eyes. I could have carried her groceries twice a week for the rest of my life and it wouldn't begin to make up for those three dead children.

Protect and Serve. I tried to live up to that increasingly difficult motto. But I was flawed. I was vulnerable to anger and ego like everyone else. I had emotional prejudice and a parochial moral view, which I tried to overcome. On the street, I tried to be color-blind and situation-neutral. Yet, with each passing year I became more fatigued by the effort.

I would have given a year's pay to have that old woman forgive me for the deaths of three children I never even knew, and that puzzled me. Why should it be so important? Why should I invest so deeply in something I wasn't a part of and couldn't change?

But I did. I guess somewhere deep down I still needed my uniform to validate me. Maybe I needed it for identity or for a sense of belonging. Maybe I had chosen to be a cop because I respected the values in the manual; and when all those values got skewed I didn't have the guts to get off the ride. I still wanted to do the right thing. I still wanted the people I served to know I cared. But more and more, nobody cared if I cared. I had been absorbed into the mix, unable to rise above the perceptions of others. Now I feared SEB and SRT were on a course that would only make it worse, and that was what was darkening my mood and ruining my day.

I looked up as Nan Chambers walked into the restaurant. She saw me and headed in my direction on those strong muscular legs, her cut arms swinging, spiky hair bristling, turning heads all over the room as she crossed toward me.

"Your office told me you were going to be here," she said, answering my unspoken question like a gypsy mind reader.

"We need to come to an understanding," I said. "You can't write about that crime scene we found across the street, at least not yet. That's gotta stay between us, Nan. And if you left any prints at that apartment, get ready for a visit from the feds."

"I didn't leave any prints," she said, and slid uninvited into the booth across from me.

Then she reached into her purse and pulled out a leather wallet, opened it, and slid it across the table. I read:

SGT. JOSEPHINE BRICKHOUSE
LASD

Pinned under the creds was a star.

NINETEEN

Brick Shithouse

"Don't take it so hard," Jo Brickhouse said. She had just repacked her badge and was leaning her muscled forearms on the table. "Besides, from what I've seen so far, you could use the help."

"I don't want any help. At least, not from you."

"Scully, we live in a democracy. Tony, Bill, and I say yes. You say no. This was voted on. Three against one. You lose. Get over it."

"That's not a vote, that's three coyotes and a poodle deciding on what to have for dinner."

I put a dollar down for my coffee, then got up and headed out of the restaurant. I didn't see her green Suburban parked in the lot, so I turned and looked through Denny's front window. She was still inside buying something at the counter. I got into my Acura feeling completely sandbagged. I'm generally not this damn gullible. I guess my feelings were hurt, or my pride—something.

She came through the swinging door of Denny's, opened my passenger side, and slid in carrying a caffe latte to go.

"Take your own car. I'm not a taxi service," I snapped.

"I was dropped. Don't have wheels. That SUV was a department plain-wrap. Vice needed it back, so I'm with you. You can drop me at the L.A. substation at EOW."

She closed the door, slamming it harder than I like, then started to pour about six packets of Equal into her latte. "Okay, Scully, we need to get something straight before we partner up. I have some issues."

"I'll bet lying isn't gonna be one of them."

"I'm gay. I don't sleep with guys, and you're not the priceless piece of ass that's gonna change that, so put your fantasies away, stay on your side of the car, and we'll do fine."

"Then a blow job's out of the question?"

"You can stow that sarcastic bullshit. I've been in law enforcement for over ten years. I've learned it works a whole lot better if I get this out of the way, up front. I pack a nine-millimeter Glock with thirteen in the clip. I'm a range-qualified sharpshooter and I have two black belts, one in karate, one in tae kwon do. Just because I'm a woman doesn't mean I'm a pussy. I don't want to be your backup. We can take turns on cover, or flip for it, whatever. But I'm not your CHCO."

"My what?"

"Coat-holder and communications officer."

"In case you're interested, you're coming off like a complete asshole."

"I can be that, too. But deal straight and you get the best. Pull any horseshit, and you can go ahead and bring it on down, frog-boy, 'cause I won't put up with it." Then she shot me that dazzling smile and took a sip of latte. "These are good. Sure you don't want one?"

I put the car in reverse and backed out a little too fast, but she was really pissing me off. Male pride. I mean, I'm happily married, but come on—you shouldn't knock what you haven't tried. I turned onto Lankershim and drove toward the sheriff's forensic lab.

Jo Brickhouse was looking around the front seat and up on the dash. "Where's your murder book on Greenridge?" she asked. "You didn't give those goat-fucks from ATF your notes, did you?"

"No murder book."

"You're the primary on a homicide and you don't keep a murder book?" She sounded stunned.

"Yeah, I would've been keeping a murder book, but I was pulled off the case before I had time to get most of my evidence back from your slow-as-shit crime lab."

"You don't have to take that tone, Scully. I wasn't criticizing. I just like to keep everything written down: keep a good event timeline, evidence records, crime scene photos, background. I'll get one going. For now, we can use my notes." She pulled out her spiral pad.

"But you're not going to be my secretary, I bet."

"Sure, I've got no problem pushing some pencil lead. But let's do it right." She opened her notebook and tore out three pages. "This lecture on latent prints was simply fascinating. You want it, or can it go in the file?"

"I know a better place you can stick it."

"Temper, temper," she said, and wadded up the papers and dropped them in the back seat.

We drove in silence for six blocks. I snuck another look at her. There was a lot of animal magnetism there. In retrospect, I could see why she needed to get her personal proclivities on the line up front. She'd undoubtedly had to deal with her share of squad-car Romeos. I tried to settle down, make the best of it. Finally she finished her coffee, slurping the last drop, then she just pitched the damn cup into the back seat with the three wadded-up sheets of notebook paper.

"This is not a department car. I'd appreciate it if you didn't throw your litter in the back."

"Sorry."

She hitched herself around and leaned over the seat. She was in a miniskirt, and for a minute she was poking a well-developed ass up in the air, nearly mooning the next car over. The driver did a double take. For my part, I almost hit a taxi. She sat back, put the cup on the seat between us, and stuffed my dumb-ass fingerprint lecture in her purse.

"Sorry about the short skirt. I was doing field interviews today. Sometimes it helps to show a little leg. Tomorrow I'll be in class-C stuff."

"Whatever that is."

"Sheriff's department dress code for plain clothes dicks. Excuse the expression."

We drove in silence for another minute or two. "So, Scully," she finally said. "Where the hell are we going?"

"Bill Messenger took our bullet, that three-oh-eight casing, out to your forensics lab for a print scan and tool marks. I figure, since you pack a star you can get the techs out there to give us a sneak peek."

"This is probably good thinking," she said, then settled back in her seat.

But to be truthful, even the way she said that was pissing me off—like she was validating a surprising idea from a total blockhead. Then she hitched sideways on the seat, snapping her short skirt down. All her movements were athletic and a little too big. She was a muscular girl who took up slightly more space than I was accustomed to.

"So, I had time to check you out before Messenger sent me to meet you," she said. "You're married to your division commander. I've seen her on the news and once at a cross-training day for detectives, out at our SWAT range at Spring Ranch. Damn fine package."

I looked over, not sure what to make of that. Finally I nodded and said, "I think so."

"Look, Shane, I'll give you the keys to the kingdom here, the Rosetta Stone for our partnership."

I waited. What do you say to shit like that?

"I have no hidden agendas, no back-channel dog wash. Like Popeye, 'I yam what I yam.'" Then she smiled. "So don't get your shorts in a bunch just because I want to lay out some ground rules. You got any stuff you want out there, let it fly."

I didn't have to ask my friends at the sheriff's what Sergeant Brickhouse's department nickname was.

Had to be Brick Shithouse.

I found out later I was right.

TWENTY

The "Old" Crime Lab

The sheriff's seventy-five-year-old crime lab is just east of Hollywood in a run-down three-story building near Elysian Park. The place is on its last legs. Since the department has already broken ground on its new, $96 million forensics facility next to the M.E.'s building on the L.A. State campus, this pile of bricks was not getting much attention. When I pulled into the parking lot I spotted deferred maintenance everywhere I looked. The cream-color paint was peeling off brick siding. Cracked asphalt and faded white hash marks lined the parking lot. Weeds grew in the landscaping.

But this was still where most crimes were solved. The ultimate revenge of the nerds, where geeks caught cheats. It encompassed all the major crime sections: firearms, biology, DNA, trace evidence, and identifications. In this high-volume facility, LASD criminalists juggled seventy-five thousand pieces of evidence each year, as the criminal justice system chugged merrily along. Getting moved to the head of the line was normally a futile exercise in this overworked battleground of egos and priorities, but our shell casing had been personally hand delivered by the big boss, Bill Messenger, so my guess was, under these circumstances, we'd be first up.

Jo and I had not spoken for almost half the ride over. She sat beside me, looking out the side window, content to say nothing. Silence can be a weapon in the front seat of a police car. I wasn't sure what game we were playing yet.

I parked in a visitor's space. We got out and she pushed ahead of me through the double glass doors into the crime lab.

"You have an evidence number?" she demanded.

"No, but it came in here through Bill Messenger."

"That oughta have Doctor Chuck E. Cheese sitting up pretty straight," she said, then went to a visitor phone in the empty lobby and dialed a number.

I looked around while she talked to somebody in the back. The place really needed help. The linoleum had turned black and was peeling up across the room, exposing the wood flooring underneath. It looked like somebody delivering a gallon of acid base had dropped the load. But I guess it's hard to spend money on a building that you know is going to be bulldozed in twelve months.

"Scully, you're with me," Jo barked, sounding like my old Marine Corps drill sergeant. A security lock buzzed and she held the door open as we entered.

"Latents got a four-point hit," she said. "They already sent the brass up to Tool Marks to graph the striations and impressed action marks. When we found that casing yesterday it looked to me like it also had some pretty good breech and pin impressions."

She was showing off now. I was tempted to say "Fuck you," but, gentleman that I am, I only muttered, "Bite me."

She smiled, pushed past, and led the way. "Latent Prints is down here."

We walked down a narrow corridor, past the weapons library and lab. Through the glass doors, I could see thousands of rifles and handguns of every known manufacturer locked behind metal bars in the armory. These guns could be used to match firing patterns on weapons seized or placed in evidence. They could also be shown to witnesses for the purpose of firearm identification.

We continued past the GSR and footprint lab, a notorious grunt station for newbies. The youngest criminalists were stuck in there doing footprint analysis or using the electron microscope to perform gunshot residue tests. Then we passed a room housing the protein base analyzer that charted DNA profiles, also known as electropherograms. Next, down the hall was a trace evidence lab devoted to hair and fiber. There was a lot of state-of-the-art equipment in this crumbling facility.

At the end of the corridor Sergeant Brickhouse swept into the fingerprint bay. The room was empty. Blown-up photographs of fingerprints were pinned up everywhere. Two long benches containing print photographs in labeled boxes were pushed against the walls. There was a large, overstuffed chair in the corner. Jo turned around and glanced out into the hall, looking for the criminalist.

"Chuck oughta be down in a minute. On the phone a minute ago, he told me he was just going to check on our print upstairs. They ran our latent through the federal print index."

We stood in the lab with the silence between us growing painfully.

"Answer me one thing," I said to break the awkward spell.

"Shoot."

"Did Bill Messenger instruct you to investigate the Hidden Ranch thing? Is that why you were up at Smiley's burned-out house poking around, and over in the apartment on Mission Street?"

"I've been sworn to secrecy," she deadpanned.

"Only, when I partner up with somebody there can be no secrets."

"Scully, grow up. I'm not telling you what I've been ordered not to, but use your imagination."

"Okay. So Messenger had you up there even after he promised the mayor and Tony he'd leave it in my hands?"

"I don't wanta talk about this. Let's just move on, okay?"

I was about to tear her a new asshole, when into the room waddled the fattest, baldest young man I had ever seen. He even made Ruta look svelte. His appearance was made even worse by his wardrobe. He had on an over-sized, bilious, lime-colored Hawaiian shirt that flapped around the thighs of his frayed, tent-like jeans. The effect was startling. His head looked like a pale medicine ball sitting atop a mountain of green Jell-O.

Jo said hi and introduced me. "Shane Scully, meet Doctor Charles Gouda."

Charles Gouda—Dr. Chuck E. Cheese. Got it.

He lowered himself carefully into the overstuffed chair, letting out a long sigh as he dropped.

"Just got back the run from the federal print index," he said. "Nada. But it was pretty thin to begin with. Only four identifiers."

He leaned over and picked up a photograph of the print, then showed it to us. "Whoever fumed this thing saved the print, but with round surfaces like shell casings we rarely get a full ten-point match anyway." Chuck pointed to the photograph with his pen. "What it comes down to is, you got two pretty good typicals here, a good core and an okay whorl, half an isle up here. This tent arch ain't too bad. Basically, it's pretty low-yield. Call it four and a half points to be generous. Since it's a sole in-dex finger, there's not enough here for the federal com-puter. If I had a comparison print to put next to it I could get some eyeballs on it and give you an opinion, but nothing you'd want to take in front of our awesome denizens of justice. In court, you need at least six out of ten identifiers or the defense is gonna feed it to you."

Then, to make that gastronomic point absolutely clear, he belched.

"How long till Tool Marks is finished?" I asked.

Doctor Gouda belched again, this time more delicately, catching the burp in his baseball mitt of a hand. He opened his desk drawer and took out a half-eaten sandwich. It looked like tomatoes and anchovies, which, in my opinion, ranks right up there with shit on a bun. He took a bite, frowned, then threw it in the trash.

After all that I really wasn't expecting an answer, but I got one anyway.

"Beats me," Doctor Chuck E. Cheese said through an ugly mouthful of chewed fish.

TWENTY-ONE

Mijares Restaurant

I met Chooch, Alexa, and Delfina at Mijares Restaurant for dinner. Chooch's sports-injury doctor was in Pasadena, and Mijares is one of the best Mexican restaurants on the east end of the L.A. Basin. I arrived last and was led to their table out on an enclosed patio. Chooch was wearing a new white cast and a glum look.

I kissed my wife, said hi to Chooch and Del, then dropped into a wood-backed chair and ordered a double margarita. Long day, so screw it. In the other room was a ranchedo duet, two guitarists in traditional dress, picking "Malagueña Salerosa" on humpbacked Martins.

"I see you didn't get the plaster off," I said.

"Nope." Chooch was staring morosely down at a Coke on the placemat in front of him. Delfina reached out and took his hand.

"But the doctor said in a week, maybe," she explained. "It's coming along good. The bone is almost healed."

Chooch nodded bleakly, as if the idea that his foot would ever mend was just too far away to grasp.

I had the Pop Warner League book with me, and I looked at Delfina and gave her a little eyebrow raise. A silent question. She nodded, so I laid the blue binder on the table, then pushed it over to him. I had called the league on the way over and had received some additional information.

"What's that?" Chooch asked.

"Pop Warner League rule book. You're good to go if you want the gig. Emo's team, the Rams, is in the Junior Bantam division." Chooch was looking down despondently at the binder, so I added: "That's twelve through fourteen. The kids can be in the hundred-fifteen- to hundred-sixty-pound range at the beginning of the season, which was August, but nobody can weigh more than one-sixty-nine by the end of the season in December. As of late, they've been holding workouts, but with no head coach they had to forfeit their last game."

Chooch opened the book and stared at the front page. Then, with no enthusiasm, he started flipping through it. Delfina frowned, as Alexa and I traded looks.

"*¿Que haces tu?*" Delfina said angrily. "We talked about this. You said you wanted to do it for Emo Rojas. Now your father has made it happen and you sit here like a troll on a rock."

"Okay, okay," he said and put the book on the floor by his feet.

"Honey, if you don't want to coach the team, don't coach it," Alexa said. "It's not going to help these kids to have a coach who doesn't want to be there."

"You guys—you don't . . ." Chooch stopped, then put his head down. "Forget it."

"Do you want me to talk to your coach?" I asked. "Make sure it's okay with him? Is that what you're worried about?"

"No, Coach Norris said it was fine. He even said he'd look at the playbook and help me with some revisions if I wanted."

"So, what's the problem?"

"It's like . . ." He paused, then took a deep breath. "It's like, by agreeing to do this, I'm saying my season is over. Maybe my college career with it."

"These Pop Warner teams play on Saturday or Sunday. Harvard-Westlake plays Friday nights. Once your foot heals, you go back on your team and set the Pop Warner practices to fit your schedule," I said.

"I know, it's just . . ."

"Then, don't do it, son," I interrupted. "Mom's right. You have to want to."

"I'll do it, okay? I said I'd do it, so I will."

But he sure didn't sound happy about it.

Then our conversation turned to Delfina's *West Side Story* rehearsals. She was excited and animated as she told us about the full run-through with music. Chooch remained strangely quiet while she talked.

When we got home I went to my office and booted up my PC. Then I typed in CACTUS WEST.

A few seconds later a welcome screen came up. There was a window for a password. I punched in: *MCAS YUMA TACTS*.

A message popped up:

ACCESS DENIED.
THIS IS A U.S. MARINE CORPS SECURE SITE.
YOUR COMPUTER WILL BE SCANNED IF YOU
ATTEMPT TO REENTER.

I logged off and was still frowning at the screen when Franco yowled to tell me he hadn't been fed. I took him into the kitchen and fixed his dinner while Chooch and Delfina sat in the backyard. She was talking hard at him.

Alexa and I decided to take a walk around the neighborhood to avoid the fallout of what looked like the beginnings of a teenage quarrel. We strolled along the walkways that bordered the canal. The wedge-cut quarter moon hung low in the night sky. It lit the water and turned the mist-wet edges of the houses and garden gates silver. A late-feeding hell-diver took off out of the water, startling us. He beat his wings savagely, disappearing into the sky.

"I talked to Tony and Bill this afternoon," Alexa said. "Bill is going to free up your request with his people at CSI. They're going out to Hidden Ranch sometime tomorrow afternoon to look for the dog's remains and check on that basement bomb shelter." She said it like she thought it was a complete waste of county time.

"I'm not scoring too many points in this family tonight, am I?" I said.

"It's just, you know how badly this is setting up. The sooner we clear it the better. I won't lie to you. I'm getting a lot of pressure, and I think checking Smiley's background and that house isn't going to get us anywhere, but I'm through arguing about it. It's your investigation, so it's your call."

"In that case, can I get you to find out what's on this Web site?" I handed her a slip of paper with 'CACTUS WEST MCAS YUMA TACTS' printed on it. "It's some kind of Marine Corps secure site that Smiley hacked into. If we can't find out through the mayor's office, maybe the geeks in our computer division can see if they could hack into it." She didn't say anything, but wrinkled her nose and put the slip in her pocket.

We walked over and stood on one of the arched bridges that spanned the main canal. I told Alexa that we had a partial print on the shell casing from the apartment, but that it was smudged, with maybe only four identifiers, and that Tool Marks would look for a match on striations after Sheriff Messenger had his SEB long rifles fired.

She nodded and we both looked across the water at our house. Delfina and Chooch were still sitting in the yard, heads together, talking earnestly.

"So, how's your new partner Joe Brickhouse?" Alexa finally asked, changing to a better subject.

"She's—different," I said.

"She? *Joe* is a girl?"

"Not in the traditional sense."

"Is she pretty?"

"Very. But she kills that impression effectively, because she's the most opinionated, in-your-face partner I think I've ever had. Present company excluded."

"I don't like this. I know how drawn you are to strong women," she teased.

"And she's gay," I said. "Apparently, I'm not the priceless piece of ass that's going to change that, either."

"I feel better already," Alexa said and held my hand.

"But *you* might qualify. She thinks you're 'a damn fine package,' or something to that effect. She's also a control freak. I'm biting my tongue trying to keep from tangling with her, but it may require more self-discipline than I possess."

We stood quietly for a long moment. Suddenly a fish surfaced. It's tail slapped the water as it swam away. Both Alexa and I looked down at the spot below us, but our scaly eavesdropper was long gone.

"Look, Shane, this is what Sheriff Messenger wants, so having her for a partner is a small price to pay. If he can test fire his SEB long rifles and prove that the casing didn't come from any of their firearms, then we've gone a long way toward settling all this down."

"Right," I said. "And if it did come from one of his long guns, then I have only one question."

"What's that?"

"Who do I have to fuck to get off this damn case?"

"Me," she said, then smiled sexily.

TWENTY-TWO

Payback

It was finally cooling off in Los Angeles. By evening the temperature had begun to dip down into the fifties, but around midnight, with an abrupt barometric change, the hot Santa Ana winds had started up again, blowing out of the desert, flaring allergies and tempers. Alexa and I were both sprawled on top of the blankets as the pre-dawn temperature in our bedroom climbed into the mid-seventies. Alexa had been restless, constantly turning over, unable to sleep. The ringing phone brought me up out of a semiconscious steambath. I fumbled it off the hook and glanced at the bedside clock. A few minutes past three in the morning. Alexa said something unfriendly and turned over again as I pushed the receiver against my ear and muttered my name.

"Scully? We're on," a female voice commanded. It took me a minute to get there, but then I realized it was Jo Brickhouse.

"It's three A.M.," I snarled. But as consciousness returned I began to realize she probably wouldn't be calling at this hour unless it was pretty important.

Just then, Alexa's beeper went off and shot a bolt of adrenaline through me. *Uh-oh. Something was definitely up.*

Alexa grabbed her pager off the bedside table. "Damn," she said, reading the LCD screen, "Tony."

"What's going on, Jo?" I asked, pulling my head further out of the vat of oatmeal I keep it in when I sleep.

"Spotter on the SEB Gray team just ate a round. Guy's name is Michael Nightingale. Same basic deal. Vertical coffin—dead on the back porch. This should be our case, 'cause he's a sheriff, and there's a damn good chance now it's connected to the Rojas killing, but the way this is falling, who knows? The FBI could even claim it."

"Right. Title Eighteen. 'Unless the FBI's absence from the case materially effects the course of justice,' or something."

"Get your ass out to two-four-six Sherman Way, Van Nuys. It's LAPD turf, so for now, we're up. Take the Cahuenga off-ramp, it's quicker. And let's see some smoke. I'm already rolling."

"Right." When I hung up Alexa was on the cordless phone with Tony and was walking into the bathroom, talking as she went. I scissor-kicked out of bed and followed her. As I walked in Alexa finished her call and pushed the hang-up button on the handset. She grabbed her hair brush, ran it through her hair once, then threw it on the counter. So much for grooming.

"Nightingale?" I asked.

"Yep. Michael. Spotter for his brother Gary on SEB."

"I know."

"Tony wants me downtown. Since Nightingale's a sheriff, he's got Bill Messenger on the way in. It's in our jurisdiction, so unless Messenger says otherwise, it's our one eighty-seven. Yours, Sergeant Brickhouse's, and Ruta's."

I was already in my Jockeys. Alexa scooped up her panties and was hopping on one foot as she put them on. Then she grabbed her bra and headed into the bedroom. I skinned into a pair of dirty jeans I had thrown into the laundry hamper, stepped into some loafers—not bothering with socks—then went into the bedroom and threw on yesterday's shirt and jacket.

"Do I really have this, or am I gonna go out there, stand over a corpse, and wrestle with a buncha feds over whose case it is, like last time?"

Alexa had on a mismatched outfit. She was taking no care with her appearance, which was unusual. Suddenly, she stopped buttoning her blouse and turned to face me. "Shane, I don't have to tell you, this is the worst thing that could have happened. Amps up everything. It's going to be a national news story now. No way to stop it. There'll be reporters hanging from the trees. Geraldo will be on the front lawn interviewing neighbors."

"Look, Alexa . . . I—"

"No. Listen. If this is two SWAT teams going at it, we've got to stop it now. You've gotta find some physical evidence, the bullet or the cartridge casing, a print, something. In the meantime I'm gonna search these two SWAT houses, bring ten or twelve sheriffs and ATF agents into custody, and hold 'em until this is sorted out."

"You can't do that without a helluva lot more evidence than we have now."

"Stop arguing with me," she said hotly.

"Alexa, you're not thinking straight."

"You want these people out on the streets after work, rolling around in SWAT vans, trying to pick each other off?"

"Of course not. But you can't arrest people without evidence."

"I can hold them for forty-eight hours without charging them."

"Cops? No chance. You try that and the U.S. Attorney will take this right out from under us and give it to the

FBI. Plus, you're gonna fire up all the rank and file from both agencies. Then come the lawyers, the unions, and the network news."

"Then get me something I can use. Fast."

As I looked at her I saw something I'd never seen before. She was frightened. Unlike me, Alexa had never had a crisis of conscience on the job. She believed in a set of rules that had always served her. But this didn't fit any of them. Nobody had ever seen fit to spit on my beautiful wife. But now she was living her worst nightmare. She believed in the system, and the system was spinning out of control. This was the total collapse of another treasured idea. She wasn't thinking straight, she wasn't sleeping, and I could see confusion in her eyes. She wasn't sure how to deal with it, or even if she had the skill. It worried me.

"You gonna be okay?" I asked.

"Just get me something. I need some leverage," she said, and turned around looking for her shoes.

I grabbed my gun and tin and took off toward my car, pausing in Chooch's makeshift bedroom to tell him that his mom and I were being called out. He rolled over in bed, rubbed his eyes, and nodded. He'd seen this before. Then I exited through the side door, jumped into the Acura, and peeled out.

God only knew what would happen next.

TWENTY-THREE

Nightingales

There were four police cars and three media vans parked in front of the neat, one-story ranch-style house in a *Leave It to Beaver* neighborhood in Van Nuys. Nobody had bothered to tape off a staging area yet. The street was wide open, and as I got out of my car another news van rolled in and three crew types hit the street and started unpacking video equipment.

The crime scene was alive with spectators. I saw a lot of strained looks and hidden agendas. If Jo Brickhouse hadn't been screwing up her end so badly I would have enjoyed watching her trying to handle this angry mess, but there were already half a dozen people on the porch standing over the body. I saw two TV news teams and a print photographer walking around inside the house shooting tape with their sun-guns on. Like the Morning News with Ken and Barbie needed to be in there handling evidence and getting shots of the widow crying in the den.

Adding to the emotion and hyperbole were Rick Manos, the SEB Gray team scout, and his long gun, Gary Nightingale, who was sitting on the corner of the porch crying, holding his dead sibling's hand. To her credit, Jo Brickhouse was trying to move all the extra people out, but this thing had already lifted off. Brady Cagel and his band of feds hadn't put in an appearance yet. *Interesting,* I thought. *Why not?*

I pulled Jo Brickhouse aside. "You're missing a sure bet here. You should be selling tickets."

"What am I supposed to do, physically throw these assholes off the porch?"

"Exactly. You're a woman, not a pussy, remember?" While she was turning a few more shades of red, I stepped up and took Rick Manos by the arm.

"Get your people off this porch," I ordered.

"This isn't your case, it's ours." He snatched his arm back.

"I'm through with that shit," I replied. "You're SWAT, I'm Homicide. You don't know how to work a murder. Look at the mess you've already got here. Besides, this is inside L.A. city limits, and Sergeant Brickhouse from your department is on it, so get your people out of here."

"We told you this was gonna happen, but you wouldn't listen!" Rick said hotly.

I didn't like the way he was facing me, too ready, too close to the edge. He killed people for a living and wasn't used to getting pushed around. I decided the best way to handle him was to put him to work.

"You wanta do something worthwhile, get those damn newsies out of the house. Who let them in?"

Manos looked at me, trying to decide if he was going to answer. Finally he shrugged. "I don't know. Barbara Nightingale probably. They were here when we arrived." But he still didn't move—not sure he wanted to take an order from me, even a good one.

"If you want me to solve Michael's murder, get all the civilians out of there. We gotta bolt this puppy down. Come on, help me out. You know this is fucked."

He nodded and started inside.

"Hey, Rick," I said, and he stopped. "Take Gary with you. Give him something to do other than leak DNA all over his brother's body."

Rick looked down at the SEB long gun, who had tears streaming down his face. Then he went over and gently took hold of Gary's arm.

"Let's go, Gar, okay? We gotta help clear out this house," he said. "Then you should go sit with Barbara."

The two of them went into the house and I heard voices raised in anger, but the blow-dries inside weren't a match for Manos and Nightingale.

Just then two more of our black-and-whites and a fourth TV news van rolled in. Jo Brickhouse was heading toward me, shaking her head in frustration. I stopped her.

"Get a patrol car blocking each end of the street and move all those news vans and press cars at least a block away. Tape off a staging area out front."

She took off and I grabbed one of our uniforms. His nameplate identified him as S. Berg. "You wanta help me, Officer Berg?" He nodded. "Get a notebook and start an incident log and crime-scene attendance sheet. Nobody gets past you without signing in. Start with me. I'm Scully, three forty-five A.M."

He pulled out a spiral pad, wrote my name down, and I signed it.

"Get everybody who was inside, including civilians. Depending on how this goes, we may need to contact all of them later for elimination prints."

It took us almost ten minutes to clear the house. It really pisses me off when news crews arrive at a crime scene ahead of us, but the midnight stringers and late shift newsrooms ride the police frequencies. Because they have mobile units all over town, they can often get to the meat ahead of us.

I had a murder once, right after I joined South Bureau Homicide, where I arrived at the crime scene and couldn't find the body. There were twenty people in the murdered guy's apartment: neighbors, friends, TV, and print news. I'm looking all over the place, and I can't find the vic. Finally I asked the person who called it in where the body was. "In the bedroom," this guy tells me. So I go back in there and I still can't find it. I start thinking, *I don't believe this! Somebody stole the damned corpse.*

Then I hear a news photographer in the bathroom firing off stills with a motorized camera. So I go in there and ask him, "You seen the dead guy anywhere around?" And now I'm feeling like a complete yahoo.

"Yeah," this asshole tells me. "I finished taking pictures in there and the body was kinda grossing me out, so I rolled him under the bed."

Amazing.

Finally I had the crime scene locked down and Officer Berg taking names at the door. Nobody could find Lou Ruta. He wasn't answering his pager, but Beverly King called in and reported that she was five minutes out, so I waited for her before I started.

When she arrived Jo kept the other cops off the porch, while Beverly and I took Mrs. Nightingale into a spare bedroom. After we calmed her down we took her preliminary statement. She told us that Michael had been on call last night, so she had taken the kids out to a movie. When she got home she came in the front door, didn't see her husband, and figured he was still at work. She went to bed, but woke up at two. Michael was still not home, so she called the squad and found out that he had gone EOW three hours earlier. She started to worry and began looking around, and finally found him head-shot on the back porch. She managed to get the kids to a neighbor, then called it in.

Basically, she knew nothing. Heard and saw nothing.

It's SOP in all homicides to regard the spouse as a prime suspect until the facts prove otherwise. But the truth was, Barbara Nightingale looked and sounded legit to me. Still, I couldn't let my suspicion that this was done by a bunch of angry commandos at SRT color my thinking. I had to keep all options open; collect information and evidence with no preconceived bias.

Alexa was right. This was going to be huge—a media frenzy. I had only Jo and Beverly to assist me, and neither had much homicide experience. I could use more help.

When I walked back into the living room I asked Beverly King, "So, where's Ruta? Think he's ever gonna show?" Even though he was a jerk, at least he was an experienced one.

Beverly shrugged, probably relieved that her partner was MIA, but came to his defense anyway. "Maybe his pager batteries are dead." Which is sort of the adult equivalent of "The dog ate my homework."

Sergeant Brickhouse was starting to direct the forensic techs onto the porch, so I went outside to stop her.

"Let's just hold off on all that for a minute. I don't want anybody to touch anything for a while."

"Why?" she argued. "We need to get on this. Bag and tag the vic, get a liver temperature to establish time of death, search for trace evidence."

"Just calm down for a minute, okay?"

"I don't work for you, Scully," she said angrily. "You don't outrank me either."

I pulled her off the porch, holding her muscled arm. She was hard to move—big and strong. I led her out of earshot of Beverly King and the CSI techs. We stood in the backyard, ten or twelve yards away.

"Let the fuck go of me," she said. "I don't . . ."

"Work for me, I know. But how 'bout working *with* me?" She glowered, but I charged ahead. "How much time did you spend in homicide before you went to IAD?"

"That's not the point. I'm here at the direct request of Sheriff Messenger, Enrique Salazar, and the county supervisors. My department has a lot at stake now. This dead officer was ours. I'm your jurisdiction on this shooting," she said hotly.

"This isn't the time or place to have it out, but I'm damned tired of fighting with you for control of the wheel. We need some guidelines."

"Here's a guideline! Stop trying to tell me what to do."

"I've done over a hundred homicides. I have a way I do it. Why don't you take advantage of that, instead of resenting it?"

She looked at me, anger still flaring. "Okay. This should be fascinating. So why don't we start with the body, since the body is the reason we're all here?"

"The body isn't going to get up and leave, so there's no need to rush."

"You don't even want SID to get started? That's nuts."

"While you and the sheriffs were on the porch holding Michael's hand, half the city desks in town were wandering around inside, screwing up the evidence. We can't change that now, but I want to take a minute and work out an operational theory. The crime scene might have been altered. I wanta think this out for a minute."

"The porch *is* the crime scene," she fired back, then added defensively, "I kept it as clear as I could."

Then the second L.A. myth made an unscheduled appearance. "Where the hell were you? I called you at three A.M. It doesn't take forty minutes to get here from Venice."

I took a deep breath to control my anger.

"We don't know what the crime scene is. Since I don't see a bullet hole in the back door or porch, we don't know where this happened. He could have been shot inside and dragged out here. The biggest mistake that is usually made in a homicide investigation is prescribing too small an initial crime scene area. If I could rope off the entire block, I'd do it. Now let's just back off for a minute and try to work up a shooting theory."

She was looking at me, her chest, rising and falling. Hyperventilating. Pissed.

"Look," I said, "this is bad form standing out here arguing. We'll have this out later. For now, let's do it my way."

She turned and walked off, leaving me standing there.

The truth was, I always stretched the edge of the crime scene to the farthest point out, and walked that area first, marking anything that looked out of place. After I had the immediate scene under control and the body was secure, experience had taught me that it's extremely hard to keep people from prowling the edges of the site. Neighbors, and even other cops, patrol the border, and if it's a large area it's easy for some well-intentioned schlub to pick something up or leave a footprint. We could find some cop's bootprint, plaster it, then start running off in the completely wrong direction of looking for a killer wearing size-ten combat boots.

Once I spent two weeks working a hair follicle our CSI techs found at a murder scene. The lab reported that the hair had undergone an amber tint dye job. It also had traces of an expensive French shampoo and a special French conditioner. A good potential lead. I put it out on the news that we were looking for an upscale killer with tinted amber hair who uses an expensive, French shampoo and conditioner.

A week later, I'm looking in Alexa's bathroom cabinet and I see all those same products in there. It turned out that the hair had fallen off my own coat and belonged to my wife. It's very hard to protect a crime scene, so I always start at the far edges first, and work in toward the body.

I walked the perimeter carefully, examining the ground, looking down, shining my police flashlight. The sun would be up in a few hours, but I couldn't wait, because I had seen the anger and pain in Gary Nightingale, the deadly resolve and violence in Rick Manos. I had also promised Alexa I wouldn't let this investigation drift.

The projectile had entered Michael's head from the front, the same as Billy Greenridge. The slug caught him square in the forehead, right between the running lights. He had fallen where he was shot and since the bullet had not hit the house or the door behind him, that meant it probably came from the side. To miss the house completely, the shooter had to have been firing from either the far right or the far left portion of the back yard.

I started walking around out there, searching for the shooting location. About forty yards away, behind an old lemon tree, I saw footprints. Boots. Big ones; size thirteen at least. The lowest limb of the tree had a fork about five feet up from the ground. A perfect place to cradle a rifle barrel. I called the crime techs over and showed them the footprints and the tree limb. They started photographing and getting ready to plaster the impressions.

I kept looking around on the ground on the right side of the tree. About forty feet away, lying under a small hedge, I spotted the casing.

I called Jo Brickhouse over and pointed it out to her. Beverly King followed. It was an ArmaLite .223, the kind of ordnance common to AR-15 assault rifles.

It didn't escape my notice that the long guns SRT had been using up at Hidden Ranch were AR-15s. The .223s were very fast rounds, with a muzzle velocity of over three thousand feet per second. The projectile is designed to tumble and break into smaller pieces on impact. After we photographed it, I leaned down and retrieved the brass, again using my pen tip. I held it up and we all stared at it.

The casing was a deadly calling card, and all three of us were thinking the same thing. Finally, Beverly King put our thoughts into words: "This seems way too easy."

TWENTY-FOUR

Warrants

The strong Santa Ana winds whipped September leaves off the elm trees that lined Sherman Way, driving the temperature up further, scattering trash from overflowing garbage cans, and blowing down our yellow crime scene tape.

Michael Nightingale's body rolled out in a coroner's van at eight-thirty that morning. Barbara Nightingale left ten minutes later in the back seat of her sister's yellow station wagon. I caught a glimpse of two children with her, young boys, little, towheaded versions of their father. Their faces tight, blank with confusion.

"The only good thing that's happened here so far is SRT hasn't shown," Jo Brickhouse said.

"No need to come out and watch, if you already know what happened," I answered.

The thought scored. I saw a silent curse cross her face. Anger followed. She hated not coming up with that herself.

Before we took off, Beverly, Jo, and I huddled on the back porch and divided up responsibilities. "We need to have that two-twenty-three casing checked and matched for tool marks and possible fingerprints. Not to jump to conclusions, but SRT's long guns are AR-fifteens, so we need to test fire all their carbines."

"The feds are never gonna cooperate," Jo said. She was probably right.

"The three of us can't make it happen, but maybe your chief and mine can talk some sense into ATF. Failing that, maybe the mayor or Supervisor Salazar can force it down. We have to play this straight up, with no favorites. Test fire and match the brass from both SWAT teams—"

I stopped because both Jo and Beverly had wrinkled their noses. My idea obviously stunk. "Let's just hope for the best," I added. "Hope they don't put agency loyalty above common sense."

Beverly and Jo remained skeptical. To be fair, so was I, but a little positive thinking never hurts.

"Jo," I said, "could you walk that casing and the footprint cast through your lab, get us squared away down there as fast as possible?"

She glanced at Beverly checking out her reaction to having me give the orders. Detective King seemed to have no problem. Finally, Jo nodded and said, "Okay."

"Beverly, you stay with the body, go to the autopsy. Hopefully, that slug broke on impact and we can retrieve a bullet fragment for lead content comparisons. Also get us a full blood panel. I'd like to know if Mike was drinking last night. If he was at a bar we need to find out. Tell the M.E. to get us a liver temp ASAP. We need a close time of death to start our pre- and perimortem timelines."

Jo made a frustrated noise in the back of her throat.

I ignored her. "Check with the vic's SEB team leader," I continued saying to Beverly. "The guy's name is Scott Cook. See when Mike left work, if there were any unusual circumstances."

"I'll call Sergeant Cook," Jo interrupted. "If we keep it inside the sheriff's department we'll get more." It was a good suggestion.

Beverly offered, "Why don't I get a team of cadets from the academy to start hunting around this neighborhood, looking for what's left of the bullet?"

"What're the odds of ever finding that? A two-twenty-three? It's probably in a zillion pieces," Jo said.

"But we gotta try."

"What're you gonna do?" Jo asked me.

The question rang with accusatory overtones, as if, while they were out doing all the real police work, I was going to be in Beverly Hills enjoying a Turkish steam and a hot oil massage.

"I'm gonna see if I can get these warring agencies on the same side." I bowed my head in sarcastic theatricality. "May justice be served. Amen."

We broke our huddle like college athletes and headed to our cars.

I called Alexa on the way back to the office and told her what I wanted. She said the chief was way ahead of me. Everybody was meeting in his office at ten. My presence was required.

"Brady Cagel gonna be there?" I asked.

"Brady, Cole Hatton, Garrett Metcalf, Supervisor Salazar—the whole *mishpucha,* but this time everybody's gonna have a chief legal counsel in tow."

"Don't you love this?" I muttered.

"Sucks," she said.

I found out later that the meeting was being held at the Glass House because Tony had a budget meeting at eleven. Always nice to know who's picking the playing field.

There were enough lawyers in Filosiani's big office to set a quorum for the local bar association. Tony and Bill had just informed Cole Hatton that LAPD had found a .308 casing across the street from Greenridge's house. His reaction to that wasn't friendly.

After a heated argument over withholding evidence from the primary agency investigating the homicide and half a dozen threatened lawsuits, that problem was put on hold and the argument quickly came down to whether there was enough probable cause for searching both SEB's and SRT's armories. The different agency lawyers were all circling that scrap like hungry reef sharks.

Then the door opened and Enrique Salazar entered, arriving late. He waved off the formal handshakes and took up a position next to his cops. Sheriff Messenger leaned over and whispered in his ear, filling him in.

"Look," Tom Neil, the mouthpiece from the sheriff's union said, "any way you cut this, everybody knows you're not asking these SWAT officers for their help. You're looking for a murder suspect. This is an active homicide investigation, so you've got to follow the normal rules of evidence. If you want to search our armory you're gonna need a warrant. That means you better come up with adequate probable cause for the search. You've got nothing that ties either of these casings to SEB or SRT."

I looked at Enrique Salazar. He was staying quiet. No good politics could come from this. Bill Messenger was rocking back on his heels, a worried look on his face. The police unions didn't care about his need to wrap this up quickly. They were only interested in the legal rights of the rank-and-file deputies and agents. I suspected he'd already tested SEB's long guns without a warrant, and now, if we couldn't shoot his police union lawyer down, he couldn't use anything he'd found without risking the court case later.

Tony didn't want to let the meeting degenerate into legal haggling, so he cut it off fast. "I have a municipal judge on standby. He already agreed to sign the search warrant, on the grounds that these cops are officers of the court and, as such, have a sworn duty to provide evidence and enforce the law."

"Reversible error," Neil said. "When you pin on a badge you don't give up your rights as a U.S. citizen under the Constitution."

"Who's gonna work up the search warrant preparation list?" Cole Hatton asked. "Is this warrant going to be delivered by LAPD SWAT?"

The warrant prep list uses a number scale to determine the level of risk assigned to the warrant's delivery. The warrant control officer checks twelve categories. A total of five risk points or more out of twelve mandates that the warrant be served by a SWAT team.

Normally warrants were served on criminals, but as I mentally ran through the warrant prep list, I saw the dilemma that serving SEB and SRT presented.

1. Was it a barricaded location?—Yes.
2. Were automatic weapons believed to be on the premises?—Yes.
3. Are the perps suspected of committing an assault on a peace officer?—Yes.
4. Were hostages believed to be at the location?—No.
5. Were assault weapons, body armor, or ballistic protection present?—Yes.
6. Were there barred doors or windows?—Yes.
7. Was there countersurveillance, closed circuit TV, intrusion devices?—Yes.
8. Guard dogs?—Yes.
9. Third strike candidates?—No.
10. Did the suspects have violent criminal histories?—No, but SWAT officers were certainly accustomed to violence.

11. Did handguns exist at the location?—Yes.
12. Had there been threats by suspects against police officers?—More or less.

By my math, nine out of twelve points were present here, which technically put the serving of this warrant at the highest risk possible and mandated a SWAT team.

You could see the indecision in the room. Everyone was asking themselves: *Isn't this different? These are cops, not criminals. Should a strict adherence to the prep list be observed? Isn't it unnecessarily provocative to serve a SWAT team with a SWAT team?*

Nobody said anything.

Alexa finally spoke: "Let's low-key it. Do it with a warrant control team; but we should recognize the risk and keep SWAT in reserve."

"No," Tony overruled sharply. "That's nuts. We do it by the book."

Alexa stiffened slightly, but she put up no further argument.

"If we serve our people, you gotta serve yours," Salazar finally spoke.

Brady Cagel and Garrett Metcalf, with their tan gabardine suits and styled hair, stood stone-faced, looking like window mannequins, or an ad for genetic engineering.

"We don't have time to argue about this." Cole Hatton stepped up, grasping the gravity of the problem.

"I can convince a friendly federal judge across the street to paper the warrant on our guys. Tony, you get the municipal judge for the sheriffs."

Metcalf and Cagel didn't like it, but what could they say? Their own U.S. Attorney had just jumped the fence.

The meeting broke up. A lot of unhappy faces crowded into the elevator for the ride down. I walked with Alexa back to her office. She was quiet most of the way. Once she was behind her desk she picked up a folder and handed it to me.

"What's this?" I asked.

"You were right about Vincent Smiley applying to the LAPD before Arcadia," she said stiffly. "We turned him down in April of 'ninety-nine. He flunked the preliminary psych interview. I made a copy of the written denial by the academy, but I haven't had a chance to read anything, except the summary. He looks like damaged goods." She seemed distracted, tense—wrapped tighter than the inside of a baseball. I was about to say something when her phone rang, so I waved good-bye and left.

When I reached the lobby I was paged. The LCD readout said: Jo Brickhouse. I found her number and called back. She was still out at the sheriff's crime lab when she answered.

"Me," I said. "What's up?"

"The crime techs have done both casings. Good striation marks and pin impressions on both. If we can get comparison casings, our lab says they have enough here to make a match."

"Good. Sheriff Messenger just covered his ass with a search warrant. He can't use the first batch—illegally obtained. He'll have to stick with the cover story, say the range captain was just adjusting sights, and do it all over again. Get in touch with Messenger's office and have him send the second batch of brass over to the lab as soon as he gets them. I'll let you know when the SRT long guns have been tested."

"One more thing . . ." she said.

"Go."

"Robyn DeYoung, the CSI for Hidden Ranch, just rolled out of here with an evidence team and two vans full of academy cadets. She's on her way back up there to search for a dog and a bomb shelter. What's all that about?" She sounded suspicious.

"Try to reach Messenger and make arrangements to get his brass out to your lab, then meet me out there as soon as you can. I'll fill you in when I see you."

TWENTY-FIVE

Digging

When I got back to Hidden Ranch Road there were two parked sheriff's academy vans and at least two dozen academy cadets up by the burned-out house, dressed in grubbies and yellow fire slickers, leaning on shovels. They seemed glad to be working on an actual case, instead of running laps and doing pull-ups at the Academy. They were eagerly looking at the large dig site, anxious to begin.

I spotted a slightly plump female criminalist with wire-rimmed glasses and red, curly, Orphan Annie–styled hair. She looked to be in her mid-thirties and was wearing a crime tech windbreaker, sweatpants, and a white T-shirt that said: *Get Off My Fucking Crime Scene*. Had to be Robyn DeYoung.

Jo hadn't arrived yet, so I walked up to Robyn, who was standing a few feet past where the front porch had once been, just about on the exact spot where Emo Rojas had bled to death. She was holding an open set of builder's plans and was issuing instructions, dividing the cadets into four teams and assigning them to separate quadrants of the dig site. When she finished, she turned to me.

"Don't tell me. You're Scully," she said.

"Guilty," I replied. "DeYoung?"

She nodded. Aside from the curly red hair, she also had freckles across the bridge of her nose and was attempting a disapproving scowl. But she possessed an instant likability, an infectious demeanor. She was mad at me for sending her back out here in all this damp ash and rubble, but for her anger wasn't a durable emotion, and it was already burning off like predawn mist.

"Sorry to put you through this again," I said, trying to soften her up.

"If you wanna grab a shovel, I have a fire slicker in my trunk that might fit you."

"Gee—me with a shovel. Now there's a heady concept."

"Didn't think so," she said. "Okay. Always good to have another supervisor." She opened the plans and studied them.

"Building department?" I asked.

"Yep. Pulled 'em this morning. No architect on these homes. Builder contracted. They all run between three and five hundred K. They seem nice, but when you look close they're just two-story, hollow-wall deals. Probably why it flashed over so fast."

"Right," I said. "The hot gas grenades and all that ammo in the garage probably didn't hurt either."

She let it pass, then asked, "What am I looking for again?"

"Rottweiler."

"Okay, have a seat and get started on your ice cream. If he's here, we'll dig him up."

I returned to the car, then opened the manila envelope containing Smiley's LAPD academy records and started to read.

The person who did the psychological profile was Doctor Hammond Emerson IV. I always love it when people put Roman numerals after their names, like inbred New England dilettante French royalty. Doctor Emerson had conducted three interviews with Smiley in 1999. He found the subject to be evasive and secretive. He felt that Smiley clearly had parental issues, particularly with his mother, which the doctor surmised could have stemmed from child abuse. Emerson noted in his summary that Vincent exhibited some gender confusion and a sense of hostility toward women that most probably also stemmed from the deep-seated problems with his mother, Edna Smiley—currently deceased.

Doctor Emerson concluded that Vincent Smiley demonstrated sado-sexual tendencies combined with latent rage. Emerson also surmised that these problems would create great stress when interrelating with females, both in the department as well as in society.

The LAPD academy employed a point system for applicants. Out of a possible one hundred points Smiley had scored forty, well below the seventy required to be considered for admission. Not even a close miss.

I closed the file, tapping it with my thumb. Was the AK-47 a deadly penis substitute? Was Smiley trying to make up for his sexual confusion by going postal and shooting up his neighborhood?

Just then Jo Brickhouse pulled to the curb in a sheriff's black-and-white. We both got out of our cars and met halfway. I handed her the file. "What's this?" she said. She still seemed angry, but maybe it was me, and I was just projecting.

"Smiley's LAPD academy app. He applied to us before Arcadia. Probably took a shot at your department, too. You might see if they turned him down and if they have a psych profile on him."

She took the file, opened it, and skimmed it while I watched the cadets moving ash and charred lumber off the site.

"Gay?" she said raising an eyebrow.

"Hey, come on, take it easy. That doesn't necessarily make him a bad person."

There was a moment while two conflicting emotions, anger and amusement, fought for control of her strong face. Finally, the dazzling smile won out. "You're not gonna stop busting my balls, are you, Scully?"

"When you stop busting mine, I'll stop busting yours."

She considered that for a second, then waved it off.

"Okay, look—the sheriff's department doesn't spike an application on the grounds of homosexuality alone. You guys don't either."

"Not now, but what was it like in the mid- or late nineties?" I asked.

"Not sure." She tapped the folder on her thumb, exactly the same way I had. "Most likely, Doctor Emerson dinged him for all this other stuff. The sado-sexual rage, the mother problem—add that to the gender confusion, and who wants an asshole like that on the job?"

"Right. But I don't think gender confusion is necessarily homosexuality."

She thought about that and nodded, so I went on.

"And there's nothing in there about depression or suicidal tendencies either."

"It's just a quick psychological scan. This doc could've missed a lotta stuff."

"Still . . ."

Just then we heard yelling up at the site. I walked across the grass again with Jo Brickhouse at my side. The Academy cadets had found a charred lump of meat about the size of a large dog. They had scraped the ash away from the mound and were all standing around, looking happily at the object like puppies who had found a ball.

I kneeled down. The smell of cooked, decaying flesh made my throat constrict. Then I saw something glistening in the ash near the corpse. Using the tip of my pen, I pulled it away from the burnt carcass. A round piece of metal.

"Dog tag," Robyn DeYoung said. "You can touch it if you want. No prints survived the heat of this fire."

I picked it up and rubbed it with my thumb, clearing the ash. "Eichmann," I said, reading the name. "Guy named his dog Eichmann."

"'Hitler' was probably already taken," Jo said from behind me.

"I wonder if he really was some kinda white supremacist?"

"Goes with the survivalist training Tad Palmer mentioned," Jo answered.

I handed the tag to Robyn and stood. "Okay, that probably answers the question of what happened to the Rottweiler. Can you get us a DNA scan to match the breed, just to be sure?"

Robyn nodded. She gave an order and two cadets ran to the crime van, returning with a plastic sheet and a rubber coroner's bag. Then they loaded the charred remains onto the sheet and Robyn wrapped him up like a burrito. She instructed them on how she wanted the remains loaded into the coroner's bag, then two cadets carried him down and left him in the back of her black-and-white Suburban.

Jo and I walked back and leaned against the hood of my car, watching while the cadets again started digging where the plans indicated the basement staircase would be.

"What are we really doing out here?" Jo asked.

"Loose ends," I said.

"Look, Scully, you were right. I never worked in homicide, but in IAD I've put down a pile of officer-involved shootings. So far, this doesn't stack up as a bad shooting. Smiley brought this on himself. Death by cop. I don't see how checking this guy's background adds anything to

Emo Rojas's death, or Billy Greenridge's and Michael Nightingale's."

"I'm not sure it does either," I admitted, annoyed again, but trying to stay frosty.

"Not to state the obvious here," she continued, "but you and I are at ground zero in a jurisdictional hurricane. I'm starting to get a lot of cold shoulders from my fellow deputies. They don't like it that we're investigating this. We've got heavy metal blowing around over our heads and you're out here looking for a dead dog and a bomb shelter."

"I gotta get it off my mind."

"What? Get what off your mind?" Frustration again.

"What Smiley was really doing."

"Committing suicide."

"Not according to Doctor Emerson."

"Fuck Doctor Emerson. He's just a guy in a tweed coat who never dealt face-to-face with a gun-toting psychopath. For him it's all theory and book work."

"Smiley was in Kevlar," I said for the umpteenth time, speaking slowly so somebody might finally get it. "He was building a bomb shelter. That doesn't sound like a guy contemplating suicide."

"So what?" she snapped. "Look, Shane, my ass is on the line too. I'm having daily meetings with the under-sheriff. My boss wants results, and all you're doing is moving backwards."

I shook my head. This was exactly what I'd been afraid of. Some silk from sheriff's IAD, who'd never worked a murder, telling me what to do.

"Is this just you wandering around on the outer edge of the crime scene again?" Jo interrupted. "Because if it is, I think we need to seriously refocus."

"There's not much we can do until we get those shell striations matched. Let's just see this through."

We both went to defense postures, leaning back and crossing our arms. She was definitely not in agreement, her face impassive but angry. The sleeves of her gray cloth jacket bulged at the biceps.

Again, I couldn't shake the feeling that I'd seen her before. *Where was it?* I wondered.

"We found it," one of the academy trainees yelled. Jo and I pushed away from the hood of my car and trudged up the lawn again toward the crowd of young cadets.

They had uncovered a staircase that led into what looked like a basement. There was ash and rubble all the way down to a lower level door. One of the female cadets was at the bottom of the stairwell, still digging with a shovel, throwing the last spadeful of sodden debris up. It landed all around the spot where we were standing. Then she scrambled up, her face smudged with soot, but she was grinning. This was a high-profile investigation, and she was thrilled. This was why she had signed on—exactly what the recruiting poster promised.

Join the tradition. Become an L.A. County sheriff. Wear the star. Shovel shit.

We looked down the staircase. It was a mess, the ash at the bottom still soggy from the fire hoses.

"I'll take you up on that slicker now," I said to Robyn.

She smiled and instructed a cadet to run to her car and get two. He returned a minute later carrying yellow ponchos with LASD stenciled on the back. I handed one to Jo, put the other over my head. Once we were rigged, we started down the steps. The door at the bottom of the stairs had burned right off its hinge. I picked it up and set it aside, then we went into the underground room.

The flashover heat from the fire had been so intense it scorched everything down there. The basement contained a laundry room, a tool area, and a few metal closets. The clothes had burned off the wire hangers. The plastic on the Black & Decker power tools had melted.

But there was no bomb shelter.

We all stood and looked at the scorched remains in the concrete block basement.

Jo said, "What now?"

"I don't know," I replied. "The neighbors claimed he was pulling dirt out of here. He told them he was digging a bomb shelter in the basement. So where is it?"

"Smiley was a lying head case," Jo answered.

"But his neighbors weren't lying. Where'd the dirt come from, if it wasn't from a bomb shelter?"

Again we fell silent. Then Robyn DeYoung said, "You through with us? Can I send these 'cruits back to the barn?"

"Yeah, I guess. Thanks, guys."

They all waved, then started to pack up their gear. But something wasn't right. Just before they headed back to the academy vans, I stopped them.

"Wait. Hold on a second. Help me pull this stuff away from the walls first."

Several cadets came down and helped move the tool bench. It was heavy, almost two hundred pounds, and took three of us to slide it to the corner of the room. Next we moved a metal closet. Nothing. Last, the washer and dryer. When we pulled them away from the wall, I saw where the dirt had come from.

Vincent Smiley had dug a hole in the wall under the drainage line hidden behind the washer. It was a foot up from the floor and measured about three feet in diameter. Just large enough for a man to crawl through.

TWENTY-SIX

Tunnel Rat

Of course, Jo Brickhouse wanted to be our tunnel rat—the one to go through the hole.

"I'm not the CHCO, remember?" she said, her attitude temporarily replaced by excitement. "Look, Scully, I'm smaller. If that tunnel narrows down you're gonna get stuck in there."

I'm sure it was one of the few times in her life that Jo Brickhouse had admitted to being smaller. But she had a point.

"Okay, but take a Handy-Talkie. Talk to me all the way to the bomb shelter."

"Of course. You think I'd even consider doing this without you bitching in my ear and barking instructions?"

I went back to the car and picked up two Handy-Talkies and a flashlight, then jogged back to the basement area.

The female cadets were all standing around Jo Brickhouse, staring at her. They were impressed. This buff, hot-looking lady sheriff had just backed off the big, dumb L.A. cop. She was going to crawl through that tunnel alone, prepared to face untold dangers in some underground cavern. You could feel the adrenaline and hero-worship flowing back and forth among the six young women and Jo. The male cadets were harder to read, but were probably thinking, *Whatta pussy this L.A. cop turned out to be.*

Finally, Jo was ready. She triggered the Handy-Talkie.

"Radio check," her voice screamed from my belt.

I took my unit off and turned down the volume, then spoke into it: "Okay, we're hot."

She leaned toward me. "This is more like it."

She looked at her audience once, then dropped down on her hands and knees and looked into the hole.

"Better take this."

I handed her the flashlight I'd brought from the car. She eased halfway into the tunnel, paused, then continued all the way in.

After she disappeared we were left standing around looking at the mouth of the hole. Me and my two dozen disapproving helpers.

"That's one brave lady," one of the female cadets said.

"Just hope she doesn't run into the gopher who dug that thing," I said.

They looked at me for a moment, trying to make sense of it. "Kidding," I added.

That remark lost me the few remaining points I had left. It was bad enough that I was afraid to go through the tunnel, but how could I make jokes about heroic Sergeant Brickhouse at a time like this? I'm telling you, it's hard to be an enlightened male. I usually end up wrong.

I looked at my watch. Two minutes. I triggered the Handy-Talkie. "How's it going?"

I could hear the squelch as she triggered her unit, then heard her grunting with effort as she elbow-crawled along.

"Gotta . . . It's kinda . . . can see . . ."

Then static—then nothing.

We waited some more. The cadets all had worried expressions as we stared at the hole. Robyn DeYoung was sitting on the bottom step of the basement stairs looking interested but skeptical.

"I triggered the unit again. "Come in. What's going on? You okay?"

All I heard back was static.

"One of us should go in after her," a dark-haired female cadet said, starting to cinch her slicker tighter.

"No—she's okay. It's just that we've lost range on the Handy-Talkie. These units aren't too good transmitting through solid matter."

"I'll go in and look for her," a blonde cadet volunteered.

". . . find . . . in . . . light . . ." I heard Jo say through a wall of static. We were all staring at the round, dark hole like a team of anxious proctologists.

A minute later Robyn DeYoung stood. Now she looked concerned. "She's been in there over five minutes."

"I guess I'd better go in," I said, and reluctantly belted my slicker.

"Won't be necessary, Hoss."

Everyone spun around. Jo Brickhouse was standing on the stairs behind us, backlit by the morning sun, spiky blonde hair dusted over with dirt.

"How'd you get there?" I said.

We all scrambled up the stairs and back into the burned-out house.

"Come on, I'll show you."

She led the way across the backyard toward a four-foot-high grape stake fence. She grabbed the top of the fence and easily jackknifed up and over—a perfect, gymnastic parallel bar move. Nothing to it. I tried to duplicate the maneuver, but parallel bars are not my event, unless they've got Coors signs in the windows.

Eventually, most of us landed on the other side of the fence and followed Jo, who was winding her way down into an overgrown gully behind the house. She stopped and pointed to the other end of the hole.

"No bomb shelter. Just a tunnel. Starts in the basement, comes out here."

Finally everybody had climbed down to where she stood and we all studied this opening with varying expressions of confusion.

"You sure you didn't miss a fork or anything in there?"

"This is it," Jo said. "The tunnel follows the washer drain pipe most of the way. The last fifty feet or so, the pipe goes right, but he dug straight through to here."

One thing I had come to learn working crime investigations is that even the most confusing things usually have some kind of central logic. If they appear not to, then what you have to do is rearrange the facts until the correct pattern emerges.

As I looked down at the tunnel I knew that I was working the wrong theory. We definitely had some pieces way out of order.

TWENTY-SEVEN

Truce at DuPar's

Twenty minutes later, Robyn DeYoung and her two dozen cadets drove off. We were standing down by our cars and Jo Brickhouse was combing the dirt out of her hair, with her fingers.

"Come on, let's grab some lunch," I said.

She followed me in the sheriff's black-and-white to DuPar's Restaurant off Vista Del Sol. We found a booth by the window and ordered. I got a hot Reuben sandwich, she had the seafood salad and a latte. We sat staring at each other like enemy generals, across a white vinyl battleground littered with napkins and scratched flatware. This wasn't working.

Finally she leaned forward. "Look—I think we need to start over."

"I agree."

"I took a department course in human relations once," she said. "They taught us that a good way to improve a strained relationship is by acknowledging each other's strengths."

"You first," I said, sounding petulant and small.

"Okay. You were right, checking the edge of the Nightingale crime scene. We found the shooter's position, got the casing and footprint casts. That stuff could've been missed or destroyed. And going back and finding that basement tunnel might be important. I'm not sure what it proves—if anything. But you're right, it's definitely weird."

"Okay, thanks."

"Now you," she prompted.

"Okay. You seem very organized and thorough."

"That's all?" She wrinkled her brow in disappointment.

"And going through that tunnel alone was a gutsball play. You showed a lot of courage."

She smiled. "It was kinda gutsball, wasn't it?"

I nodded, and she began tearing open half a dozen packets of Equal and dumping them into her latte. I couldn't believe how much artificial sweetener she used.

She looked up and caught me staring. "So let's hear your next big theory, Scully." Looking down again, stirring her sweetened blend. "I can hear lots of shit grinding up there in the old gear box, but nothing's coming out your pie hole."

Cute.

I took a moment, then leaned back and sighed.

"Okay, you probably won't like this, because nobody else does, but I don't buy the death by cop thing. Here's my reason and my timeline, so check me for flaws."

She pulled out her spiral notebook, flipped it open, and clicked the point down on her pen.

"Vincent Smiley has a bad childhood. He doesn't get along with his mother. Maybe she sexually abuses him, maybe she just yells a lot. Whatever the reason, he's got anger problems. For some reason, his parents pull him out of Glendale High and he's home-schooled for most of his high school years. He gets a GED, goes to junior college, then decides he wants to be a cop. Maybe so he can push people around and prove he's a real man. Next, he applies to the LAPD and fails. Emerson says he has mama problems, sexual identity problems, and can't relate to women. But somehow, even with all these deficits, he bullshits his way onto the Arcadia P.D. Finally they get wise and throw him out as a probationer, probably for all the same reasons. Now he's pissed. The cops dissed him, so he hates cops; but he also wishes he was one. He becomes a military nut and a survivalist. Hacks into a secure Marine Corps Web site called Cactus West."

She wrote that down.

"He even buys a dog and names it Eichmann. All that lines up with what Tad Palmer told us."

She nodded. "So far we're on track. But what's with the Marine Corps Web site?"

"I don't know yet. Our computer people are trying to penetrate the site." She nodded, so I went on. "After dear old Mom and Dad hit the slab, Smiley cashes in their death benefits and buys a three- to five-hundred-thousand-dollar home up on Hidden Ranch Road."

"Do we know he used his parents' insurance?"

"I'm guessing. It's what Palmer said, but you're right, we should check that out. Otherwise, where does this guy who doesn't work get enough money for a place like that? If it's not insurance, maybe it's hooked to some other kind of nastiness."

She kept making notes as I continued. "Okay, so he's up there in Hidden Ranch, walking around, pretending he's a cop, and at the same time saying he hates them. Basically acting nuts. Sometime last year ATF says they got a complaint and braced him on a suspected weapons charge. They claim when they talked to him he was docile, and it turned out he was clean. No weapons in the house. So they let him go. Didn't even bust him."

Jo was scribbling notes.

"Now, a few weeks ago something happens. For some reason, Vince goes into overdrive. He's still showing the phony badge, only now he says he's working on the anti-terrorist squad. But he's such a loosely wrapped package, nobody believed him. To prove it, he takes some of his neighbors into his garage and shows them his weapons stash. Palmer and the Bellinghams get spooked, call the sheriff's department, and find out there's no Vincent Smiley on the county roster. So they make a complaint to the ATF for automatic weapons and impersonating.

"ATF looks the complaint over and says we already braced this jerk-off once and it turned out to be an air ball. Since they think he's docile, they kick the impersonating beef over to the sheriff, figuring if the LASD finds guns in there, so much the better. But on second thought, SRT isn't completely sure, so when Emo calls to tell them he's serving the warrant, they give him a little covert ATF backup and wait to see what happens. Emo walks up and knocks on the front door, Smiley opens up, and it's welcome to Dodge City. The fed SRT van is just around the corner. They hear the gunfire and roll, which explains how they got there so quick. But Smiley knows it's coming, so he's waiting for them, all dressed in Kevlar with a gas mask. Next we have Waco in the foothills."

I looked up at Jo. "So far, is all that pretty much the way you have it?"

"Pretty much," she said, putting down her pen and sipping her latte. "Eat your sandwich, it's getting cold," sounding like somebody's mother now.

I took a bite and swallowed it. "Okay, so now he's pinned in that house and he's greasing off lead-core three-oh-eights. The guy's dog is in there with him. After half the cops in Southern California are finished raining shit through the windows and burning the place down, he ends up dead in the bathtub, looking like a pot roast somebody left in the oven. His dog is downstairs, also cooked. Roof falls in, end of incident."

I took another bite of the Reuben and looked at her again. "All of that still seem right?"

"Yep. At least as far as we know."

"Okay, then here's what's wrong."

I took a deep breath. "Smiley obviously had this all carefully planned. He shows Palmer and Bellingham the stash of bullets, the grenades, the AK-forty-sevens and boxes of C-four. Smiley's gotta know it's gonna freak these guys. They have children. He's gotta know they're gonna call the cops."

"Probably."

"He's gone to all the trouble of spending two months last summer digging an escape tunnel out of the basement to the gully below. He could have easily crawled through there and gotten away, but he didn't. He crawled into the bathtub instead and let the whole fucking house fall on him."

"Makes no sense, does it?"

"Only if we put him down as a mental. And all the rest of this is too organized, too planned for a real head case. Why go to all that trouble to build an escape hatch and then not use it?"

"Maybe he was overwhelmed by the fire," she offered. "Maybe it went up faster than he planned."

"I was under that porch with Sonny Lopez when the house was burning. Smiley was downstairs at the end, running around shooting. The house was completely ablaze. He had to know it was about to come down. I did. It was hot as hell. I could barely stand it, and I was outside. He could have easily gone to the basement, pulled the washer away, crawled through the hole, and gotten out of there, but he chose instead to die a horrible, painful death. Why?"

"Maybe he just lost it."

I frowned at her. "Come on, you don't like this any better than I do."

"Okay, you're right. But it's still a dead end. Excuse the pun. I think all the stuff about SRT, and how they got there so quick, is good. We can write that up. It adds to our investigation; but everything about the tunnel and why he didn't use it is irrelevant. Vincent Smiley is in the morgue. Where does all that take us?"

She waited patiently for my answer, so I finally told her why I couldn't let go.

"When I first started working homicide it was the last year that John St. John worked as a consultant for the LAPD. He used to come around and talk to us, tell all the new humps how to work cases, how to follow the evidence trail."

"Jigsaw John?" she said, remembering the legendary LAPD homicide detective who had retired after he took a bullet in the back fifteen years ago.

He'd moved to Oregon, but back then he still rented his services out on big cases. He especially liked to work with and train young detectives.

"John told me once, when you have a twister like this, where the logic doesn't track, it's usually one of two things that are causing the confusion. One: because you're looking at the timeline wrong. Something important is out of place. Or two: because there's a factual piece missing."

"But what if there isn't? What if he was just overcome by smoke and couldn't get down to the basement?"

"John said it was like when you reconciled a checkbook. If you're off even one dollar you can't just forget it, because that one dollar could be hiding a much bigger error."

"So, what do we do?"

"We start over. Start with Smiley's backstory again. Work it from the ground up."

"You kidding? We've probably got SEB and SRT running around killing each other. We're under heavy pressure from your chief, my sheriff, your wife, and every cop and deputy in L.A. We have to find something fast that we can take to the D.A. Something that will allow them to sack up those two units until they can get it sorted out."

"Look, I don't . . ."

"No. Listen. If any other cop gets sniped on either side, you and I both go in the bag and stay there."

"But, what if all the theories they're working on are wrong? What if we're building this investigation on a bad foundation? If we are, we'll never come out at the right place."

She studied me for a long moment, then pushed her plate away. "Are you asking me?" she said.

"Yeah. Damn right," I answered. "Since we finally agree we're in this together, just tell me where you think we oughta go from here. I'm open for suggestions, but we have a lot of stuff that doesn't line up, and I only know one way to do it, and that's to start over."

She sat for a long time, then took her wallet out of her purse, opened it, and threw ten bucks on the table.

"You don't have to buy lunch," I said.

"Don't you wish. Get your dough out, Scully. Since I guess I'm going on this dumb-ass, career-ending ride with you, the least you can do is pay your half of the food bills." She got up without waiting for an answer and walked out of the restaurant.

We had a truce. I think.

TWENTY-EIGHT

The Rams

The way it was explained to me by my stressed and emotionally frayed wife, two plainclothes lieutenants from the Warrant Control Office, along with an LAPD Special Weapons and Tactics Team, under the command of a captain from our Internal Affairs Division, drove out to 130 South Fetterly Avenue in East L.A. and served a search warrant on the captain in charge of the Sheriff's Enforcement Bureau. Scott Cook, who had commanded the Gray team at Hidden Ranch and his scout, Rick Manos, watched angrily as two LAPD SWAT team members in body armor collected five Tango 51s and seven 40-X long guns. They were put in one of the sheriff's ARVs to be driven out to Spring Ranch and test fired.

A warrant was also served on SRT by two SWAT teams about an hour later, at 4 P.M. SRT had nine AR-15s, which were very versatile weapons that could be switched in seconds from a sniper rifle to a fully automatic carbine simply by swapping the upper receiver. All nine SRT guns were picked up and taken out to their training facility in Moorpark to be test fired.

The collection of the weapons had gone down without incident, but Alexa told me that nobody was happy about it. "An insult," is what she'd heard Scott Cook had called it.

In the past I'd found out that the best way to get the pieces of a confusing case to line up correctly was to focus my head on something else for a while. Let some fresh air in. It was five in the afternoon when I called home, and Delfina told me that Chooch had driven out to Agoura High to run his first Pop Warner football practice for the Rams. I was only a few miles away, so I said good-bye to Jo and drove over.

The high school was in the foothills, not far from where this had all started. I parked behind the athletic building and walked around the big fieldhouse until I saw the practice fields on a terraced level about five feet above me. There were fences everywhere. The Agoura High football team was also running a practice using the two full-sized fields, but the Rams were on a fifty-yard overflow field on the far right. The problem was, I kept hitting locked gates when I tried to get up there. I had to ask a student for directions.

"Gotta go around by the administration building." Then he added: "You can't get there from here."

Story of my life.

I eventually found my way onto the grass, snuck up into the bleachers a short distance away, and watched Chooch without letting him know I was here. He had a clipboard under his arm, a walking cast on his foot, and was working with two twelve-year-old quarterbacks. Both boys were wearing red no-contact jerseys, watching Chooch, with his broken foot, trying to demonstrate how to throw a quick out off a three-step drop. Across the field, Sonny Lopez was working with the linemen—the wide bodies, such as they were. The heaviest kid on the field was still under 170.

Finally Chooch blew a whistle. "Okay, everybody over here and take a knee," he yelled.

The twenty or so members of the team surged toward him. You could spot the serious athletes from the wanna-bes, even from where I was sitting in the bleachers. The committed players ran all the way to Chooch, some even raced each other. The other kids, the ones who were just there for their fathers, walked. I got up from the bleacher seat, and, trying to stay unobserved, moved down closer so I could hear.

"Okay," Chooch said, "good warm-ups. In a minute we'll start walking through plays, then do a half hour of scrimmage. I'm not gonna have all of your names for a while, so when I talk to you, if I don't call you by name, you guys tell me who you are. I'll get it straight pretty quick."

I watched Sonny Lopez pulling a blocking sled out of the way, getting the short field ready for play.

"I've been studying Coach Rojas's offense, and even though I've never had much experience with a Veer, this one looks good. But I'm gonna have to put you guys through some new speed tests. Forty-yard dashes. Sorry about that, but I need to see for myself where the quick-ness is."

The kids were a little subdued, all of them down on one knee, helmets off, looking at the grass instead of at Chooch.

He sensed it, so he said, "On this team, anybody can say anything. I'm only a few years older than you guys. I'm your coach, but I also want to be a friend. I feel a lot of stuff going on under the surface—stuff you're thinking about me, or what happened to Coach Rojas. We gotta get that all behind us if we want to have a winning spirit."

Nobody looked at him.

"I want you guys to tell me what you're thinking. How you feel about all this—Coach Rojas dying. If it's on your mind, let's get it out in the open and deal with it."

Still nothing.

"Can't somebody please say something?" he said, smiling slightly.

One of the larger boys in the back raised his hand. He was an African-American wearing number 58 on his jersey. Probably a linebacker.

"Yeah," Chooch pointed at him.

"How come we . . ."

"First gimme your name," Chooch said.

"Deshawn Zook."

My blood chilled a little.

"Okay, Deshawn. How come what?"

"How come we gotta play for you when your dad is trying to fuck ours?"

I almost got up and walked over to Chooch to answer that, but before I could move, Chooch was talking.

"I know most of you guys have sheriffs for dads, and I know a lot is going on between the LAPD and the sheriffs right now, but whatever happens down there, it isn't part of this team. This team is about us. You and me. It's about our values and how much we want to win, for ourselves and each other. It's about that and nothing else."

Now they were listening. Most had their heads up watching him.

"I was friends with Emo Rojas. That's why I'm here. I wanted to do this for him. What happens between our fathers can't be part of what happens on this field, but I'll tell you this, Deshawn, my dad is one of the fairest people you'll ever meet. I met your dad, Darren, on an Iron Pig rally this summer. He seemed really cool and really nice.

With your dad and mine working on it, I just don't think whatever's going on is gonna be that big of a problem."

Deshawn Zook nodded his head. He was a smaller version of his father.

Then Chooch looked down at his clipboard and said, "Deshawn, you're playing inside linebacker, right?"

"Yes."

"You like that position?"

"Not really."

"Why not?"

"Used to play fullback. Like that better."

"Okay, then here's the deal. All positions are open again for two days. Everybody write down the position you prefer, the position you'll take, and the position you're playing now. Hand 'em in after practice. I'll work with each of you to try and get you where you want to go. I can't promise to move you, but everybody can have one tryout at any position he asks for. By Tuesday any position changes will be posted, and then we'll get back to work. Fair?"

The boys started nodding, some were even smiling.

Half an hour later, when the scrimmage started, I left, slipping out behind the bleachers. I don't think Chooch ever saw me. As I walked back to the Acura I was thinking how proud I was of the way he handled that—how smart. Throwing everything open and giving everybody a second chance was a great idea. The kids were now focussed on the future, not on Emo, or me, or any of the other angry nonsense that had washed over them.

When I reached my car I had another surprise. Scott Cook and Rick Manos were standing there with Darren Zook and Sonny Lopez. As I took out my keys, Rick Manos intercepted me.

"You know what happened this afternoon?" he asked, not waiting for an answer. "Warrants got served on us.

They think we shot that fed. Your SWAT guys rolled in and took all our long guns."

I stared at him, not sure how to play it. Then I glanced over at Sonny. "You call these guys when you saw me arrive?"

"No sir," he said, leaning on the *sir* so it sounded more like a curse than anything else. "All our kids play on the team. Pickup is in half an hour."

I turned back to Manos. "I'm getting sick of this. I'm just doing a job, what do you want from me?"

Now Scott Cook leaned forward and fixed me with a level, no-nonsense stare, frightening in its focus. "You don't know where this is headed, Scully. If you did, you'd play it differently."

"Then you know something," I said.

They started to walk away, but Scott Cook turned back.

"I know what those assholes at Treasury are capable of," he said. "I know whatever those casing striations show, we didn't shoot Greenridge. And I know this has just started, Scully. Nobody can stop it now."

TWENTY-NINE

Meltdown

"I'm worried," Alexa said.

I was barbecuing chicken in the backyard, basting on my beer butter sauce and nervously watching the Santa Ana winds blow briquette smoke and sparks across the fence into the yard next door. I hoped my surfboard-shaper neighbor, Longboard Kelly, wasn't watching and cursing as my embers sailed over the fence. Franco was right at my feet, purring. He liked my barbecued chicken, so he was watching carefully.

"I'm worried too—these hot embers. Maybe this wasn't such a great idea," I said, trying to refocus the conversation.

"I'm not talking about the wind or the damn barbecue," she snapped.

"I know you're not, honey."

"How long until the sheriff's ballistics lab can get us a match on those casings?"

"I don't know."

The phone rang and Alexa jumped. She was that stressed.

"Delfina will get it," I said. "It's probably just Chooch telling her he's gonna be late getting home from football practice."

I wanted to tell Alexa about what I'd seen and how proud I was of the way Chooch had handled the team, but I didn't want to compromise the story by telling it while she was this upset.

After a minute Delfina walked outside. "It's for you, Shane."

I handed the barbecue tongs to Alexa. "Don't let my little chickadees burn," I said, doing a bad W. C. Fields. Then I gave her some Groucho eyebrows, trying to lighten the moment. But she was in no mood to smile.

I went into the den and picked up the phone. It was Jo.

"You want the bad news, or the bad news?" she said.

"Shit."

"We got a positive match on the three-oh-eight you and I pulled out of the apartment. The pin impression and ejection striations line up perfectly with a long gun from the sheriff's SEB armory. A Tango fifty-one. Serial number X-one-five-seven-eight. Brand new sniper rifle bought three months ago."

"Whose gun is it?"

"That's the problem. They don't assign individual weapons at SEB. They have an armory, keep 'em in the van when they roll, and pass 'em out when they hit the event."

She was right. That's what I had seen happen at Hidden Ranch Road.

"So anybody could have taken this gun out of the armory and used it," she finished.

"Great."

"Sometimes one of the snipers will check a long gun out and take it home if he's on standby. That way they can roll to a call from home. When that happens, they sign them out. I imagine certain guys get attached to certain guns. They like the way the sights line up or the way the trigger pulls, the balance—stuff like that. I figure, if this long gun kept getting checked out to the same guy, maybe that leads us somewhere. I'll get the records."

"Right. Good thinking." I tried to guess where this was going. No doubt we would now have to take the whole SEB Gray team off duty, print everybody, and hold them somehow.

"I called Sheriff Messenger," Jo said. "He's not a happy camper. ATF went out to our crime lab with a court order and took the two-twenty-three casing we found at Nightingale's house. They're doing their own ballistics match. Messenger's gonna send a print team out to our SEB SWAT house at South Fetterly. With that three-oh-eight casing match, we have enough PC to force a print check on everybody in our enforcement bureau. That's all the updates."

I stood looking down at the desk, trying to figure out what our next move was.

"Whatta you bet we also get a positive on that two-twenty-three casing from SRT?" she said.

"No bet," I replied.

"Your place or mine? We've got a lot to do here."

"Whatta we gotta do, besides wait?" I asked. "You figure we should go out and roll prints ourselves?"

"I've been working on your angle. Rebuilding Smiley's backstory—his history. Isn't that what you wanted? I've been doing computer runs all afternoon. I've got reams of county and city printouts. I could use some help sorting."

So, while I'd been at football practice Jo Brickhouse was down at the sheriff's computer information center doing runs on Vincent Smiley. I was impressed, and okay, a little embarrassed. I should have been on that, instead of watching my son coach. Figuring out priorities are a bitch.

"Your place," I finally said, because Alexa was in a foul mood and I wanted to get some air. Also, she hated my background approach, so I'd just as soon not do it right in front of her.

Just before Jo hung up I said, "Hey, Sergeant Brickhouse?"

"Yeah?" Her voice was wary.

"Thanks for the help."

"We're partners, aren't we?"

"Yeah, but it was very thorough. The gun info, the background search—everything."

"Just doin' police work, Hoss," she said. "Nothin' special."

"Take the fucking compliment, why don't ya?"

"You sure it's a compliment, or are you finally trying to make up for being such an asshole?"

I could picture the dazzling smile spreading across her face. "See you in half an hour," I said, smiling myself as I hung up.

Outside, Alexa had her back to the house, facing the canal, talking on her cell phone. When she turned around, I knew it must have been Tony telling her about the casing match, because her face was pulled tight.

"You heard?" I said.

"They matched the casing," she said.

The chicken had been forgotten and was blazing merrily on the grill. Alarmed, Franco jumped up on the table to watch it burn. If a cat could frown, Franco was frowning. I grabbed the tongs and plucked a piece off the grill, but it was too late. Chicken briquettes.

"Now we're gonna have to get everybody on SRT off the street and printed," Alexa said.

"SRT?" I said. "Whatta you talking about?"

"Brady Cagel just called Tony. The two-twenty-three matched one of their AR-fifteens. What were you talking about?"

"I was talking about SEB," I said. "That was Jo. She said sheriffs matched the three-oh-eights to one of their Tango fifty-ones."

Alexa stood holding her cell phone, looking lost, her face a dark mask. She had always been my strength. Even though I hated to admit it, I looked to my wife for moral clarity and emotional guidance, because I was often at sea in those two critical areas. Now as I watched her I saw only confusion and fear on her lovely face. Suddenly she pushed past me and went quickly into the house, leaving me and Franco in the backyard.

"Not good, buddy," I said to the cat.

I had never seen her like this before. I turned and headed into the house after her. She was in the bedroom with the door locked. She never locked the door.

"Alexa?" I called through the wood panels. Nothing. "Alexa, please let me in." No answer. "Don't make me break this open," I said.

"Go away, Shane. Please." She sounded like she was crying. She wasn't a weepy woman. I had only seen her cry once, and that was when her ex-boyfriend and commanding officer, Mark Shephard, was murdered.

"Alexa, please. Please open up."

I heard the lock being thrown and she stood in the doorway, her face contorted, her mascara running. "What?" she said angrily.

"I'm not the problem here."

"Look, Shane, I'm having a meltdown, okay? Occasionally it happens."

She turned and went into the bathroom. Then I heard that door lock.

I sat on our bed and waited. Ten minutes later the door opened and she came out. She looked more composed, but she was still stressed. There was a tightness around her eyes. She saw me and paused, looking down without expression.

"Honey . . ." I started.

"No, look. I'm okay. I just caved in for a minute. Leave it be."

"Most of the time you're propping *me* up. Most of the time I'm looking to you, but when *you* get down, if you won't let me be a part of it, how's that supposed to work?"

Now she had the strangest expression. An ugly mix: confusion, anger, dismay. Her eyes were swollen from crying and lack of sleep.

"It's just a job," I said.

"No—no, please don't." She moved to the bed and threw herself down on the far side—on her side. Then she grabbed the extra pillow and held it in front of her, wrapping her arms around it as if it would protect her from me.

"We need to talk about this," I said softly.

"I was always the good little sister, the one who did it right. After Mother—after she and Dad . . ."

She stopped and her eyes started welling up. Her mother and father had died in a car accident when she was sixteen.

"I know how you feel about my brother Buddy," she suddenly continued, "and part of that is justified. It's just . . ."

Where was this going? Her older brother sold supermarket products to chains all over the country. Buddy was sort of the ultimate Bubba. I didn't much care for him because, when he wasn't being self-centered he was loud and overly friendly. He also treated Alexa like a servant. But she loved him and mothered him unreasonably.

"I always wanted to do the right thing," she went on. "People counted on it. I took care of Buddy until he left for college. My life was so confusing after he left. I had nothing. It was like I'd lost my job—my reason for being alive. Then I decided to become a cop. I don't know why it surprised everybody. Police work is about order. About rules and social design. All the things I was good at." She stopped.

"This is absolutely ridiculous." She pounded the pillow savagely.

"Honey, you haven't slept a full night since we got handed this case. Is it Tony?"

"Fuck yes, it's Tony. He's putting more pressure on me than I ever would have guessed. Every morning he calls me in and shouts at me. Nothing I do is right."

"Then I'll go over to his place and dial him down a notch."

"Jesus, Shane, would you stop it? This isn't a school-yard. He's the chief of police. He's got major pressure coming down. The press, the mayor, Salazar, the governor. The feds are all over him; so is Bill Messenger. That dickhead Cole Hatton is threatening a malfeasance lawsuit." She stopped again.

"We're being threatened constantly. Not just lawsuits—the police commission. They could fire Tony. We could both get axed. Everybody's looking for a scapegoat, and if we don't handle this right we're it. So he's been hammering on me, telling me to keep you focussed. I'm trying to hold the line for you, but . . ."

"Is this because of the way I want to work the case?" I was stunned.

"It's about that. It's about us trying to investigate two sister agencies. I'm getting threatening phone calls at Division. Can you believe it? Right in the Glass House. A whispery voice telling me I'm next."

My heart almost stopped. She hadn't told me any of this. It was just like her. Taking it all on herself, never complaining until she broke from the strain. I came around to her side of the bed and tried to put my arms around her.

"Honey, I'm sorry."

"Just—just . . ." She stopped, and the tears started coming again.

She shouted at the ceiling. "Stop crying, Alexa!" then rolled over and buried her face in the pillow.

I lay down beside her and started stroking her back, whispering to her, telling her how beautiful she was and how she was the most important person in my life. After a moment she stopped crying and turned again to face me.

"It's not just about the job. It's the way I feel about a lot of things. It's all changing."

"Come here," I said and held her close.

We embraced for a long moment, until, male libido being what it is, I started to wonder if making love would help her. Would a priceless piece of Scully ass make things right here?

Shane Scully, the Loooove Doctor.

I rubbed her back and shoulders. She started to relax a little and cuddled close to me. I was still trying to figure out what to do when she initiated it.

We caressed each other for a long time, making the beginning moves. Then she unbuttoned her blouse and in moments we were naked.

Emotions are the basic currency of police work, yet sometimes I'm surprised at how little I understand. We made love once diligently, then a second time with abandon. The air conditioner clattered in the window, but our combined heat and the Santa Ana winds had us slick with sweat.

When we finished I lay in her arms. "You're the best," I told her. "You make all things worthwhile."

She snuggled closer and nuzzled my ear. "Sometimes I'm so lonely and afraid," she said in a voice so tiny I barely heard her. "Sometimes I don't have any of the answers I'm supposed to, and I'm just down there faking like a gypsy."

I said, "We all do that."

"I can take pressure. I'm good under pressure. It's self-doubt that I can't deal with."

"It's that way for everybody," I told her.

"Except, you always seem so sure."

I couldn't believe she said that. I always felt so unsure. Always following in the footsteps of other people, like Jigsaw John, or Tony, or Alexa.

"I'm never sure," I told her. "Every time I'm sure, I turn out to be wrong."

But then I started to work on a way to solve her problem. If it was my investigative technique that was causing trouble, I could change that. I could focus on the SWAT teams like she wanted, leave everything else, the tunnel and all my hunches, for later. Also, I had an idea how I could get Tony off her back.

I was just getting ready to lay some righteous stuff on her when she said, "I'll get past this. It's just a hitch in the road." Then she whispered, "And thanks."

"For what?"

"For just listening. Not doing what you usually do, trying to solve it."

So I scotched all my brilliant solutions and just held her.

An hour later I changed my clothes and got ready to go to work with Sergeant Brickhouse. As I was passing through the living room the phone rang. It was almost ten, and I was pretty sure it was Jo wondering where I was. I almost didn't answer it, but then changed my mind and snapped up the receiver. Immediately, I heard a whispering, threatening voice.

"You been warned, Scully. Shut this down now or you pay the price, bitch."

"Wrong Scully, asshole," I said, anger and violence flaring. "When I find out who you are—and I will—I'm gonna reach down your throat and pull your asshole out."

Before I could finish the sentence he had hung up.

THIRTY

Star Trouble

I immediately hit star-69, but the number was blocked. Alexa was already under enough stress, so I didn't tell her about the call. Instead, I got in touch with Tony. The chief promised to run a phone check on my line and to increase the patrols in our neighborhood, keep an eye on our house.

I was almost two hours late getting to Jo's house off Alameda, in Glendale. It was in a middle-class neighborhood full of small one-story houses and duplexes. It was nine-thirty in the evening as I pulled slowly up the street, looking for her address. I spotted the number painted on a mailbox and turned into the narrow drive of a nondescript painted brick house. There was a black Navigator parked in the driveway facing the street. As I was setting my hand brake, a very pretty woman with black hair and long legs stormed out of the rear of the house, carrying a laundry basket full of clothes. She threw the basket into the back of the SUV and slammed the door. When she came around to the driver's side, I could see a mask of fury on a beautiful, structured face dominated by high cheekbones. She motioned for me to back up, then jumped into the Navigator, started the engine and blasted the horn angrily.

"Okay, okay, I'm trying," I said to my dash. I fumbled the key into the ignition and backed out into the street.

The Navigator came out of the driveway like a getaway car after a 7-Eleven robbery. She whipped the wheel right, squealed rubber, and roared away up the street.

I pulled back into the drive, parked, then went up to the front door and rang the bell.

Nobody answered. I rechecked the address. No problem there. I looked around the front yard. It was neatly trimmed, but bland. The flowerbeds were organized, but mostly planted in white. Colorless. The brick house was gray with white paint on the sparse wood trim. It was a square, uninspired structure. The whole feeling of the place was clean efficiency. No energy had been wasted on frills. *A brick shithouse,* I thought.

I rang the bell again. Still nothing. So I walked around to the rear.

The backyard was small. Two recliner sun chairs and a portable Jacuzzi with wood sides sat out on the lawn. There was a utilitarian concrete patio that held a coiled hose and a flower potting area.

The back door was ajar. I knocked loudly, then called out, "Jo. It's Shane."

No answer.

I was beginning to feel alarmed. Sheriffs were getting shot, Alexa was being threatened. Who was the angry woman who had raced out of the driveway in the Navigator, almost hitting me?

I checked my gun, but left it in the holster and entered Jo Brickhouse's sparse kitchen. It was neat, but like everything else, colorless and efficient. Lots of stainless steel.

I moved into the living room. Wood floors, plain walls, Danish Modern furniture, which always struck me as the ultimate triumph of form over function.

As I passed through the dining room, I could hear someone crying down the hall. Large, wracking sobs.

"Jo, it's Shane," I yelled out again, and the crying abruptly stopped.

"Just a minute," she called, in one of those fake brave voices. "Go wait in the den."

I turned and went into the den, which was really just an alcove off the living room. More Danish Modern furniture, gray upholstery, white walls. No art. All the warmth of a G.E. refrigerator. Her desk, on the far side of the little nook, was piled high with Vincent Smiley printouts.

I decided not to futz with it, but to let her pass out the paper. A minute later I heard her in the bathroom running water. Then her footsteps came down the hall. When she walked into the den her eyes were rimmed red and badly swollen.

First Alexa, now Jo. My female karma was in serious retrograde. "You okay?" I asked.

"Dandy," she said sharply, to cut off further discussion.

"You don't look dandy," I pressed, thinking even as I said it: *Don't get into this, Shane. Whatever it is, you can't solve it.*

"Where were you?" she snapped. "You were supposed to be here two hours ago." She was pissed at the pretty, black-haired woman in the SUV, but she was taking it out on me.

"I had to deal with something at home," I said.

"Really?" Focusing more anger. "Well, that can happen I suppose. But it never hurts to call. It's why we all carry beepers and cell phones."

"Who was that who almost took off my front bumper pulling out of here?" I asked, thinking again: *You don't want to know, Shane. Don't get into this.*

"That was Bridget."

"Who's Bridget?"

"Somebody I'll probably never see again." She said it so bitterly that it sounded like a curse. Then, little by little her composure began to crumble. It started with a slight lip quiver, then spread upward, eventually crashing her entire face. She hiccupped a loud sob at me, spun and ran out of the den, up the hall, leaving me standing alone.

Again, I had the same strange feeling that I knew her from somewhere before, but where the hell was it? The feeling was circling close, just out of reach. I tried to pin it down. Sometime, a while back. It was something about her build, or the way she moved. What was it about those muscular arms, those developed calves and thighs?

Then it hit me.

"Son-of-a-bitch," I said softly to myself.

I went out through the kitchen into the backyard, then crossed to the small garage and opened the side door. Parked inside was a department black-and-white. I walked around to the far side and there it was.

Jabba the Slut's yellow-and-black Screamin' Eagle Deuce.

THIRTY-ONE

Jabba the Slut

I was back in the tiny den waiting for her, thinking: *She must have remembered me from the Iron Pig's rally.* But, just like me, she wanted to pretend to have emotional distance on Emo's death. If I'd known they were friends I would have questioned her objectivity, as she had undoubtedly been questioning mine. It explained some of her argumentative attitude. At least, I hoped it did.

After a while she came out of the bedroom and sat in the swivel chair across the room, maintaining a careful physical distance from me. She looked crushed. Emotionally shattered.

"Look, Jo, this is probably a bad time to work on this. I could come back tomorrow."

"No. No, we have to do it now. There's a lot at stake."

"Right. But I can see you've just—I don't want to add to your emotional problems."

She looked at me, then shrugged her big shoulders. The motion said: I don't count, I'm nothing. Don't worry about me.

Then she added, "My brother sheriffs want this solved. I'm getting threatening calls at work."

She went to her desk and sat looking down at the papers. I decided not to complicate things by telling her Alexa was being threatened, too. I needed to get her focused on something else for a minute.

So I said, "I saw your bike in the garage. Why didn't you tell me you were on that ride?"

She shrugged again. "I didn't like you. From the first moment I saw you up in Trancas Canyon you sorta pissed me off. Sitting on that big Roast King that wasn't even yours, acting like some bullshit Willie G, highsiding and countersteering every turn. You ride like a girl."

"Jesus. That bad?" I smiled at her.

"Hey, I have female issues. I won't deny it. I also make snap judgments, so I'm wrong a lot. I've befriended a lotta assholes, alienated a lotta friends." She rubbed her hand under her one green eye, taking away some excess moisture. "Look, I do the best I can. Everybody doesn't see my virtues."

"I do," I said softly.

"Gimme a fuckin' break, Scully. I piss you off. But that's okay, I piss everybody off. If you could throw me overboard ten miles out, tied to an anchor, I'd be strolling the Catalina Trench right now."

"Don't be so hard on yourself."

"Right." She shook her head in bitter frustration. "Bridget says deep down I'm cold. I don't let people in. I suppose she's right, but I never know what to expect from people. I get scared, so I play a lot of defense."

"Me too."

She spun the swivel chair around and regarded me with frustration. "Don't try and get inside my head, Shane. It'll scare the hell outta you."

"What's in your head probably wouldn't scare me, Jo.

My own devils seem worse than yours, because they're mine."

"I'm sure," she said skeptically.

For some reason, at that moment I needed to get something off my chest. Maybe I was feeling guilty and isolated over Alexa, or maybe it was that I sensed that in her current state, Jo wouldn't judge me. Whatever it was, I took a deep breath and let go.

"Most of the time I feel pretty lost and unsure," I said softly. "And deep down I usually don't think I'm worth very much."

She was watching me carefully now, waiting for a punch line. But there wasn't one. This was one of my dark spots, a place I rarely go. Her mismatched eyes softened, so I went on.

"That can happen when you're left at a hospital when you're six weeks old, and the county can't give you away, even if they're paying people to take you. I'd go with somebody for a week and they'd spit me back—too fussy, too hyperactive, too old, too hard to handle. Mostly I was raised by the county. So, like you, for most of my life I never let anybody get close.

"I wanted to be a cop because cops got respect just by wearing a badge. Being a cop gave me standing in the community. It made me part of a brotherhood—a family. I stood for something important that didn't have to be explained to be understood. But there was something else—something less noble. As a cop I didn't need to have a personal relationship to affect the relationships of others. I was great at police work, but as a person I was hiding out. I was good with assholes, because at least I understood them. I knew what to expect. Nothing. And I was used to getting nothing."

She sat quietly listening, so I went on.

"But in the last few years I've been trying to change that, to take more chances and be more vulnerable. I'm learning that vulnerability doesn't have to signal weakness. In fact, it draws people to you. Little by little, my personal life is getting richer. But it's like everything is balanced on some kind of complicated teeter board. The more vulnerable I become the happier I am personally, but the more inept I feel as a cop. I'm getting played more, and I'm having trouble finding a reason to care about anything on the job. This case we're working is threatening to end my career because it is the ultimate breakdown of everything I once believed in."

"So you're taking a chance with me now. Is that what this is? Showing how open and nonjudgmental you can be?" She was sort of sneering as she said it.

"I don't care whether you're gay, Josephine. It's just a choice and it's yours to make. But if you want some unsolicited advice, don't let your sexuality define you. You're worth more than that. I have my own issues I'm working on. Nobody gets through life without getting ambushed occasionally. Stop thinking it's only you. Everybody's out there looking for their own answers."

She remained silent, her face hard to read.

"You and I are in this thing together," I said. "My wife is getting phone threats like you are. I'm worried about her safety, and now yours, too. Everybody wants us to ditch the Smiley background and start focusing on those two SWAT teams. Only, I can't shake the feeling that the answer is hiding in his past. Putting our rocky beginning aside, you've been a good partner, and I don't usually do well with partners, because trust is another one of my issues. But maybe we could develop some trust. If you wanta let down some personal boundaries, just say the word."

She didn't respond for a long moment, then finally

nodded her head. "Lemme think about it. I'll get back to you."

She reached over and scooped up all of her background material on Smiley and handed me half the stack.

"Wanna get started?"

She still seemed shaken, but she had a lot of will power, just like Alexa, and I knew she wouldn't break again.

"Sure. What's this?" I said, pulling the top sheet off the stack.

She glanced at it and said, "It's a bank payout to Vincent Smiley for four hundred and eighty thousand dollars. I'm guessing it's the Firemen's Fund Life Insurance policy for Edna and Stanley Smiley. Stanley had a one-truck plumbing service, Smiley, The Happy Plumber. Both he and Edna died in a car accident in 'ninety-five. Insurance premiums were fifteen thousand a year."

"So that's where the house came from."

"Exactly."

"Fifteen thousand a year?" I said. "Isn't that a pretty big premium?"

"Why?" she wondered.

"I don't know. Guy's a plumber with one truck, pays fifteen grand in life insurance premiums? Sounds kinda high. How much life insurance would that buy?"

She scribbled a note. "I've got a friend who sells insurance. I'll check it out."

"Can't you just call the broker who handled this policy?"

"No."

"Why not?"

"You don't want to know."

I frowned. "Don't tell me you hacked this bank's computer to get this."

"Ve haff our veys," she said, using a corny German accent. "I have a friend in computer sales who doesn't mind skating the edges, and she knows how to write spaghetti codes. I'll get her to hack the insurance company's computer. Because of the medical file, all this life insurance stuff is confidential."

"Shouldn't we just serve a warrant on Fireman's Fund?"

"Smiley's dead, so whatever we find now can't hurt him. This isn't going to end up in court, anyway. You want to waste time we don't have getting a no-recourse warrant that we can't file until Vincent is buried?"

"Probably not. What else?"

She reached over and picked up more printouts. "Here's everything I could hack and track on Smiley from the county and municipal sites. Most of it's probably useless, but at least it's a start."

She divided the stack in two. "I've arranged it chronologically by date, starting with county health records, preschool, middle and elementary, his GED in 'ninety-five, on through to the shoot-out statements and death certificate. Couldn't find his birth records. What do you want, Smiley in short pants or Smiley in Kevlar?"

"Smiley in short pants."

She handed me one of the stacks. We spent the next hour reading and making notes. At midnight we were both cranking off yawns, but we had a record of his life as far as county and municipal records took it.

"I'm shot," she said. "Wanta meet first thing for breakfast? Work out a doorbell schedule?"

"Yeah. My brain is fuzzed." I closed my notebook and got to my feet. She followed me to the door. I was just starting to leave, when she reached out and took my arm, stopping me. It was the first time that she had actually touched me.

She looked earnestly at me for a moment, then let go

of my arm and cleared her throat. "Listen, Shane, you say you used to be a loner, that you didn't let people in, but now your personal life is richer. Exactly how did you change that? No matter how hard I try, I'm afraid to trust anyone."

"It was pretty easy once I got the knack," I said, and she leaned forward as if I was about to give her the secret of life.

"When you don't like yourself, it's damn hard to have much of a relationship with anybody else. All you've gotta do is start finding things to like about yourself. Once you learn what they are, find somebody you care about and give those feelings away. What it boils down to is: In order to get, you've gotta give."

"That sounds like New Age bullshit," she replied skeptically.

"Some of the best answers are the easiest," I said. "But at the same time, the easiest answers can be the hardest to understand."

THIRTY-TWO

Matches

Doctor Gouda called Jo at 8 A.M., just as she was leaving her house to meet me for breakfast. She called me and we changed our plans. It was a little after nine when we walked into the print bay of the sheriff's old lab. Doctor Chuck E. Cheese was bent over, studying two enlarged blowups of a fingerprint through a magnifying glass the size of a hotel ashtray.

"I think I got something," he said without turning around. "Enough, at least, to have a serious talk with this guy." He straightened up, hefting his big belly off the table. This morning he was decked out in a tent-sized dashiki large enough to camp under.

"This is the comparison print we rolled at the sheriff's SWAT house yesterday afternoon." He handed Jo a blowup of a right index finger. "We think it belongs to a guy named Pat Dutton. It more or less matches that partial on the three-oh-eight you guys found. Dutton's one of the long guns on the SEB Red team out there."

"The Red team?" I looked over at Jo, surprised that it wasn't someone on Scott Cook's Gray team.

"How sure are you of this match?" Jo asked, holding the blowup and examining it carefully. She had regained her composure from last night, and looked fresh in a crisp white blouse, black slacks, and a blazer.

"As I told you before, this is not a great latent." Doctor Gouda picked up a second photograph, which was of the partial taken from the casing we'd found across the street from Greenridge's house. He laid it next to the photo of the print they'd rolled yesterday, then started pointing out similarities.

"These two tented arches are pretty good matches. Here's half a central pocket whorl that's pretty much on the money. This isle ain't a bad match. Would I take it to court? Probably not. Would I make an investigatory judgment based on it? You bet."

Gouda looked up. "That footprint you plastered was identified by the grunts in Soles and Holes," referring to the footprint and gunshot lab. "Follow me," he said, and waddled out of the fingerprint bay into the room next door.

The GSR lab was a windowless room given over to several large electron microscopes, used for breaking down and reading barium and antimony, the chemicals used to determine gunshot residue. There was one long table for identifying footprints. The three young criminalists working on the equipment sat, heads bowed, eyes pressed to various viewfinders.

"Hey, Ruben, you got that bootprint from Mission Street?" Gouda asked.

An African-American criminalist rose up from a microscope and handed Gouda a photograph from a stack on the footprint table. Clipped to the back of the footprint photograph was some catalogue material from the Danner Boot Company.

"Your print came from a Striker CTX Danner Terra Force jump boot, size twelve," Gouda said. "The print was pushed out a little, but it looks like a narrow foot. Maybe a double-A."

Gouda handed it to Jo, who glanced at it before passing it to me. I knew that Danner boots were big with most cops. They came in a lot of styles. Police officers bought them because they were light, durable high-tops with thick rubber soles and good traction.

Gouda took the photo back. "This one looks pretty fresh. Right from the box. No nicks, cuts, or flaws. It'll be hard to make a positive match."

Thirty minutes later Jo and I were standing in the parking lot of the old crime lab watching for Chief Filosiani to arrive. Ten minutes later he pulled his maroon Crown Victoria into the lot. He was talking on his cell phone as he got out, just closing it up as he approached.

"That was Bill Messenger," he said, holding up the phone. "He got an arrest warrant. We're staying off the scanners to keep the news crews away. Gonna meet our SWAT unit out at South Fetterly in twenty minutes and pick up Pat Dutton."

"Chief, we only have four identifiers," I said. "The criminalist inside says this print's probably not going to stand up in court. We need to polygraph Dutton, if he'll sit for it."

"That'll be up to his lawyers," Tony said.

Just then Sheriff Messenger arrived in the passenger seat of a LASD black-and-white. His face was drawn. He had the arrest warrant in his hand.

We piled into our separate vehicles and followed Sheriff Messenger out to East L.A.

An LAPD SWAT van and a support SUV, along with three black-and-white escort vehicles, were lined up at the curb across from the public library, a block down from the sheriff's SEB building. LAPD SWAT was or-

ganized, more or less, the same as SEB, only each LAPD
team had ten guys, instead of eight.

Tony and Bill had elected not to tell the Justice Department about the arrest until after it was over. ATF was
the agency investigating William Greenridge's murder,
but both chiefs reasoned that emotions were running way
too high. If they were notified, SRT would want to serve
the warrant. Under these sensitive conditions, that
seemed like a really bad idea. Messenger reasoned it
would be far easier and less risky for him to arrest his
own officer, but to keep the LAPD SWAT in reserve.

After they briefed the LAPD SWAT team leader on
how they wanted to serve the warrant, the four of us got
into the Crown Vic. We drove up to the corner and parked
next to SEB's long driveway. Sheriff Messenger used a
cell phone to call the captain in charge of his SWAT
house.

"This is Sheriff Messenger," he told the switchboard
operator. "Who's on the desk this morning?" We waited,
then he said, "Put Captain Otto on please."

A minute later the SWAT commander came on the line
and Messenger told him what he wanted.

I took my Beretta out of my ankle holster and jacked a
round into the chamber, then repacked the nine on my
belt.

"Okay, Captain," Sheriff Messenger said, "I want you
to take Sergeant Dutton to the side door. Make sure he's
not armed. Stand there with him and wait."

He paused while the captain spoke, then said, "Good.
See you in five."

We drove down the winding drive. There were almost
twenty sheriff's black-and-whites of all makes and sizes,
along with four big SWAT vans, parked in the lot beside a
one-story ranch-style building.

Tony pulled around to the side door where a middle-aged, dark-haired captain with a Marine's combat bearing was standing next to a freckled, red-haired man about twenty-five who was chewing a wad of tobacco, occasionally spitting juice into a Styrofoam cup. This was Sergeant Patrick Dutton. He had a confused look on his Irish face.

Tony set the brake and we all got out.

Sheriff Messenger walked over to his SWAT commander and handed him the arrest warrant, then he turned to the red-haired man.

"Sergeant Pat Dutton?" he asked.

"Yes sir," Dutton replied, clearly puzzled.

I looked down and saw that he was wearing Danner Terra Force jump boots laced up over his tan, SEB Weapons Team jumpsuit. But so did the captain and probably two-thirds of the SWAT guys stationed here.

"You're under arrest for suspicion of murder," Messenger said as Captain Otto handed Dutton the warrant.

Dutton's expression barely changed. All that happened was he shifted his tobacco chaw to the other side of his lip, then spit a line of juice into the cup.

"Whatta you kidding?" he said. "Who'd I kill?"

"An SRT agent named William Greenridge," Messenger said.

Dutton looked from me, to Jo, to Chief Filosiani, then back at Sheriff Messenger. An entire new range of emotions now played like a wide-screen movie across his open face: first humor, then disbelief, followed by fear and panic. I knew a split-second before it happened that he was going to bolt.

He lunged away from Captain Otto and headed across the parking lot. I threw myself at him, low and head first, tackling him with a body block below the knees. The move took his legs out and he tumbled over my back. The cup of tobacco juice went flying, but Dutton was a commando and he hit and rolled, coming up to his feet almost immediately.

I've seen fast moves in dojos, seen plenty of black belts working out with each other on police mats, but I wasn't prepared for Sergeant Jo Brickhouse. As Pat Dutton regained his footing, he spun and Jo blocked him with her body, then threw three quick blows: A straight-hand finger strike to his neck, followed by a closed fist shot to the solar plexus. The last was a knee to the groin.

Patrick Dutton went down hard, and seconds later Tony and I had him cuffed and in custody.

"I want an attorney," Dutton gasped at Captain Otto. He was holding his balls and must have swallowed the chaw, because he suddenly gagged, leaned forward, and puked it up at our feet.

THIRTY-THREE

The Other Shoe

The next morning Jo and I were unceremoniously shifted to the backwater of our own investigation.

The ABC news desk had gotten wind of Pat Dutton's arrest. Somebody at SEB or Parker Center had leaked it, along with all of the evidence we had against him. The story about two L.A. SWAT teams gone wild broke nationally on *Good Morning America*.

Alexa called me into her office at 9 A.M. and told me that, for political reasons, the U.S. Attorney was taking charge of the investigation. Jo and I could stay on background, but Cole Hatton had strong-armed the city council and Mayor Mac off the case and was using his own investigating officers. Starting this afternoon, we would report to a couple of GS-12s from the local bureau of the FBI.

There was a press conference scheduled on the fifth floor of Parker Center at 10 A.M. Jo and I were told it was not necessary for us to attend.

We were two blocks away, sitting in a back booth of the Peking Duck restaurant while keeping one eye on the TV that was on in the bar. Half a dozen off-duty dicks from the Robbery-Homicide P.M. watch were sitting in there having a 10 A.M. after-work beer and watching KTLA's field reporter, Stan Chambers, do a pre-event standup in front of an empty podium. The volume was just loud enough to hear from our booth in the next room.

"Sources inside the department indicate that these two SWAT team murders might be connected to the fiery shoot-out that occurred on Hidden Ranch Road ten days ago," Chambers announced. "We'll be waiting right here at Parker Center for this all-important press conference to convene. Back to you, Hal."

I kept one ear on the TV, but turned back to Jo while weather and sports drifted in from the bar.

Jo was saying, "This insurance guy I called says a fifteen-thousand-dollar premium on a universal life policy would pay out almost a million dollars in benefits if it was whole life, which, according to this printout my friend hacked, it was."

A Chinese waiter came over to bring us coffee. Jo asked him for some Equal and he recovered a dish from another table. She immediately began tearing open little blue packets while I sat back and took a sip from my cup. Unfortunately, the blend at the Peking Duck was watery, just like their tea. I guess it's okay when green tea is weak, but weak coffee really sucks. I'd forgotten how bad it could get in here.

I set my cup down and said, "So if Smiley buys a house in Hidden Ranch for five hundred K, where's the other half mil?"

"Don't know. Here's the exact financial picture." She looked down at her notebook. "I went through his tax returns. He deposited four hundred eighty thousand in Glendale S and L at five percent when the policy paid out in 'ninety-six. The house didn't cost five hundred K. He paid three hundred thirty thousand for it in 'ninety-nine, all cash, leaving him with one hundred fifty grand in the S and L. He's been drawing down on that to live. He still has a little under eighty thousand left."

"So, if there's eighty grand in his estate, and nobody is stepping up to collect his body, we gotta figure there's nobody left in his immediate family to claim it."

"Would seem that way. I checked all his bank accounts. No safety deposit box. So, if he did have the missing five hundred thou, maybe it burned up in the fire." She started making her gruel, mixing in the six packets. She was going to end up with brown sugar water. "Or maybe the other half mil's in a fruit jar buried in the backyard," she added as she stirred.

"I can hardly wait to ask Robyn DeYoung to head back out there with a metal detector and her trusty cadet shovel squad."

"I wouldn't do that. There's too many better ways to hide cash these days."

"So, where's the rest of it, then?"

"Don't know," she said. "Boat? Foreign investments? Unlisted house in the Bahamas? Money isn't the motive anyway. Neither was suicide. Pure, kick-ass anger got this done. Vincent was a wannabe cop and a cop-hater with deep psychological problems. He goes fruitcake and barricades himself in his house and starts shooting our troops. He was just killing cops. That was his whole program."

"So you're buying that now?" I said, looking up.

"It took me a while to get there, but yeah, I think that's the reason this all started. But we're just jerking off with all this background. The U.S. Attorney doesn't want to hear it. The case went that-a-way." She jerked a thumb at the TV in the bar.

"I'd still like to know what happened to the five hundred thousand dollars. I get nervous when half a mil is missing."

"Maybe he didn't inherit all of the insurance benefits," she said. "Maybe someone else got some of it."

"Who else is there?"

"His parents could have had debts that needed to be paid off before the insurance could be disbursed."

"Half-a-million-dollars' worth?" I asked skeptically.

She took her first sip of coffee and swallowed it. A faraway look spread across her face, followed by a slow grimace. "That is truly shitty," she said softly, looking down at her cup in disbelief.

"Welcome to the culinary environs of Parker Center. What else did you find?"

She flipped a few more pages in her notebook. "He applied to the L.A. Sheriff's Department in two thousand, like you figured, but was turned down. Nothing in here about why. Our academy doesn't include a psych package in their A-elevens. I called, but nobody there remembers him. They burned me a copy of his file app. Nothing on it looks too different. He was blown out on his preliminary interviews, same as at LAPD."

"Two for two. He must have been a pretty twitchy guy even back then."

She mimicked a high voice. "Mr. Smiley, why do you want to be a deputy sheriff?" Then, in a deep voice, " 'So I can carry a big gun and kick the shit out of people.' . . . Wrong!"

She closed her notebook and looked at me, then added, "No military service, which seems strange. They have guns, grenades, armor-piercing ordnance. Sounds like Smiley's kinda deal. In the mid-nineties enlistment had fallen off so badly that the military would take anybody who had a heartbeat and a temperature above ninety-six degrees. I'm doing a follow-up to see if I can get an answer.

"Oh yeah—he also belongs to a mountain climbing club. The Rock Stars. I put a call in to their president, Marion Bell. Marion's a guy, by the way. We don't need any more gender confusion on this case."

She looked up, waited for my grin, and got it. "He agreed to meet me this afternoon. Didn't sound like a big Smiley fan. Said Vince wanted to learn rock climbing as part of his survivalist training. Apparently he told some of the other members of the club that he was part of some survivalist group, but he was very secretive about which one, or where they hung out. The Rock Stars is a sports club, so Smiley didn't really fit in. Marion said he wasn't surprised when he saw the shoot-out on the news."

She took another tentative sip of her coffee, then pushed it away. "That's Smiley in Kevlar. Let's hear about his roller skate days."

I looked down at my notes. "Went to Glendale Elementary School K to fifth grade, then through Mrs. Kimble's Country Day Middle School in Eagle Rock in sixth and seventh. Then he was in high school for a year, but got pulled out and homeschooled through twelfth grade. GED in 'ninety-five. I'm still looking for his birth records, just in case there's something missing—medical problem from birth, like maybe he was born with a tail and horns and nobody thought to tell Geraldo. I put a wire out to all the county hospitals in Southern California, most should get back to me sometime today or tomorrow."

"Juvie record?" she asked.

"He's got one. But, as you know, according to California State law it was sealed when he turned eighteen."

"Man, I'd like to get my hands on that."

"I'm working on it."

"You little devil," she said. "How?"

"Ve haff our veys."

She smiled at that, so I added, "His doctor retired professionally as well as physically, so we can't get anything there, unless you wanta dig him up and try to restart his heart. That's all I could find by nine thirty this morning."

"We're really sucking wind on this thing!" She was looking at her coffee, twirling her spoon in the cup. "Now that the U.S. Attorney is in charge, we're just doing busy-work." She frowned. "But to be honest, you know I never thought the answer was gonna come out of his past. Now they're just using that to keep us out of the way."

There was certainly something to what she was saying. With the murder of Michael Nightingale this case had turned into a hot grounder. I was pretty sure Alexa was looking out for my career and had put me and Jo on background checks to keep me out of the line of fire.

"Even if we come up with more questions to ask, Hatton's IOs aren't gonna be interested. They're focused on those two SWAT units. We might as well spend the day at the beach," Jo said bitterly.

"Look, we're still officially on the Hidden Ranch investigation. Let the U.S. Attorney's investigators run the Greenridge and Nightingale murders, but for the next four to eight hours, while they're all doing press conferences and organizing evidence, we can still work our case. Nobody is even thinking about that anymore.

"We probably have less than a day before we're gonna be assigned to do grunt work for the FBI. Let's put the time to good use."

She dropped her spoon into her cup and looked over at me. "One thing you said doesn't track," she said, and held my gaze with those incredible mismatched eyes.

"What?"

"This is a nitpick, and it's definitely in the who-gives-a-damn column, but middle school is sixth through eighth grade, not just sixth and seventh."

"So there's a year missing," I said, waving it off. "He drops out of eighth grade, home-schools, then goes back into the ninth grade at Glendale High, drops out in tenth, homeschools again, gets his GED two years later . . ."

"That's a lot of dropping in and out. Whatta you think happened to cause that?"

"Who knows?" I said. But since she mentioned it, I guess it was a little strange. "So you think something is wrong there?"

"Look, Shane, as far as I'm concerned, we're on the sidelines. I'm just saying it sounds screwy."

I thought about it some more. I had to agree.

I glanced over at the bar TV. Tony and Bill Messenger were just stepping up to the podium, along with Brady Cagel and Cole Hatton. Mayor Mac and Supervisor Salazar, politicians that they were, knew a no-win when they saw it and elected not to attend. The press conference was starting. "Wanta see this?" I asked.

"Nope," she said. "My bullshit meter is already red-lined."

I slid out of the booth and drifted into the bar. The Robbery-Homicide detectives made room for me. One of them was a big street monster named Griff Hover, who I'd worked with way back when I was in Valley Patrol. He looked over and smiled.

"Hey, Shane. That's a good-looking pile a bones you got sitting over there." He glanced back at Jo, who had her head down, again going over her notes.

"Yep," I agreed and turned to watch Sheriff Messenger at the microphone.

"We've arrested an L.A. sheriff's deputy named Patrick Dutton and are holding him as a material witness in connection with the murder of ATF Agent William Greenridge. We have identified a shell casing that appears to have been fired from a sniper rifle belonging to the Sheriff's Special Enforcement Bureau. A partial print from that same casing appears to match Deputy Dutton's."

Then Sheriff Messenger stepped aside and made room for Brady Cagel, who was dressed in his tan gab, with his tan face and tan, freshly barbered hair. Everything tan and perfect. A fed.

"Good morning," he said. "I am sorry to have to also confirm that one of the AR-fifteen sniper rifles belonging to the Bureau of Alcohol, Tobacco, Firearms, and Explosives Situation Response Team appears to have been involved in the shooting death of Deputy Sheriff Michael Nightingale. At this time we have not determined which ATF agent, if any, might be involved. The weapon could have been obtained by anyone with access to our armory, even civilian personnel. We are currently requesting that all agents and civilians with access to that particular SRT armory remain in the SWAT house under voluntary curfew. It is our hope that they will also cooperate with polygraph examinations."

He quickly gave way to Cole Hatton, who looked like ten million bucks in a tailored black pinstripe. Hatton cleared his throat, then spoke in his booming baritone.

"There is currently no evidence tying these two murders together. Sheriff Messenger, Agent Cagel, and I are all appalled at the suggestion that members of the ATF Special Weapons units and Sheriff's SEB Special Weapons Team might be gunning for each other after hours. However, until this investigation is complete, I urge the news media and the individual members of both the Los Angeles Sheriff's Department and ATF to please stand down and cooperate with us in every way possible. I promise that, in the end, justice will be served."

"Serve this, dickhead," Griff Hover said as he grabbed his crotch. "These humps at ATF are dirty."

"What about the sheriffs?" one of the other detectives said.

"Hey, the sheriffs might be square badges, but at least they back us up when we need 'em, and they roll on our calls," Griff said.

I went back into the restaurant and paid our bill.

"Dare I ask?" Jo said.

"Come on, don't put me through it. I saw you listening."

"This is about to get a lot messier," she said.

What happened was it got a lot deadlier.

THIRTY-FOUR

Pieces

Jo and I split up and I used the walk back to Parker Center to gather my thoughts. I climbed up the stairs to the fourth floor, taking them two at a time, using the brisk climb to clear my head. Frankly, my spirits were a little low.

I was beginning to think maybe I *had* been wasting my time, like everybody kept telling me. When you got down to it, Jigsaw John retired twenty years ago. Things were different when he was on the job. Back then, each division only had two or three homicides per week. Now we have that many a night. With the growing caseload, there just wasn't time to investigate this way anymore.

In theory, you study pre-event behavior to determine mindset. You look at the victim to see what might have been going on in that person's life to draw the perp in.

If something didn't fit, it could signal a mistake in reasoning, but it didn't have to. It was entirely possible that Smiley had just gone nuts and started shooting like Jo said, and then, because he was completely delusional, had chosen not to use his carefully dug tunnel.

What had been eluding me was a plausible alternate theory. Without that I had no line of logic to follow, nothing to work on.

I suppose it was always possible that these two SWAT teams were shooting at each other, but that was a hard concept for me to buy into. SWAT teams were supposed to be the cream of any law enforcement agency. All the evidence to the contrary, I just couldn't believe that SRT and SEB would try and settle a grudge with long guns. Was that valid reasoning, or just me trying to prop up the last vestige of a once-treasured idea? I wasn't sure any longer.

This afternoon I'd probably be getting a call from one of Hatton's federal IOs, with a new list of things to investigate. They'd treat me like a stupid lackey, ordering me to do scut work they were too busy for. They'd want me to background every member of SRT and SEB, looking for somebody with anger-management problems, or a history of unprovoked violence. There was no chance that the police union was going to let any of them be polygraphed.

I reached my cubicle in Special Crimes on the fourth floor, out of breath from running the stairs, and sank into the chair at my desk. Jo and I had divided our workload. She was going to see if she could get her computer genius to run down the insurance policy. Then she was going out to talk with Marion Bell and any of the members of the Rock Stars mountain climbing club she could locate.

We both had Vincent Smiley down as a loner. It would be worth finding out if he really belonged to some survivalist group or Nazi wilderness outfit. If that proved to be a reasonable alternate theory, it would move this investigation off SWAT and onto an antigovernment hate group. Skinheads always make convincing bad guys.

While Jo was running that down I was going to stay on the few hot trails we'd turned and work my way through Vincent's school years.

Busywork?

I looked up Mrs. Kimble's Country Day Middle School in Eagle Rock and placed a call. When I asked for the director, somebody named Rose Merick came on the line.

"Mrs. Kimble is retired," the sweet-sounding woman said.

One of my little games is to see if, over the phone, I can guess a person's age by their voice tonality. She sounded about sixty. I wrote *60* and put a question mark after it, then circled the number.

This was one of the many ways I attempt to alleviate boredom on the job. Innocent enough, I guess, but boredom, like violence, can change you. Some cops become so tweaked, they carry their emotional remedies to dangerous extremes.

Back in the late seventies, the entire night shift at Devonshire Division was so far into the ozone they devised a weird photo contest. They each put up ten bucks, then ran a monthly competition to see who could come up with the grossest photo. These guys were crawling onto beds with overdosed hookers while their partners snapped Polaroids. That's how screwed up you could get.

Humor is the shield that protects cops from the grim realities we're forced to deal with every day. As your view of life darkens, you can quickly come to believe that most of humanity is primal, corrupt, and deadly. Little by little, if you're not careful, your humor becomes so sick that you're crawling into bed with a dead sixteen-year-old junkie just to get a laugh. The more death and human depravity you see, the more disillusioned you become, until one day you find yourself sitting on a toilet in some restaurant bathroom with the door locked and your service revolver in your mouth. After you pull the trigger nobody you work with even has to ask what went wrong or why you did it. They all know you just couldn't find a way to laugh anymore.

Angrily, I scratched out my *60*, thinking I had better find a more constructive way to dodge my boredom.

"I'm sorry I can't be of more help," Mrs. Merick was saying.

She was about to ring off when I had a thought.

"Do you still have records of your student body from the late eighties?"

"My goodness, no," she said. "That's over fifteen years ago. And if we do, they're in storage someplace. This is a very small facility."

"Were you teaching there during that time?" I asked.

"No. Except for Midge Kimble, I don't think anybody from the eighties is still around."

"Is Mrs. Kimble still in the area?"

"Yes she is."

"Could you give me her number?"

"I could, but I'd need to see your badge first. We can't just give out phone numbers anymore. Times have changed."

"How about you call me back at Parker Center? I'm in Special Crimes. Sergeant Scully. You can get the number out of the book so you'll know it's legit."

"I guess I could do that . . ."

Three minutes later my phone rang. Rose Merick again. She gave me Midge Kimble's number and address.

I called and reached a recording. If Mrs. Merick sounded sixty, Midge Kimble sounded a hundred. *I'm out right now*, a raspy voice shouted. *Leave your number and I'll call back.*

I did as she instructed.

I was gathering my notes, getting ready to head out, when the phone rang again. I snatched it up.

"Scully, it's Cletus."

Clete James was a friend who worked in the Juvenile Justice Division. He was going to try to cut through the red tape and pull Vincent Smiley's early record.

"Your guy Smiley had some juvie busts in 'eighty-eight and -nine, but I'm in a tug of war with the Pasadena City Attorney," he said. "She's being bitchy and set her heels on me. I'm gonna need a court order to open them."

"Pasadena?" I said, writing that in my crime book with the years '88–'89.

"Yeah, that's where all his juvie cases were filed."

"Nothing in my records about Pasadena. I have him living in Glendale, Burbank, and Agoura, going to middle school in Eagle Rock, but nothing in Pasadena."

"Well, Eagle Rock is only a few miles west of Pasadena. I think it's even in the same school district," Clete pointed out.

"Listen, in the late eighties Smiley had to have been about ten or twelve. Can you check to see if there's a bicycle license in Pasadena or Eagle Rock for a Vincent Smiley? Could be under his dad's name, Stanley, or maybe Edna."

"No problem. Hang on for a minute while I log on." Clete came back a few minutes later.

"Got it. Stanley Smiley. A Schwinn Scrambler, registered in March of 'eighty-eight—2346 Mountain Circle, Pasadena."

"Thanks, Clete. I owe ya."

I hung up and pulled a Thomas Street Guide out of my bottom desk drawer. Midge Kimble now lived on the far east side of the L.A. basin, way out in Duarte. I decided I'd start in Smiley's old neighborhood in Pasadena. Once I'd canvassed that, I'd move on east, check out Mrs. K., then head back and stop in at the hospital in Pasadena. I figured, if Vincent lived there in '88, there was an outside chance he was born in Pasadena at Huntington Hospital. I packed my stuff and headed out.

Mountain Circle is a side street off a main drag called Fair Oaks Boulevard, which runs north and south, stretching up into the Pasadena foothills. The further up Fair Oaks you go, the more sketchy and run-down it gets. I quickly found myself in a mostly black and Hispanic neighborhood. Single-story, run-down houses sat next to three-story, brown stucco project buildings that, when they were built, were heralded as the answer to urban blight, but within years had turned into urine-soaked, graffiti-marked monstrosities.

As I passed the Foothill Projects I witnessed a drug deal going down through a chain-link fence, right in plain view. The seller was a thirty-year-old banger dirtbag in a hooded blue sweatshirt and satin basketball shorts. The buyers looked like two fifteen-year-old girls. I didn't stop. *Not my turf. Why sweat what you can't change?* I told myself.

I knew, even as these thoughts hit me, that I was wrong. Every time I see something like that and instead of stopping choose to just drive on and give it a wave, I know I'm losing a small part of myself. I become a little more jaded and skeptical with each lost opportunity. But experience taught me that if I did stop and chase that dealer and those teenagers through the projects and caught them, I'd likely face angry parents who would claim that I'd used unnecessary force during the arrest. They would file charges against me and then the crowded court system would plead the busts down to misdemeanors rather than prosecute. In the end, nothing much would have changed, except that a few more 181 complaints would be added to my IAD file.

Why bother? It won't change anything. But, of course, it does. It changes you.

I found Mountain Circle almost in the foothills, turned right, and eventually pulled up across the street from 2346. It was a small wooden house that had definitely seen better days. The long-dead lawn had been beaten into a hard dirt playground littered with broken plastic toys. An old black Cadillac Brougham with a single hubcap and primered trunk was parked in the driveway.

I walked up to the door and rang the bell. The broken ringer snapped and buzzed like an angry wasp. Moments later the door opened to chain width and an angry black woman of indeterminate age glared out at me.

"Police?" she said, before I could even get my badge out. Something, some vibe had warned her that I was The Man and up to no good, even though I was smiling.

I showed her my shield and she glared at it with contempt. She'd seen dozens of badges, and experience told her it always turned out badly.

"Are you the owner of the house?" I asked.

"Got a warrant?"

"No, ma'am," I said. "I'm just trying to find out if there's anybody living here who remembers Stan and Edna Smiley. They owned this house back in the eighties."

"Ain't no Smileys here," she growled.

"No—I know that. They *used* to live here. I wonder if there's anybody still in the neighborhood who might remember them from back then."

She looked at me with shrewd distrust. "What dis be about?" she said. " 'Nother nigger goin' down?"

"No, ma'am, the Smileys were Caucasian."

Maybe she was glad to see some white assholes finally getting popped, or maybe she just wanted to be done with me. Either way, she blurted out the answer:

"Try the Phillips. They 'cross the street on the corner. Been here forever."

Then, without waiting for my thank you, she slammed the door in my face.

Across the street I saw a set of curtains close. You could almost feel a warning pulsing through the neighborhood. *Cop on the block.* How many eyes were watching me? Hard to say. I felt exposed, like a soldier caught behind enemy lines. I walked up on the Phillipses' front porch and rang the doorbell.

"Who is it?" a high-pitched man's voice yelled.

My estimate? Seventy-five at least. Call that my last guess. One for the road.

"Police," I called through the door. "Mr. Phillips, I have a few questions about a case we're working. Maybe you can help us," trying to sound like Ed McMahon delivering a million dollars.

After a moment I heard half a dozen latches being thrown. The door creaked and a very old man was standing in front of me. His skin was so white I could see blue veins on the backs of his hands and around his temples. I'd undershot my guess by at least twenty years. A complete Magoo—round, hunched, half blind, and almost bald, he was dressed in a frayed checkered shirt, tan slacks, and old tennis shoes. A hearing aid the size of a bottle cap stuck out of his right ear, and thick, horn-rimmed magnifiers rode his bony nose.

"What was that you said?" he shouted at me, reaching for the volume on his hearing aid.

"Can I come in, sir?" I held up my badge.

He squinted at it. "Pasadena police?"

"Los Angeles."

"Fucking drugstore glasses," he mumbled.

Without saying anything further, he turned and hobbled into his living room.

I followed, breathing in Vicks VapoRub and mildew.

"Who is it, Albert?" a woman shrilled from the back.

"I got it. Go back to yer soaps," he yelled.

We sat on his uncomfortable coil-sprung sofa and he leaned forward.

"We don't give to no charities," he shouted, without warning. "Police included. Food Stamps. Social Security. You want money from us, gonna have to knock out our teeth and steal our fillings." Then he laughed. It was a strange, high-pitched, braying hee-hee.

"No, sir. This isn't for money. It's about a case we're working on."

"A what?" He leaned in and again cranked up the volume on his hearing aid. It started screeching, but he didn't seem to notice.

"Sir, I think you should maybe turn that down a little."

He looked at me, blinking like a lizard on a flat rock, but made no attempt to adjust the volume.

I plunged on. "Do you remember the Smileys?" I asked loudly. "Stanley and Edna? They lived across the street at 2346 back in 'eighty-eight or 'eighty-nine."

"Right," he said. But I wasn't sure he'd heard me.

"Edna and Stanley Smiley," I repeated.

"Yeah—that fucking plumber," he said. "I had him work on this place once. Fucked up everything. Had shit running out the overflow pipe in the backyard. We was on septics back then."

"Do you remember their child? He would've been about eleven or twelve."

"Which one?"

"What?"

"Which kid? Had two—boy and a girl."

"A boy and a girl?" I said, taking out my notebook.

"Ain't that just what I said? What's wrong? Y'deaf?" He actually said that to me while his hearing aid was wailing like an air-raid siren.

"How old was the girl?"

"Shit—how do I know? They was little kids 'bout eight or ten, both around the same age."

"Albert, who is it?" the woman demanded impatiently from the back.

He ignored her, or maybe he didn't hear her.

"Can you tell me anything else about them? What were their names?"

"The girl was Susan, the boy—can't remember what they called the little bastard. Both were assholes. Loud. Playing outside all hours. The parents were drinkers. Them kids was out sometimes riding their bikes around after ten o'clock at night, makin' noise. Edna and Stan inside, drunk as skunks."

"Was the boy's name Vincent?" I asked.

"Don't remember, mighta been. It wasn't like all I had t'do back then was watch the fuckin' plumber's house," he snapped. "If you say he was named Vincent, fine. Ain't gonna get no argument from me."

"How long did they live here?"

"One year. One year and one year only. Just one year." Why he said it four times, I have no clue.

"And then what? They sold the house and left?"

He thought about that, then nodded and sliced a withered hand through the air between us. "Good riddance. Fuck 'em."

He finally reached up and turned down the ear piece.

"You don't happen to have any pictures, do you?" I asked.

"Why would I take pictures o'assholes?" he said reasonably.

"And you have no idea where they moved to?"

"Nope."

"Albert, who is it?" the woman yelled again.

He didn't answer, but I knew he heard her this time, because an annoyed look followed.

"Well, thank you, sir. You've been a big help."

I walked to the front door, then turned back to say good-bye. A strange, troubled expression appeared on his pale face. I thought he was about to say something, but he just lifted one haunch and farted. I let myself out.

Once outside I called Jo on my cell phone. She picked up on the second ring.

"I might know what happened to the other five hundred thou," I told her.

"Let's hear."

"Smiley had a sister named Susan. Maybe she got the other half. The old man I talked to said he couldn't remember if Vincent was the boy's name or not, but the guy was ancient. Waiting for the chariot."

In light of that, we decided to scotch what we were doing and meet to reorganize at a restaurant I knew in Pasadena.

THIRTY-FIVE

Twin Palms

The Twin Palms Restaurant was developed by Cindy Costner in the mid-nineties. It's located on Green Street, just one block south of Colorado Boulevard in Old Town Pasadena. Old Town is one of the great redevelopment stories in Southern California. Back in the eighties it was a slum. Situated at the west end of Colorado Boulevard, it had become a hangout for winos, hookers, and hugger-muggers. Drug dealers hung on every corner selling bags of cut. Low-end secondhand stores were lumped in with all the urban decay, and the entire nine- or ten-block area had completely slid off the human spectrum into some sort of environmental hell.

Then a group of entrepreneurs saw an opportunity. They bought the land cheap and tore down the slums, while saving the period architecture. They lured in retail chains and designer shops and sprinkled in some upscale sidewalk restaurants with colorful Cinzano umbrellas shading decorative wrought iron tables. Presto! Four years later, Old Town became a shopper's mecca. Caffe Mocha and sushi bars, Tommy Bahama and The Gap. The winos moved east and started camping out under the freeway.

I pulled to the curb in front of the white-tented patio restaurant, then handed my keys to a red-coated valet and walked around the corner to the gated entrance. I didn't have a reservation, but it was a large place and there were enough tables so that you could be seated without too long a wait. I spotted Jo over at the bar. In one fist she had a Coors Light, the other was up to her mouth, head tilted back, tossing salted peanuts down her throat. Nothing too delicate there.

"You beat me," I said.

"Story of our short little partnership," she said, then slid off the stool and followed the hostess to a table over by the wall, taking the preferred gunfighter's seat looking out at the room, leaving me with the chair facing a slab of concrete. I settled in and ordered a Corona with a lime squeeze.

As I watched our hostess walk away to give my order to the bartender, Jo said, "So the neighbor says there were two kids. A boy *and* a girl."

"That's right. Susan and a boy, probably Vincent, both around the same age."

"Twins?" she said, looking up at me with a hunter's predatory gaze.

"I don't know. He didn't say."

"Twins would have the same DNA, right?" She was leaning forward now, a pointer on scent. "What if that was Smiley's twin sister they found in the bathtub up at Hidden Ranch Road? What if he *did* go out through the tunnel like you thought?" Loving her connect-the-dots theory, looking intently at me, waiting for me to pump my fist and go "Yesss!"

Instead, I felt myself frowning. "To begin with, we don't know if they were twins or not. Second, a girl and a boy would be fraternal twins, not identical."

"So what?" she said brushing that aside with an impatient gesture.

"We have an identical DNA match at the morgue. A boy and a girl can't have identical DNA. Fraternal twins don't look the same or have to be the same sex, because they come from two separate female eggs fertilized by two separate male sperms."

"You're sure about that?"

"No, I'm just saying it to mess up your theory."

"Look, you don't have to be copping attitude all the time. It was just a question."

"I was dealt off to a foster family in Torrance when I was seven. They had fraternal twins. Tom and Morgan Weiss. I had it explained half a dozen times. To have identical DNA, they have to be identical twins. That's the way it is."

"But all of a sudden we've got an extra kid here. Maybe his sis can fill in some of the blanks." She was jazzed. "So how do we find Susan?" she asked.

"We go back through county records. Start hunting. Of course, Susan might be married now. Different name."

She thought for a minute, then finally said, "How do you want to do this?"

"Huntington Hospital is only a mile or two from here, down Arroyo. If they lived here, maybe that was where they were born, and you can access Edna Smiley's prenatal records for the mid- to late seventies, find out for sure if they were twins, or if they were just brother and sister. Susan could have been a few years younger or older than Vincent. Mr. Phillips wasn't too sure of anything. Maybe there's other family listed on that form that we can contact."

"What're you going to do?" she asked.

"I'm gonna go see Midge Kimble. Maybe Susan went to that school with her brother and she can remember something."

Just then my cell phone rang. I looked at the readout: Jeb Calloway.

"Who is it?" she asked.

"My skipper." I turned the phone off and put it back on my belt.

"Aren't you gonna take it?"

"It's just him telling me to contact the IOs at Justice. The minute I do that we're gonna both get turned into info humpers for the FBI. Turn yours off, too. Let's be out of cell range for a while." She reached into her purse and switched off her cell.

The waiter came over and handed us menus. "Something for lunch?" he asked.

"Sorry, we're going to have to leave. Something just came up," I told him.

While we were waiting outside for our cars Jo touched my arm, and I turned to face her.

"I hate to tell you this, Hoss, but you were right. If we hadn't been reworking Smiley's background we would have completely missed this. Feels important, like it might lead somewhere."

"But let's not get carried away. So far, all we have are questions and we only have a few hours to get the answers before we're yanked in another direction."

"Maybe you should learn to take a fucking compliment yourself," she grinned. Then she did a strange thing—she reached out and took my hand. "Don't get the wrong idea here, Scully, this is purely professional, but as partners go, you ain't half bad."

Our cars arrived. She had managed to get the green Suburban back from Vice. She got in and, without looking back, roared off toward Huntington Hospital. A few minutes later I was in the Acura on my way to see what Midge Kimble had to offer.

My nose was definitely twitching. Or, as Jigsaw John might have said, "We got our first whiff of something good here, boy."

THIRTY-SIX

Midge

Royal Oaks Manor turned out to be an upscale assisted-living facility. As I pulled up the drive I saw a large expanse of rolling lawns and neo-Spanish Colonial buildings. This wasn't your standard linoleum floor and vinyl couch old folks' home. There were attractive, tile-roofed buildings separated by expensive floral landscaping. The residences all had their own two-car garages. There was a large medical facility off to the east side of the property, next to a tennis court and a large common patio. I pulled in and parked between a new red Mercedes and a black Lincoln Town Car, then walked up the manicured path to the main building. Inside the spacious contemporary lobby I found a house phone, dialed zero, and asked for Midge Kimble. A minute later I heard the familiar shouted greeting from her answering machine.

I hung up and went to the front desk. An elderly man working over some papers glanced up at me.

"I'm looking for Midge Kimble," I told him.

"Today is bridge day," he said. "She's out in the Culture Center Annex."

"Where's that?"

"Through the main lobby, down the corridor. It's the pavilion on the right."

I thanked him and made the trip. If you were stuck waiting for the Grim Reaper, this was certainly the place to do it. The windows offered views of beautiful trees and flowering bushes. Purple bougainvillea trellised off latticework set up in each of the small, landscaped areas. Outside the main sliding glass doors, Brown Jordan outdoor furniture sat on a large, pebbled, concrete patio, all of it washed clean, sparkling in the afternoon sunshine.

The Culture Center Annex was an art exhibit area off the main building. I walked into a high-ceilinged room filled with older, well-dressed men and women studiously playing bridge. There were at least ten card tables, all fully occupied, everybody bent forward, intent on their cards. For a room full of people, it was strangely quiet. I didn't quite know where to start. This place seemed so upscale, I couldn't just shout out Midge's name. Sensing my dilemma, a woman seated at the table nearest me reached out and touched my arm. I turned toward a pleasant octogenarian in a pink pillbox hat.

"You look lost," she said sweetly.

"I'm looking for Midge Kimble."

"In the blue dress over by the window." She smiled, so I smiled back. "Nice to have such fine young people come visit," she said.

Right then I didn't feel very fine or young, but I thanked her and walked over to the table and waited until the foursome finished a hand and started throwing their cards into the center.

"Excuse me, are you Midge Kimble?" I asked the woman in the blue dress.

"I am." Her voice was strong and didn't even resemble her shouted message on the answering machine. She was close to eighty, but there had been a time when she would have stopped traffic. The remnants of beauty still clung stubbornly to her strong, wrinkled face.

"I hate to interrupt your game, but I have a few questions."

"In that case, you have excellent timing," she said a bit too loudly.

"I do?"

"I'm the dummy."

"I beg your pardon?"

"It's a bridge term," she said, smiling. "After the bid on the next hand I lay my cards down. Don't have to do anything after that. It's called being the dummy."

"Oh—I never played bridge."

I watched as the cards were dealt and a round of bidding started.

"Three spades," one of the women said.

"Four hearts," another answered.

"Four spades," a third said. It went on like that for a while until finally Midge said:

"Trump." Then she laid down her hand face up, rose, and accompanied me to an alcove in the adjoining room.

Midge Kimble was spry and athletic. She moved with authority and purpose. We sat down and she fixed a polite smile on her face, waiting for me to begin. She had inbred grace and refined social bearing.

"This is nice out here," I started, apropos of absolutely nothing. I hate to admit this, but, sometimes when I'm in the presence of money or culture my normal self-confidence can suddenly desert me. Another curse visited on me by my childhood. I had a sudden revealing thought: *Did I become a cop so I'd have social authority and could use my badge to gain emotional status, and to build a wall between me and my insecurities?*

"My husband was a developer," she was saying. "He actually put up two of these buildings when we moved out here. The Kimble Rec Center across from B unit was his. You can see it on the right when you drive out."

"So the school was just a hobby?" I said, putting the pieces together thinking, her husband had the gelt and she ran the country day school for kicks.

"Not a hobby—a treasured vocation," she said, fixing me with a stern look.

My smile felt hot on my face. I immediately pulled out my badge and showed it to her.

"Oh my goodness," she said. "I knew I shouldn't have borrowed Lillian's jewelry and not returned it."

"I'm sorry?"

She smiled. "I'm just fooling, Sergeant. When you get to my state in life, you need to take your laughs where you can find them." The same argument the humps in Devonshire had used.

But I liked her. Instantly I felt more at ease.

"This is about a young boy who I believe went to your school, named Vincent Smiley. It was around 'eighty-eight or 'eighty-nine. Do you remember him?"

"Yes." Her expression softened slightly, or maybe it saddened. "Vividly," she added.

"I was wondering if you could tell me a little about him?"

"It was one of the strangest things that ever happened during all the years I ran that school."

"Start at the beginning," I said, and whipped out my trusty notebook, clicked down my pen, then poised over a fresh page, all business now. Sergeant Scully on the case.

"The Smiley children first came to school in the sixth grade. Paul and Susan."

"Paul, not Vincent?"

"If you'll let me finish, I'm getting to that."

"Sorry."

I wrote down PAUL AND SUSAN SMILEY, underlined PAUL, then wrote KIMBLE COUNTRY DAY—'88.

"Paul was very bright and outgoing. His twin sister, Susan, was extremely shy. Almost never said anything."

So they were twins, I thought, writing that down.

Midge was saying, "They didn't get along, which seemed strange for twins, but they were both excellent students."

"Sixth grade—that made them about twelve."

"Yes. Twelve."

"At the end of seventh grade something very extraordinary happened."

"What was that?"

"Susan Smiley was in the girls' restroom when one of the other little girls happened to open the bathroom stall. Susan had forgotten to lock it and this other girl saw that Susan had a penis. She was standing up in her blonde ringlets and dress, urinating right into the toilet."

"Susan was a boy."

"Yes. It turned out that Susan was really Vincent. We took the child into the nurse's office and called his parents in. Stanley Smiley didn't come, but his mother Edna did. We forced an inspection in her presence so we could see for ourselves. Well, I must tell you, nobody was prepared for what happened next. Mrs. Smiley went into a white rage. I think she was a drinker and was maybe a little drunk at that meeting. She started shouting that she didn't care what I or anybody thought. She didn't want twin boys, always wanted a daughter. So she raised Vincent as Susan. She let his hair grow long and had been dressing him as a girl since he was an infant."

She sat back and looked at me, the sad memory of this rich on her face. "Once Mrs. Smiley told us that, it explained everything. Vincent's shy behavior when he was being Susan, the fact that the twins seemed to hate each other. It was an impossible situation. All over school the children were talking about it. We had to call a school assembly with everybody's parents to discuss the situation. Twelve is an awkward age, and sexuality becomes a growing concern. I knew that it would be a mistake to try and keep the Smiley boys at school. The school year was almost over, so I made arrangements for them to finish the grade work at home."

"And then they were homeschooled the following year?" I said.

"Yes. We called in Child Services. There was a major argument about taking the children away from the Smileys. But, since they weren't being physically abused, there was no way to remove them from the home, because, when you came down to it, they had only violated a school dress code. We signed an affidavit and the boys were homeschooled for the eighth grade. We supplied the curriculum, then the boys went off to Glendale High in ninth grade."

"As boys this time?"

"Yes. Vincent and Paul registered at Glendale High."

"Do you know about the car accident that killed their parents?" I asked.

"Strange you should mention that. When it happened I think the police suspected Vincent. They came and talked to me. Back then he was still a juvenile, around seventeen I believe."

"So the results of that investigation would be locked in his juvenile record," I said, making a note. This explained why the C.A. wouldn't release Vincent's file. She obviously had read all of his juvie records for Pasadena and Glendale and knew it would be used at the SWAT trial. Without a court order mandating its release, she'd have a lot of explaining to do.

"I think the police suspected Vincent of foul play," Midge was saying. "I know they picked him up and talked to him. The Smileys had moved to a house off

Cliff View in Glendale. There was a steep incline that went down from their house. One evening, Stanley and Edna's brakes failed. They went over the cliff on the last turn. The car burned, so nothing much was left for the police to examine. Eventually, it just went into the records as an accident."

Fat chance, I thought.

"He was out of high school after that—in junior college," she went on. "That was the last I heard of him, until that shoot-out two weeks ago." She frowned. "That poor boy probably never had much of a chance, did he?"

"Thank you, Mrs. Kimble. You've been a huge help." I stood to go. "If you think of anything else call me at that number." I put down my card.

"You should try and get in touch with his brother Paul. I think he lives up in San Francisco. He might be able to tell you something."

"I can't," I said. "Paul's dead."

THIRTY-SEVEN

Union Park

I couldn't reach Jo on the phone, but then, like an asshole, I'd told her to keep her cell off to avoid getting called in by the FBI. My next try was Alexa.

She was in Cole Hatton's office and stepped out of a heated debate to take my call. Since the meeting was just breaking up, she agreed to get together with me in Union Park across the street from the Federal Building in thirty minutes.

I hit the gas and cut through traffic, banging on my horn, going Code 2, breaking red lights all the way to the freeway. Then I slammed the pedal down, doing almost ninety on the 110 and took the Chinatown off-ramp to Union Park. It was a little past one o'clock when I grabbed a metered parking place and got out. I saw Alexa in a great-looking black dress I'd bought her for her birthday. She was standing over by a hot dog vendor buying a foot-long, saw me coming, and met me halfway.

"Sit down," I told her. "So you don't drip mustard on my favorite outfit." We settled on a bench nearby.

"What is it that couldn't wait an hour until I got back to the office?" she said. She still looked way too stressed to me.

"If I told you that Vincent Smiley was alive, that he went out that tunnel Jo and I found under his house, what would you say?"

"That it's impossible. His DNA was crossmatched. The man's positively dead."

"Smiley had an identical twin brother named Paul. Identical twins have identical DNA."

She sat there taking this in. Then she said, "Had?"

"My bet is it was the twin who did the flambé in the bathtub. It's a long story why, but Paul and his twin brother Vincent hated each other. My theory is Vince lured his brother down from San Francisco, or maybe even kidnapped him. Either way, he gets Paul out to Hidden Ranch. He ties him up and waits. When Emo shows up he starts a shoot-out, conks his brother, and leaves him in the tub, then crawls out through the tunnel we found."

"And you think Vincent is the one murdering the SWAT team guys." She furrowed her brow, trying to fit the pieces.

"That's my guess. He hates cops because they wouldn't accept him so he arranges his death using Paul as a stand-in. Then he crawls out through the tunnel. He pops Greenridge first, then does Nightingale to get a SWAT war going between the sheriff's department and ATF, sits back, and watches it go down on TV. I've been looking at this guy's early life, and we have a very sick puppy here."

"What about the shell casings? We found shell casings at both crime scenes that match long guns at both SEB and SRT. One of them has a partial print that matches an SEB deputy."

"I've been thinking about that on the way over here. SRT does their SWAT training out in Moorpark, at a range they have there. Sheriff's do it at Spring Ranch,

near Agoura. I've been to Spring Ranch. You can see the
firing range from the road. How hard would it be to hide
out on the road until an SEB SWAT team shows up for
target practice, wait till they leave, and sneak in and pick
up the brass from the long guns?

"It never quite worked for me, that Patrick Dutton was
on the SEB Red team and not Scott Cook's Gray team.
Now it makes a lot of sense. Smiley couldn't tell who
fired which casing. He just knew it was all SWAT ordnance that would eventually be matched to one of their
sniper rifles."

Alexa sat looking at me, the hot dog forgotten in her
hand. "Shit," she said softly, then dropped the uneaten
dog in the trash.

"My guess is Vince got the two-twenty-three casings
from the SRT range in Moorpark and the three-oh-
eights from the sheriff's SWAT range. He set up the
phony shooting sites, the secondary crime scenes, left
the three-oh-eight casing in the apartment across the
street from Greenridge's house and the two-twenty-
three behind Nightingale's, along with the Danner boot
prints, for us to find. We all thought the shooter was
making it too easy, not picking up his brass. That's
why! He needed us to find them. He was setting a
frame."

"I'm going to go talk to Tony and Bill. Then we need to
take it to Cole." Alexa stood. "Where are you going to be?"

"I've gotta find my partner. She's disappeared."

"Okay, but turn your damn phone on. I got a call from
Cal. He said he can't reach you. Who do you think you're
fooling with that shit?"

"If I'd answered that call, I'd have spent the morning
downtown sorting through SRT folders, and we wouldn't
have any of this, so you tell me," I said.

She nodded, turned to go, then turned back and unexpectedly kissed me. A bright smile suddenly appeared on her face. The first one I'd seen in two weeks.

"You're the best damn detective on the force," she told me.

"Wanta fuck?" I asked.

"Hold the thought. I'll get right back to you on that."

Then she spun and ran across the park toward Parker Center.

THIRTY-EIGHT

Where's Brickhouse?

Jigsaw John was a genius. No wonder the guy cleared 85 percent of his cases. I sat in the park, looking up Union Street at Parker Center, trying to pin down the last pieces of the puzzle. Smiley had used identical weapons from his own armory to shoot Nightingale and Greenridge. Mr. Magoo couldn't remember the correct ages of the twins. He'd guessed too young. They weren't eight or ten, they were twelve. An easy enough mistake for an old grump with no kids. The Smileys moved away in one year because of the fiasco at Midge's school. Changed school districts, left Pasadena, went to Glendale.

My guess was that Jo Brickhouse was still out in Pasadena at the hospital. I called and asked for someone in admitting or records, did my badge number boogie, and was told that nobody from the L. A. Sheriff's Department had been there looking at birth records.

Okay—so, where was my strong-willed partner?

I called the Sheriff's Bureau, reached Jo's office at Internal Affairs, and asked them if they'd heard from her. Nada.

Where are you, kid? Then uneasiness struck. A sense of impending disaster swept down on me. A fluttering of dark wings in my mind, stirring dead air in my empty head.

Why did I tell her to keep her cell off? Stupid.

But I'd solved it. *We'd* solved it.

From here on it was just a straight-up system bust, put out a BOLO: Be on the lookout. Wait until some passing squad car made the spot, take Mr. Smiley off to jail, or if he wanted to do the dance, plant him right where we find him. Either way, Jo and I were out of it. For us it was over. Nothing bad was headed our way. I tried to ignore my premonition of disaster.

"You got five dollars?" a gruff voice said.

I looked up at a homeless man, about fifty, with matted hair and taped-up sneakers.

"I'm starvin'. Ain't et for a day."

"I know where you can get a good meal."

I reached down into the trash and fished out Alexa's uneaten hot dog. It was still warm and wrapped in white paper. I handed it to him.

"What the fuck am I gonna do with that?" he said.

"Eat it. Nothing wrong with it."

He shook his head. His expression, a symphony of disgust.

"Ain't the way it works, asshole." He dropped the dog back into the trash, turned, and limped away.

Yeah? So, how does it work? I wondered. *I give you the fin, so you can buy more malt liquor? Keep you drinking malt 40s until your leaking kidneys finally rot? That how it works, asshole?*

I had a moment of sweeping remorse. I had been so focused on the case for the last ten days, it had completely consumed me. Now that it looked like we had the answers, I was feeling empty and alone, sitting on a bench in a park full of strangers. Again, my case had moved on without me. I needed to clear my head, so I decided to call and see if Chooch was having football practice this afternoon. He'd said he would leave a message on the phone to give me the time and location. I called our answering machine and, sure enough, Chooch's voice greeted me.

"This is for Dad: four o'clock—same place in Agoura. It's looking up. I've got some real animals on this team."

Just as I was about to hang up I heard another voice.

"Hoss, this is Jo. I found Susan Smiley's address." She sounded jazzed. "I had someone in my office go through all the phone books. We found a listing. She lives in Inglewood, off Centinela, near Vincent Park. Three-four-six Hillside. Since we're running out of time, I'm on my way over there now. If you get this message you can meet me there. In the meantime, I'm going to go ahead and brace her woman-to-woman, see how much I can get. Wish me luck."

I hit the ground running before the message was complete. Jo didn't know that Susan was Vincent.

I reached the Acura and squealed out, jamming my finger on the GPS to bring up the map screen. The most direct route to Inglewood was straight down La Brea. It was just a little past one in the afternoon, so, with the lunch traffic, I'd probably make better time on surface streets than by trying to get over to the freeway.

I roared down Exposition, breaking lights, then hung a left onto La Brea. I don't have a MCT in my personal car, so, with no computer, I turned on the police scanner under the dash and put out a call for backup.

"This is L-nineteen. Officer requests backup at three-four-six Hillside in Inglewood. One plainclothes female officer with blond hair in a blue jacket is already on the scene. Perp at this address is a possible One-eight-seven P. Request a unit respond Code Three."

The RTO came back immediately and put out the call division-wide. Unit A-22 was assigned Code-3.

All the way down La Brea I cursed myself for having Jo turn off all her communication equipment, a complete breach of police procedure. How could I have been such a jerk?

I passed Slauson.

I was praying this was another Susan Smiley, but the way my luck had been running, I doubted it. Vincent had been Susan Smiley all the way through seventh grade. Susan was his alter ego. In trouble, hiding from the law, I was pretty sure he'd choose to be Susan again. If he did, then Jo Brickhouse was walking right into another vertical coffin.

After I passed Fairview, I heard a siren converging on my left. In the LAPD, only one unit at a time can go red-light-and-siren. The reason is, if two units both have their sirens on, they can't hear one another. As they both get close to the address, the chance of a high-speed collision grows exponentially. Way too many units crashed before this rule was in place.

I could hear the crosstalk on the scanner. One-Adam-22 was about four blocks to my right as I turned on Hyde Park. I was now inside of Inglewood. All the way down La Brea I had been trying to dial in my GPS. Finally I had the address programmed in. Hillside was about four blocks up, off Field Street.

I saw Field, hung a right, then turned right again. Finally I was on Hillside. I'd beaten the squad cars. Half a block away I saw Jo's green Suburban parked at the curb. I didn't want to come sliding in hot, squealing rubber because I didn't know what kind of a situation I had and didn't want to announce myself with a high-speed, tire-smoking stop. I pulled over half a block up, unholstered my Beretta, then made a low run across the street and up the grass onto the front porch at 346.

Nobody seemed to be home. The house was a small one-story, wood-sided number, badly in need of paint. The yard was overgrown. It looked deserted, but if Vincent had bought it as a place to hide out after the shoot-out, I didn't see him wasting a lot of time on maintenance.

Then I heard a gun shot.

Seconds later I heard a car start in the back of the house. I ran to the corner of the porch and peeked down the driveway. A huge black Ram 2500 truck, with high-suspension and dual tires on the rear, came flying right at me. Smiley was behind the wheel. At least I think it was him. He was wearing a woman's blonde wig, lipstick, and hoop earrings. Man-sized muscular forearms gripped the wheel. I jumped back as he roared past. Then I fired three shots at the fleeing truck. I broke some glass, but that was about it.

The black-and-white patrol car was just screaming up Hillside, going Code-3. Smiley steered the bigfoot Dodge right at it. In this deadly game of chicken, the huge, high-centered, pipe-grilled truck was bound to win. At the last moment Adam-22 swerved, hit the curb, and blew out its suspension skidding up on somebody's front lawn, tearing deep furrows in the grass. The Dodge disappeared up the street, smoking rubber around the corner. I knew Jo had to be in big trouble, but my first duty was to get Adam-22 back into the pursuit. I ran toward the squad car holding my badge out in front of me.

"LAPD! Take the black Acura. Go after him." I threw my keys at them. "He's a cop killer! Get it on the radio! Ida-May-Victor, five-eight-seven." I yelled the truck's plate number and immediately one of the cops was putting it out on the air while the other ran to my car. He got in my Acura, his partner finished his broadcast and dove in beside him. They squealed away up the street after the Dodge truck.

I ran back to the house with my gun drawn, heading up the driveway, moving fast, but carefully.

Jo was lying up on the back patio, a messy hole high in her chest. I ran to her and kneeled down, put my hand on her throat to check for a heartbeat. The bullet had entered just above her heart and had gone through her lung, blowing out a large exit hole in her back.

After a minute, Jo opened her eyes, looked up at me and started to speak.

"Save your strength," I said. Then I took off my jacket and slid it underneath her, putting it over the larger exit wound in her back, making a compress, pushing it tight.

She started to cough.

I grabbed my cell, dialed 911, ordered an ambulance, and put out an officer down. Then I prayed they'd get there in time.

Jo's face was turning pale and slick, her eyes were losing focus. I stroked her forehead and held her hand.

"This still ain't gonna get you laid, Hoss," she whispered softly.

THIRTY-NINE

E.R.

Jo didn't speak again and lapsed into unconsciousness. I was holding her in my lap, watching the life leak out of her. Finally I heard the ambulance siren arrive out front, and the EMTs pulled into the drive. I yelled out and they quickly found us in the back.

The rest was a blur. I wandered around in the backyard trying to keep my wits about me as they loaded her on a gurney and set up an IV bag. I felt weak and nauseous. I was shaking, beginning to come unstrapped.

They lifted Jo into the ambulance and I hitched a ride, sitting in the front seat of the rescue unit with Jo's black leather purse in my lap.

"Get this thing moving," I snapped at the driver who was slowly edging the big ambulance out onto the street.

Then we were speeding out of Inglewood on the way to the L.A. County King/Drew Medical Center, which was only five miles away. The siren heehawed, clearing traffic all the way down Crenshaw Boulevard to the hospital.

I found a spot in the E.R. waiting room as anxious surgeons ran down from the O.R. upstairs. Finally, I opened Jo's purse and used her cell phone to call her office. I told her lieutenant supervisor what happened, then hung up and scrolled through the numbers. I found a listing for BOLLINGER, BR. *Bridget?* I pushed dial and in a moment I had Sheedy, Long, and Bollinger Advertising.

"Is Bridget Bollinger there?"

"Ms. Bollinger? Just a minute," the operator said. Then I was connected with some guy in New Accounts.

"I'm trying to speak with Bridget Bollinger," I told him.

"Who may I say is calling?"

"I'm a friend of Josephine Brickhouse's."

"Moment, please," he said and put me on hold. I was listening to an inane muffler shop jingle.

He came back on a minute later.

"Ms. Bollinger cannot be disturbed. She's with an account," he said.

"Hey, Sonny—this is Sergeant Scully, LAPD, and it's a police matter. You tell *Ms.* Bollinger to get her ass on the phone right now or I'll come down there and put the whole building in cuffs."

I was shaking, my nerves and emotions in a boil. *Calm down,* I lectured myself. *This isn't the way you get results.* I was back on hold. Then a minute later I heard a female voice that was smooth and coldly inquisitive.

"What's this concerning?" she asked.

I pictured the pretty, black-haired woman with the high cheekbones and structured face.

"Ms. Bollinger, I'm Sergeant Scully, LAPD. Jo Brickhouse and I have been working a case together. She was shot this afternoon. She's in critical condition in L.A. County King/Drew Hospital. I thought you might like to know."

"Oh, my God!" Bridget said, attitude replaced by anguish. "Where is the hospital?"

"Wilmington Avenue, south of the one-oh-five."

"Is she . . . is she going to be . . ."

"I don't know. She was hit in the chest, lost a lot of blood. She's in a coma. To be honest, it doesn't look too good. If you want to see her, you'd better get here quick." I hung up.

They moved Jo upstairs to an O.R.

I waited on the surgical floor while the docs opened her chest and started picking out bullet fragments. The asshole had shot her at point-blank range, using a hollow point, which broke up on impact. They were desperately trying to tie off the bleeders and fix the mess inside her.

I called Alexa and told her what happened.

"Oh my God, Shane. I'm sorry," she said.

"I tried to get there to warn her. She didn't know about Vincent. She thought she was going to see his sister Susan. He came to the door in a wig, shot her, and took off in a black Dodge truck. I don't know what happened after that, whether they caught him or not. Two blues crashed their unit, so they borrowed my car and went after him."

"I'll find out. Keep your phone on." She hung up.

Ten minutes later she called back.

"You won't believe it," she said, "but the two guys from A-twenty-two tried to bust through an intersection against a red light and got broadsided by a city bus. Both of them are in Baldwin Hills Emergency. Your car is totaled."

"And Smiley got away?"

"Looks like it," she said.

Ten or fifteen minutes later people from the Sheriff's Department started showing up. Among them was Jo's boss at IAD and the undersheriff, a nice-looking guy with silver hair, named Bert Clausen.

They began filtering in one by one, some in uniform, others in civvies, off-duty officers and civilian personnel. I wondered if they were sorry now that they had been dogging her all week for just doing her job. As more of them arrived, I was pushed to the side and ended up sitting alone on a vinyl sofa trying to keep my chin up.

If only I hadn't told her to turn off her cell.

Why didn't I go out there with her?

Ifs and whys. Questions that never get answered.

Twenty minutes later Bridget arrived looking drawn and nervous. I saw her come off the elevator and I went to intercept her.

"I'm Shane," I said.

"Thank you for calling me." Her voice was faint, almost a whisper.

I didn't respond. I was all out of pleasantries.

"Is she . . ."

"In trouble."

You can generally tell how bad it is by the way people move in the hall outside the operating theater. Too many nurses were running to suit me.

Bridget looked like she was about to break.

"We were having—she and I . . ."

"Look, Bridget, that's between you guys."

"No—I mean—I walked out. I've wanted to call her half a dozen times since then. It's just—Jo can be so definite. She's not someone who lets you get too close."

She sank down onto the sofa. Her face crumpled, her eyes brimmed with tears. I reached over and took her hand.

"You're wrong. She's not definite, and she wants to let you in. She's just scared. It's how she covers it."

"She thinks I don't care, but that's not the problem. The problem is I care too much."

"Bridget, she needs you now. She needs somebody to sit with her. I can't stay. I've got to catch the guy who did this. But somebody needs to protect her from the mistakes that can happen in big medical factories like this one."

"I can do that," she said valiantly.

"And she needs somebody to hold her hand. Somebody to pray for her and—"

I stopped because suddenly I was on the verge of tears, myself.

"You really care for her, don't you?" Bridget said.

"Yes," I said. "I really do." Then I thought for a minute before I went on.

"Jo is one of a kind. She makes her own rules. You gotta love someone who walks their own trail, no matter the consequences."

"I do," Bridget said softly, and from the sound of her voice, she meant it.

Ten minutes later the surgeon came out and told us that Jo was critical and had been moved to ICU.

"The next forty-eight hours will tell the story," he said.

I decided to put them to good use. I couldn't help Jo sitting around here. I was going to even the score, get some payback for Josephine Brickhouse. I'd failed Jo just at the moment I realized how special she really was.

I was going to catch this son-of-a-bitch or die trying.

FORTY

Climbing

At three-forty-five I was back at Smiley's hideout house in Inglewood. Since I'd left two hours ago it had become a full-fledged LASD crime scene. CSI had chalked the spot where Jo fell. She was facing the back door when he shot her. The techies from Soles and Holes were searching the backyard with metal detectors, looking for bullet fragments. I found the man in charge. Deputy Douglas Hennings was a fifty-year-old plainclothes drone with a vanilla personality and hair the color of poured concrete.

"You were working this thing with her?" Hennings said, after I had shown my creds and explained who I was. He started motioning to his second, another deputy sheriff in a suit, who wandered over and stood behind me, blocking my exit as if I was the problem.

"How come an LAPD Special Crimes dick is working with one of our IAD advocates?" Hennings said. "That sounds screwy."

"Look, Deputy Hennings, if you want to call Sheriff Messenger . . ."

"No, I don't wanta call the sheriff. I'd like you to answer my question."

"We were working a joint reinvestigation of the Hidden Ranch Road shooting at the request of Mayor

MacKenzie and Supervisor Salazar." I saw a little shadow pass across his eyes at the mention of the politicos. "Sergeant Brickhouse left me a message that she was coming over here to conduct an interview. I arrived right after Vincent Smiley shot her. He blew out of here dressed in women's clothing, driving a new black Dodge Ram twenty-five hundred, license number Ida-May-Victor-five-eight-seven. Surely, you must already have all this." My frustration was mounting.

"Let's get this on tape from the beginning," Hennings said, motioning again to his partner, who moved in and cracked his knuckles like a gunfighter about to upholster a six-gun. Instead, he reached for a Sony minitape and placed it under my nose.

For the next twenty minutes Hennings took my statement. What I wanted to do was get past this guy and search the house before the sheriff's department criminalists bagged everything for evidence and hauled it out of there.

After I finished my statement, I asked Hennings if I could take a look around. He regarded me skeptically.

"I know how to work a crime scene," I assured him. Then, to show him I meant business, I pulled out my latex gloves. *See?* He finally nodded, so I snapped them on and went down the hall into the master bedroom.

It was immediately obvious that Smiley had been living here as Susan. The clothes in the closet were all large-sized dresses and skirts. In the bureau, women's blouses and underwear, extra large. The cosmetics in the bathroom were pancake and rouge. His preferred shade of lipstick was Bozo-the-Clown red, something called Torche. Pinned up over the mirror were several Polaroids of Vincent in drag—close-ups of his face in full makeup. Janet Reno on steroids. I broke my promise to Hennings, and filched one, putting it in my side coat pocket. Then I stood surveying the bathroom, trying to get a grip on the methodology here. Was this just a place to run after he shot Emo and barbecued his brother Paul, or did he actually live here as Susan half the time? How long had he owned this house, or did he just rent? I made a mental note to check the local Realtors.

I left the house twenty minutes later and walked out to the driveway. I wondered if anybody had gone through his garbage yet. Not wanting to let this normally important crime-scene treasure trove get away, I moved behind the garage and opened his cans. Both empty. The sheriff's crime techs had beat me to it. Then I noticed some sheets of paper on the ground, partially hidden behind some bushes. One was an old market list, but the other was some kind of computer printout that had "YUMA TACTS" on the top. Under that was a series of columns and boxes:

7S	MECH INFANTRY REIN	1335	PG783783	N 33 13 57.1	W 115 05 16.6	LIVE ORD	1, 2
8S	MECH INFANTRY REIN	1539	PG726796	N 33 14 39.9	W 115 08 58.2	LIVE ORD	1, 2
10S	SA-6 Site	2240	PG771820	N 33 15 56.5	W 115 06 01.1	LIVE ORD	1, 2
11S	ARMORED COLUMN	2203	PG773815	N 33 15 38.1	W 115 05 54.3	LIVE ORD	1, 2
12S	SAM SITE	1348	PG735806	N 33 15 12	W 115 08 18.5	LIVE ORD	1, 2
13S	MECH INFANTRY	1444	PG718803	N 33 15 02.9	W 115 09 27.5	LIVE ORD	1, 2
14S	MECH INFANTRY REIN	2350	PG771772	N 33 13 14.5	W 115 05 57.4	LIVE ORD	1, 2
15S	NE-SW AIRFIELD W/SAM, AAA, RADAR SITES	0205	PG736809	N 33 15 23.6	W 115 08 17	LIVE ORD	1, 2
MT. BARROW	NE-SW AIRFIELD W/SAM SITES	0545	PG895707	N 33 09 42.1	W 114 58 10.8	LIVE ORD	1, 2, 5

Tad Palmer told me he'd seen this site on Smiley's computer out at Hidden Ranch, and I had tried unsuccessfully to access Cactus West on my PC. With words like INFANTRY and LIVE ORD, I knew it was some kind of military site.

I put the paper in my jacket pocket with the Polaroid

and headed back toward the driveway. As I passed the garage, I noticed that the side door was ajar, so I pushed it open with my toe and walked in.

Nothing much was inside. A few recent oil stains on the pavement, but nothing was piled up against or hung on the walls. I noticed some old cardboard boxes up in the rafters that looked like they'd been broken down, folded and stored up there. Probably nothing, but most people don't go to the trouble to store broken-down boxes, so I found a ladder and dragged it over, climbed up, and started pulling at the edges. They cascaded down and landed on the floor.

I climbed down and started opening them up. The shipping labels indicated they had come from a mail order catalogue called The Mountaineer. The UPS dates indicated they were all delivered within the last week. I started to pull out the manufacturers' packing lists that had been left behind.

The first box I went into had contained a GPS—a mini-unit for exact global satellite positioning. I reached into another box and found the printed instructions for installing something called "crampon metal spikes." They attached to the bottom of boots and were used for ice climbs. There was a box for an ascender and one for fifi hooks, which had a complicated set of instructions for a hanging belay. There was a box for an SLCD. The instructions indicated that it was a spring-loaded camming device, used to improve handholds on a cliff face.

What it all came down to was Vincent had recently ordered one hell of a lot of expensive mountain-climbing equipment. The boxes had been opened here, but since the gear wasn't in the house or garage, it was probably in the back of that bigfoot Dodge 2500 that had roared out of here, almost hitting me. Detective logic at its tip-top best.

I left the garage by the side door, walked down the drive, and climbed into a slick-back D-car that I'd picked up at the motor pool downtown after leaving the hospital. I drove slowly up the block, trying to figure my most effective next move. Jo's purse was on the seat beside me. Nobody had asked me for it at the hospital, so I just held onto it. I drove up the street and found a quiet place to park, then pulled over and turned off the engine.

I opened the purse and pulled out Jo's crime book, then began flipping pages until I found what I was looking for.

FORTY-ONE

If It's a Bell, Ring It

I pulled into the parking lot of a one-story showroom office in Sunland a few minutes past five in the afternoon. The window art advertised Sprint contracts and the latest in digital communications. The company's name and slogan were in big white letters:

BELL COMMUNICATIONS
IF IT'S A BELL . . . RING IT

I got out and walked inside. Most places that sell computer and phone equipment keep the air-conditioning on way too low. This was no exception. They hadn't wasted much thought on décor either. Like a lot of yuppie businesses these days, the trend was toward open space and hard surfaces. The color scheme was overpoweringly gray. The showroom had concrete floors and the ceilings were crisscrossed with exposed aluminum air ducts. Every kind of cell phone imaginable was displayed in glass cases.

I asked for Marion Bell and was told by a sneering pair of pleated pants that I couldn't see Mr. Bell without an appointment. I showed this arrogant dweeb my badge and cocked a suspicious eyebrow, which is the cop equivalent of "Wanta bet, asshole?"

He had an immediate change of attitude and led me into the back where the sales offices were. After a whispered conversation on the phone, I was shown into the boss's corner office. Decoratively, more of the same.

Marion Bell was one of those compact, thirtyish, yuppie packages whose stiff body language suggested a lack of grace, despite an athletic appearance. The best word to describe him was "severe." His physicality screamed nononsense, from the half-inch buzz cut to his ugly, Velcrofastened shoes. His eyes were so blue, I suspected contacts.

"Police?" he asked as I entered. "I talked to Sergeant Brickhouse yesterday. She said she was going to set up a meeting, but she never called me back."

"She's my partner," I said. "This won't take long."

"About Vincent Smiley?" From his expression and tone, I could tell that Jo was right. Smiley was not a favorite.

"The cops are spending a lot of time on that guy, considering the fact that he's dead," he said.

"There are potential lawsuits surrounding that Hidden Ranch Road shoot-out," I said, electing not to tell him that Smiley was still alive. People are generally not all that anxious to rat out paramilitary psychopaths.

"Go ahead, ask away." Marion said, lowering himself behind his gray metal desk.

I took the uncomfortable gray chair across from him and opened my casebook. "Just tell me a little about Vincent. I understand he joined your mountain-climbing club, the Rock Stars, sometime last year. What month was that?"

"June," Marion said.

I wrote it down, thinking that was about the same time Smiley started digging the escape tunnel at his house in Hidden Ranch. Important? I wasn't sure.

Marion went on. "He wanted to do some organized mountain climbing. We're an outdoor club."

"As opposed to what?" I asked him.

"That means that our climbs are on real mountains. Some clubs are strictly gym climbing clubs. They scale indoor, artificial walls, that sort of thing."

"What was your take on him? What kind of guy was he?"

"Well, on a personal level he was a jerk. Frightening, if you want to put a better word on it."

"How so?"

"He was always right on the edge of going off on you. Even when he was laughing, it could turn ugly in a second. You said the wrong thing and you'd set him off. He had real anger-management problems. We took him in originally because he said he was YDS fifth-class qualified. YDS stands for Yosemite Decimal System. It rates climbing ability. To be fifth-class rated, you have to have expertise in all forms of technical free-climbing and be proficient with specialized techniques and equipment. Once he became a member of the Rock Stars, and we took him on his first climb, we realized it was all BS."

"So he lied."

"Big time. He was basically a Gumby. His equipment was a mess, mostly second-hand stuff. His haul bag was a disaster, full of the kinda stuff mountain shops sell to newbies, but nobody ever uses. Since we do outdoor climbs, not gym climbs, we have to travel to our sites. Sometimes it's a two- or three-hour drive, so I like to get an alpine start."

"A what?" I was writing all this down.

He smiled. "Alpine start—early, like three A.M. We'd meet in a market parking lot, or some agreed-upon place, and take off from there. You go early, especially if it's a snow climb, because the hard pack starts to melt after noon and you want to be off the mountain by then. Once the snow starts melting, all your protection starts pulling loose and it can get treacherous."

"Protection?" I was still scribbling like mad trying to keep up.

"Anything you pound into a rock face, or screw into ice to tie you off, is called protection."

I nodded.

"He always escalated any disagreement past the place you were willing to go. It's how he won arguments. There was something about Vincent. You never knew what he was capable of, and you didn't want to find out."

I nodded. Pretty much exactly what Tad Palmer had said.

"On the first climb he went on, we saw how dangerous he was, so we made him a belay monkey. That's basically somebody who stays at the belay station and minds the anchors."

"I'm sorry, I'm afraid . . ."

"Somebody who stays below and holds the end of the climbing rope, keeps it from getting tangled. It's a job anybody can do. If a guy brings his nonclimbing girl-friend, we always give her the job. Make her our 'Belay Betty', so to speak, okay?"

"Right."

"But after the first time he didn't want to do that, so the next time we went, we had to take him up as a rope man. He was long on nerve and short on skill. Basically, a screamer in training."

I raised my eyebrow again.

"A screamer is somebody taking the big drop. A screamer is dangerous to everybody, because he can zip-per out all the protection and kill everyone on the line with him."

"Got it."

"So we asked him, basically, to stop climbing with us and resign from the club. As president, that was my job. I actually considered putting a gun in my belt when I talked to him. He was that unstable."

"Sergeant Brickhouse told me you'd mentioned that he belonged to some kind of survivalist club."

"That's what he said. He was always talking like some ex-military, antigovernment fanatic. But if you want my take on it, he was just mouthing off. He didn't have any tats on him, no swastikas, or any of that other antigovernment nonsense those survivalist guys like. I think it was just talk."

"Anything else?"

He thought for a moment, then said: "Well, one thing. He was always wanting us to climb the Chocolate Mountains."

"Where's that?"

"Way the hell on the other side of the Salton Sea. It's a mountain range between California and Arizona, which is, to be honest, not all that challenging. But he wanted to go up there anyway. Said there was a high altitude SEAL training camp he wanted to see. Even had maps."

"When was this?"

"All the time. He never stopped talking about it, until we threw him out. Most of the club members like the big face at Pinnacle National Monument, or, if we're going to overnight, we like Yosemite National Park. There's hundreds of great V-five climbs up there, some as high as thirty pitches, that require two or three days to complete."

I didn't know exactly what pitches or V-5 climbs were, but I more or less had the idea, so I didn't ask. "If he was going to make a climb somewhere, you think it would be in these Chocolate Mountains?" I asked.

"If he was still alive, yeah, I'm sure that's where he woulda gone. To the SEAL camp up there. It's almost four thousand feet up."

"Do you have a map?" I asked.

"Yeah, I think I have the Chocolate Mountains in a book—right here."

He crossed to a bookshelf where he had a library of climbing books. He pulled down a volume labeled Bradshaw Trail Climbs.

"The Bradshaw Trail is out past Indio by the Salton Sea in Riverside County," he explained as he started flipping pages. "It runs between the Chukwalla Mountains and the Chocolate Mountains. There's some spectacular views from the Chukwalla Bench of the Palos Verdes Valley."

Then he found the page he wanted. "There's a Navy SEAL camp known as Camp Billy Machen down here at the base camp. They used to use it for desert training. It's closed now. The other SEAL camp, the one he wanted to visit, is at altitude." He pointed at a spot on the map. "'Bout here, above Silver Pass."

"Could I make a copy of this?" I asked him.

"You can take it, if you bring it back."

He gave me the book and I pulled out the sheet of paper that I'd found by Smiley's trash. "You recognize anything here?" I asked him. He scanned it for a moment.

"YUMA TACTS," he read aloud. "Looks like some kind of military operation."

"Yeah, but for what?" I wondered out loud.

He shrugged and handed it back. "Beats me."

I thanked Marion and walked back out to the car, wondering how to go about this.

If Smiley wanted to go to the Chocolate Mountains, then that's where I wanted to go.

My problem was, I didn't know the first thing about mountain climbing.

FORTY-TWO

The Deal

By six fifteen the Rams were halfway through practice. I pulled the borrowed D-car into the upper parking lot at Agoura High School and walked through the campus. It was Friday afternoon, and the school sign announced that the Agoura football team was playing at San Marino High that night at eight, so the high school team wasn't out on the field. I stood for a minute on the top steps, looking down to where Chooch and thirty or so kids in their practice uniforms were running plays on the main field. There was still almost an hour of fall sunlight left.

Chooch was with the offense. Across the field, working on breakdown drills with the defense, was Sonny Lopez, the man I'd come to see. He was coaching the boys to come to a partial balanced stop, setting their feet, running in place before making an open-field tackle.

Chooch saw me and waved. "Hey," he yelled. "This is a closed practice."

I flipped him the bird and he laughed, then turned and limped on his walking cast back toward the offense. Sonny looked up when Chooch yelled. He was dressed in sweats and football shoes, with a towel around his neck. When he saw me, he scowled and immediately started walking in my direction. We met about midfield.

"I came to make a deal," I said.

"You got nothing I want."

I told him about Smiley's twin brother Paul, how Jo Brickhouse and I had found the tunnel at Hidden Ranch, and my theory about how easy it would have been for Vincent to steal those casings from the shooting ranges, commit the Nightingale and Greenridge murders, and frame both SWAT teams. When I was finished, he had lost the attitude.

"You and Jo Brickhouse turned all that?" he said, a little respect creeping into his voice and eyes.

I nodded, then added, "Jo was shot by that bastard this afternoon. She's in critical condition at L.A. County. She went to a house Smiley was using in Inglewood and he dumped her. It's all over the department and on the news. I'm surprised you haven't heard about it."

"I've been at practice here since two."

"I think I know where Smiley might be," I continued, "but I have a few conditions."

Sonny stood with his hands on his hips, his face a mask. I couldn't read him at all.

"First, I can't go after him alone. I need your word that if I tell you where I think he is, you'll do your best to deliver what I want."

"I'm not gonna promise anything, Scully. At least not until I know what you have in mind."

"All I want is your best effort. If you can't deliver, then you can't deliver."

"Let's hear." He took off the towel that was around his neck and dropped it on the grass. His team had stopped practicing, so he turned and yelled, "Hey! Keep that drill going. This ain't a break! We have the Chargers on Saturday!"

The boys again lined up and continued the tackling drill. Sonny looked back at me.

"I think Smiley went up into the Chocolate Mountains. It's a range out by the Salton Sea, south of Indio."

"So call the FBI. It's their case now. Turn it over to them."

"I want to arrest him myself. Two weeks ago he shot Emo, a guy I really cared about. This afternoon he dropped my partner. I really want this guy, Sonny."

"It's not like Sergeant Brickhouse was your real partner." He was hedging.

"Hey, she's my partner! And she's also my friend!" I almost shouted this at him. *Calm down*, I lectured myself for about the tenth time in two days. Then I put my hand on his shoulder. "Listen, Sonny, if not for me or for Jo, then do it for Emo. You cared about him. Smiley deserves some first-person payback."

"You said you had a few conditions. I got the first one. What're the others?"

"I don't know how to mountain climb, and from what I've found out, I think he's going into some pretty rough terrain. I need help to get up there."

"How can I help you with that?" Sonny said. "I don't know how to mountain climb."

"SEB does. They teach their SWAT teams mountain rescue. I want you to get in touch with Scott Cook, tell him to bring the Gray team, or as many of those guys as he can, and have them meet me here and bring their climbing equipment. I'll call Cagel at SRT and see if I can convince him to loan me that unit too."

"SEB and SRT are barely speaking. Put 'em in the same place, and you could end up with people getting killed."

"Think about it. These are the two units that were hurt the most by all this. They weren't out killing each other, Smiley just made it look that way. What better way to bring these guys back together?"

"A joint op."

"Exactly. We work it together. Go up there and drag that asshole off the mountain."

"You oughta sell this to the Discovery Channel," he said dryly. But I could tell from his expression and the glint in his eyes, that I had him.

"Tell Sergeant Cook that my condition for giving him Smiley's exact location is that I go up there with them."

"He's not gonna go for that."

"He is if he wants to catch the guy who killed Billy Greenridge."

FORTY-THREE

Good to Go

"Whatta they doing here?" Gordon Grundy said, standing in the back of the SRT SWAT truck, which was parked in the Faculty Only area of the Agoura High School lot. He was looking across the tarmac as the SEB SWAT van's headlights swept across us pulling in. It was just after sunset.

"So far, the only thing all of us are guilty of is having a stupid fight in a bar," I said. "Nobody shot anybody. SEB didn't light up Greenridge and you didn't shoot Nightingale. Maybe it's time to bottle up some of this testosterone and aim it at the real shooter."

Grundy was a tall, hard-edged man, dressed in black Kevlar. A collection of right angles and hard surfaces, his jaw jutted and his knuckles looked like unmined calcium deposits. He was flacked and jacked. His first scout, Nacho Rosano, was behind him, also glaring across the tarmac at the sheriff's van.

Grundy, Rosano, Happy Zant, and Ringo Wagner, the two other members of the ATF Situation Response Team, climbed out of their truck. They stood in a tight huddle watching the Sheriff's SEB team dismount from their van twenty yards away. From this distance, it looked like only SEB team leader, Scott Cook, and his first scout, Rick Manos, had come. Then I saw Sonny Lopez jump down out of the back of their van. He was only supposed to be the messenger, so what the hell was he doing back here? Scott, Rick, and Sonny moved across the parking lot toward us.

"Let's talk to these guys," I said to Grundy.

He nodded, and along with Nacho Rosano, walked with me toward the SEB team. Once we got to within a few feet, everybody stopped. There was enough electricity here to start a power company.

The sheriffs wore tan jumpsuits with Glocks in low-slung outside rigs strapped with Velcro to their right legs. They were carrying long rifle cases called drag bags. Each one was folded up around a long gun and contained a shooter's mat and sniper's pack, with a multifrequency radio and several bullet trays. All of them, including Sonny, were wearing heavy Cover 6 Plus tactical vests.

ATF was in black jumpsuits with "SRT SWAT" in gold letters on the back. They also carried big holstered sidearms, wore Ultima flak vests, and were carrying fifty-pound mission packs.

Everyone traded appraising looks. It seemed it was up to me to perform the marriage ceremony.

"Okay," I said. "We need to get some stuff behind us before we start." Nobody said anything. "I think somebody needs to own up to what happened at Hidden Ranch."

Grundy shifted his weight. "We told your warrant control desk there was a possibility of automatic weapons in there."

"Not according to them," Cook said immediately.

"Excuse the expletive, but fuck 'em," Grundy said dangerously.

"Whatta you mean, fuck 'em? Fuck *you!* They said you only told them about the impersonating bust."

"That's bullshit." Grundy was getting hot. "Somebody, probably some six-dollar-an-hour civilian in your warrant office, is covering his ass. We told them there was a weapons complaint and that there was a possibility of ordnance at that address. We also—" He stopped and everybody waited. "Okay," he went on. "We put a low assignment risk on it because we'd braced Smiley before and, quite frankly, he looked to us like a feeb. We didn't see any trouble coming. In retrospect, we shoulda assigned a higher risk to the warrant delivery. That was a mistake. But we're not fucking mind readers. Nobody thought the shit was gonna jump off like it did. We backed up Deputy Rojas. We were just around the corner."

"Why didn't you serve your own damn warrant?" Cook asked.

"We thought it was unnecessarily provocative to roll in there with a SWAT team. We didn't think he had an AK-forty-seven, but we wanted to give your guy cover, so we parked nearby."

They were all silent for a long time.

"Look, we're sorry," Grundy said. "I know that doesn't cover the loss of Deputy Rojas, but the fact is, we feel pretty damn bad about it. We tried to come to the funeral, but you guys ran us out."

Scott Cook looked at Sonny Lopez. It was almost as if he was asking Sonny's permission to go for this. Finally Sonny nodded.

"Okay," Scott said. "We accept the apology." Then he put out his hand and Gordon Grundy shook it. After that we shook all around.

"I understand this guy is in the mountains up on rough terrain." Grundy was getting right to business.

"Right," I said.

"Okay, we're good to go," Grundy said. "We're all V-five-certified climbers."

"So are Rick and I," Scott said. "But Sonny Lopez couldn't climb off a whore's ass in the middle of a vice raid."

"Then what's he doing here?" Grundy asked.

"He came over to the SWAT house to give us the word, then wouldn't get outta the damn van."

"I'm going," Sonny stated bluntly.

"We can't take anybody who isn't certified. It's dangerous and it'll slow us down," Grundy said.

"I'm going," Sonny repeated.

"Me too," I said. "I didn't put this whole thing together so I could read about the capture in the newspaper."

"You're not going either, Scully," Scott Cook said. "Neither of you are."

"Then you're not getting the map," I answered. "I'm the only one who knows where on that mountain Smiley went. Those are the terms."

Scott and Gordon glowered at me. Again, I was the problem.

"Okay, if that's the way you want it, you guys can come. But we're not waiting for either one of you. If you can't keep up, we're leaving you."

"Fine," I said. Sonny nodded.

"Is that all you've got to wear?" Grundy said, looking at my jeans and cotton shirt.

"I'm sure you guys have another one of those snazzy-lookin' bunny suits in the truck."

Grundy turned to Rosano. "Nacho, get this asshole suited up."

Nacho headed to the truck and I followed. As I was changing my clothes inside, putting on the jumpsuit and Tac vest, Gordon Grundy and Scott Cook walked over to the back door.

"Okay, so where the hell am I going?" Grundy asked.

I pulled the book that Marion Bell had given me out of my briefcase, and flipped it open to the Chocolate Mountains. "He's heading for a Navy SEAL camp. Right here."

I put my finger on the spot marked Silver Pass.

FORTY-FOUR

The Chocolate Mountains

We were all in SRT's SWAT truck, because it was bigger, newer, and had better toys. Gordon Grundy drove, while Sonny, Rick, Scott, Nacho, Ringo, Happy, and I sat on the benches in the back facing each other with tight, blank expressions, dressed like Gulf War commandos. We sped along the 210 on our way toward Palm Springs, lost in our own thoughts. Too many friends had died or had been injured in the last two weeks.

I thought of Emo, remembering his easy smile, the way he had of looking at you without judgment. I had once seen him in a booking cage telling jokes to a guy he had just busted, both of them doubled over with laughter. He could arrest somebody without making a power trip out of it. He understood human weakness and always seemed to be able to communicate, even with the most hardened criminals. Emo was the kind of cop I had joined up to be.

Before we left Agoura, I had called the hospital and Bridget reported that there was no news. Jo was still in ICU and critical. Bridget sounded like she was beginning to come apart, her voice tight, verging on shrill.

As we rode toward the desert, I was feeling very alone in the crowded state-of-the-art SRT truck. I knew I had been going through a simultaneous process of growth and degeneration. I was slowly exposing the vulnerable parts of myself, taking the chance that the people I cherished the most wouldn't hate me for those weaknesses. While this helped me in my personal life and on the job, I no longer saw the landing lights, unsure of why I was even on the mission or if I would ever find the answers. Then along comes this one moment of moral certainty. Find Vincent Smiley and make the sonofabitch pay. As if his destruction would somehow restore order to my fractured value system.

Jo Brickhouse and I were coming from the same place emotionally. The order we both craved from police work had only produced confusion and disillusionment. But she was lying in a hospital close to death as a result of my bad police work, and I was in this SWAT truck roaring across the desert to avenge a shattered sense of justice, telling myself I was doing this for Jo, a woman I hadn't even liked a few days ago and had badly misevaluated, and for Emo, a man I'd admired but hadn't spent that much time with.

Was this just a big, ugly piece of street theater? Was I making a splashy move to convince myself I was still relevant? Could I put an end to my moral slide by stepping on the back of Vincent Smiley's neck and jamming his face in the dirt? Would that restore my values, make my work seem worthwhile again?

Even as I raced toward the Chocolate Mountains to apprehend him, I couldn't forget the look of hatred in that Compton grandmother's eyes. What the hell was I really looking for?

We turned off the interstate past Palm Springs at Indio, traveling south, toward the Salton Sea. Nacho Rosano stood, bracing himself in the jouncing truck, and started going through drawers, passing out communications equipment.

"Since we don't share a frequency, let's all use one of

these." He handed each of us a small radio transmitter with an LCD faceplate, and pointed to the small screen. "That's a GPS. If you get lost, it'll tell you where you are, within half a meter." After he showed us how to operate it, I loaded it into my vest.

I had my cell phone on and checked the battery. It was at three-quarters, but there was no signal out here.

It was after 10 P.M. by the time we took State Highway 111 to the Salton Sea Recreation Area, then continued south. After about half an hour Grundy pulled to a stop, set the brake and came back into the rear of the truck. He filled the door to the driver's compartment, his crewcut tickling the ceiling.

"Okay, we're outside of Niland," he said, looking right at me.

I opened the map book. "Go on up Coachella Canal Road to Camp Billy Machen. The Chocolate Mountains are on the left. There should be a parking area at that old camp. There's no more road, so we hike into the mountains from there."

"Okay. Everybody saddle up now," Grundy said. "Smiley had an AK up at Hidden Ranch and he knew how to use it. I don't wanta be climbing out of this truck, hooking our shit together, while this jerk-off is up in the trees somewhere picking us off with three-oh-eights."

Everybody started buckling up vests and chambering weapons. Then Grundy went back up to the front, put the truck in gear, and we were rolling again. Scott and Nacho gave Sonny and me a short course in mountain climbing, showing us the belt harness and how to use the carabiners.

"You're gonna feel like you want to climb using your arms," Scott said. "But that's a huge mistake. Use your legs. Your glutes are much bigger muscles than your biceps. Your glutes won't tire. Most newbies try and pull themselves up. You do that, you'll burn out in less than an hour."

"In a lead climb," Nacho said, "a leader and a second go up first, set the protection, get to the top, tie off, and then bring the rest of the team up. Last up are the belay monkeys; that's you two. We change lead and seconds after each leg of the climb. Each leg is called a pitch. A pitch is a section of the climb that is slightly shorter than the rope. The ropes we use are a hundred meters long."

I remembered Marion Bell saying that some of the climbs in Monument Valley were thirty pitches.

"The first climber, or leader, wedges a piece of protection into the rock halfway up the first pitch," Nacho was saying. "We mostly use SLCDs, which are spring-loading camming devices."

He held one up. It matched the printed picture Smiley left in his garage.

"An SLCD can fit in a crevice and attaches to the rope with carabiners. We can use it for protection or for handholds on sheer cliffs. If somebody falls, the idea is the protection should catch and hold him until the rest of us can reel him back up. If the lead climber sets this thing too far down, then a fall will zipper out the protection and we're all toast. The last man on the climb is called the belayer. He holds the rope steady until the lead climbers make it to the top of the pitch. Once the lead and second have tied everything off and the others are secure up top, we pull the belay monkeys up and start all over again."

Sonny and I glanced at each other. It sounded doable.

We were all rigged and ready to go when the truck pulled into a parking area at the old Camp Billy Machen.

Scott Cook opened the door and we stepped out into the darkness. The temperature was forty degrees and dropping. We were standing in the parking lot feeling exposed under a slim slice of desert moon.

Parked ten feet away, next to a weathered maintenance shed, was Vincent Smiley's black Dodge Ram 2500 pickup. It looked evil and predatory, sitting up high with its Bigfoot suspension on huge, tractor-sized tires. We approached slowly and looked inside. There was an empty box of .308s down in the floor well.

"Looks like he's locked and loaded," Grundy said, pointing at the cartridge box. "Let's decommission this truck."

He and Nacho shinnied under the Dodge and checked the engine compartment for booby traps. "Looks clear," Grundy shouted, and they both rolled back out.

Scott Cook popped the hood and removed the positive battery cable. "Souvenir," he said and handed it to me.

I put it into my pack.

"Now let's go get this guy," Rick Manos growled.

We all turned and walked through a gate marked "Gas Line Road," and started the long trek across the sandy desert toward the dark brown Chocolate Mountains.

FORTY-FIVE

The Alpine Start

We hiked in the freezing desert until midnight, picking our way across dry, sandy gullies and parched ground. Unseen cacti tugged at the bloused ankles of our jumpsuits. About a mile out we crossed a small trickling stream in a gully. In the damp sand were footprints. We all kneeled down and looked at them. Nobody had to mention that the cross-hatched sole prints came from Danner Terra Force jump boots. We continued on, then finally bivouacked at a little past midnight.

I lay on my side in the still warm sand and prayed I wasn't parked over a scorpion nest. Almost before my head hit the crook of my arm I was asleep. I was so tired I didn't dream. Before I knew it, someone was shaking me.

"Okay, we're heading out," Scott Cook said. I rolled over and looked at my watch: 4 A.M. "We need to get a jump on it," he added.

By sunup we were four miles north in the foothills, working our way up through the crevices and canyons. I won't say it was easy, but for the first hour of the climb we had no need for ropes, carabiners, or harnesses. Then we reached the first huge rock, fifty feet high with no way around it. We had to go up and over, a feat Nacho called "bouldering."

Before we started Gordon Grundy took out his binoculars and, using the first rays of morning light, focused them on the face of the giant rock, looking for the best ascent.

"There's something there," he said. "Halfway up, somebody left a piton jammed in the rock."

I took the binoculars and focused them on the metal spike. It had been pounded into the face of the boulder, and had a carabiner hanging off the threaded end.

"Probably part of his protection," Grundy said. "He had to leave it behind because he's climbing alone and couldn't yank it free."

"Time for some white courage," Scott Cook said. "Let's chalk up." The SWAT members all dug into their haul bags and broke out tin shakers full of powdered chalk. They chalked their hands like gymnasts, sharing it with Sonny and me. Then we faced the first part of the climb.

The initial boulder was surprisingly easy. We were warned again by Grundy and Cook not to pull ourselves up by our arms. The problem was, pushing up with my legs felt dangerous, as if I would fall backward off the mountain. The leg climbing technique fought all my instincts. Grundy did the first lead climb, with Nacho as his second. He put in the protection halfway up the pitch, pounding in a spike with his belt hammer, testing it by hanging from it, using all of his weight. Then he and Nacho went the rest of the way up to the top of the rock. The climbers following scrambled up using nubbins for footholds, taking advantage of the tiny flutes and chimneys, jamming the toes of their hiking boots into crevices for traction before finally reaching the top of the first boulder.

Nacho yelled, "Off belay!" which was Sonny's and my signal to climb up and join them.

Lopez went up first. I was last. My job was to yank out our protection and bring it up with me. It was a rush, making that first pitch, hanging from my harness a thousand feet up. My heart pounded while my eyes swept the landscape below. As I passed Smiley's piton, I looked carefully at it. Stenciled on the side it said MOUNTAINEER. It had come from one of the boxes in his garage.

When I finally got to the top I was expecting a lot of praise, but nobody said anything, except Nacho. "Stop using your arms," he growled. Then they all turned and started the next pitch, with Scott Cook taking over as climb leader and Rick Manos as his second.

By ten o'clock I was so wiped out that I was unable to go much further. I had spaghetti arms from pulling myself up. Sonny Lopez was in the exact same condition.

Nacho said, "I told you to use your legs. Your arms won't hold up on a long climb like this."

"I warned you guys if this happened I was gonna leave you," Grundy said. "You're gonna have to get down on your own. Here's the spare key to the SWAT truck," he said, handing it to me.

"You're not leaving me," I said.

"This was your call," Grundy responded. "The deal was, you could go as long as you didn't slow us down. This guy is just up ahead. He's killed three cops and put a fourth in ICU. We're gonna get him, but not with you two holding us back. The last two pitches, you guys barely made it."

"We'll be along in a minute," Sonny said as the two SWAT teams turned away and took off up the next boulder. Sonny and I lay on our backs on a narrow ledge, out of breath, and watched them climb away from us. Despite the fact that the sun was out, at this altitude it was still cold. Scott and Gordon had left us some rock pitons, carabiners, and two lengths of rope for our descent.

"Let's go on up," I said, pulling myself to my feet and moving to follow. "I'm not being left behind."

I approached the boulder and tried to do a solo lead climb, scaling the rock, going up about ten feet, pounding in some protection with my belt hammer. But I was shot. My arms were shaking from the effort.

"Whatta you stopping for?" Sonny said sourly as he watched me, still on his back. I was dangling ten feet up.

Then suddenly I lost my handhold and fell, zippering out my poorly set piton. As I landed I felt a rib crack. I lay on my side moaning in pain.

"That was encouraging," Sonny said, his face strained with exhaustion. "I especially liked the eekie little scream."

"Let's get off this damn mountain," I said angrily.

Climbing down was easier, but not a complete snap. We had to tie off and belay from above. We didn't get back to the foothills until almost two in the afternoon. I was monitoring the small radio Nacho had given me and could hear the two SWAT units talking to each other as they neared the SEAL camp at Silver Pass. Once we reached level ground, Sonny and I started the long, hot hike back to Camp Billy Machen. The temperature had soared on the desert floor, so we stripped off our Tac vests in the dry hundred-degree heat and carried them.

By five o'clock we were almost there. I triggered the radio. "This is Scully. We're one or two klicks from the Billy Machen camp." Scott Cook came right back on the radio.

"We just left that SEAL camp at Silver Pass. The place was empty, no sign of him. No tackle, foot, or rope marks on the climbing faces. You want my take, this guy hasn't been up here."

"But we saw his piton," I said.

"Roger that, but he's not on this side of the mountain.

We're gonna check the back side, but if he's not over there. I think we've been messed with."

I clicked the transmit button twice to indicate I understood.

Sonny and I didn't say anything but we were both walking faster, now afraid that Smiley had for some reason lured us out toward the Chocolate Mountains, then doubled back.

We got to the end of the Gas Line Road and pushed open the gate. The black Dodge was gone. Somehow he'd rewired the battery system. I wondered where he'd found a cable way out here. Then I looked over at our SWAT truck. The hood was up.

Spray-painted on the side in black paint was a message:

NICE TRY ASSHOLES

FORTY-SIX

Cactus West

The back of the SWAT truck, where the spare ordnance was kept, had inch-thick metal doors with a bolt lock, impossible to penetrate. But Smiley had pulled the engine alarm wires and opened the hood. The emergency alarm had probably brayed until the system's battery went dead. As we approached, I could see that our battery cable was missing.

I reached into my pack and pulled out the one that Grundy had given me, then opened the truck with the spare key and found a toolbox in the back. Sonny went to work reattaching the positive cable to the engine battery.

"Yeah, nice try, asshole," he said softly as he finished. We opened the driver's side door on the truck. Sonny slid one of the keys into the ignition and started the engine, then backed the truck out while I walked over to where Smiley's Dodge Ram had been parked when we pulled in. I knelt down and studied the tracks in the gravel, as Sonny rolled up and stopped the SWAT truck behind me.

I pointed to a service road. "Cochise read many signs. Track many assholes."

Sonny grunted, and was already talking on the radio by the time I had the passenger door open. "You guys, he's down here. He got his truck going and went west, down the service road. We're tracking him in the SWAT truck. What's your ETA the parking lot?"

"We're losing light up here. It's gonna be slow going down at night. We can't get back there until around twenty-two thirty," Scott Cook said.

Not till 10:30 P.M. I looked over at Sonny and he said, "Looks like it's up to the dumb-ass arm-climbers to fix this mess."

We put our SWAT Tac vests back on, then drove along the fenced perimeter of camp Billy Machen. It had once been a tent city, but now all that was left were some poured concrete pads. It looked completely deserted. We kept going until we hit the Niland Blythe Road, which wasn't really a road, as much as a narrow dirt trail. Sonny slowed the truck to a stop and we looked to the left out across open desert. We were trying to decide which way to go, when I thought I saw something flash way out in the distance.

"What's that?" I pointed toward the spot.

We focused on the dark landscape, working on our night vision. After a minute it flashed again.

"See if they've got any infrared stuff back there," Sonny said.

"Good idea." I ducked through the opening into the back of the truck and started reading the labels on the equipment drawers, finally spotting one marked: LIGHT-GATHERING SCOPES. Inside was a single pair of heavy-duty infrared binoculars. I brought them forward, then settled back into the seat, turned them on, and focused them through the windshield, toward the spot where the flash of light had been.

As they heated up, the picture first turned green, then slowly brightened. I was looking at the same landscape, only now I could see details, almost as if it were daylight. Something was racing around on the desert floor at least two miles away. It was still too far away to tell if it was Smiley's black truck.

"Something's out there. Some kind of vehicle," I said.

Sonny turned the wheel toward the spot and drove up the dirt road, heading deeper into the desert valley full of Joshua trees and cacti. Suddenly, the road veered right and we were running beside a ten-foot-high industrial-strength chain-link fence. Every quarter mile or so there was a large painted sign:

CHOCOLATE MOUNTAIN AERIAL GUNNERY RANGE
DANGER EXPLOSIVES!
KEEP OUT!
BY ORDER OF THE U.S. GOVERNMENT

Then under that:

PELIGRO—EXPLOSIVOS!
PROHIBA LA ENTRADA!
POR ORDEN DE LA GOBIERNA
DE LOS USTADOS UNIDOS

Sonny had his eyes on the rutted road, trying to keep from breaking an axle, when I reached over and turned off his headlights.

"What're you doing?" he barked. "Can't see."

"I have a feeling we're gonna end up going in there." I pointed at the range. "I don't think we oughta be advertising our location."

Sonny grunted, but made no move to turn the lights back on.

We were soon passing what appeared to be a massive automobile graveyard. Bombed-out wrecks, old county and state vehicles, yellow bulldozers, garbage trucks, and decommissioned road-maintenance equipment loomed behind the chain-link. Most of them were scorched by fire or blown to bits, some barely recognizable, others had signs painted on the sides in large white letters: *Armored Column, Russian T-62 Tank, SAM Missile.*

"What the hell is all this about?" Sonny said, slowing to look as we passed.

"I've heard about this place. Navy and Marine pilots fly practice sorties against all this old junk."

"Is it safe for us to go in there?" Sonny said, suddenly apprehensive.

"If that's where Smiley is, we got no choice."

Then I remembered the slip of paper I'd found out by his trash. I dug it out of my pocket and opened it up. "Pull over for a minute."

Sonny stopped the truck and I turned on the map light.

"Whatta ya got?" he said.

"I found this at his place in Inglewood. I couldn't figure it out back then, but you know what I think it might be?" Sonny shook his head, puzzled.

"A Marine Corps firing mission. MCAS could stand for Marine Corps Air Station. YUMA is the Yuma air wing. TACTS could be like Tactical Air Combat Training or Combat Target Systems—something."

We both studied the sheet.

7S	MECH INFANTRY REIN	1335	PG783783	N 33 13 57.1	W 115 05 16.6	LIVE ORD	1, 2
8S	MECH INFANTRY REIN	1539	PG726796	N 33 14 39.9	W 115 08 58.2	LIVE ORD	1, 2
10S	SA-6 Site	2240	PG771820	N33 15 56.5	W 115 06 01.1	LIVE ORD	1, 2
11S	ARMORED COLUMN	2203	PG773815	N 33 15 38.1	W 115 05 54.3	LIVE ORD	1, 2
12S	SAM SITE	1348	PG735806	N 33 15 12	W 115 08 18.5	LIVE ORD	1, 2
13S	MECH INFANTRY	1444	PG7718803	N 33 15 02.9	W 115 09 27.5	LIVE ORD	1, 2
14S	MECH INFANTRY REIN	2350	PG771772	N 33 13 14.5	W 115 05 57.4	LIVE ORD	1, 2
15S	NE-SW AIRFIELD W/SAM, AAA, RADAR SITES	0205	PG736809	N 33 15 23.6	W 115 08 17	LIVE ORD	1, 2
MT. BARROW	NE-SW AIRFIELD W/SAM SITES	0545	PG895707	N 33 09 42.1	W 114 58 10.8	LIVE ORD	1, 2, 5

"I don't know what column one is, but column two is the target description," I continued. "Mechanized Infantry, Armored Column, SAM site. They drag these old garbage trucks and bulldozers out on the gunnery range, set them up to look like armored columns or a SAM missile site, then the jet jocks roll in and hit all this stuff with Tomahawk missiles. Column three is something. Numbers—I don't know what."

"Could be the coordinates of the target. The latitude and longitude," Sonny said.

"No, it looks more like military time. Thirteen thirty-five hours is one thirty-five P.M. Columns five and six look like the coordinates. That N33.13 would be longitude, W115.05, latitude. Then the next column says LIVE ORD. Means they're shooting hot ammo."

"As opposed to what?" He grinned. "Rubber pellets?"

"Inerts. We trained with the air wing when I was in the Corps. Inert ordnance is like bombs made out of concrete. They use that stuff to test for target accuracy, but it doesn't explode."

"And that last column?"

"I don't know," I admitted.

"So why did Smiley print this out?" Sonny asked.

"I don't have a clue," I answered. Again, we sat in silence. "Okay, we have a couple of ways to go here. Your choice," I said.

"Don't do that 'your choice' BS on me again, Shane. I remember the choice you gave me up at Hidden Ranch Road."

"Hey, Sonny, if we call the authorities, the Marines are gonna chopper out here in those big double proppers, bullhorn this place, and before they can catch him, Smiley will be long gone across the border into Mexico. Let's just go under the wire and get this puke."

"With no backup."

"Our backup is five miles south of this range, still up on the mountain, and we've got the truck."

He thought about it for a minute, nodded. "Okay, I'm down. Let's see if we can find where he went in."

I checked my cell phone again. Still no signal. We continued past the auto graveyard until, off to the right, I saw a wash leading away from the gunnery range with a lot of dune buggy tracks marking the deep sand.

"Turn down there," I said. "Follow those tire tracks. Somebody must live down there. Maybe we can find out more about this place and use their phone to call in the locals."

Sonny hung a right and headed into the wash. The SWAT truck was muscular but heavy, and the minute we slowed, the tires started to dig in and spin. Sonny had to keep the speed up or we'd be stuck. We followed the tracks. Then, off to the right, I spotted a small homestead. A trailer and junkyard sat next to a fenced parking area containing a bunch of radical-looking sand rails. I estimated we were about a mile east of the gunnery range.

"Pull up," I said.

"If I stop we're never gonna get dug out," Sonny answered.

"We have to take a chance. We can't off-road in this truck. Look what's parked back there. Just stop," I said.

We rolled to a stop and our tires immediately sank into the soft sand. Behind the six-foot-high fence we counted half a dozen unpainted dune buggy–like vehicles of various sizes. All were equipped with big, exposed V-8 engines and had massive tractor tires on the rear wheels, with smaller ones up front. The buggies were light and lean with open cockpits, bucket seats, and no windshields. A few had large flatbeds resting between the rear axles. None of them had headlights.

The chain-link gate was bolted shut with a large heavy-duty padlock. Off to the left an old, rusted-out silver Airstream trailer was parked under a lone olive tree. All the lights were off inside. No phone wires anywhere. Whoever lived here was some kind of recluse. I walked to the trailer, climbed up on a creaking wood porch, pulled out my badge and knocked on the front door. It didn't look like anybody was home. Sonny followed and stood behind me.

"What kinda fool lives out here, less than a mile from a live gunnery range?" he asked.

"Desert rat," I said. "Since nobody's home to lend us one of those dune buggies, whatta you say we just borrow one and call it a police emergency?"

"How? They're all locked up," Sonny said.

"I think I saw some bolt cutters in the back."

Sonny nodded and took off running to the truck. He returned with a set of heavy-duty bolt cutters, put them on the padlock, and easily clipped through it. Then he carried the cutters back to the truck and disappeared inside.

When he reappeared he was carrying two AR-15s and

four circular C-mag hundred-round clips. He reset the complicated alarm on the truck, while I swung the metal gate open. He handed me one of the AR-15s and two of the heavy C-mags. Then we surveyed the motor pool.

"How 'bout this one here?" Sonny said, checking out a two-seat racer with no flatbed. He unscrewed the gas cap and stuck his index finger inside. "Full. I can hot-wire it easy."

A few minutes later Sonny had unhooked the ignition wires, twisted them together, and we had the sand rail going. It had straight pipes with no muffler, and the roaring engine fractured the still desert night. I climbed into the passenger seat. The owner had screwed in a metal pole between the seats, about where the windshield would be. The thick mast went up about a foot above our heads and had a huge bolt welded to the top.

"What's this thing for?" Sonny said, pointing at it.

"It probably ain't for water skiing," I quipped. "Let's get out of here."

I stacked the two automatic weapons between us, then Sonny hit the gas and we careened out of the enclosure, passing our SWAT truck sitting low in soft sand.

We raced back up the wash to the gunnery range fence, turned right, and continued running on the road beside the range, which was situated in a desert valley halfway between the Chocolate and Chuckwalla mountains. We were speeding along under a quarter moon, without a windshield or headlights, the wind stinging our eyes, tears streaming down our faces, running almost blind at about forty miles per hour in a two-seat dune buggy with no suspension. I was bouncing hard and holding on with both hands. Every time we hit a pothole my cracked ribs talked to me. After this ride, I was going to need to get my prostate checked.

Up ahead I saw a spot where somebody had cut a hole

in the government fence. I pointed at it and Sonny steered over and parked. I got out and peeled back the wire flap. He slowly edged the rumbling, vibrating dune buggy through the opening and I jumped back aboard.

We were inside the restricted area of the Chocolate Mountain Aerial Gunnery Range.

I still had the night vision binoculars around my neck, so I pulled them up and focused them toward the center of the vast area. There had to be thousands of acres out here. I saw burned cacti and sand charred black from Nadaum drops. It looked apocalyptic, as desolate and bombed-out as any place on earth. Then I noticed a small outcropping of low buildings a mile or two away. I pointed them out to Sonny but didn't speak, because the straight pipes on the sand rail were so loud I would have had to scream to be heard. Sonny floored it and we were off again, heading toward the buildings, flying over the sand, jumping berms, Sonny driving like a man who had lost his mind.

As we approached I saw that this was some kind of target town. There were two or three transecting streets and a main drag. The houses were all one-story, built out of adobe bricks and corrugated metal. Many of them had been leveled by past bombing runs, then rebuilt and tumbled down again. We slowed the sand rail and came to a stop on the outskirts of this little unmanned village. Our engine idle filled the night and vibrated the sand rail energetically. A hand-painted sign was posted directly in front of us. It said:

CACTUS WEST CITY LIMITS

FORTY-SEVEN

Deadly Premonition

Sonny pulled slowly into Cactus West and drove through the little empty village once, taking each street to the end before turning around and retracing the route. After we looked the place over he turned off the engine.

"Wait here," I told him and found a building that had a tumbled-down wall I could use to climb up to the roof, one story up. I stood gingerly on the flexing corrugated metal and surveyed the flat, ugly terrain. From up there I had a good view of the desert gunnery range. I could see more vast, blackened napalm drops. The few yucca trees that had survived were also scorched black. I slowly scanned the landscape with the night vision binoculars. The strong lenses pulled the eastern mountain range into focus.

The Dodge was parked about half a mile away. I saw a figure that had to be Smiley, walking around examining things on the ground. He picked up something large and loaded it into the back of his truck. It was hard to make out what he was up to, because he was so far away. The night scope bathed everything in a strange green hue but afforded me a lightened view of the area. As I watched, Smiley got behind the wheel, the truck started up, then turned and headed right toward us.

I scrambled down off the roof and ran back to the sand rail.

"He's coming this way," I shouted.

"The black truck?"

"Yep. Pull this thing around behind that bombed-out shed." I pointed to a structure that had only three sides. "Back it in so you're heading out. Gimme one of those AR-fifteens."

Sonny handed me a carbine with a hundred-round clip, then twisted the ignition wires, restarted the rail, and drove it around to the back side of the nearest building. He put the dune buggy in reverse, backed it in, and shut it down. Suddenly the desert was very still. A second later Sonny ran toward me carrying the second AR-15, jamming in one of the large C-mags and tromboning the slide.

The temperature fluctuation out here was amazing. Over a hundred degrees at noon, it was now close to freezing. The stars twinkled and winked as if somebody had punched a load of buckshot through a dark blue blanket. The quarter moon shed almost no light on the little uninhabited town.

"Let's set up a cross fire," I said.

"I'll take that wall over there." Sonny pointed to a bombed-out structure that would give him waist-high cover if he was standing, and would completely hide him when he kneeled. I picked a little square adobe shed with an open front window and corrugated tin roof. I pointed to it and we split up to take cover.

Way off across the desert we began to hear the sound of the truck approaching, its engine growing louder, growling in low gear. It sounded like he had it in four-wheel drive to keep from sinking into the sand. Less than a minute later headlights appeared around the far end of the last building in Cactus West. The high beams shot light up the center street of the empty town. I was hunkered down under the small window, holding the AR-15 at port arms, listening to his truck engine idling. Then I rose up cautiously and peeked over the top of the window frame.

"I see you, asshole," Smiley shouted, then opened up on my position.

The walls all around me started to disintegrate. I immediately knew from the sound and fury of his weapon that this time he wasn't firing an AK-47. He was shooting at us with a .50-caliber Browning machine gun. The huge antitank exploding rounds were cutting the bricks in half, knocking my cover down around me with devastating efficiency. The .50 slugs contained exploding tips. If he kept this up, my little adobe shack would soon be dust. Sonny opened up on him trying to take some pressure off me.

Smiley laughed maniacally, then turned the weapon on the low wall where Sonny was hiding. I heard the exploding shells tearing Sonny's cover down. I popped up and squeezed off a twenty-round burst. The .223 bullets ripped into the truck, but didn't seem to be doing much damage. Before I could fire a second burst, Smiley spun back and started unloading on my little adobe shack again.

The AR-15 is a good assault rifle, but it's no match for a .50-caliber antitank weapon. Adding to the problem were the truck's high beams, which were shining right at us, blinding me.

Sonny made a move away from the crumbled wall, firing the AR-15 as he ran. I popped up and gave him some cover fire. He dove behind an old burned-out van just as Smiley started ripping holes through it. Suddenly he stopped shooting and I heard his engine accelerate. The black truck sped right down Center Street. I caught a glimpse of him as he roared past. His eyes were wide, the cords of his neck bulging. Then his tail lights receded as he headed back out into the desert.

Sonny was on his feet, running toward me. "He's got us outgunned with that thing!"

"Get the rail. We're going after him," I shouted.

Sonny ran for the dune buggy and got it going, while I stood in the center of town with the night vision binoculars up, watching the truck disappear into the dark desert night, trying to see if he made a turn before I lost sight of him. Sonny skidded to a stop beside me.

I jumped into the passenger seat, Sonny popped the clutch, and we shot out into the gunnery range speeding after Smiley.

We were running at breakneck speed across the desert. The moon was almost no help. The ravines and gullies were hard to see and came up fast in the dark. Sonny was not slowing for any of it, swerving at the last minute to miss the few tall cactus plants that had managed to escape the napalm drops in this charred, bombed-out no-man's-land. Occasionally we were airborne, landing in soft sand, throwing a rooster tail off both of the giant rear tractor tires. We were slowly gaining on Smiley, who was forced to use four-wheel drive and couldn't run the truck as fast.

We were only about a hundred yards behind him when he turned off his headlights and swerved right, heading down into a gully. Sonny whipped the wheel and followed. We raced along the sandy wash, narrowing the distance between us until we were so close the flying dirt from the truck tires stung our cheeks and filled our eyes with grit. We rounded a turn and roared past a line of trucks and old bulldozers situated to look like a stalled armored column. Each one was identified in large, white letters that read: T-62 or ARMORED TROOP CARRIER.

Was this out here for a reason? Why had he turned off his headlights? Why was he leading us here? Suddenly I had a deadly premonition.

Just then, off to our right, a loud siren started blaring in the distance. I turned to see where it was coming from but couldn't locate it. Seconds later, five state-of-the-art FA-18 fighter jets dropped out of the moonlit sky, heading right at us. The Super Hornets roared down toward the column of parked trucks and bulldozers. Just as I looked up, a Maverick missile launched from under the wings of each plane. The pilots were a mile out and I doubted they could even see this little sand rail down here. Had Vincent turned off his headlights so they wouldn't see him in the low light of the quarter moon?

The air-to-ground weapons streaked toward us and five loud metal clicks sounded from above. I'd only heard this once before when I'd done cross-training with the air wing, back in the Marines.

"What's that?" Sonny screamed as we roared along.

"Detonators!" I yelled as the warheads went hot overhead.

The Mavericks vectored in over our shoulders. The first one blew an old dump truck off its axles and ten feet into the air. Little pieces of it rained down all around us. The other four hit seconds later, blowing up a bulldozer and some old trucks.

Smiley had already turned right, driving the Dodge Ram out of the gully. But Sonny and I were stuck in the middle of this night fire mission. Suddenly, five more Mavericks came streaking in. Their detonators clicked on, followed ten seconds later by huge explosions. A bulldozer on our right turned into deadly shrapnel.

I grabbed Sonny and threw him out of our speeding sand rail just as two more missiles struck, blowing up vehicles on both sides of us. We burrowed down into the sand as the four fighters screamed by low overhead, climbed into the night sky, and banked right to come around for a second pass.

"We gotta get outta here now!" I pulled Sonny up and we started running back toward the sand rail, which had come to a rolling stop twenty yards away and was miraculously still upright with the engine idling. There were destroyed garbage trucks and bulldozers blazing all around us while the strike fighters climbed, making a sweeping turn, their wings glinting in the moonlight.

"They're coming around!" I yelled. "Listen for the sound of the detonators. They click on about a hundred yards out. You can hear it happen. Means you got about five seconds to get in a hole somewhere."

Just then, I saw the Dodge nose up to the lip of the wash, fifty yards away. The door slammed, and without warning he was firing the .50-caliber at us again, pinning us down. The huge slugs whined all around, tearing holes in the night and exploding anything they hit.

The Super Hornets had completed their turn and were coming back. Smiley saw them, dove into his truck, and backed up out of range of the missile attack. It gave us a precious few seconds to get out of there.

"Let's go!" I yelled as we jumped into the bucket seats. Sonny put it in gear. We hung a right, climbing up out of the wash just as the FA-18s leveled out and started another pass. I saw more bombs light up and streak out from under the wings heading our way again, then seconds later: click, click, click, click. The detonators snapped on.

"Now!" I yelled.

Sonny and I dove out of the rail while it was still moving and started eating sand.

The trucks and vans parked in the wash exploded like a

chain of fireworks, shooting sparks high into the air. We were further out of the fire zone this time, so none of the shrapnel or falling debris landed on us.

The Hornets completed their pass and climbed out again. Our sand rail was again miraculously still unscathed. It had a low center of gravity and wasn't prone to flipping. We raced toward it as the .50-caliber started up again, chopping loudly from a sand hill on the right.

Sonny screamed and went down in a heap. His right leg was missing from the knee down. Blown right off.

"Shit!" I stopped short and kneeled over him.

Smiley's laughter rang out from a distant hillside. The jets roared low overhead, passing over us again before they careened to the left, turning for another pass. Once they were gone, climbing to come around again, I heard Vincent yell:

"Having fun, assholes?"

I took off my belt and cinched it tightly around Sonny's thigh.

"How bad is it?" he asked, lying on his back, straining to look down at his leg.

"It's fine. Just a scratch," I told him, pushing him back down so he couldn't see.

When I had it tied off, I threw him over my shoulder and made a run for the rail. I could barely see Vincent up on the sand hill. He had the big Browning thrown across the hood of his truck and was squeezing off long bursts. The massive exploding slugs dug holes all around me as I threw Sonny into the passenger seat, and jumped behind the wheel. The FA-18s were coming in again, wingtip-to-wingtip. Five more Maverick missiles launched. Smiley backed the truck away fast, out of the line of fire.

I threw the sand rail into gear and floored it, roaring back across the desert toward Cactus City. The buildings loomed on the night horizon as we approached. I looked over my shoulder, but Smiley was nowhere behind me. I needed to get back to the SWAT truck and get a first aid kit for Sonny, then radio for help. With his leg shot off, and his arteries open, even with my belt tourniquet, he would bleed out soon and die. I headed back toward the hole in the fence.

Suddenly, off to my right, another silver dune buggy was heading right at me. Where it had come from I didn't know. The same huge rear tractor tires threw sand out behind as it closed in. The same metal mast jutted up between the seats.

A skinny man wearing a checked shirt and John Deere ball cap was at the wheel. He angled in to head me off, then pulled alongside until we were wheel to wheel, running at breakneck speed. I looked over and saw that he was driving with only one hand. The other was holding a big Army .45 pointed right at me.

He raised the muzzle and fired one shot over my head. My AR-15 was on the floor, banging around uselessly at my feet. I fought the wheel with both hands, flying along half blind at over forty miles an hour.

The man extended his arm and aimed the gun at my head. His meaning was very clear.

Stop or die.

FORTY-EIGHT

Royal

I had to make up my mind fast. Do I pull over for this ass-hole in the John Deere hat and risk Sonny's life, or keep going and pray for the best? I decided to make a run for it. Out of the corner of my eye, I saw the truck closing in from the right. Smiley had sped across the hard-pack that rimmed the edge of the gully, but now he was back in the soft sand. I heard the truck shift back into four-wheel drive and start growling. I knew he wouldn't be able to keep up if I just kept going.

Suddenly the black Dodge braked to a stop and the Browning started chattering. One of the bullets hit the metal mast in the front of my rail, blowing the large welded bolt away. The bullet ricocheted and metal fragments stung the side of my face. One piece blew a pretty good hole in my forearm, knocking my hand off the wheel. The rail spun right and finally shuddered to a stop.

I heard the .45 popping and looked back to see that the guy in the John Deere hat was now firing the large semi-automatic pistol at the truck. Impossible to hit at that distance with a handgun.

I pulled up the AR-15. With blood running down my arm and dripping off my fingers, I aimed at the truck and squeezed off a burst, holding the trigger down until the

C-mag was dry. Then the man in the checked shirt spun his sand rail around in a circle and roared up on Sonny's side.

"Follow me," he yelled. Now we were teammates.

"My friend is wounded. He needs help!" I shouted over the roar of both sets of straight pipes.

He waved for me to follow, then floored his sand rail and sped out in front of me.

My arm was bleeding and the blood made my grip slick on the steering wheel. I fought the rough terrain. The hard suspension on the sand rail kept jerking the wheel from my grasp. The man in the John Deere hat roared ahead of me, back into Cactus City, but he never stopped. He exited the far end, then turned right and drove down into a sandy gully. I followed, wondering where the hell we were going and if he'd heard me about needing a doctor. I glanced over at Sonny. He was holding on with both hands, a ghastly expression on his face.

"Where's my leg?" he yelled across to me, the sick realization turning his expression into a mask of horror.

The man in front of us drove his dune buggy up to a large bush, then stopped, jumped out, and pulled it aside to reveal a metal drainage pipe about five feet in diameter. I could see from the tire tracks leading inside, that he'd used this before. He pulled his rail into the pipe, then motioned me to follow. I pulled in behind him. He ran past me and replaced the bush. As he passed back again he shouted, "Follow me! Stay close!" He jumped in his rail and took off before I could reply. It was suddenly pitch black and my tires were chattering across the ridged metal. I navigated by following sparks from his exhaust.

The tunnel angled slowly to the right. I found that the rail would almost steer itself inside the pipe. All I had to do was keep it from climbing the walls and flipping over. After about a quarter mile we came out the other side. There was an old wood shed next to a concrete, windowless building that was about twenty feet square. The man stopped the dune buggy and jumped out. He still had the .45 in his hand, but no longer looked like he was going to shoot me.

"Come on," he said and motioned for us to follow him.

"He's lost his lower leg," I said.

The man came back and stared at Sonny, who was now white and pasty, going into shock. Then without a word the skinny man lifted Sonny out of the rail, threw him over his shoulder in a fireman's carry, and ran with him across the sand to the concrete building a short distance away. He had a padlock key and was struggling to get it out of his pocket, with Sonny still over his shoulder. He finally opened the place up and carried Sonny inside. I followed, bringing both AR-15s and our two remaining C-clips.

Once we were inside, the man put Sonny on a mat on the floor, then closed the door and threw a bolt, locking us in. With no windows, it was again pitch black.

"I can't see," I said.

"Shut up," he answered. "Ya sound like a feckin' pussy."

A match was struck and a Coleman lantern hissed, throwing a dim light into the area. I looked around. We were in some kind of old water-control building or pumping station. There were rusted pipes and valves everywhere. Off in the distance I could still hear bombs exploding.

"This here's a no-impact area, inside the gunnery range," he said. "I found it three years ago. I wait here durin' fire missions."

Then the man came over and looked at Sonny's stump. "This here boy's gonna have to be tough as stewed skunk ta get through what we gotta do. But we cain't wait, gotta fix this mess now." He reached down and pulled a piece of Sonny's pant leg away, exposing the bloody stump.

"Don't touch him," I said. "He needs a doctor."

"We don't get this fixed up now, this Mexican won't need no doc. He'll be upstairs with Jesus. I was a medic. Vietnam. Seventy-fifth Army Rangers," he said. "I seen a lot worse than this. But we gotta triage the fecker now."

He had a deep cracker accent—Virginia, or South Carolina. He took off his hat, revealing a snow white forehead above a tan line on his weathered face. Gray hair, growing long, covered his ears. His teeth were a mess and he hadn't shaved in at least a week.

"Gimme yer shirt," he said.

I took off the SWAT vest, then removed my shirt, leaving me in a T-shirt. My forearm didn't look so bad, now that I saw it in the light. It had more or less stopped bleeding.

The man started ripping my shirt into strips. Then he took off the tourniquet belt I'd put on Sonny's thigh.

"Gonna let this bleed out a little, clean her out some," he said, and Sonny looked at his newly shot-off right leg in horror. Blood started spouting out onto the floor around us. Then the man cinched up the belt again, stemmed the flow, pulled a pint of scotch out of a backpack, and handed it to Sonny.

"Get this down," he ordered.

Sonny took a sip.

"Not like that. Give yerself a party, boy."

So Sonny started swallowing the scotch until the bottle was empty. The man crossed to one of the valves and turned it. When the water started to flow, he washed his hands, then brought the lantern closer. He knelt down, and picked up Sonny's stump in both hands.

"Whatta you gonna do?" I asked, feeling a little sick as I looked at what was left of the leg.

"Cain't git no lard without boilin' the hog," he said softly. "Ain't gonna be much fun, but I gotta tie off them bleeders, or this boy's gonna be tradin' his guitar for a harp."

He crossed to his backpack, pulled out a small nylon combat medic's bag, and returned to Sonny. "Keep this handy and gimme what I ask for."

For the next ten minutes, while Sonny screamed in pain, this man, whoever he was, searched Sonny's bloody stump for the main arteries, then one by one, pulled them out, then clamped and sutured them.

Somewhere in the middle of this Sonny stopped screaming. He had fainted.

The FA-18s had completed their run and were gone. It was strangely quiet in the little concrete room. Finally, the man completed this field surgery and bound up the stump with strips of my shirt. He did it all in thirty minutes.

"Help me move him over there to the bed," he said.

We carried Sonny to a futon by the far wall, laid him down and elevated his leg. I sat on the floor next to him while the man went back and washed Sonny's blood off his hands. Then he returned and slumped down next to us.

"Who the hell are you?" I asked.

"I'm the guy you stole that feckin' sand buggy from," he said, flat Southern vowels ringing on poured concrete.

"I'm a police officer," I said.

"Then ya oughta know better," he replied.

He had iridescent blue eyes—the kind of eyes I'd sometimes seen on the criminally insane. Madness glinted there. Everything else screamed hillbilly. The bony hips and the lean frame with the bulging beer belly, an Adam's apple that looked like somebody had shoved a tennis ball down his throat.

"I'm Shane Scully," I said. "This is Sonny Lopez."

"Royal Mortenson," he answered, but made no move to shake hands.

"I've gotta get him to the hospital," I persisted.

"You go back out there before the twenty-three-fifty strafing run and Blackie will drop you with that big Browning. He's pretty damn good with that thing. Knows the terrain. He'll set up over at the wall, or north a' Cactus West where he can see us coming. Before we get to any of my through-holes, motherfecker will rip us all new assholes."

"What the hell do you do out here?" I asked, wondering why he and Smiley were wandering around at night on an active gunnery range.

"I'm a scrapper," he said. "All this shit lyin' around out here—the fins on the inerts and stuff—is worth money."

He wiped his hand across his mouth, then pulled out a can of Skoal, took a pinch, and put it behind his lower lip.

"Aluminum on them fins of the two-thousand pounders is worth plenty." He pronounced it *al-ow-min-eum*.

"Depending on the market, I kin git ninety bucks a fin on them thousand-pound inerts. Sometimes I'll disarm some of the smaller unexploded stuff. A seventy-pound fin is worth thirty-five bucks a blade. Then, twice a week them Cobra assault choppers with twenty-millimeter cannons, swoop in here, blow up some dump truck. Brass cartridges coming down all over the place. Fifty cents a round, like it's raining money." He smiled at me, his brown, uneven teeth looking like a busted-down fence.

"And Smiley? Does he scrap too?"

"Who's that?"

"The guy in the black Dodge Ram."

"Ya mean Blackie? Blackie is a big feckin' problem. I'm out here pickin' up scrap, tryin' to make me a livin'. He's bringin' the EOD down on us."

"Don't you need a permit for this?"

"I got me a permit." He held up the .45. "The EOD don't got no problem with me, on account they know I'm an ex-Ranger and I'll do the right thing, by God. Yessir!"

"I was a Marine," I said, looking for some connection. He seemed to think about that. Then he went on.

"Blackie's a problem 'cause he don't give a shit. I only take fins off the inerts and the low-yield ordnance. Them's the blue bombs and the yellow stripers. But we got a lotta UHE shit out here—that's undetonated high explosives, and it's stuff EOD doesn't want messed with."

"What's EOD?" I asked him.

"Explosive Ordnance Disposal. They shut this place down once a month and go searching for unexploded JADAM two-thousand-pounders and up. Hot ordnance that didn't detonate. Them's the bombs got C-four packages in 'em. Gotta disarm the warhead to get a one-pound package out, but it's worth fifteen grand or more on the black market, especially now, with terrorists tryin' to buy it. I could mine C-four easy, but I never do it. I'm an American. Ain't gonna help no sand nigger terrorist assholes get shit to blow us up. That's why EOD kinda leaves me alone. Fifteen years out here and they coulda busted me easy, but they let me be. Blackie, he's a whole 'nother story, 'cause he's in the C-four business. He's out here three times a week pullin' warheads off the reds, takin' out C-four packs. I been tryin' to catch the fecker myself, but he's tricky, and smart as a windmill fixer."

That explained where Smiley got the C-4.

The strange man spit a stream of tobacco juice across the room into a Folgers coffee can. He hit it pretty much right in the center and it rang loudly. Bull's-eye.

"With Blackie puttin' the heat on, EOD's gonna end up throwin' me out, right along with him."

"How soon till we can we get out of here?" I asked.

"Now that I got the bleedin' stemmed, yer friend's probably gonna hold up for a while, but he's gonna be needin' some regular doctorin' soon, antibiotics, a proper stitchin'. 'Course, we try to get outta here now, Blackie's gonna make some trouble. That big Browning's got some bite to it." He looked at his watch. "Like I said, ain't got another firing mission until eleven-fifty. Warthogs gonna be takin' out a phony SAM site. That's our best chance fer gettin' outta here. While they kick ass on them targets on the east ridge, he's gotta keep his head down. That's when we go."

FORTY-NINE

The Wire

We sat on the floor of the old pumping station, the Coleman lantern hissing loudly, Sonny lying unconscious beside us. The Warthog fire mission was scheduled to begin in an hour. Then we'd put Sonny in the sand buggy and make a run for it. Royal was talking softly, his voice droning in the dimly lit room.

"Ain't nobody comes out here much. 'Round April, it gets so dry the jackrabbits is all totin' canteens." He shook his head sadly. "After Nam, didn't have no place to go. Seemed there was no place I fit in. Folks spittin' on me, callin' me baby killer. But how do ya tell some snotty draft dodger who never served that some o' them kids over there would ask ya for a Hershey, then trade ya a hand grenade for a candy bar? After I got back, seemed weren't nothin' much to give a shit about no more. I seen my share of misery and there's no doubt it changes ya. Out here I don't gotta explain it to nobody. It's just me and the range. Takes my chances, makes my livin'. If I pull the wrong wire, it's adios, motherfecker. Nobody's even gotta come to my funeral, 'cause there ain't gonna be nothin' left t' bury."

I listened to him ramble on like that, talking about South Carolina and Vietnam. Royal Mortenson was what you became if you gave up and withdrew. A lonely, angry old man who had retreated to a spot so unforgiving and desolate that he no longer had to deal with life. As he talked, my thoughts about my own future sharpened. I knew one thing: Whatever happened, I didn't want my journey to end up there.

Royal suddenly switched to current events. "Blackie, he seems t' want you dead pretty bad."

"He hates cops," I said flatly.

"I can get behind that one," he joked, then spit some more tobacco juice.

Another bull's-eye.

"'Course, bein' as you're a cop, I know y'all gotta do things a certain way. You probably got some penal code tells you when t' shit and how far out in the woods to bury it. But sometimes I've found things work better when ya skin yer own possums."

He looked at me with a sharp twinkle in his eye.

"I'm listening."

"Ol' Blackie, he's clever. He hacks into the Yuma Range Management computer, just like me. Gets the time of the firing missions. Them Marines are always right on time, Drop their loads, regular as Presbyterians. So he knows, just like me, when them planes is comin'. Once they start bombin', he's ducked down in a safe place like this one. Rest of the time, he's out there on the range, prospectin' C-four."

He looked up at me, shrewdness a cagey visitor on his weathered face. "So here's the way I see our choices. We could wait for that flighta Warthogs to come in at twenty-three fifty, then make our move, get yer Mexican to the hospital. But looks to me like this boy could go inta shock. Blood pressure gets too low and his heart could just plum quit. Not wantin' that ta happen, maybe you and me oughta advance up the timetable a smidge." He started picking at a loose thread hanging off his pant leg. "I seen ol' Blackie shootin' at you in Cactus West, then lettin' you chase him out by Kill Hill, down inta Jackrabbit Creek, leading ya in there right on time, so them Hornets could have their shot at ya."

"Are you telling me he knew they were coming?" I asked.

"Yep." Royal kept picking at the loose thread. "Knew the exact time and exact coordinates. Got 'em off the range computer. Took ya down there specifically so you could French-kiss a Maverick."

He snapped the thread off, then looked over at me. "If ya wanta get Pancho to that hospital a scootch ahead of schedule and keep him from singin' in the celestial choir, then I might have a way we fix ol' Blackie. Make it so he loses his head and makes a mistake. Or, if it pleases ya, we could arrange it so that happens the other way around."

Then Royal told me why he had the metal masts screwed into the front of the sand rails. The government strung low wires at various places on the range to make it dangerous for scrappers that were running fast without headlights at night. The EOD kept moving the wires to new locations so the scavengers wouldn't know where they were. The masts on the sand rails were up front to catch a missed wire and snap it.

" 'Course, I don't hit many of them things, 'cause I make it my business to know when them EOD boys change a wire. But ol' Blackie, he's in that big truck with a cab to protect him so he don't pay them wires no nevermind. Maybe we can arrange it so things happen a little different tonight."

He looked up and flashed his yellow smile. Then he told me his plan. When he finished, he looked over at me, his criminal blues blazing.

"Can't shoot the fecker, 'cause if EOD finds him fulla

lead, it looks like a murder, and I got a lotta explaining to do. This way it looks like he just got careless and paid the price." Then he stopped talking and a crafty look followed.

" 'Course, with you being a cop, I wouldn't want to be facin' no bullshit trial afterwards. You want my help, you and me gotta come to an understanding."

I stayed quiet for a minute, thinking. He could call it an accident, but what he was really talking about was murder.

Then I thought about the last two weeks, and about Emo and Jo. I remembered how Emo's son Alfredo, had held on to Elana's hand at the funeral, standing tall, refusing to cry, knowing he and his mother would have to go on alone. I remembered Emo up on Smiley's porch, dead in the vertical coffin. Smiley had opened the front door and shot him at point-blank range. He'd had no chance.

I thought of Jo, lying in her hospital bed, hovering near death, a victim of the same situation. Only with Jo, I had to share the blame and it weighed heavily on me. I looked down at my shirt wrapped around Sonny's stump, his life slowly seeping out, his blood staining the cloth. I needed to get him out of here before he died. Add in Greenridge and Nightingale and the score was five to zip. I was getting pretty tired of losing.

I could feel Royal's eyes on me as I weighed the decision.

"We do this right, it'll go down slick as snot on a doorknob," Royal drawled. "But you and me, we gotta swear us a oath, first. We gotta swear to both take this piece'a business to the grave."

Then Sonny coughed and moaned, helping me make up my mind.

"Let's do this guy," I whispered.

Royal looked up, smiled widely, then nodded.

I put my Tac vest back on and we left Sonny lying on

the futon with the empty scotch bottle now filled with water. Royal and I exited the pumping station and stood outside in the moonlight.

"Things're goin' so good, I might have to hire me somebody to help enjoy it," he joked, then turned to me. "You know what you're gonna do?"

"Right," I replied, thinking I shouldn't be taking tactical orders from a withered old hick who was probably half insane. But as he'd said, this was his backyard. He knew the rules and the terrain.

Royal unscrewed the mast on the front of my sand rail and leaned it against the pumping station. "Now git, and keep your head down," he warned.

I nodded, fired up the buggy, and drove back into the drainage tunnel. Royal was already removing the mast from the second rail as I pulled out. The engine echoed loudly in the metal pipe. After a quarter of a mile, I stopped at the end of the tunnel and removed the bush blocking the opening. Then I drove back out onto the desert floor heading toward Cactus West. My forearm was aching where the shrapnel hit me and my fingers were going numb, but I ignored it and kept driving.

I pulled in five minutes later, parked off the main road in a bombed-out adobe structure, and turned off the motor. I grabbed the AR-15, jammed in another C-mag, then found a spot up on a roof where I had a clear view of the main street. I proned out on the cold corrugated metal, put the assault rifle to my shoulder, and waited.

Half an hour later I heard the sound of Royal's rail way off in the distance. He was roaring toward Cactus West, the straight pipes blaring faintly across the desert, changing pitch every time he shifted gears. Then slowly, an octave lower, I began to hear the distinctive sound of the black Dodge. I pulled the night vision glasses up and focused them in the direction of the noise. The sand rail was out front, jumping berms and ridges, going about forty, spewing rooster tails of sand from its rear tires. About two hundred yards behind him, the Dodge Ram growled loudly in four-wheel drive, going about thirty-five, trying to stay up. In the strange green hue of the night scope the scene appeared ghostly and surreal.

Then the truck stopped and Smiley jumped out, threw the Browning down across the front fender, and started firing. The Browning was winking death silently, then the chattering bark of the huge weapon reached me a few seconds later. But Royal was almost in town. Smiley jumped back in his truck and continued the chase. Royal flew past my position and drove right out of town, dragging the truck like a tail behind him, much the same way Smiley had dragged Sonny and me down into Jackrabbit Creek.

In a few seconds he would pass my firing position. I tromboned the slide, kicking a .223 out of the breech to make sure I wasn't jammed, then waited. The black truck sped toward me, the engine growling ominously. I had the Dodge in my sights as it sped past. Then I opened fire, shooting at the tires, squeezing off at least fifty of the hundred rounds in my C-mag.

The truck tires all exploded. The Dodge shuddered and spun to a stop. Even before it came to rest, Smiley was out with the .50-caliber cradled in both hands. He swung it around towards my position and fired, but I was already up and running, jumping down off the roof. As the exploding shells tracked me, I dodged between the disintegrating adobe buildings and quickly reached my sand rail. Royal Mortenson was in the driver's seat with the engine running.

"Where'd you leave it?" I asked.

"Right on the edge of town. Fecker can't miss it." He down-shifted, popped the clutch, and the rail exploded forward, out of the bombed-out building and up the street. Royal turned right onto Main and powered out of town.

Smiley, on foot, saw us make the turn and started firing. The slugs blew holes in the last building on the street as we swerved around it and headed out into the desert. I turned around in the passenger seat with the AR-15 in both hands and squeezed off a short burst at him, aiming high.

Smiley was firing the Browning at us from the edge of town where Royal had stashed the other sand rail, but we were out of range. He finally spotted the second rail parked over to his right, and moved cautiously to check it out, not sure if it was booby-trapped. Then, without much delay, he was in the driver's seat and coming after us, the big .50-cal propped in the bucket seat next to him.

We vectored toward the north end of the gunnery range. I thought Sonny had been driving fast, but nothing like Royal was driving now. We had to be going at least sixty, maybe more, screaming across the desert. When we hit a berm or a gully, it seemed we catapulted at least five feet in the air.

"Yeeeeeaaaaahhhhh!" Royal screamed every time the rail flew. We headed toward two large fenced-off areas where it looked like they dragged the unusable bombed-out truck carcasses. The fenced lots were about fifty yards apart and filled with torched wrecks.

"There she blows," Royal screamed, slowing slightly. "Give the sidewinder a little encouragement."

I fired off another burst and saw him swerve, then speed up, closing fast. He had somehow managed to prop the Browning up on the dash and now he squeezed off a short burst. It was surprisingly accurate. The chain-link fence on the left side of us sparked with bullets.

"Keep down, wires ahead!" Royal shouted as we roared between the two fenced lockups.

Smiley was a hundred yards back. Royal had his head

way down, almost between his knees. I was laid out, facing backward, holding the AR-15, the sand rail throwing sand out behind us on both sides. I could see the glint of a wire flash past inches over our heads.

Unexpectedly, Royal screamed a bad joke at nobody, yelling it into the night air: "Hey, Blackie, ever hear the one about the fecker who bought hisself a blow job but forgot his wallet so he lost his head?"

Almost as he yelled it, Vincent Smiley's head flew from his shoulders, cut off clean by a bridging wire. It sailed up into the air like a bloody jumpball and landed ten feet away. The headless torso now drove the dune buggy, which swerved wildly, crashing into the fence.

"Yeeeeeaaaaahhhhh!" Royal Mortenson yelled. He slowed to a stop. We got out and ran back toward the spot where Smiley's torso had landed when his sand rail crashed. We were careful to duck under the taut wires that EOD had strung between the fences. They were nearly invisible in the dark.

The second sand buggy was still upright. Royal reached in and shut off the engine. Then we walked over and looked down at Vincent Smiley's head lying on the sand. The final expression on his face was a terrible, ugly grimace.

Royal leaned down and stared into the lifeless eyes. He giggled, then looked up with mad eyes that revealed to me, in that instant, the landscape of his tortured soul.

FIFTY

Inheritance

Royal Mortenson helped me get Sonny back to the SWAT
truck. He used his tractor to pull it out of the sand, but he
didn't want to go with me.

"Towns're like a booger you can't shake off yer finger,"
he said, charming and understated to the end. We shook
hands and that crazy bastard walked out of my life forever.

I raced to the hospital in Brawley with Sonny in the
back of the SWAT truck. Like my other partner, Jo, he
went right into ICU. I sat in the waiting room while doc-
tors were paged and people ran back and forth. Too many
nurses were running.

The two SWAT teams arrived an hour later and sat
with me in the waiting room. They told me they had seen
the Super Hornets bombing the desert from the mountain
as they climbed down. I explained that we'd chased Smiley onto the gunnery range and that Sonny was hit when
Vincent opened up with the big Browning. I told them
we'd been trying to get away with Smiley chasing us
when he had unexpectedly hit the wire and decapitated
himself. It fudged the truth but nobody had asked too
many tough questions. At least not yet.

I called to check on Jo and was told that she'd taken a
turn for the worse. She was having a lot of secondary

problems, low blood oxygen and a troublesome infection that was slowly taking her resistance down.

After Sonny was out of surgery the doc came back and told us that he was going to make it. The good news was they had been able to save his knee so he would eventually be able to walk with a prosthesis. I left Sonny with his fellow sheriffs, Scott Cook and Rick Manos, then caught a ride back to L.A. with SRT.

"The military really strings cable out there to stop these guys from scrapping metal at night?" Gordon Grundy asked, having trouble believing it. "Why would they want to decapitate people?"

"Because of the C-four," I explained. "They don't want terrorists to get their hands on it. The whole place is posted. You enter at your own risk."

"Well, if somebody had to lose his head, I guess Smiley's a good choice," Rosano said, putting the best spin on it.

The news treated the story and me very kindly. ATF was in charge of all investigations involving stolen C-4. That gave Brady Cagel control of the case. A good break for yours truly. Nobody seemed inclined to question EOD's description of the event. The way they told it, Smiley had been scrapping out there for months. They had tried to run him off, even got him on a radio frequency once and warned him about the wires, but he had cut off the transmission.

They had tried to apprehend him, but he worked mainly at night and had always been able to escape. EOD said Smiley had stolen the sand rail he'd been driving when he died. It belonged to a local Coachella Valley resident named Royal Mortenson, who the newspaper said was a Vietnam vet and recipient of the Silver Star.

When Smiley's truck was finally found in Cactus West, all four of the tires that I'd shot out had been miraculously replaced. I'd been worried about what questions would be asked when that Dodge was found full of .223s.

Who had done that little piece of cleanup for me? Royal? EOD? The gunnery range good fairy?

I'm not asking, so I'll never know.

Life settled, more or less, back to normal. My overweight partner, Zack Farrell, returned from Miami. He was wearing a new dark green outfit, and he filled his swivel chair across the desk from me, looking like three hundred pounds of gristle wrapped in a Glad Bag.

"Man, I leave town for a minute and all the action starts," he groused. His mother had made a miraculous recovery, so Zack was back in my life.

Jo Brickhouse continued to lose ground. I spent most of my spare time at the hospital, looking across a chipped linoleum table into the worried eyes of Bridget Bollinger.

"I know she's going to get better," Bridget said. "She just has to."

"We're not in charge," I told her. "It's in God's hands."

Platitudes. Why do people think they have to say stuff like that? I've been on the receiving end of those same remarks, and they never help.

Bridget looked more frightened every day. "Y'know, Jo really liked you," she said one afternoon, unexpectedly. "She said you were attractive. We even had a fight about it."

"You never had anything to worry about there," I told her. "Our friendship worked on different levels."

Every evening after visiting hours Bridget and I went down into the little chapel at the hospital and said prayers for Jo's recovery.

She lingered like that for days, sometimes rallying before taking a turn for the worse. And then, slowly, we started to lose her.

Two days later she was gone.

Bridget and I were sitting in the waiting room, playing gin, when Jo's surgeon came in and told us she had passed on. Bridget started to cry and I held her, feeling the huge, wracking sobs, realizing my own tears were mixing with hers.

The Rams' first game with Chooch as a coach was against the Chargers. Sonny Lopez was on the sidelines in a wheelchair with a blanket over his lap. Alexa and I wheeled him onto the field. The sheriffs who were there, and all the players, came over and shook his hand.

Darren Zook had taken over for Sonny and was coaching the defense. He and Chooch had the Rams in pretty good shape, but they were behind by seven points at the half. I walked over to the end zone where the team had their helmets off, sitting on the grass eating oranges and getting instructions from the coaches for the second half.

"Who has that middle linebacker on the inside blitz?" Chooch was saying as I joined them. "He's killing us."

"I do, Coach," a tall Mexican kid said. "But the guy's been using his hands and the refs don't call it."

"Forget that. Knock this guy on his butt. He can't sack our QB if he's seeing sunshine."

Chooch made the halftime speech. "You guys are playing great. But they have a good team, some great athletes, so we gotta dig a little deeper. Emo's up there watching," he said simply. "He'll give us the plays. He knows the game plan, and his offense rocks."

"Coach," Deshawn Zook said, and Chooch looked over at him. "Thanks for sticking with us," the boy said softly. "We're gonna win this for Emo, but we're also gonna win it for you."

An hour later, with ten seconds left on the clock, they did.

A week after the game, on Sunday morning, we were

sitting around after breakfast looking for something to do with the day. Delfina and Chooch decided to go to the park to study under the trees. I went out to the backyard with Franco and sat looking at the Venice Canal. So much had happened. So many people had died, and I had to figure out how to accept my part in it. *What could I have done differently?* I had prayed for Jo and Sonny until my knees were sore, but one had died and the other was in a wheelchair, and the answers still hadn't come. I felt culpable and out of touch with myself. I was in an emotional echo chamber—a moral cul-de-sac.

Alexa came out to join me and handed over a beer. We clinked bottles.

"Chooch was really happy about winning the game," Alexa said, smiling. "With three college coaching visits scheduled this week, his cast coming off on Tuesday, and Delfina's play about to open, things are definitely looking up in the kid department."

"Yep." I was trying to feel the upper, but not getting there.

"And Tony—yesterday he actually called me in and apologized."

"Really?"

"Yep. He said he knew that he was acting like a jerk, that he was just passing his misery down, and that it was lousy command tactics. He promised he'd never do it to me again."

"Tony's a good guy, but if he hadn't eased up on you he'd be wearing a few new knots on that shiny bald head."

She hit me in the arm. "Cut it out, tough guy."

"Sorry, some parts of me won't ever change. You gotta take the good with the bad."

She looked over, sensing the strange place I was in, seeing how uncomfortable I was with how all this had ended.

"You know, Shane," she said softly, "we can only do the best we can. If life was so easy to predict, nobody would ever get hurt. You can only view your culpability in any situation by the choices you made looking forward. If you view it looking back, it's called second guessing."

"When you look into the future, what do you see?" I asked her.

"I see things I want to do. I see Chooch in college, getting married, raising children. I see us growing old together, always being in love." She reached over and took my hand. "What do you see?" she asked.

"Nothing. I see nothing. I've always been afraid to have dreams, to look too far into the future."

"We'll just have to work on that." She smiled sadly, but I could tell she was worried about me when she said it.

"From the time I was a baby, my future only held disappointment," I said, trying to explain. "Maybe if I'd seen more, felt more, taken more chances . . . maybe I coulda changed what happened."

"Honey, don't go there. Coulda, woulda, shoulda. You're not to blame. Jo Brickhouse was a good police officer, she signed on to do a dangerous job. She made a mistake and she paid the full price. I didn't know her, but from what you've told me, she'd tell you to let it go. She'd want you to know it's not your fault."

"Okay," I said, but I was just ducking her now, and she sensed it.

"I know something happened out there on the gunnery range, because a lot of this doesn't add up. But Shane, whatever happened, whatever you had to do—you did the right thing. You reached down into a vat of goo and pulled out a rabbit. You saved this for me and for Tony, and you kept something terrible from happening. What happened to Jo and Sonny wasn't your fault. You could just as easily have been the one to get hit."

"Cut one and we all bleed," I said softly. I finally understood the full extent of that slogan.

Later that afternoon, there was a knock at my door. I opened it and Darren Zook was standing there.

"Come outside, I want to show you something," he said.

I followed him out.

Parked in my driveway was Emo's beautiful red Harley Softail. The chrome glittered, the lacquered black paint sparkled in the sun.

"Isn't that Emo's?" I asked.

"Not anymore," he said. "It's yours."

"Mine?" Looking at the bike, not understanding.

"Elana Rojas is grateful for all you did. She wants you to have it if you'll teach Alfredo to ride it when he's sixteen."

He handed me the keys.

An hour later I was riding Emo's bike through Trancas Canyon, going fast, leaning hard on the turns. Not oversteering this time—taking chances, just letting it all happen. The wind was tugging at my shirtsleeves and flapping my pant legs. The engine filled my ears with its throaty roar. Finally, I pulled into the place where we'd started the Iron Pig ride last summer. It was a spot high in the Malibu hills that overlooked the ocean. I shut off the engine, kicked down the stand, and reached into the hand-tooled saddlebag, taking out the beer I'd brought with me. Then I opened it and walked over to the lip of the hill, sat on a boulder, and looked out at the Pacific. The sun was just setting, turning the water and sky a purplish-orange.

In my heart and head I was always racing toward something I could never quite define, my ambition and ego pushing me, my final destination, unsure. Along the way, there were many places to stop. Some of them were havens where people I loved were waiting—Alexa, Chooch, Emo, and Jo—places where lessons could be learned. Others were simply hideouts. There were also dangerous spots where demons waited. Where I stopped, and what happened to me when I did, was not only controlled by fate. I had a lot to do with those decisions. They defined my destiny. All I had to do was simply own it. I had spent two hours with the ghost of the future, and knew I didn't want to end up like Royal Mortenson. In the end, life was all about choices. Alexa was right. I had done the best I could, and it hadn't quite worked out the way I wanted. I had to find a way to accept that, but not second-guess it.

I had told Jo that in order to grow she needed to be vulnerable. Maybe that's all this was. Vulnerability. Maybe I didn't have that down quite as well as I thought. Maybe vulnerability was just going to take some more getting used to.

The funerals had all been delayed by the forensics. In the next week, after the coroner finished with the bodies, I would stand at four grave sites while more empty words and hollow platitudes were spoken.

But this was my time.

I raised my beer and said all of their names softly.

"Emo Rojas, Josephine Brickhouse, William Greenridge, Michael Nightingale." Soldiers who had fallen while I marched on. It was just the way it was.

As the sun went down, I said good-bye to all of them.

God, how I hate cop funerals.

AUTHOR'S NOTE

I trust Californians will forgive me for rearranging the geography of the State a bit to suit my fictional designs, with special apologies to the municipalities of Palm Springs and Indio.

THE COLD HIT

A Shane Scully Novel

by Stephen J. Cannell

Shane Scully and his partner are assigned to the case of "the Fingertip Killer"—a serial murderer preying on homeless Vietnam vets in Los Angeles. Every two weeks he strikes: He beats his victims, then shoots them in the back of the head. Once they're dead, he cuts off their fingertips, closes their eyes, and tosses them in the river.

Into this explosive mix comes another killing, and this one does not fit the pattern. It has clearly been staged to look like the work of the Fingertip Killer, but Scully suspects something else: an elaborate copycat murder that may hide a far more dangerous criminal conspiracy—with connections high up in the American government.

COMING IN SUMMER 2005
FROM ST. MARTIN'S PRESS